RAINMAKER TRANSLATIONS *supports a series of books meant to encourage a lively reading experience of contemporary world literature drawn from diverse languages and cultures. Publication is assisted by grants from the Black Mountain Institute (blackmountaininstitute.org) at the University of Nevada, Las Vegas, an organization dedicated to promoting literary and cross-cultural dialogue around the world.*

Elias Khoury

YALO

Translated from the Arabic by Peter Theroux

archipelago books

Archipelago Books
232 Third Street #A111
Brooklyn, NY 11215
www.archipelagobooks.org

Library of Congress Cataloging-in-Publication Data
Khuri, Ilyas.
[Yalu. English]
Yalo / by Elias Khoury ; translated from the Arabic by Peter Theroux.
– 1st Archipelago Books ed.
p. cm.
ISBN-13: 978-0-9793330-4-0 (alk. paper)
ISBN-10: 0-9793330-4-0 (alk. paper)
I. Theroux, Peter. II. Title.
PJ7842.H823Y3513 2008   892'.736 – dc22
2007038964

First published as *Yalo* by Dar-al-Adàb, Beirut, 2002

Distributed by Consortium Book Sales and Distribution
www.cbsd.com

This publication was made possible with the support of the Black Mountain
Institute of UNLV, Lannan Foundation, the National Endowment for the Arts,
and the New York State Council on the Arts, a state agency.

As Christ walked upon the sea
I walked in my visions
But I came down from the cross
Because I am not afraid of heights
And I do not preach of Resurrection

MAHMOUND DARWISH

Yalo did not understand what was happening.

The young man stood before the interrogator and closed his eyes. He always closed his eyes when he faced danger, when he was alone, and when his mother . . . On that day too, the morning of Thursday, December 22, 1993, he closed his eyes involuntarily.

Yalo did not understand why everything was white.

He saw the white interrogator, sitting behind a white table, the sun refracting on the glass window behind him, and his face bathed in reflected light. All Yalo saw were halos of light and a woman walking through the city streets, tripping on her shadow.

Yalo closed his eyes for a moment, or so he thought. This young man with his knitted eyebrows and long tan face, his slender height, closed his eyes for a moment before reopening them. But here, in the Jounieh police station, he closed his eyes and saw crossed lines around two lips that moved as if whispering. He looked at his handcuffed wrists and felt that the sun that obscured the face of the interrogator struck him in the eyes, so he closed them.

The young man stood before the interrogator at ten o'clock that cold morning and saw the sun refracted on the window, shining on the white head of the man whose mouth opened with questions. Yalo closed his eyes.

Yalo did not understand what the interrogator was shouting about.

He heard a voice shouting at him, "Open your eyes, man!" He opened them and light entered, into their depths like flaming skewers. He discovered that he had had his eyes closed for a long time, that he had spent half his life in the dark, and he saw himself as a blind man sees the night.

Yalo did not understand why she had come, but when he saw her he dropped onto the chair.

When he entered the room, the nameless girl was not there. He entered stumbling because he was blinded by the sun refracted on the glass. He stood in the whiteness, his hands cuffed and his body shivering with sweat. He was not afraid, even though the interrogator would write in his report that the suspect was trembling with fear. But Yalo was not; he was shivering with sweat. Sweat dripped from every part of him, and his clothes were spotted with the odd-smelling moisture emerging from his pores. Yalo felt naked under his long black coat, and smelled the odor of another person. He discovered that he did not know this man called Daniel, also known as Yalo.

The girl with no name arrived. Perhaps she had already been in the interrogation room, but he had not seen her when he came in. He saw her and dropped onto the chair, feeling that his legs had betrayed him. A slight dizziness came over him, and since he was unable to open his eyes, he closed them.

"Open your eyes, buddy!" shouted the interrogator. So he opened them, and saw an apparition that resembled the girl with no name. She said that she had no name. But Yalo knew everything. While she was dozing, her body delicate and naked, he opened her black leather bag and wrote down her name, address, telephone number, and everything else.

Yalo did not understand why she said she had no name.

Her breathing was uneven and the breeze around her face seemed to

< 10 >

suffocate her. She was unable to speak, but she was able to say this: "I don't have a name." Yalo bowed his head and took her.

There in the cottage, below the Villa Gardenia owned by Monsieur Michel Salloum, there, when he asked for her name, she said in a voice filled with gaps, lacking the air that was closing her lungs, "I don't have a name. Please, no names." "Fine," he said. "My name is Yalo. Don't forget my name."

Yet she stood here, her name beside her. When the interrogator asked for her name, she didn't hesitate before answering, "Shirin Raad." She did not tell the interrogator, "Please, no names." She did not stretch out her hand as she had done there in the cottage where Yalo had slept with her after she had stretched out her incense-scented arms. He had taken her palms and put them over his eyes, then started to kiss her white forearms, inhaling the fragrance of incense and musk. He inhaled the fragrance of her black hair and buried his face in it, intoxicated. He told her that he was drunk on incense, and she smiled as if a mask had vanished from her face. Yalo saw her smile through the shadows the candlelight threw against the wall. It was her first smile on that night of fear.

What was Shirin doing here?

When he opened his eyes after the interrogator's shouts, he saw himself in Ballouna. He told her, "Come," and she walked behind him. They walked from the pine forest below the Church of St. Nicholas and climbed the hill to the villa. The girl fell to the ground, or so it seemed to Yalo, so he turned to raise her, grasped her hand, and they walked on. When she fell a second time, he bent over her again, to carry her, but she shrank from him and stood up. She grasped the trunk of a pine tree and froze where she stood, panting heavily. He offered her his hand. She took it and walked beside him. He listened to the sound of her breathing and her panting fear.

When they reached the cottage, he left her at the door, entered and lit a candle, tried to arrange his rumpled clothing and accessories, yet abandoned this quickly, realizing it would take too much time. When he went back to her, he found her resting her head on the leaf of the open door, making crying sounds.

"Don't be afraid," he told her. "Come. You'll sleep here, I'll make you a bed on the floor, don't be afraid."

She went in hesitantly and stood in the middle of the room, as if looking for a chair to sit on. Yalo jumped up and removed his pants from the chair and threw them on the bed, but instead of sitting down she remained standing and confused.

"Do you want tea?" he asked her.

Instead of answering, she reached out pleadingly. Yalo took her outstretched hands, but when he saw the fear forming concentric circles in the depths of her little eyes, he drew back. He said he was afraid, he would say that he felt fear, but at that moment he did not know, he did not feel afraid before writing the word. He said it and felt it, then wrote it. Today, when he remembered her little eyes in the trembling candlelight, when he saw how the pupils of her eyes shrank into concentric circles, he felt fear, and said that he was afraid of her eyes.

When he drew back, he saw her coming toward him. Her hands were suspended in the air as if she were appealing to him for help. He came close to her and took her palms and placed them over his eyes, and she became quiet. He held her hands and felt their trembling, as if the lines of fear that throbbed within each of them had become like the arteries that circulate tension throughout the body. He placed her palms over his eyes, and saw the darkness, and felt how her body calmed down and quieted, and gave off the scent of incense.

"What's that sweet smell?" asked Yalo, drawing back. He sat on the chair and covered his face with his hands as though exhausted, and remained there unmoving. The candlelight flickered in the piney breeze rising from the forest. The girl with no name stood beside him to regain the breeze fear had stolen from her when she saw the black phantom approaching, from the car stopped at the corner of the dense pine forest, below the Orthodox Church.

Why was she wearing her short skirt that showed her thighs?

She sat in front of the interrogator in her short red skirt and crossed her legs, and spoke as if she had swallowed all the air in the interrogation room.

Yalo had told her not to wear short skirts. "What is that supposed to be, huh?" But she did not answer. She looked down at her knees, which is where he was also looking, and her lips moved in the hint of a smile, and she shook her head. They went out together in the morning and he stopped a taxi for Beirut for her, then went back to his cottage.

But now she sat, wearing that same red skirt, or one like it, her legs crossed, speaking without any stammer or hesitation, as she had done there.

They were in the car like two shadows. From the top of his lookout hill, Yalo could see only the man's gray hair. Yalo aimed the beam of his flashlight at the car just as the shots were fired. He felt, as he dodged among the pine trees, carrying the Russian Kalashnikov, and the flashlight, that he was going hunting. The cars were traps for prey like him. He was like a sparrow hunter, he knew the seasons, and enjoyed them. This is what he tried to explain to the interrogator. He said that the point for a hunter like him was not robbery or women, but pleasure. The pleasure of hunting, the love stolen inside the cars with sealed windows, and the pleasure of the first moment, the moment the light fell on the two faces, or on the hand reaching for the thighs, or on the head bent to the breasts free of the folds of clothing.

The beam that Yalo aimed hit its target directly. Yalo was not playing with the light, it immediately hit the right spot. Had the beam not hit its target, he would have considered his adventure a failure; he would have retraced his steps or hid in wait for the car to pass, withdrawing quietly, dragging his failure behind him.

The first shot, or nothing; that was his hunting philosophy. For him the best thing was the gray hair that shone in the light. The best moments were men's heads covered with white hair as they bent over a forearm or a thigh. The beam penetrated the old gray hair, lit it up, and froze it in place. The light entered the bending white and drew a complete circle around it. The beam lifted up from the gray hair and moved to the other side, drawing eyes, and there were the woman's eyes, dilated with a mixture of fear and desire.

The light came closer. The phantom emerged after turning on the flashlight and playing it over the car. In the first moments of the hunt, Yalo focused the light, making it sharp and narrow as a ray. After the eyes were frozen, he enlarged the beam and flashed it around as he approached the closed window and rapped it with the muzzle of his rifle. The window opened and revealed terror. The phantom's head drew close to the man's window, but he did not allow the woman's eyes to escape his own alert hawk eyes, wide open in the dark. He penetrated the dark and flashed the beam of light, and the shadows rose. He approached within the shadows, and rapped the window with the muzzle of his rifle, and ordered it open. He looked into the woman's eyes and contemplated how wide they were, with the pupils shrunk to nothing. Then he withdrew quietly with his booty: a wristwatch, a ring, a gold chain, a necklace, and a few dollars, nothing more. Of course. Once he had asked a man to remove his necktie because he felt that fear was choking the man through the necktie that hung over his opened belt, like a noose. Once he had asked a woman to give him her yellow shawl, for no reason at all. But he wanted nothing more; more came to him with no strain or effect. Yalo was not looking for anything more, but he did take it when it showed up, because he had learned from his torment in the city known as Paris never to refuse grace.

Things were different with Shirin, however.

Why did she say he had raped her in the forest?

"I did not – " Yalo said, but heard the interrogator's shout:

"You confessed, you dog! And now you say no. You know what happens to liars!"

Yalo was not lying, however. It was true that he had agreed that what he had done could be called rape, but . . . it was not a question of that night. Shirin had not leveled any charge against him having to do with that night, only with the days that came after.

Things had been different there with her. Yalo had not known the right words to use to tell her that the smell of incense her arms gave off that night had surrounded him like white clouds and then penetrated his very spinal column.

When he told her that he loved her from his spinal column – this was three months after the forest – she laughed so hard that tears ran down her face, and she kept having to blow her nose. At first he thought she was crying, and he bent over the table loaded with appetizers at the Albert Restaurant in Achrafieh, then he saw that she was laughing.

"I'm laughing at *you*," she said. "You're an idiot, all appearance and nothing more. What is this third-rate crap?"

And she started to speak English, telling him, "Finished, you must understand, everything is finished."

He said that he did not understand English, so she spoke to him in French.

"*C'est fini, Monsieur Yalo.*"

"What's *fini?*" he asked.

< 15 >

"Us," she said.

"So you want to *finish* me?" he asked.

"Please, Monsieur Yalo, I can't go on like this, please leave me alone and go, let's understand each other, tell me what you want and it's yours."

She opened her bag and brought out a handful of dollars.

Why had she told the interrogator that he had slapped her because she refused to eat?

No, he had not slapped her because she refused to eat sparrows, as she had alleged to the interrogator.

"Who would eat music?" she said when she saw the plate of fried sparrows swimming in a broth of lemon and garlic.

"I don't eat sparrows – it's wrong!"

Yalo prepared a morsel of a small sparrow wrapped in bread and dipped in sauce, and brought it near her mouth.

"*Non, non*, please!"

But the hand that brought the bread-wrapped sparrow stayed there, outstretched, then began to approach her mouth and hover around it, before brushing it against the closed lips. The girl gave in, she opened her mouth, accepted the morsel, and began to chew, yet the muscles of her mouth contracted in repulsion.

She swallowed the sparrow and then stopped eating and talking.

Yalo kept drinking arak and gazing at her face. Her face was as small as a small white moon hung over her long neck. He wanted to tell her all about the moon. He wanted to tell her how he had discovered the moon and the stars and the Milky Way, which looked like a swath of milk in the sky, there in Ballouna, below the villa to which Parisian fate had guided him, but he was afraid she would laugh at him.

"So it seems like you don't speak Arabic or think much of Abd al-Halim Hafiz."

He told her that, or something like that, but she said nothing in reply. The little white moon rested still on the long neck, then tears streamed from her eyes. She grasped a paper tissue, wiped her tears, and blew her nose. But the tears did not stop. He started to tell her stories about the "Brown Nightingale," about Suad Hosny and Shadia, and the song "Jabbar" he loved so much.

He told her that he had come to love the poetry of Nizar Qabbani because of Abd al-Halim Hafiz, and that "A Message from Underwater," in which a man is sinking in the water of passion, was the most beautiful poem he had ever heard in his life. And that he had not believed that Abd al-Halim did not write the lyrics to his own songs until he read about it in the newspaper.

"It's impossible, Shirin, the words melt in his mouth like sugar, he spins the lyrics into fine threads, impossible that he didn't write that poem, but later I believed it, and went and bought a book called *Drawing with Words*, but I didn't understand a single word. Poetry doesn't make sense unless it's sung by someone like Abd al-Halim. You don't like Abd al-Halim?"

The moon was silent, flinching with muscle contractions, and he saw the small eyes suspended on its round white surface.

Yalo had not noticed how small her eyes were before they had come to the Albert Restaurant. There in Ballouna he saw, and yet did not see, because the fragrance penetrated him and made him unable to see.

"Do you remember? I don't know how you felt, but there, I felt like I was drowning in the smell of incense, I couldn't see anything. Look at me close up so I can see the color of your eyes."

Shirin had selected this restaurant and they drove there in her white Golf. He sat beside her but could not think of what to say. She had told him on the telephone to wait for her in Sassine Square in front of the Bashir

Gemayel memorial at one o'clock in the afternoon. He had stood there and waited in the rain, never budging from his spot. In vain he sought shelter from the torrents of rain under part of the memorial. He did not go to the Café Chaise nearby. He was afraid that she would not find him, afraid that she would not recognize him, afraid that he would not recognize her car. And when she arrived, he did not recognize her because he had been gazing at the passing cars without really seeing them. The car stopped beside him. She opened the door and motioned to him. He saw her and fell onto the leather seat, droplets dripping from his long black coat forming puddles on the floor.

"You're still wearing that coat?" she asked.

He did not know what to say. He had worn it for her so that she would remember that night. But he was lying without even opening his mouth, because this was a coat he could not bear to be without. He wore it in Beirut, he wore it at the war barracks near Adlieh, he wore it in Paris, and he wore it in Ballouna, and he could not bear to take it off. He even hated summer for its sake. He never parted from this coat on his hunting trips in the forest. But he did not know what to say. The spinal column idea occurred to him, and he wanted to tell her about love that could unhinge vertebrae, but he said nothing. He waited in silence until they arrived at the Albert Restaurant, where she stopped the car and they got out. She went in ahead of him and found a private corner where they were seated. Before he had a chance to tell her that he had missed her, as he had planned to do after she had agreed to go out to the restaurant with him, the waiter appeared and she asked what he wanted to drink.

"Arak," said Yalo.

"Arak," said Shirin with a little hesitation. "Why not."

Yalo began to order *mezze*. Shirin seemed oblivious to the different

< 18 >

dishes, or was not listening. Yalo was certain that her consent to have lunch with him would lead her, in the end, to his house in Ballouna or her house in Hazemiya.

When he had bathed at eleven o'clock that morning, as he worked the green shampoo into his hair, standing under the hot shower and closing his eyes, he saw Shirin. Water cascaded over him and his love poured out. He felt that everything was surging off his shoulders, his whole life was rushing by with the hot water, and he felt a strange elation. He pleasured himself without knowing it, and everything flowed away as he finished. He came to her, leaving his sexual desire at home. He came to her naked, without desire. His desire had washed away and he came to her with love. Love alone, he said to himself, love for the sake of love, like Abd al-Halim. A love that he did not know how to express, but he would express it. From the first time he met Shirin, he had not stopped listening to the songs of Abd al-Halim. True, he had gone out on hunting parties but did so without any real desire. He had stopped seeing Madame Randa; he had slept with her only three times in six months, and each time she had put a pornographic movie in the VCR, for he never slept with her without a movie on.

Shirin said that she would meet him in Sassine Square. So Yalo parked Madame's car at a corner near the Lala Grill and walked toward Sassine Square.

When he had caught Shirin with the gray-haired man bent over her neck, he had thought she did not own a car. The man had sped off in his car and left her alone, shivering in the forest, and Yalo took her to his cottage because he had no other solution.

Why had she told the interrogator that he had ordered her to get out, and had asked the man to leave?

"She is lying, sir."

When he said that she was lying, he raised his palm to his right cheek, and felt small white circles spinning out of his eyes, and then everything was a blur.

Was this really what had happened?

Yalo would spend long days in his cell trying to re-create the event exactly as it had happened, but he would fail.

When the light shone on the two victims and he ran toward them, he heard nothing. His footfalls, the sound of his cheap shoes smacking the ground, filled his ears. As always happened with him, the sound of his footsteps rose when he was on the hunt, and he heard nothing else.

He cast the beam of the flashlight on them and then advanced. When he reached the car, he saw the gray-haired man lift his head in terror before getting out of the car and standing before Yalo. Yalo looked at the girl and gestured with the muzzle of his rifle, and while his movement was not intended as an order to get out of the car, the girl opened the door and got out. Yalo turned and walked toward her, and at that moment the gray-haired man jumped back into the car, took off fast in reverse, then turned and sped off with the wheels spraying dirt. Yalo lifted his rifle and aimed it at the car, cocking it in preparation to fire, or so he thought, and he heard the girl crying. He lowered the rifle and went to her side, and silence fell between them.

Yalo guided the girl to his house after asking her to remove her high heels. He held her by the hand and stopped her and then walked with her, and when he realized she was stumbling because of the high heels, he looked at them and she understood, so she removed them without being asked. She carried her shoes in her right hand and walked beside him. Still, she kept stumbling and also fell down at one point. She bent over as if about to fall, and he bent over her, but she regained her balance and stood up.

He grasped her left hand and led her to where he had smelled the radiating scent of incense from her beautiful white arms.

Why had she lied to the interrogator, telling him that she had been with her fiancé?

Yalo did not remember that he had told her that her arms were like rice pudding, but there in the restaurant, after he had slapped her, and they had finished eating, Yalo ordered rice pudding. Shirin had smiled because she remembered that he had told her that her arms were sweeter than rice pudding.

No, he had not slapped her because of the sparrows as she claimed to the interrogator, but because she had offered him money and he despised money. He ate a dozen fried sparrows and drank half a bottle of local arak before slapping her for insulting his honor.

No, what she said was not true. He had not ordered her to kneel, she and her fiancé. She had knelt down after the gray-haired man left. Nor had she been with her fiancé. The young man who sat in the interrogation room had not been with her there in the forest.

She told the interrogator that he had ordered them to kneel and then pointed his rifle at them, intending to kill her fiancé, Emile Shahin, but she implored him to spare him, and he did.

"You are Emile?" asked the interrogator.

"Yes, yes, Emile Shahin," replied the young man.

"Do you have anything to add?"

"Shirin said it all," said Emile.

She said that he had ordered Emile to say his prayers before he was killed in front of his lover. "Then I began to plead with him, and I cried, but he was still stubborn, with his gun aimed at my fiancé's head, so I screamed, I don't know where I found the strength. Emile jumped up and ran to the car

< 21 >

and escaped, thank God, my fiancé was able to escape, but I was trapped with this bandit.'"

"Daniel, what do you have to say in response?" the interrogator asked.

Yalo felt tongue-tied, he fell mute. The pebble came back. His mother used to put a small pebble under his tongue so that he could learn to speak without stuttering. Then he forgot the stutter when he saw the blood, that is what he would have written had he been able to see his life in the mirror of days, but he was standing here, feeling his mother's pebble under his tongue, and found no words to speak.

"Why didn't your fiancé report this incident immediately?" he would have said.

"How was he a man of fifty, who became a young man today?" he would have asked.

"Why did you run away and escape?" he would have asked.

But he said nothing, and the interrogator did not press him for a response. He considered his silence to be a response, and a confession.

"Is this the man who raped you, robbed you, and continues to stalk you?" asked the interrogator.

Shirin nodded in reply.

Emile looked at his watch and asked the interrogator if they might leave now.

"Of course, of course," said the interrogator, and escorted them to the door of the guard desk.

But at the Albert Restaurant, no.

He slapped her and she shut up. Then when he ordered rice pudding she smiled, and he told her that he loved her.

"I'm engaged, Yalo," she said.

"I love you," he said.

"Please," she said.

The waiter appeared with the bill, but Yalo asked him for another glass of arak. He took a sip and looked into the girl's eyes before closing his eyes for a long time.

"Please don't fall asleep," she said.

"Shut up," he said. "Leave me alone. I'm talking to God."

The girl began to talk, and Yalo listened to her with his eyes closed.

"I respect your feelings, but as you can see, I'm engaged, so I can't," she said.

"That's the shit who abandoned you in the forest and ran away?" he asked.

"No, no, I left him, my fiancé is someone else."

The girl talked, and Yalo listened.

"It's like an Egyptian movie," he said. "It's like I'm sitting in a Ustaz Wahid movie."

She said that she would listen to Arab songs only to please him, and that she respected him. She said that she cherished him, and apologized and said that he was free to slap her because she had hurt his feelings when she had offered him money.

"Stop it!" shouted Yalo.

He got up and mimed the scene in "Daughter of the Nile" where Farid Shawqi slaps Hind Rostom and how the actress falls to her knees and says, "I love you – you beast!" "That's how you should be," he said. "You have to love a real man, not these shits, one geezer your father's age, the other one afraid of his mother."

"You're right," Shirin said, "but what can I do? I love him. He was my classmate at the American University, and we slept together. I took birth control pills, but one day I forgot, I don't know why, and when I told him I was pregnant and we had to get married, he ran away and said he was afraid of his mother. So I took care of myself. I had such a *dépression* and one of my girlfriends took me to Dr. Said, who made me a *courtage*, and who loved me. He told me he loved me because I'd cried so much. I got to his place, to the clinic, and I started crying. I couldn't speak. I sat on the chair and placed my head between my hands, and I started gasping, and the tears just ran from my eyes, and the doctor didn't say anything. He let me cry and sat there watching me. He told me later that he sat and watched, and that he became infatuated with me 'for my tears' – that is exactly what he said, in Classical Arabic, 'for your tears,' then he took me in his arms. I don't know how long I stood there crying before he said, 'Come on, let's go to the room next door.' Then he said, 'Get undressed.' I took off my skirt and stood there. But he said no, and motioned with his hands that he meant everything. So I took everything off, and he stared at my breasts, and I felt, I don't know why, his gaze penetrating my breasts like pins, and I heard him say: 'Very nice.' But I didn't respond. I was shaking with fear, and I told him, 'Doctor, I'm cold,' and he said, 'Stretch out there,' and I stretched out on that strange bed, sort of a half-bed. I was on my back, with my legs dangling, and the nurse approached me with a needle, while he looked down below, and he had a strange look on his face, I don't know, I was afraid I was in trouble and I tried to speak, but my tongue was heavy in my mouth, like rubber, and after that I don't remember anything. No, before I passed out, I told him, 'I'm cold, please give me a cover,' I was so cold and ashamed, and his eyes were like, they could see everything, and then when I opened my eyes, it was all over. I heard the nurse saying, 'Thank God, get dressed and go see the doctor.'"

As Shirin told her story, her tongue had a life of its own as she talked, cried, and blew her nose, as Yalo gave her tissues and burned, everything within him was inflamed. The half-bed inflamed him, and the doctor's motion for her to take off her clothes inflamed him, and the sight of the nurse as she gave her the shot of anesthesia inflamed him.

She said she had taken off all her clothes, and drew what seemed to be circles around her small breasts. He smelled the fragrance, the fragrance of nakedness, but he was like a paralyzed man. She talked and he listened, and his eyes felt as heavy as if he were on the verge of sleep. She spoke of the bleeding she suffered two days after her abortion, and how Dr. Said al-Halabi took her to his private clinic, where she spent three days until she was better, and how she had fallen in love with him by the third day.

"I let him sleep with me without feeling any real desire. No, he didn't really sleep with me." She said that on the third day, at about six o'clock in the evening, when she was alone in the room, overcome with sleepiness and craving a cigarette, she saw him coming in the twilight that obscured the room with gray, making everything uniform. He sat by her on the bed, and said, "It's done. Thank God you made it through. Now you're able to go home." He pulled the blanket off her so she could get up, and took her hand.

"When he held my hand, I felt that I loved him."

She said that she loved him for his hands. His long fingers, like those of a piano player, were interlaced with hers, when she fell in love with him.

"He put his right hand on mine and ran the other through his white hair, and I fell in love." She said that she loved him, and was hoping he would pull her against his chest.

"I told him, 'I don't want to go – I'm so comfortable with you, Doctor.'"

Describing that evening, Shirin said that night crept up on them and she had no idea what happened after that.

"I don't know what happened, I don't remember. You know, I never remember these kinds of things, not just with Dr. Said, but, like, with anyone, with you I don't remember either, and I don't remember with Emile. Of course, I remember the room and the doctor beside me, and I did sleep with him, but I don't remember the details. Why does this happen? Do you know?"

"How do I know?" said Yalo.

"That's strange. I don't remember a thing," she said.

"You mean now you don't remember how you slept with me?" asked Yalo.

". . ."

"You don't remember the second time, when you said that you could smell pine, as if there were pine trees in the room?"

"I said that?"

"Of course!"

"No way."

"You were talking about the pine smell, and I felt as if my spinal column were coming apart."

"I never said a thing," said Shirin. "It is just not possible. When I was with you I was dying of fright, anyway, please God, let us forget."

Why did she forget everything?

She had forgotten how she had told him, in the Albert Restaurant, about Dr. Said and her new old fiancé, Emile. She sat like a stranger, and from her small eyes gleamed something like the savagery of youth on that day that Yalo had decided to forget, and had indeed forgotten. They dragged the three men to the cemetery, and crucified them on the ground under the cypress trees in the cemetery of St. Demetrius. They crucified them before shooting them, then they began to curse them and spit on them. Terror haunted their eyes. That day, Yalo vomited, then started to cry, then went home, then . . . No, he did not want to remember now. He closed his eyes.

She said that she had kissed the doctor, she lifted her head a little for her lips to meet his, and she fell in love with him.

"I let him sleep with me but with no desire, but he didn't . . ." she said.

The doctor told her that the complete sexual act was forbidden, for now.

"So he slept with my breasts," she said, crying and blowing her nose.

"Like how?" quavered Yalo.

"Like this," she said, tracing with her fingers a line between her breasts.

"And I didn't feel anything," she said, "except, of course, I felt hot."

She said that she started a long-term relationship with the doctor, that he had strange ways, and that he "always slept with her that way."

"What do you mean 'that way'?" Yalo asked.

"I mean, here," she said, and traced an invisible line between her breasts.

"Always like that?"

"Pretty much," she said. "He said he liked my tits."

"Don't say that word," said Yalo. "It's not nice for women to use words like that."

"Fine, so what am I supposed to say? I'm talking facts."

"Say *sahro*."

"What does *sahro* mean?"

"It means 'moon.' You've forgotten? I taught you that word when you were at my house, that night."

"I told you, I don't remember anything."

"At the time, you asked me what it meant and I explained it."

"Fine, explain it to me now."

"Now, no," Yalo said. "Just don't use that word."

She said that the doctor never slept with her, even once. He was content with just playing around, and with "those." "He said he was afraid of really sleeping with me because we were in the clinic, and I told him, Fine, let's go to a hotel. He said everybody knows him, and he's a married man, so we spent the evening in either the clinic or the car, there in Ballouna, where you raped me."

"I raped you? What's that supposed to mean?"

"I mean, when you took me to your place and slept with me. We were in the car, and he told me to put my head down."

"Maybe he saw me."

"No, he didn't see you, he wanted me to – "

"He wanted you to what?"

"He wanted me to put my head down, and that's when your excellency showed up, and we practically died of fright. I don't know how I held my head up again and how he managed to tidy himself."

"I'm an idiot!" shouted Yalo. "An idiot! A jackass!"

"Lower your voice," said Shirin. "Please. The restaurant is full of people. Do me a favor, don't raise your voice."

Yalo repeated quietly that he was an idiot and a jackass.

Where was the scent of incense?

Why did Yalo not smell the scent of incense when he saw her sitting in the interrogation room?

At the Albert Restaurant he had smelled that scent. Her incense was stronger than the arak, the fried sparrows, than everything. But here, in the white interrogation room, he could smell nothing. His nose picked up a smell like rubber. When the interrogator forced him to write his life story, he would write about the smell of arrest. He would say that the smell of prison was like the smell of damp rubber. The smoking, burning smell of oil, diesel fuel, and tires.

When he saw her in front of the interrogator, he dropped down onto the chair and closed his eyes, searching for the smell of incense. He saw Emile sitting beside her, and saw her slender, naked thighs and short skirt, and her round breasts, and waited for the incense. But the incense did not emerge, and the other smell grew stronger, like the smell of burned rubber extinguished with water. A sun penetrating everything and making it impossible to see.

Then Shirin spoke.

She spoke and reached out and clasped Yalo's hand, in the restaurant, before withdrawing it and saying, "Please."

"Please let me leave. I don't want anything from you, I'm sorry, forgive me but let me leave."

"Where are you going to go?" Yalo asked.

"I want to go home and back to my life," she replied.

"Go. I'm not keeping you."

"Yes, you are keeping me, let go of me, and let me go. I'm grateful to you for everything, but you have to understand that this is over, it's all over."

Yalo wanted to slap her again but didn't. The slap seemed logical when she opened her purse, pulled out a handful of dollars, and offered them to Yalo, asking him to leave her alone.

"Take everything," she said. "If you want more, I'm ready to pay, but just stay away from me."

Yalo stood up and slapped her. He heard the sound of footsteps approaching and guessed it was restaurant staff approaching. He put his hand in his pocket and felt his knife, prepared for a fight. But the footsteps grew fainter and faded away. He sat in his place and drained his glass in one swallow. Silence fell, broken only by Shirin's coughing and sobbing.

He gave her a tissue and she put the money back in her purse, and then he fed her a bite of *kibbeh nayeh*. She ate it and they resumed talking.

He described to her the Egyptian movies he loved, because Madame had made him love them. She used to ask him to go down to Beirut once a week so he could bring her Arab movies from the video store in the Sodeco district. She spent her mornings watching the movies, and sometimes asked him to watch them with her. He did not tell Shirin about the other movies, except that he did not know where Madame got them, but she only watched them at night. Daytime was for the Arab movies and night was for those movies that she only watched with a bottle of Black Label scotch. Yalo did not want to talk about those movies now, because ever since Shirin he had begun to see life through new eyes.

Why did Shirin not believe him?

Why did she insist on thinking that he was robbing her and that his love for her and the songs of Abd al-Halim Hafiz were meaningless?

In the restaurant, when she described her relationship with Emile, he felt a need to slap her again. She said that she had started to believe that Dr. Said did not love her.

"I mean, how can I explain it. I don't know. Only I just felt that he didn't really love me."

She said that her relationship with the doctor ended after that hellish night. "It was like all the gates of Hell opened up. I went to see him at the clinic as usual, around six o'clock in the evening, because he would go home in an hour. We sat and talked, and he moved closer to me and reached out to unbutton my blouse, and asked me about Emile. At that time I'd go home and then go out with Emile. I was so fed up with life, living with secrecy and lies and missed appointments, and anyway, the only way he slept with me was the way I told you about. I got back together with Emile. I won't tell you how it went when we talked. He said that he felt guilty, and so on and so on, and that he was going to bring his mother and we'd get officially engaged. I didn't tell Dr. Said about Emile, so I don't know how he knew. I guess I told him Emile called, but I didn't tell him I went to the movies with him and that we slept together."

"You slept with him?" asked Yalo.

"What's wrong with that, when he's going to be my fiancé?"

"You mean you were sleeping with two men at the same time?"

Shirin did not reply. She hung her head and said nothing.

"Why so quiet?"

She said that she no longer understood him. He had taken her and raped her and was now stalking her on the phone, and demanding to meet with her in cafés, waiting for her in front of her home and her job, robbing her, threatening her, and now here he was lecturing her on morality because she had slept with two men.

"What about you – how many women have you slept with in the forest?"

"No, I'm not like that."

"What are you? Who are you? I swear to God, I have no idea why I got mixed up with you."

"So, what?" asked Yalo.

"So what, what?" asked Shirin.

"You told him about Emile, and then what?"

"Oh! You're asking me about the doctor."

She said she was very surprised when she saw Dr. Said's reaction. When he asked her about Emile, Shirin decided that the time had come to tell him the truth. When he heard that they had gone to see the movie *Scarface*, that they went to an Italian restaurant afterwards, and that they then spent the night in his apartment, he did not get angry and throw her out of the clinic as she thought he would. He began to bite his fingernails uncontrollably, and then he came closer to her and grasped her breasts.

"No, no," she said. "I don't want this."

"I know what you want," he answered, as he began tearing at her clothes and leading her to his couch. She took off all her clothes and helped him take off his, and Hell commenced.

Shirin said that she didn't know what happened, whether he slept with her or not. She said that he had an erection, and that she held it, and that

< 31 >

he entered her, but she did not know, perhaps he ejaculated quickly, but there was no sign, so perhaps he had suddenly gone soft and claimed he had finished, and began to try again. He was up against her the whole time, as if he were sleeping with her, but he did not . . . then he said he wasn't able to, because she had castrated him. "You are a woman who castrates men."

Shirin looked at Yalo and asked him, "What do you think?"

Yalo said that he did not understand exactly what happened.

"Neither do I," said Shirin.

"God doesn't test us," laughed Yalo.

"So it's true that I'm a castrator?" asked Shirin.

"With other guys I don't know, but with me, I'd be glad to prove that you're not, right now."

"That's all you ever think about!"

"What do you want me to think about?" said Yalo, sipping from his glass of arak.

Shirin went back to her story, saying that the doctor got up then, put his clothes on, and left, leaving her alone in the clinic.

"I dressed quickly, without washing. I was afraid he had locked the door and left me stranded there, but when I tried the door it opened. I got myself out of there and went home, and that's it."

"That's it?"

"Well, then there was the whole story in Ballouna. He begged me, and I went out with him in his car. And you know the rest."

"What about Emile?" asked Yalo.

"No, no, Emile knew nothing about my relationship with Dr. Said. Anyway, what kind of a relationship is it when it's no fun?"

She said that even with Emile she did not feel the pleasure of things, but she was going to marry him. She slept with him without any real desire, though she felt affection for him, especially since he was so weighed down by his feelings of guilt. As if he were afraid for her. Shirin said she would marry Emile and wanted Yalo to understand her situation, and to stop harrassing her with his phone calls, because the official engagement would be announced soon.

"Engagement? What engagement?"

"My engagement to Emile," said Shirin. "We decided to get engaged. So please, that's it."

"Now the truth is out!" shouted the interrogator.

Why did the interrogator say that the truth was out? Because Shirin had shown up with Emile and lied? Was that how the truth came out?

The interrogator said that the truth was out, "So it's no use lying anymore."

"Yes, sir," said Yalo. He wanted to confess. He bowed his head, closed his eyes, and sensed his confession, and heard the hoarse voice of his grandfather the *cohno*, deep in his throat, "Confess." Yalo was afraid when he heard his mother say that her father had "swallowed his voice," he was afraid and even stopped swallowing entirely, in order not to swallow his voice and become like his grandfather.

"Confess, boy," shouted the *cohno*.

Yalo saw nothing but a white beard with an odd smell around it.

"That's the smell of incense," his mother said. "Your grandfather is a *cohno*, my boy, he chews frankincense and musk before starting prayers. You too, someday when you're grown, God willing, you'll be a *cohno* like your grandfather."

"I hate all the *cohnos*," said Daniel.

But his grandfather, Abuna Ephraim, as he became known once he entered the priesthood, forgot everything. He forgot his first name, which was Abel, and his second name, which the Kurdish mullah had given him, and forgot his work as a layer of tile in construction projects all over Beirut. He forgot his mother, who had died in a faraway village called Ain Ward, and he forgot his first wife, who died after a long illness.

All Cohno Ephraim remembered of his mother was her long black hair, with spots of congealed blood over it like open eyes. Ephraim chewed the resin of the pine tree and perfumed his beard with incense, and was afraid of the open eyes.

"Close your eyes, boy, and confess."

"This lad's eyes frighten me. Why are they so big and his eyelashes so long? Where did he get these eyes from? We don't have big eyes like this in our family."

Yalo did not know how to answer his *cohno* grandfather's questions, but he closed his eyes and confessed that he had lied or stolen an apple, or not studied, or anything that came into his head. When the *cohno* listened to his confessions, he was transformed from a *cohno* who heard the sacrament of confession into a grandfather, and instead of preaching to the lad who confessed before him with bowed head and closed eyes, he would beat him with a bamboo stick.

"I don't want to confess to you, Grandpa."

"I am not Grandpa, I am Abuna Ephraim, and if you don't confess, you won't eat tomorrow."

He forced him to confess, then would beat him, and the boy became afraid of the hoarse voice which heralded the whack of the bamboo stick on his bare feet.

Yalo did not cry. He held back, and trembled with misery before his grandfather.

He called him Black Grandfather – that stocky, honey-eyed, big-nosed man whose white beard occupied his whole face, and spilled over his chest, he was the master of this little family made up of Yalo and his mother, Gaby. Yalo was fatherless. His father had long since emigrated to Sweden and had never been heard from again; nor was there a brother or sister.

"There are just three of us," is what Yalo told the interrogator when he was asked about his family.

"We are a family of just three persons: Abo, Bro, and Ruho Qadisho. I'm Bro."

"What are you talking about? Do you think I'm joking?" shouted the interrogator.

"No, sir, but my Black Grandfather talked that way. He's Syriac, even though I think he's really Kurdish, but I don't know which is his strange mix. That's what we are, the Father, Son, and Holy Spirit. My mother is the Holy Spirit, that's what I learned when I was little, but my grandfather stopped calling me Bro, he said I was not a good Bro, because the Bro is the Christ, and I was growing up like Judas, a crook, a good-for-nothing, and that's why he started calling me Yalo, and when he heard my mother calling me Bro, he shouted at her and told her to stop it."

Why didn't Yalo tell the interrogator these things?

When the interrogator asked him about his family, he did not know how to respond. He closed his eyes as if he did not hear.

"Confess!" shouted the interrogator.

Yalo decided to confess, and he said: "Yes, but that isn't the way it happened."

"What happened? Tell us."

Yalo said that Shirin had not been in the car with Emile but with another man.

"Liar! Why didn't you say that when Mr. Emile was sitting here?"
Silence fell.

Yalo felt the silence pervading his whole body, a complete silence swallowing him, and his voice, and his ears. That is how he had felt when he got to the villa. The lawyer had told him, "Come," and he brought him from Paris to his dwelling. And there, in the village of Ballouna, he heard the voice of silence, and got used to it, and it became a part of him. He discovered that the night had a body, and that the body of night swooped down on him and covered him.

A night like a black coat, a silence like silence, and stars spread out above him as if they were the opening to eternity, an eternity taking him to the end of fear.

Michel Salloum, the lawyer, said that he had taken him here in order to guard the Villa Gardenia. He said that he had brought a Kalashnikov rifle and a box of ammunition and guided him to the cottage below the villa, where he lived.

"Yes, yes," said Yalo.

"Go down to the house, clean yourself up, and then follow me up so I can introduce you to my wife, Madame Randa, and to my daughter, Ghada."

"Yes, yes," said Yalo.

"Have a bath – the water's hot – and change your clothes. I bought you fresh clothes. And then follow me."

"Yes, yes," said Yalo.

"I don't want any tricks, you understand? The rifle is not to be used unless something happens, God forbid. I don't want anyone seeing the rifle, and I don't want my wife to know."

"Yes, yes," said Yalo.

"My wife's afraid of dogs, otherwise we would have gotten a watchdog, I mean, to help you, but she's afraid, that's why you can't trust anyone. Just trust in God and yourself."

"Yes, yes," said Yalo.

Yalo went down to the cottage below the villa owned by Monsieur Michel

Salloum. The house was small and lovely, but to Yalo it felt like a palace – that's what he thought once he found himself alone in his new home. A spacious rectangular room, about forty meters square, walls painted white, the floor carpeted in green. To the right was a wide wooden bed covered with a blue blanket, and to the left was an old flowery sofa beside a wooden table and three rattan chairs. A single bare lightbulb hung from the ceiling. There was an iron wardrobe to the left, which Yalo opened and saw three pairs of new pants, several old but clean and ironed shirts, and an olive green woolen sweater. Off the room to the left was a kitchen with a small refrigerator, a gas canister with three outlets, a small table, a white cupboard holding pots and plates, and beside it a small bathroom with a toilet, shower, and a half-length mirror. There was a white first aid kit with the emblem of the Red Cross, and an electric water heater. Yalo lit the water heater, went back to the room, and sprawled on the sofa. He noticed cobwebs in the right-hand corner of the ceiling, and saw that the paint was flaking at the top of the wall to the left, but he still felt like a king. He took a shower, but the water wasn't hot enough, then put on a green shirt and gray pants, only to find out that the pants were too short and that the three other pairs of pants hanging in the wardrobe were a little short too. So he decided to put his old pants back on again, and to buy new ones the next day.

Yalo thought that for the first time in his life he would live in a house of his own. He thought he could bring Gabrielle, his mother, here, but then dropped the idea, for she'd said that she wanted to return to her old house, that she hated the suburb of Ain Rummaneh where she had been compelled to take refuge after their forced flight from their home in the Syriac Quarter in Mseitbeh at the outset of the war.

She said that her clients were waiting for her to go home to her neighborhood and that she would go back to her old trade because she was the best seamstress in Beirut.

She said that she could not bear this life anymore, that she longed for her old neighbors, that the civil war had ended or it had to end now.

She said that her father, Abuna Ephraim, had died alone here, like a stranger, and that she did not want to die in this neighborhood; she wanted to die at home, in her own house.

She talked and she talked, she stood for a long while in front of the mirror and talked. Yalo began to be afraid of his mother, that's why he decided to leave. He left the house two years ago and has never gone back. The days pulled him in all directions, and there, in the Paris Métro, the lawyer Michel Salloum discovered him and took him back to Lebanon.

Yalo had not visited his mother since his return to Lebanon, and he could not justify this to the interrogator – there was no legitimate excuse that could prevent a man from visiting his mother.

"I saw your mother," said the interrogator. "She said she knew nothing about you. I went to see her in her house in Ain Rummaneh and asked about you."

"She's still in Ain Rummaneh?" asked Yalo.

"Why don't you know where your mother lives?"

"Sure, sure, only I thought she'd moved back to Mseitbeh."

"Do you mean to say that you haven't visited her since you came back from France?"

"No."

"Why not?"

"I don't know. I didn't want to. There was no reason to."

"Why did you do that?"

"What did I do?"

"You know."

Abuna Ephraim swallowed the syllables when he said: "You know well enough." The interrogator also swallowed his syllables, as if he were choking on the words. He took a sip from the glass of water before asking him again why he had not visited his mother.

Yalo knew that in spite of everything his mother was not a problem. He had not visited her because he didn't know, or because he did know, that she had gone back to her old house, and he did not like the old house, where there was nothing but a picture of Black Grandfather hanging on the wall.

But Yalo never confessed his real sins to his grandfather, because he was convinced that there was only one sin, and that he committed it in spite of himself and unthinkingly. He would find himself alone with his sin, he'd go into the bathroom, grasp his sin, and see stars.

He told Shirin that he loved her because he saw stars. This impression of stars, opening like eyes within the body of the night, came to him anew only when he was with Shirin, there in his little home below the villa. With other women, forest women, Madame, the war girls – no.

"I love you for the sake of the stars," he told her in the restaurant, but she did not understand a thing. She said she was ready to give him all the money he wanted, all at once, but on condition that he leave her alone once and for all.

In tears, she said that she was begging him, that she was afraid of him, that she did not love him, but loved another man whom she was going to marry. He slapped her. He had spoken to her of stars, and she understood that he wanted money! Before leaving the restaurant, he looked at the bill in front of him on the table and wanted to take care of it, but she was quicker than him and paid it.

"I'm the one who invited you," she said.

"No, that's not right. You pay every time."

"Never mind, let me, this time too," she said.

She paid and went out without her escorting him to Sassine Square where his car was parked. She got into the car without opening the door for him, started the engine, and left. Yalo was left standing on the sidewalk of the narrow street. She said she was busy and had to get back to work. But this was insolence! That's what he would tell her on the phone the next day, though instead of her reply he would hear the sound of the line going dead as she hung up on him. He would call her back dozens of times but never hear anything. Yalo was sure that she was hanging up the phone every time she heard his voice saying *allo* into the receiver. He began to dial the number, and when she lifted the receiver he was quiet and tried not to breathe. But she did not even say *allo*. She let the silence hang over the telephone receiver, then hung up. Yalo spent three days playing the silent telephone game, then sound blossomed again and Shirin resumed speaking to him, and made appointments with him, though she always tried to contrive excuses not to keep them.

Why did she say that he came over on the night of her birthday and he had terrified her?

Yalo hadn't done anything. He would say that he hadn't done anything. He'd stood under the streetlight in his long black coat, and didn't budge from the spot, and she had seen him. There was no way she could have not seen him, since his eyes were bright and he cast them on her bedroom window.

Yalo was able to swear that he had done nothing but shine his big black eyes on her window. He had stood still for long hours without moving, then Shirin opened her window and steam came out. Yalo did not know what they were doing inside there, but he saw white smoke coming from the window and becoming a cloud. He saw Shirin, a white halo of smoke encircling her head.

"That's right, you dog, that's right, you stood beneath her window the night of her birthday?" shouted the interrogator.

Why had she said that he carried two flashlights and stood under the streetlight, pointing both beams at her bedroom window?

Why did she lie and say that he was carrying a Kalashnikov? And that he had focused on her window as he had done that night in the Ballouna forest when he had attacked her and her fiancé, in his long black coat and his shoes that crunched on the dirt and gravel, and his white woolen hat that covered his face, and the blinding beam of his flashlight?

Why did she tell the interrogator that he had stood beneath her window with a rifle and two flashlights?

The rifle was impossible – who would dare carry a rifle openly in the street, and in Beirut, and with the war over? And as for the flashlight – Yalo had never carried more than one flashlight in his life, and it was the best in the world; Madame had given it to him when the power went out. A thin black flashlight, which emitted a piercing light, like a laser, as bright as lightning. Yalo had not used his flashlight that night, nor had he stood threateningly beneath her window, nor had he rapped the windowpane with the muzzle of a rifle.

True, he had gone and stood there, with his flashlight unused deep in his coat pocket beside the knife he was never without. But he had not brought his rifle with him.

He stood there, his eyes ablaze with love.

"It was love, sir," Yalo wanted to tell the interrogator.

"Love is humiliation, sir," he wanted to say.

"Love is like the cross, sir," he wanted to say.

But Yalo did not know how to say these things in front of the interrogator, because when he did he heard the voice of his mother, Gabrielle, coming out of his throat. She would stand in front of the mirror and say that her face didn't look like her own face anymore. She cried, then turned on the faucet and washed her face, washed her tears away. She would stand for hours in front of the mirror and say that she was washing the age from her face.

"Only water can wash away age, my son," she said.

He went away and left her, and her face, washed with the water of age, remained etched in his memory, and her voice followed him with its light rasp and a lisp that made the words that she pronounced only vaguely resemble words.

"How do you understand what your mother says?" asked his friend Tony, who would take him to Paris.

"Everyone understands her," replied Yalo. "People understand speech from facial expressions, not from words."

Yalo was not philosophizing when he talked to Tony about facial expressions, for he knew only a few words of Syriac, but he understood everything from the tear-filled eyes of his grandfather, and answered in Arabic, except for the one word *lo*.

He wanted to tell the interrogator to go away, *lo*, not like this, but Shirin pained him. Why had she said those things? Why had she looked at him as if she hated him?

When Yalo entered the interrogator's room, Shirin pointed at him and said, "That's him."

At that moment Yalo looked over and saw her bare thighs, and saw the man sitting beside her, and dropped onto the chair set in the middle of the room for the suspect, with everyone looking at him, under the stern gaze of the interrogator.

He sank under the stares and closed his eyes. Shirin had told the interrogator everything before Yalo was brought into the room, and once he was there she said little. She sat quietly behind the paleness of her slender thighs revealed by her short red skirt. She hid behind the paleness as she had hidden behind the white cloud that had drifted out of her window, there.

"I went and stood under the window to tell her I love her," Yalo said.

I wanted to surprise her for her birthday. I went at ten o'clock at night and stood under the window, and I stayed there until morning, and I thought, this way when she wakes up tomorrow and sees me standing there like a lamp post, she'll get a surprise, and understand how much I love her.

But Yalo did not say that. The interrogator's words shocked him like the lashes of a whip on his face.

The interrogator said that Yalo had carried two flashlights and a Kalashnikov rifle, had stood beneath Shirin's window, and aimed the beams of both flashlights at the window, and as she opened the window, he raised the rifle and aimed it at her. When she screamed, Yalo escaped.

The interrogator did not use the word "escaped." His whole sentence was, "And when she screamed, he ran like the wind."

"What does 'ran like the wind,' mean?" asked Yalo.

"It means you ran away, coward," said the interrogator. Yalo pictured himself running as fast as he could with the wind chasing him, and he smiled.

"What's so funny?"

"Nothing, nothing." Yalo saw the wind and saw the words. The words took shape before him, and he felt as if he were bumping into them instead of hearing or reading them. He had been afraid of his Black Grandfather because he feared the old man's words. He heard the phrase, "Approach, Bro," and felt as if there were shears hanging over his head. He shielded his head with his hands and approached his grandfather, as the shears hovered above as if they might sweep all the hair off his head at any moment. When his mother told him to go to school, he would not see a school but naked girls running behind the nuns, and he'd feel his mouth watering. When his grandfather asked him to fry an egg, he would see an expanse filled with stray dogs. He lived his whole life this way, hearing a word and seeing something else, but this did not mean that he did not understand what was being said. He went to school, and knew that *bro* meant son, and that his grandfather's requests must be obeyed, because a *cohno*'s orders could not be ignored.

The *cohno* met his death in an unusual way. At first he stopped eating meat entirely, and ate only eggs, milk, and vegetables, then he cut out the eggs and concentrated on fruit and vegetables, before being struck with amnesia.

Gaby said that her father got lost and Yalo believed her. He began to picture his Black Grandfather inside a labyrinth of crossed lines. The old man no longer knew how to get out of his bedroom or the bathroom. He would enter a place and get stuck there, not leaving until Bro came to the rescue. Toward the end, Bro had to go searching for his grandfather all night long through the streets of the city, to bring him back home.

When the interrogator used the expression "ran like the wind," Yalo pictured himself climbing the wind, and felt that the sleeves of his coat had become the wings of a bird, and that when he stood there under the window he didn't look like himself, but had become instead a falcon with a long beak. Yalo lifted his arms up as if about to fly, when he heard the interrogator shouting at him.

"Put your arms down and confess, you dog, did you have a machine gun with you or not?"

"No," said Yalo.

"And the flashlights?"

"No."

"Why did you stand beneath her window, pointing the flashlights at the home of Miss Shirin Raad? Is it true that you wanted to kidnap her? Is it true you wanted money? Is it true that you told her you wanted to marry her and take her to Egypt? Why did you frighten her all the time?"

Why had she lied, saying he had forced her to buy him a plane ticket to Egypt?

She had bought the ticket and offered it to him with a thousand Egyptian pounds. She said it was a gift, and that she believed he needed a change of scenery, and that she couldn't leave her job to travel with him. That day she did not mention the name of her fiancé, Emile, and that same day Yalo was convinced she had begun to fall in love with him. It never occurred to him that when he took the ticket and the money he had stepped into a trap and was incapable of seeing things as they really were. He told her to come with him to Egypt, he told her he'd take her to Luxor, where she would see God, but she told him she could not. He took the ticket and put it in a drawer. The thousand pounds, which he decided to hide in the hope that Shirin would agree to come with him to Egypt, he ended up having to convert into Lebanese lira and spend. He had thought of the money as a gift, and as a pledge of love. Anyhow, he was certain that he had not taken money from her, though the interrogator said, quoting Shirin, that he had robbed her.

Why did the interrogator shout at him, "What is the truth?"

Should he have replied that the truth was love? But how could he talk to the interrogator of love.

"Love is humiliation, sir," he told the interrogator.

"I loved her, and I still love her. No, now, after what happened, I don't know, but the thing is that I loved her and I was ready to do whatever she wanted."

"And the money?" asked the interrogator.

"The money, sir. There was no money. Money means nothing."

"You liar! Is that why you frightened her, and forced her to pay?"

How could Yalo talk to the interrogator of love, when the interrogator held a thick bundle of papers and was saying that in them he had all the information about Daniel, and all the members of the gang, and everybody? At this point Yalo understood that "everybody" meant Madame Randa and her husband, the lawyer Michel Salloum, so he decided to refuse to respond to all the questions relating to this topic. What could he say about the wife of the lawyer who had saved him from starvation and homelessness in Paris, and brought him back to his homeland? No, he would say nothing. It was true that he was depraved, as Madame Randa told him when she found out about his nighttime adventures in the lovers' forest, but his depravity would not extend to his confessing his relationship with Madame Randa, and harming the reputation of the good man who had saved him. Even if he confessed, the interrogator would not believe him, even the husband would not believe it. But it was certain that the Madame would not be able to say that he had raped her. Shirin could, if she wanted, talk about rape, because her situation was different, but the Madame, no. Shirin came to the interrogator's room and sat beside her fiancé, and said that he had raped her in the forest.

Why did she say in the forest, why not in the hut or at his house?

The forest was better for rape, thought Yalo, there a rape was the real thing. What did this poor girl know about rape? But that other one, now she was a woman. A woman of forty, with the taste of cherry. Her boyfriend sat on the ground and put his head in his hands when Yalo took her behind the huge oak tree. He had stalked her by chance. That summer night, with the road jammed with cars fleeing Beirut's heat for the mountain, he was sure that he wouldn't find anything. He wore his long black coat and crossed the road that divided the Villa Gardenia from the forest, sat in the pine shade, and waited without waiting. He dozed off, or so it seemed, because he did not see the car approaching the trap. He awoke to the sound of tires screeching to a stop. He opened his slumber-heavy eyes and saw the woman. He felt the flashlight in the pocket of his coat and straightened up. Yalo would never be able to describe how he succeeded in standing up and catching his victim in the beam of his flashlight at the same moment. Then things happened quickly. He approached the car window and motioned with his rifle. The man got out first, then the woman. He motioned to the woman and she followed him, and there under the oak tree he took her, while her companion sat on the ground, head in hands. All Yalo remembered was the taste of cherry. He laid his rifle on the ground and approached the woman, pulled her to him, then put his hand behind her waist and she sank to the ground. She did not undress, neither did he. He even kept his coat on and pictured himself immersing himself in water. Never in his life had Yalo tasted anything like this. The woman's water gushed out pure and soaked everything, and he shuddered with bliss. Everything trembled within a man and woman entwined inside a black coat, making love beside an idle rifle and extinguished flashlight. When Yalo finished, his spirit spent and his trousers drenched in feminine water, he tried to pull away but he could not. The woman was holding him tightly, so much that it hurt. A cry started to gather in his throat; it was as if he were on the verge of starting again when he saw her hands pushing at his chest and pulling him out of her. He stopped, zipped up his pants, bent over to pick up his rifle, and went home. He did not wait for them to leave. He craved a hot cup of tea so he left. When he turned back toward the car, he saw the woman opening the door as the man started the engine without daring to turn on the headlights.

"But I . . . but not in the forest," said Yalo. "I did not rape her."

What did Shirin tell her fiancé, Emile?

He sat here in the interrogation room, beside her, nodding as if he knew everything, but he did not know anything.

Had she told him the truth, or lied to him?

Had she told him that she went to Ballouna with her doctor lover, where they had sex in the car? Or did she say that she had gone with him on an innocent drive, when they had been attacked by a wild beast in a long black coat, that raped her?

Why did the fiancé agree to play this role? Did he think he was gallant? Had he been gallant, things would have ended differently, thought Yalo. Why had he not called him and settled the matter with him man to man? He could have invited Yalo to the café and spoken with him, told him that he loved her too. He could have proposed that one of them give in to the other as befitted a noble-minded man, as Cohno Ephraim had done with the tailor Elias al-Shami when he learned that his daughter had gone back to her original lover.

Cohno Ephraim had told the story to his grandson, and at the time Yalo understood nothing, but now he understood everything.

At the time, his grandfather ended the affair gallantly, and told his grandson the story to teach him the meaning of gallantry. "Life is a word of honor that you say, and that remains etched into the earth."

When Gaby found out, she went crazy. She went to her father and started cursing him, and dragged him out of his room. The *cohno* was wearing white pajamas with blue stripes when his daughter dragged him by his arms, staggering as if pleading with her as she ordered him to leave the house. He spoke unintelligibly, swallowing his words, and swore by all the saints that his intentions were honorable and that he had wanted to explain to his grandson the importance of telling the truth. Then suddenly the *cohno* dropped to his knees and stretched out his arms crucifixion-style, and his tears flowed.

The story had disappeared into the depths of Yalo's memory and resurfaced now before this white interrogator with his snub nose and deep-set eyes.

The interrogator raised his finger as if he wanted to say something, or perhaps he did say something, but Yalo was not listening to him. Yalo couldn't stop asking himself the question posed before him as if it were up on a blackboard.

Why had Emile not done as Ephraim had?

Ephraim had demonstrated courage; he told his grandson that he had castrated his rival. "He came like a puffed-up rooster and left crowned with shame, he went in a rooster and left a hen. I didn't do a thing. I just brandished the weapon of speech before him. Humans are weak when faced with speech, my boy, and that is why God the Father called his son Word. What is meant by the Word of God? It means his mystery and his truth. Your son is your word, and you are my word, my boy. Be my word, just as the Son was the word of the Father."

Ephraim sent for Elias al-Shami. The tailor thought that the *cohno* wanted him to sew a white robe for an imminent elevation to the head of the priesthood, as he told all the *cohno*'s congregation: "Someday, in a year or two or three, you'll call me, sir." And the years passed and the *cohno* waited, as since the death of his wife after that journey to Homs to seek healing from St. Elian, he had told everyone that it was the will of God. He did not shed a single tear at his wife's funeral. He stood and accepted the people's condolences, but instead of saying the traditional words like "May God compensate you" or "Live on," he only uttered, "Christ is risen," and waited for the mourners to respond, "Truly, he is risen." The *cohno* said that God had yearned for his servant, meaning his poor wife who had died of cancer, because there was wisdom that we mortals could not comprehend. The misfortune was yearning, and God yearned for his servants through misfortunes, and perhaps this misfortune was a yearning of a special kind, as if God wanted something we knew nothing about.

Of course, no one took what he said seriously, for Almighty God had not been diminished to the point of naming the old prelate the shepherd of his humble flock. But in spite of the scornful looks, Cohno Ephraim still dreamed of being head of the priesthood. White hair overtook him and old age preyed upon him, but he performed his prayers as usual, awaiting the moment of glory.

The tailor arrived, thinking that he would joke with the *cohno* about becoming an archbishop, when he found himself facing the most difficult test of his life. The tailor Elias al-Shami was sixty years old and seemed eternally youthful; he sucked in his stomach to appear slender, and smiled broadly so that people could see his clean white teeth. The tailor was one of the first residents of Mseitbeh in Beirut to discover an Armenian dentist, Nobar Bakhshigian, and exchanged putting in a plate of false teeth for a set of permanent bridgework, which looked like real teeth.

The tailor sat across from the *cohno* as he had been asked to do – "Come, my son, and sit before me." He bowed his head, which he dyed with henna, producing a reddish result, and kissed the hand that resembled the branch of a dead tree, then heard a strange request and gave a strange reply.

"You love the girl, right?"

The tailor did not understand the question, or claimed not to understand. "What girl, Abuna?" he asked.

"You love Gabrielle, my daughter Gaby. I know everything."

The tailor did not know what to say, because if he denied it he would seem vile to this elderly *cohno*, who was watching his only remaining daughter drifting into nothingness in her relationship with this man. But if he said yes, he had no way of guessing what the *cohno* would ask of him. So he just nodded his head downward in order to let the *cohno* understand whatever he wanted.

"So take her."

"…"

"I am telling you take her, what are you waiting for?"

"What?"

"Take her, my son, I will take care of the legal aspect. I will divorce her from her husband, because he has been gone ten years now, and that way you can marry her."

"But I am married."

"I'll divorce you too."

"Me?"

"Yes, you."

"But that is hard, Abuna, you know these things take time with Greek Orthodox."

"We'll make you Syriac, and that way I can divorce you in twenty-four hours."

"Me, Syriac?"

"Why, is there something wrong with the Syriac?"

"I love the Syriac, Abuna, only . . ."

"Only what?"

The *cohno* had told him to take her. The tailor kept his head bowed for a long time before answering.

"Where should I take her, Abuna?"

"Take her home with you and live with her lawfully. You have to find a way to take her. What's going on now is shameful, and a sin."

The two men did not speak for a long while, and sat immersed in a silence broken by Gabrielle when she came into the living room with a coffee tray.

"Sit down, my girl," said the *cohno*.

Gabrielle sat down, all her limbs trembling.

"I told him to take you. I told him: If you love her, take her." He gazed at Elias and asked him, "What do you say, my son?"

"I don't know," answered Elias, after taking a sip of his rosewater-scented Turkish coffee.

"What don't you know?" asked the *cohno*.

"I don't know, Abuna, why don't you take her yourself." Elias's reply came like a rattle from deep inside him.

"What did you say?" asked the *cohno*.

"I swear, I don't know what I want to say."

"No, please repeat what you said. I did not hear you well," said the *cohno*.

". . ."

"You said I should take her? Me!"

"I can't," said Elias.

"You're telling me to take her, my own daughter! What is this, get out, you shit! I thought you were a man but you are shit! Get out and get away from me, and I warn you, if you come near my daughter I'll crack your skull."

Yalo did not know how the visit ended, or how Elias al-Shami got out of the house, but he imagined that Elias had staggered off.

"He came in a young kid and left an old man," was how he would have reported it to Shirin, but he has never been able to tell her the story of his mother. When he met up with her she was frightened and in a rush and just wanted to go home. He wanted to tell her that it was up to a man to take the woman he loved. Had Emile dared to demand that he take her, he would have taken her. How could he abandon her? They all told him to take her so how could he not? It was unthinkable. And now if the interrogator told him, take her, he would take her. But the interrogator told him he knew everything, and everything meant that he knew about Madame Randa. No, that one he would not take. He imagined the lawyer Michel Salloum before him. He saw him sitting with him in front of the stove in the villa and telling him to take Randa, and then Yalo would say, "*Lo.* No, you take her. I don't want to."

Shirin, she was another story. No one would tell him: Take her. When you are truly in love, that's not the way things go. But there, at the villa, when Monsieur Michel would return from one of his trips to France or elsewhere and ask Yalo to come up to the villa, Yalo was afraid, he felt in his hands the shudders of Elias al-Shami. Yalo would trudge up, his back hunched like Elias al-Shami's, afraid that such a command would escape the lips of his mentor. For he was certain that he could not take her, just as he did not want her. But he went to her when she summoned him, and slept with her when she wanted him. With her, he felt as if he were entering, in moments he had stolen, a world whose essence he did not understand, and when he tried to write about those moments in his cell, with nothing in front of him but a pile of white paper provided by the interrogator, he would never know what to write. Was he supposed to write that he had felt that he was stepping into flames of emotions that were cooking him alive? Or lie and say that he did not like having sex with her? Or what?

Yalo was writhing in the fire of Madame and getting as hard and sharp as a spear, and she was shouting at him to stab her with his spear, and he was swaying, burning and whistling like a wild gale, as she was moaning and telling him to say her name: "Say Randa, say Randa." He repeated it after her and she kept it up. He even started to call sex randifying. He randified her, randified while he waited for her, randified himself, and randified in the shower.

"Don't look up until I call your name," she told him.

He came when she called him, and waited when she did not call him, and she came to him whenever she felt like it, and told him that she missed nature.

"I'm in the mood to sleep with your smell," she told him when she came to his small house for the first time, and they randified in his bed as they had randified in hers. She told him his smell here enchanted her, and that she loved the smells of thyme and pine mingled together, and he randified and speared her. He told her, "What do you say we trade places? You get down here and I'll get on top." She laughed and said he was outrageous, and that she loved him because he made her laugh. Then she left, going home to her bathtub filled with hot water and foamy soap, while he stood in the shower, shivering from the cold, in his little house.

"How did you start hunting people?" the interrogator asked.

"I never in my life was a sniper in the war, sir," Yalo said.

"Don't play innocent! I'm asking you about the forest, the cars, and the women. When did you start going after cars?"

Truly, how had it begun?

How could he answer a question as vague as that?

"It started by chance. I saw a car and I went down."

"Alone?"

"Yes, I was alone."

"And then?"

"After that I was still alone."

When Yalo tried to remember, he saw himself alone, he saw the night. How had the night begun? How was it possible for anyone to ask the night how it became night?

He wanted to tell the interrogator that the hunting he was asking about was like the night. But his throat was dry and he couldn't find the words. There he was, lacking words when he wanted to speak. His mother said her son had a heavy tongue, but he did not find his tongue heavy. The words were hanging in his throat, but instead of spitting them out as other people did, he swallowed them, and prayers, pledges, and pebbles were of no avail.

When Yalo remembered those days, he saw a different person. He saw a child enveloped in his mother's words, they glided over him, yet he was unable to speak. The words began forming in his mouth and he felt them to be whole, then he tried to utter them but they slipped down his gullet and would not emerge. He strained until the veins in his neck stood out, and his mother guided his words with her eyes, then saw how they slipped inside and would only emerge broken. So she'd start the lesson over again:

"Isn't it clear, darling, isn't it clear? I explained to you how you have to get it out. Try to spit. Come on, spit, you see how it all comes out at once? That's how words are, they should come out like spit. Go ahead, try."

He tried, swallowing his words and his saliva, feeling that he would be a mute when he grew up.

But one day he overcame it. At the barracks near the museum, when he shouted out that he had become a billy goat like the others, Tony had told him to spit it out, so he spat it out and learned how to spit.

The war was us spitting, that is what he would say, if he were asked to define the war.

But he did not know how to say or write these big words. He knew how to spit. When he spat, the words would no longer hang in his throat; he spat and became a billy goat, in other words, a hero. It was true that after that he went back to swallowing his words, but he knew why, so he did not fear turning mute. His stammer came back after he and Tony stole the barracks' money and fled to Paris. There Yalo tasted banishment and homelessness, and yearned to be the animal he had been. Yalo would not agree that war was animalistic work; it was basically heroism, but heroism was impossible without a certain animal component. Military training was not complete without awakening the wolf inside you.

"You are wolves," the trainer had said.

"No, we're billy goats," shouted Tony, standing in the first row of the training formation. And they became billy goats. It was not Tony who had nicknamed their battalion based near the museum. Yalo did not know why, but people started calling them billy goats, and they became the Billy Goats.

Yalo felt that there was something like the spear awakening within him. But Madame Randa had not understood him, or did not care, and when she asked him about his spear, that thing that never left him awoke within, and he became a goat or a wolf. He speared her, and when M. Michel Salloum found him in the Paris Métro and brought him to his home in the Sixteenth Arrondissement, he told him not to be a sheep. "That's not right. You're a young man. Why are you behaving like this, like a sheep?" But Yalo was not acting like a sheep; he felt that he had actually become one, and that he had lost his inner spear. Suddenly he found himself in a strange country; Tony, who knew French, stole their money and disappeared from the hotel in Montparnasse where they were staying. Yalo found himself to be like a lone sheep. He did not speak the language and had no money. Suddenly he was a beggar and a mute, how could he not be a sheep? His grandfather had told him that animals were brutes, that was why the Arabs called those who did not speak their languages brutes, or mutes.

In that faraway country Yalo felt as mute as a brute animal and was no longer able to spit out words as he'd learned during the war, and even after M. Michel Salloum took him home to Lebanon and gave him a job as guard of his villa in Ballouna, Yalo remained practically unable to speak. Words came to him only with the help of a flashlight that would light up his night with desire.

Yalo saw his mother, Gabrielle, only here in prison. She came to visit him after he had been detained for two years, but instead of bringing him cigarettes and food as the other prisoners' families did, she stood on the other side of the iron bars and wept, then told him about the room she had rented, and her poverty and fear of hunger. She extracted a little mirror from her handbag and told him, "Look at what's left of me, I can't see myself in the mirror anymore, is that possible? The mirror has begun to consume my image and suck out its essence – can you believe that, son? Look in the mirror and tell me what you see."

When Gaby opened her little handbag, Yalo thought she'd take out a packet of cigarettes, and his mouth watered at the thought that he would get to smoke like the other prisoners instead of waiting for one of them to offer him half a cigarette, or for one of the cigarettes of the lame beggar who specialized in collecting the cigarette butts and sifting them only to reroll them into small cigarettes, which he called recycled cigarettes.

Gaby did not pull out a pack of American cigarettes from her handbag; instead she extracted a small white mirror and began to talk in a way that made Yalo want to escape.

Yalo tried to explain to the interrogator that he had gone to France to escape his mother, but the interrogator didn't seem to understand.

He said that he went to France because he had become afraid, so the interrogator thought that the suspect had fled Lebanon from fear of prison. Many such youths had left after the end of the war; Yalo was only one of them. More likely than not, thought the interrogator, he had been implicated in some crime.

The interrogator asked him who he was afraid of, but Yalo did not reply, since he could not think of any way to tell him about his fear of the mirror. Should he talk about that? And what would he say?

It was nighttime and the power was cut. The woman lit the house with three candles. How old was she? How old is my mother? Yalo never asked himself this question because mothers are ageless. When his grandfather spoke of his mother, and of the red eyes spread through her hair where blood had frozen, he became like a little boy; his shoulders reared up just as children straighten their shoulders when they try to appear taller than they actually are. Now, when Yalo remembered his mother, he squared his shoulders and saw a woman full of life, carrying a candle in her hand, approaching the room of her only son. She was wearing a long blue nightdress, her hair down to her shoulders. Yalo opened his eyes and saw the long chestnut hair, curly and shoulder-length, and asked her about her chignon.

"Where is your *kokina*, Mother?"

It was as if Gaby did not hear. She murmured a few nervous words from which he gathered she wanted him to get out of bed.

"What's going on, Gaby?"

"Follow me, for God's sake."

Yalo got up and followed her to the bathroom, where she stood in front of the mirror and put the candle close to her face. She asked him what he saw.

"How do I know?" he answered. "Tell me what's going on."

She said that she had undone the *kokina* and let her hair fall down over her shoulders because she was afraid, because when she looked into the mirror she did not see her image.

"I look at the mirror and I don't see my face. The mirror has swallowed it. Do you see anything?"

Yalo looked at the mirror and saw his long tan face next to his mother's round white face and her curly chestnut hair.

"Tie your hair up again. It's hanging down like a witch's."

"Can you see my face?" his mother asked.

"Is this what you woke me up for?"

The woman lowered the candle from her face and froze in front of the mirror.

"Take a good look. Do you see anything?"

"Of course I do. Now go to sleep."

"I can't see myself," she said. "Poof! Gaby's gone. The mirror has swallowed my face, it's as if I've disappeared."

"That's enough of these games. Go to sleep."

Yalo went back to bed but his mother stayed in the bathroom. Then she started spending nights in front of the mirror and Yalo grew afraid of her. He did not understand what was happening to her. During the day she was fine and did not talk about her image, but would stand in front of the mirror, combing her hair. At night, however, the mirror became her obsession, her face disappeared, and the woman was terror-struck.

Gaby began coming into her son's room almost every night, would wake him and ask him questions, claiming that all she could see in the mirror was a white spot.

"My face has become a white spot. Oh my God, that means I'm going to die."

And the fear set in.

The fear led Yalo to agree to run away to Paris with Tony.

"I went with Tony. Yes, we robbed the barracks, and left."

However, the interrogator did not believe a word of what he said, so how could he tell him about his mother?

Why had his mother said that he had fled Beirut?

The interrogator said that his mother had told him everything, but he did not divulge what that was. So, what could she possibly have said when she did not know anything, indeed when there was nothing to know? And what did this man want, bathed in sunlight, blocked from Yalo's closed eyes?

"Yes, sir, I confess that I raped her."

". . ."

"Yes, yes, I took money from her."

"…"

"Yes, I called her every day."

"…"

"Yes, I used to wait for her below her house, and then when she left I'd follow her to work, and wait, and then follow her home."

"…"

"No, I wanted her to see me, I did not hide. I wanted her to know."

"…"

"I was wrong, yes, but she was wrong, too. Why did she come to Ballouna with that man who left her and ran away like a rabbit?"

"…"

"…"

"…"

"Men are all afraid. Women are braver than men, sir, I saw then, how they abandon the women as soon as they catch sight of my rifle. Women are different. No, no, I did not rape her because I am a coward. Just as you say, sir, just as you say."

"…"

"I am ready to confess to everything I've done."

"…"

"That's untrue, love killed me and disgraced me and humiliated me, if it hadn't been for love, if she hadn't known that I loved her, she wouldn't have come and complained about me."

"…"

"Sir, it never occurred to me. She made me feel that there was hope. I wanted her, I don't know what I wanted from her, she's the one who made me feel that way."

Yalo smiled.

< 61 >

He said nothing, but he smiled at the thought that he was on the verge of saying these things. These things could never be said in an interrogation, but he said them to himself.

Tony got angry and asked him about so many things, and Yalo replied that he had already told him all about them. That made Tony even madder, and made Yalo enter the lethargy of one who was persuaded of having said things that his friend denied and pretended not to have heard.

Then Yalo discovered that Tony was right, in fact he had not spoken, he had only been talking to himself, thinking that he had spoken to his friend.

When Tony fled from the hotel in Paris, leaving him stranded, and when his tightened throat made him swallow his words before Monsieur Michel and turned him into a lone sheep, he imagined Tony saying to him: "But I told you I was going to rub her out, I had to, man, do you get it? Forgive me, man."

"Stop calling me man, you piss me off when you say man."

But Tony said nothing, nor did Yalo.

Yalo stood alone, wishing that his image would disappear like Gaby's, wishing that he could be invisible to all those who probed his soul with their questions.

"Sir, I confessed, and that's it. Put me on trial and let the court rule as it pleases, but that's it."

However, the interrogator was deaf to Yalo's entreaties.

"We want to know everything," said the interrogator. "Do you really think we're going to swallow this story of voyeurism and perversion? We want all the information about the network that planted the explosives that blew up downtown."

"Me?!"

"Yes, you. Maybe you thought I'd be satisfied with the story of your love life that I know all about now. What we want to discover is the stopper, the plug. Listen to me – I know there is a stopper. Pull it out for me and you'll be fine, and we'll be fine with you."

"I swear to God, I loved her and I'm sorry, I did wrong by her. I raped her, and I loved her, and I'm sorry, and that's it. Now I don't love her anymore, please, sir."

Why did the interrogator ask him about the sea?

"Yes, sir, I took her and we went to the beach at Ramlet al-Baida."

"..."

"Yes, I combed her hair for her there, and asked her never to cut it."

"..."

"Yes, I told her I could walk on water, like Christ."

"..."

"Yes, I walked on the water, and I didn't sink."

"..."

"She said, too, that that she saw me walking on the water."

"..."

"Yes, I tied up her hair for her, and made a *kokina*."

"..."

"That's what we call it in Syriac."

"..."

"No, actually, I mean, I know a few words that I heard from my grandfather."

"..."

"Yes, I told her I'd bury her if I saw she'd cut her hair."

"..."

"Bury her, yes, I said bury her."

"..."

"No, that wasn't a death threat, it was just talk, I mean, a way of talking."

"..."

"Yes, yes, it's all true, but a boat, no, we didn't see boat lights coming from the sea."

"..."

"Me, no. Yes, I had a flashlight with me, only no, I did not use it to send signals."

"..."

"That's what she said!"

"..."

"She's crazy, sir, yes, she is a crazy woman."

"..."

"What does it have to do with me, what she thought? I wanted her to learn things, and learn about life, and be convinced that love can work miracles."

"..."

"Yes, yes."

"..."

"After that she wanted to go, but I told her that she couldn't."

"..."

"She's a liar! I didn't take money from her."

"..."

"She put a hundred dollars in my pocket and left. I discovered the money when I got home and I got very angry, and I meant to hide it for later – someday I'd marry her and spend the money on her."

"..."

"Yes, yes."

"..."

"No, there was no boat."

"..."

"I was wearing my black coat because I never take it off."

". . ."

"I had the flashlight with me because it's always in my pocket."

". . ."

"Sir, that is just a habit from the war."

". . ."

"And now I don't feel whole, not only because you took my coat and consider it a piece of evidence, I'm lost because I don't have my flashlight, so I feel blind, even in broad daylight. I only see right when my flashlight is on."

". . ."

"When the guys came and grabbed me, the flashlight was about to go out."

". . ."

"I swear to God, sir, it's a habit, just a habit."

". . ."

"No, no, that was not my intention."

". . ."

"That's just the way I am, that's the way I've been all my life. I didn't want anything. I swear to God I did not want anything from Shirin, right now even if she wanted me, I wouldn't want her."

". . ."

"I was thinking . . . I wanted . . ."

". . ."

"I don't know – I don't know."

Yalo tried.

He listened to the questions and answered them, or tried to answer them, but the interrogator kept going back to the flashlight, to the fact that he forced the girl to drink seawater, and kept insisting that he was sitting here not with another human being, but with a savage beast.

"I have seen plenty, I've interrogated a lot of criminals, but I have never seen a beast like you. I want you to tell me everything, why you committed these deeds. And I'm warning you, it's not enough to tell me that you put that fellow in the trunk of the car and fucked the girl, it's not enough to tell me that you ripped off the watch and the money and told them good-bye. And I don't want the story of that guy who asked you to sleep with his girl-friend, or the one about Bernadette who pretended to be hitchhiking and you found out she was a whore. When you got to the forest and the guy tried to do her, she began to scream that she wanted money, and you got out and made him pay her, and you divided the money up with her, and you laughed like crazy people, and that poor guy, what was his name? I can't remember. Tell me, what was his name?"

The interrogator started searching through his papers without success.

"Tell me his name. What are you waiting for?"

"I don't know his name, sir, you told me his name was Najib Hayek and that he was a lawyer. I didn't know his name. In my line of work we don't ask names, they don't mean anything. But her – I wish I'd never heard her name. I don't know what happened to me."

"What happened to you? Now you're pretending to be innocent and that this has nothing to do with you. I don't care about these stories. I want to get to the bottom of this flashlight story, why you had it, and who you were signaling to from the beach at Ramlet al-Baida. And you can explain to me how anyone could drink seawater and make others drink it."

How could Yalo respond? What could he say?

He said that there was no boat. He said that the flashlight was part of him, exactly like the long black overcoat, but what could he say about the seawater? Should he tell the interrogator about Cohno Ephraim and the night of the baptism? Should he tell him about Gaby and her hair, which flowed golden in the moonlight as her father combed out the long wet strands and young Daniel sat at their feet, shivering with cold.

The *cohno* would take his small family to the beach to await the Sacred Spirit that would arrive when it could. On the beach at Ramlet al-Baida, after night fell and the small stars appeared through the clouds over the sea, the *cohno* bent over the water and drank, took a few steps in the cold water and high waves, grasped his grandson's hand with his right hand and his daughter's hand with his left, and they proceeded into the sea. When the water reached the child's waist, the *cohno* bent over, murmured a few strange words in a strange language, then filled his hands with water. He let the mother drink from his hands, then her son, and then finally drank himself. After each of them had drunk three times, they went back, walking backwards. When Yalo's hand slipped from his grandfather's and he ran back to the beach, shivering with cold, the *cohno* ran after him and led him back into the water, holding his hand tightly.

"You must not turn your back on the sea, boy. Does anyone turn his back on the Sacred Spirit?"

When the three reached the beach, the mother opened her bag and took out a large white towel to dry Yalo's body after making him take off his pants and giving him fresh ones. The boy was blue with cold, fear, and the taste of salt permeating his tongue and insides.

"The water became sweet and pure," pronounced the *cohno*.

"Amen," said the mother.

"Amen," said Yalo, waiting for a piece of nougat, to put its fine sugar against his rough salty tongue.

Gaby stood in her father's arms undoing her *kokina*. She pulled the clips from her hair and placed them on the woolen blanket she'd laid out on the sand. She told Yalo to sit on the blanket, and she waited.

The *cohno* went to the water and filled his cupped hands with seawater, sprinkled it on his daughter's hair, then began to comb it. Her long hair dropped down to her shoulders, then extended down her back to her waist before reaching her ankles.

The night of the baptism, on the feast day of the Baptism of Christ the Redeemer, Gabrielle would let her hair down and spread it out in the light of night so that it might, by miracle, change color. Her long hair, full of ringlets, flowing under the *cohno*'s comb, turned to gold.

Yalo said that his mother's hair turned to gold, glinting and shining, melting in the water and under the comb. The *cohno* made his grandson stay and keep his eyes open so that he could see how his mother's hair turned to gold.

"Look at this wonder, my boy," the *cohno* said.

Yalo watched the miracle and felt the taste of briny sugar under his tongue, and saw the colors emitted by the *cohno*'s lips, surrounded by his great white beard. The *cohno* moved the comb tremulously as the faint light that penetrated the shore's night traced a spot on his hands and eyes, and the comb rose and fell without pause. The young Yalo sat on the woolen blanket, shivering with cold, and entered into the miracle of the water and the golden hair.

Should he tell the interrogator that he was looking for a miracle?

After they were home, his mother said that she had found the miracle. Shirin, on the other hand, said nothing, because she understood nothing.

The *cohno* finished his combing and the mother began gathering up her golden hair from around her legs, back, and shoulders. She gathered it into rolls that she fastened up with the clips that Yalo handed her. Gaby stood with her back to her son, looking into the distance, out to sea, the *cohno* by her side.

Yalo did not ask his mother why she turned her back to him and looked out to sea, for he knew that his mother was in a contest with the sea. Once a year the sea became a miraculous mirror and the boy saw his mother, and saw her hair that reached the water, which reached to the end of the sky.

That is what the *cohno* told them.

He said that the sea ended at the sky. "The sky is the extent of the sea, my son, and the sea is the mirror of the world." For Ephraim, despite his belief that the world was round, and all the scientific discoveries that Yalo studied at the St. Severus School in Beirut, insisted upon a special connection between the sea and heaven. "Otherwise, how can you explain the story of the prophet Jonah, who spent three days in the belly of the whale before returning safely to the shore?"

Ephraim said that the story of the prophet Jonah was simply a symbol of Christ's death and resurrection. But even the symbol would not have been possible without the special connection between God and the sea.

"In the beginning, God created the heavens and the earth, and the earth was without form and void, and darkness covered the deep, and the spirit of God moved over the waters."

The *cohno* went to the sea with his small family for the sake of the spirit that hovered over the waters, believing that the miracle could occur only on that date in January, when the spirit met the salt water and became sweeter than honey.

However, Yalo had not seen at his neighbors' or friends' the anointing of this Spirit that radiated through his house the next morning as his mother prepared cakes with milk and fried doughnuts. It was only in that little house in whose garden seven acacia trees were planted, shading the place and clinging to a huge China tree that stood like a sentinel at the entrance, that the miracle took place and the shadow of Christ's hand anointed their heads with honey and gold.

Yalo remembered nothing of the return from the beach to the house, as he returned asleep, wrapped in the woolen blanket. He got up in the morning and smelled the fragrance of oil and sweets, and saw the *cohno* sitting chewing incense before going to the church.

Yalo did not see the anointing of the Spirit on his comrades, nor did he ask them about their trip to the beach; whether they too had gone and drunk the salt water that became fresh water. When his grandfather cupped his hands and gathered the seawater, and raised it to his mouth, he said, "It's like honey." Yalo drank, trembling in anticipation of the piece of sugary nougat, which he ate sitting on the woolen blanket covered with the clips removed from his mother's *kokina*.

Was this a tradition common in Beirut, or just a private family tradition the *cohno* had brought with him from his faraway village?

Yalo didn't know the answer, and it did not occur to him to ask his grandfather. He relived the scene now, in the silence of prison, where voices reached him like vague murmurs without words while he tried to write, to end this story that had lasted too long.

He saw the scene on the beach, where dozens of women stood on the white sand, spreading their hair out over their backs. Behind each woman stood a middle-aged man with a comb, and with each stroke of the comb the locks of hair turned golden. The combs slid downward, dozens of combs glistening gold, and the spirit of God hovered over them all.

Yalo felt a cold that crept into his bones and heard the *cohno*'s voice preaching and telling him that the reason he always felt cold was because he was tall and skinny. "You have no meat on your bones to protect you from the wind."

Yalo felt the wind blow through him, as if his body were full of holes. He shivered and clung to the woolen blanket, and the hair clips bored into him from every side.

Dozens of women were being combed golden, were drinking seawater, then carrying their sons and daughters home in woolen blankets to prepare cakes with milk and doughnuts to celebrate Christ's baptism in the Jordan.

"Follow me in half an hour and don't be late for mass!" his grandfather told him in the morning before going to church. "And you better not put a thing in your mouth, my boy. It's forbidden to eat and then take the sacrament, it's a sin. I know everything, and God knows everything."

But Yalo stole the cake from the pantry and ate it, then brushed his teeth to get rid of the scent before accompanying his mother to church, where he fell into a deep sleep. Yalo had never once gone to church on his own; the moment he entered the church, his eyes got dry from the incense and he would doze off on the pew beside his mother, and wake up only to stand before the altar with the others, to receive the bread and wine, and feel the taste of blood on his tongue.

In the war, when he was up to his knees in blood, he experienced the same taste, the taste of salt mixed with sugary nougat, and the smell of the sea full of white mist, which intoxicated him and put him to sleep.

< 71 >

When he returned home, his mother would kiss him and hold her nose, saying that he stank of blood.

"I hate the smell of blood, and look at you, you're drenched in it!"

He replied that blood tasted like honey.

"Why are you afraid of blood? Your father filled a cup with blood every Sunday, and drank it, and offered it to others at mass."

"Shut up. May God forgive you for talking like that. That was not blood, my boy, that was a symbol."

"And this isn't blood either, Mother, it's a symbol."

"God forgive us both, my son."

"I'm like my grandfather, Mother, I fight with symbols."

"You don't know anything about your grandfather, about symbols, or about life. You think this world's a joke, you and your friends. May God protect us from all of you."

Yalo did not think this world was a joke as his mother said, but in this city called Beirut, which was sinking toward its death, he could smell an aroma of the sea, salt, and incense. The image of his grandfather appeared to him always, chewing incense and drinking salt water. But he did not tell Gaby about this image, because he was worried about her. He was afraid she would think her son was going to die. For Gaby had learned from her father that whoever saw death would die. The *cohno*'s mother had died after seeing the ghost of her aunt calling to her, and on the night of his death he had dreamed that he had returned to Ain Ward, where he saw his mother winding her bloodstained hair up in a red *kokina*.

"My mother's hair was wound into a red *kokina*, she was laughing. Maybe she did not die. Maybe she was kidnapped by the Kurd," Ephraim said before closing his eyes against eternal darkness.

Gaby told her son not to talk about blood. "What do you know about blood? Me, I know, my father told me about it. There was blood in Ain

Ward. The blood gushed from the spring after the massacre, and seeped out of the walls of the church."

Yalo used to sleep at church, sitting beside his mother, his eyes closed, rapt with the Sultan of Sleep.

When his grandfather said "the Sultan" had abandoned him, Yalo understood, at the age of ten, that the *cohno* was going to die.

"My grandfather is going to die," he told his mother.

"Shut up, boy. That's God's business, not yours."

"The Sultan abandoned him," he whispered to his mother.

Night became a torment for the *cohno* and to all the members of the small family. He spent the night roaming through the house. He would go to bed at ten o'clock, but then get up within two hours to recite his prayers and rattle around the house. He'd burn incense to drive out evil spirits, and cough and cough.

"My grandfather kept coughing until he died, because the Sultan abandoned him, but me, the Sultan is still with me," he told Shirin.

"Come to the beach with me so I can introduce you to the Sultan."

Shirin didn't understand this insistence on going to the beach at night. She grew accustomed to Yalo's daily phone calls and his constant harping on meeting her. She was determined that their rendezvous be in the afternoon, at the Bistrot in Achrafieh. He would arrive enveloped in his long black overcoat, on tiptoe, peeping to the right and left like a frightened man, before locating his table in the upper corner of the café. He sat down, relaxed, and ordered a beer from the waiter.

"You're so tall, why don't you play basketball?"

That is what she asked him before sitting down.

"Well, here I am, tell me what you want," she said.

"Nothing. I just wanted to see you."

"Okay, you've seen me. And?"

"And, let's go."

"May I go?"

"How about you have dinner with me at my place?"

"Where?"

"In Ballouna."

"Ballouna! God help me! *Jamais*!" she laughed.

Yalo told her unending stories, and made one up about his cousin that he killed in the war.

"You killed her?"

"Of course I did."

"You killed your own cousin?" she asked, shocked.

"I killed her – shot her."

"Why?"

"Because she wanted to marry a Kurd."

"And that was a reason to kill her?"

"It wasn't just that. He slept with her, and she was pregnant, so I had to defend the family honor."

"Family honor!"

"Of course. My uncle couldn't even see straight, he was shamed and felt that he couldn't show his face in public. But he was a coward, he wanted me to help him."

"And you killed her?"

"Like drinking water. I put the gun to her head, one bullet and it was over."

"Over!"

"Of course, over."

"And that's how you saved your family's honor?"

"Honor is the main thing," he said.

"Good grief – honor!" she said.

He told her the story in order to see admiration in her eyes, but instead of admiration, he saw her little eyes fill with terror.

He told her about the tailor who raped his mother.

"Raped her?"

"She was young, she was seventeen, and worked for him. And he raped her."

"Did you kill him too?"

Yalo smiled, flashing his big white teeth. "No – that one, my grandfather the *cohno* killed."

"Your grandfather, the priest, killed a man?"

"Of course he killed him."

"A priest who kills?"

"No, you've got me wrong, he didn't kill him like you think, he didn't use a gun or a knife, no, he killed him with talk. He talked with him, and the tailor couldn't take it, and so he died."

Shirin laughed. "Talk is all you're good at."

"Give me your hand," he said, and offered her his hand above the table.

"Not here, please God."

"Give me your hand – I'm telling you," he said.

"Fine, but down there."

Yalo brought his hand under the table and Shirin reached her small white hand out. He held it, and pulled it toward him and put it onto his hip, so that the girl felt a chill from the steel that tingled from her fingertips to her shoulders. She quickly withdrew her hand and asked, "What is that?"

"That's my piece. You want me to take it out and put it on the table? For you I'm willing to do anything."

Why did she say that when he met her at the Bistrot, he had put his gun on the plate in front of her?

He heard the interrogator reading about the gun and the plate and could not believe his ears.

"He placed the gun under the plate, then lifted up the plate and said, 'Look.' I almost died of fright, while he was laughing like mad."

The interrogator read this sentence from the notebook in front of him, then asked Yalo what he had to say.

"How should I know?" asked Yalo.

"Is it true, you put the gun under the plate to frighten her?"

". . ."

"Is it true you told her you wanted to play the gun-in-the-plate game?"

". . ."

"What is this game? Tell me so I understand."

". . ."

"Is it true you told her she had to get used to the plate?"

". . ."

"In front of everybody you pulled out your gun, as if there were no laws?"

"I only . . . I mentioned the plate, but not like that."

What did she say about that plate? Yalo had only said that he would put the gun on the plate in front of everyone, so that she would believe his love for her, and now she was saying that he put the gun on the plate to frighten her, that she begged him to stop, that he burst out into a tremendous belly laugh that rose above the murmuring conversations that mingled Arabic and French of all the diners seated nearby.

". . ."

"I forced her to speak Arabic with me?" marveled Yalo.

". . ."

"She said that she loved seeing me so she could speak Arabic, anyway,

< 76 >

what do I have to do with Arabic? Arabic is not my language, sir – we have a dead language. When I speak, I feel something dead on my tongue."

Yalo did not say this, and would not have even had he been able, in this difficult circumstance, to remember what his grandfather had said, for he was unable to formulate sentences in this way.

His grandfather, at the time the Sultan of Sleep deserted him, used to say that he felt his tongue dying in his mouth. He stood under the icon of the crucified Christ and spoke to Him:

"Your language is dead, O God, how can you let your language die this way? I feel the taste of death upon my tongue. Who after me will recite the Our Father in your language after my death?

"*Abun dbashmayo, netqadash shmokh, tite malkutokh, nehwe Sebiyonokh, aykano dbashmayo of ar'o, hablan laHmo dsunqonan yawmono, washbuq lan Hawbayn waHTohayn, aykano dof Hnan shbatayn lHayobayn. wlo ta'lan lne-syuno elo fasolan men bisho. meTul dilokh-i malkuto wHaylo wteshbuHto l'olam 'olmin, amen.*

"How can we pray, Yishou, when the words are dying? I can sense the worms emerging from them, as if my mouth has become a graveyard. Your language is dying, and You are doing nothing about it. With whom do You wish to speak upon Your second coming? There is no longer anyone in the world left but me who can understand You. And me, the Sultan has abandoned me, and death is approaching. Someday when Your servant Ephraim has died, what will You do?"

Yalo told Shirin that he wanted her to come with him to the beach at Ramlet al-Baida after Christmas. She said no. Yalo got mad, grabbed her by the arms, and made her feel the pistol on his hip. He said that he was prepared to put the gun on the plate, even in front of everyone, just so that she would believe his love for her.

"But no, no, sir," Yalo said, "I did not force her to come to the beach."

Yalo called Shirin more than ten times that day, and she repeated over and over that she did not want to go to the beach; she preferred to meet him at the café. In the end, however, he convinced her. He told her that he would show her a miracle, that he would speak to the fish in Syriac. She agreed to come, on the condition that their meeting be short, because she had to be somewhere for dinner. But their meeting lasted until late into the night, not because Yalo forced her to stay and drink wine, as she told the interrogator, but because the miracle indeed occurred.

They walked along the beach at Ramlet al-Baida, then he asked her to go into the water with him.

"It's cold, please just cut it out."

He left her standing there and plunged into the waves without taking his clothes off, then came back with salt water cupped in his hands and asked her to drink of it before they sat together on the cold damp sand. He pulled from the pocket of his overcoat a bottle of red wine and a loaf of bread. He drank from the bottle and had her drink from it, ate some bread and fed some to her.

"The wine is too sweet. I don't like sweet wine," she said.

"That is sweet fresh water, not wine."

Then he stood up, walked to the water, and walked on the water. He left her sitting on the sand, and began to see himself through her eyes. He saw his back draped in the black overcoat, he saw his shadow that stretched to the sky. When he returned to her, dripping wet, his teeth chattering with cold, he saw her sitting with her head down on her pulled-up knees, and when he raised her head to kiss her, he tasted tears.

She wept and said she would die here.

"Please, let me go home before I die."

Why did she say he had forced her to eat bread and that she had vomited up the sweet wine mixed with salt water? The water had turned as sweet as honey but she did not understand, and now as he stood in front of the interrogator who appeared to him through blinding sunlight, he discovered all at once the secret of the bread.

He wanted to tell the interrogator that he was sorry. He had suddenly discovered the secret of the bread, and this whole story with Shirin appeared ridiculous to him, not even worth discussing. Yalo burst into laughter, much to the interrogator's consternation, and after this hearty laughter he sank into thoughtful silence and stopped responding to the questions. What could he say? That the bread – that everything except for the bread was nonsense.

"Don't tell me the world has changed, my boy," said his grandfather. "Whatever has happened or is going to happen, nothing changes. The real thing that mankind has discovered is bread. Apart from food, show me one single invention and I'd be willing to believe that the world has changed. The world does not change, it is round, like a loaf of bread. Everything, my boy, is the same as it was except for the unpleasant taste in my mouth, but I continue to chew incense or pine sap every day. And all because the Sultan has left me. My boy, there are only two things in life, sleep and bread. That is our faith. Christ is a grain of wheat, that died in order to rise, and transformed death into sleep. A man sleeps every night in order to get used to death. When the Sultan of Sleep starts to abandon you, and you start to lose your craving for bread, that is when real death is drawing near. Only what's the difference? There is no difference, it's like sleeping. In sleep we dream, and in death we'll dream."

Yalo wanted to tell her, he wanted to inform her, but she was crying. How could he tell her about his mother's hair, gleaming with gold, amid the white sand, when Shirin was bent over her knees weeping, not daring to look up.

"Please let me go home," she said.

"Did you see the miracle?" he asked her.

"I saw everything, but I want to go."

"When will I see you?"

"Call me tomorrow and we'll set something up, but let me go."

He saw her disappear into the night. She took off her high heels and ran on the sand until the shadows swallowed her. Yalo remained alone on the beach with an empty red wine bottle and what was left of the bread.

He had not told Shirin about his mother. He had wanted to tell her how his mother drank seawater, how she opened her eyes, how she let her hair down. He wanted to tell her that he saw dozens of women on the beach, standing beneath flowing hair, intoxicated with the gold wrought by the small moon that swung between the clouds, swallowed up by one cloud which then cast it out to another. The light dimmed and then reemerged, and the long hair covered the boy trembling with cold, huddled up on the woolen blanket.

Why did she say that he had made her eat the bread and drink the wine and then stole all the contents of her handbag? Why did she say that when she met him, she made sure not to put more than one hundred American dollars in her handbag? Why did she say that every time they met he took a one-hundred-dollar bill?

"But she did not tell the whole truth, sir."

"And what is the truth? Please tell me."

"The truth is that no one but God knows the truth."

Yalo was no longer sure of anything, but in those encounters he felt that Shirin was dissolving under his gaze, as if she wanted him to pull her to him, but something prevented her from speaking her feelings, as if she were connected by a hidden wire to another world, which she could not leave. Yalo's gazes reached out to her to come to him.

"Come to my place," he said.

"Where?" she asked.

"My heart."

"Yes, yes," she answered.

She was afraid. Now Yalo understood that she had been afraid. Fear was a deceiver, it inspired fear of things that did not even exist. Now – that is, in a torture chamber – Yalo understood. Confessions under torture were like lovers' confessions. Suddenly a lover loses control of his tongue and says things that destroy love.

Now Yalo was convinced that he had made a mistake. He should not have told Shirin the truth about what he had experienced, yet he did. When he told her about Madame Randa, and how he randified her, and about her daughter, Ghada, and how her eyes flashed with jealousy as she told him about her friend in college who had moved to Canada, and that she would follow him there soon, and how when he told her about his adventures in the forest and his compassion for Monsieur Michel Salloum, he had fallen into a word trap. His trick had been discovered.

Had he not told her that he was sure Madame would report him to the police, this nameless girl would never have dared go to the police station to lodge a complaint against him.

It was the disease of truth that he came down with when he fell in love.

He told her that he did not know why he felt that way, or why he was no longer able to lie. He told her everything, and when the love flowed off his tongue he found himself in the police station, where he saw her, in her short skirt with her slender white thighs, pointing him out as a criminal.

Yalo told the interrogator, he wanted to tell him, but he suddenly fell mute. He recalled how he had fallen into the abyss and fallen from her favor. As he fell in love, he wasn't able to hide the truth, even if meant losing her esteem. He was telling her about his mother's relationship with the tailor Elias al-Shami when he sensed the sinking, he could see his own image crumbling in her eyes, and there was nothing he could do.

How could he save a fallen image?

Instead of ceasing to speak, and repairing his image anew, he saw his speech become the mirror of his fall. He saw as in a mirror how he had fallen to earth, with his image shattered into small pieces. He felt he was drowning, and all a drowned man can do is struggle to continue his journey into the depths that have swallowed him.

So, exposed by love, Yalo drowned, and when he spoke, he fell to earth.

"I swear I did not kill her, sir."

Why did the interrogator ask him about a cousin he had not killed?

Yalo had lied to Shirin when he told her about a crime that existed only in his imagination. He tried to salvage his image, which was sinking and drowning, so he invented a lie about a crime, and now this lie was being used against him as a fact as the interrogator described it.

Why did he say that he would send an interrogation team to Al-Qamishli to look for the Jal'u family?

"There is no such person as Maria Jal'u, sir, I swear there isn't. The whole story is that I was fibbing to Shirin. I don't have a cousin, because I have no uncles on either side. Well, it's true that I have an aunt Sara on my mother's side, but she left for Sweden a long time ago. I don't know her. My mother told me that she got married and left, and became a Swedish citizen. Then the war came and we heard nothing more from her. That's what my mother said."

"What about your father? I'm asking you about an uncle on your father's side."

"I don't know, I swear I don't know. He might have brothers or sisters, but I don't know them. I don't know my father. I've never even seen his picture, I asked to see one once, but my grandfather didn't want me to talk about that."

Why did the interrogator not believe Yalo, who stood before him with his long eyelashes, his hands shaking, his back bent, his stammering, and the words that hardly made it out of his mouth?

Yalo had known that no one would believe him. That's why he said whatever he wanted, because in the war no one believed anyone. But now the war was over, as he told Shirin. He told her he hated the war because of all its lies, and that when he met her he was sure the war was over because he had stopped lying; he wanted to start his life all over again, he loved her.

No, before the war ended, Yalo decided to emigrate. It was his friend Tony Atiq's idea. Yalo did not know whether Atiq was Tony's actual family name, or a nickname he had acquired, as people tended to acquire nicknames in the war which took the place of their real names.

Tony said he was *atiq* – old.

"I'm an *atiq* Syriac," he said, and told so many stories about his heroic deeds that Yalo did not believe. "How can I believe what you say when your eyes are lying?" But the words were eyes. He tried to explain to his friend that words were like eyes, but Tony was blind when it came to words. He said whatever he pleased, and bragged all the time. No one believed him, but he did not care, he kept talking, because talk leads to more talk.

"Words are eyes," the *cohno* told his grandson as he opened a book, in order to teach him the basics of reading the Syriac alphabet.

"Look closely at the words, my boy. Do you know why mankind is so absorbed with reading? You understand, it is the words, they watch us, because they can see and breathe."

But the war taught Yalo to believe his own eyes, not the eyes of words, and he would make his peace with words only in prison, where the interrogator would force him to write his whole life story, from beginning to end, several times over. That was when he would discover that his grandfather was right, that when speech was written down, it looked up at the writer and carried on a discussion with him, forcing him to write what needed to be written.

In the war, however, words flowed just as blood flowed. Blood flowed and speech flowed, and people no longer believed a thing, neither blood nor words.

Yalo believed Tony Atiq only once, when he convinced him to rob the safe of the Georges Aramouni Barracks so that they could flee with the money to France, where they would start a new life.

Yalo broke into the safe and robbed it, and Tony got hold of tickets for the boat to Larnaca in Cyprus, and from there, plane tickets to Paris.

In the luxury hotel in Paris, Tony disappeared with the money, leaving Yalo alone, with nowhere to go except the Métro tunnel at Montparnasse, where he found some warmth in the bitter cold of Paris. Yalo found himself in a strange land without even the means to buy a dry crust of bread. He sat in the Métro and begged. There Monsieur Michel Salloum found him and took him back to Lebanon, and from that point the story was known, because it all alternated between the interrogation room and his jail cell.

Yalo said that he had lied to her so that she would be impressed and fall in love with him.

He said it was love.

He said that Shirin let him languish for a whole year waiting for her. A year during which all he saw were promises in her small eyes. A year during which he called every day and waited under the window of her house or in front of the Araissi Advertising Company building, where she worked. A year during which he haunted the Beirut night searching for her and her middle-aged lover, and later on for the young man with the thin mustache she said was her fiancé.

Yalo wrote that he was surprised when he saw the young man sitting beside Shirin in the interrogation room, squinting through his thick, black-framed eyeglasses as if he couldn't see. A short, full-bodied young man, fair-skinned and pink-cheeked, with plump thighs, sitting quietly in the interrogation room, Shirin at his side, proud of her fiancé and gazing gloatingly at Yalo, who nearly fell over when he saw her. He steadied himself on the chair before sitting on it.

"Stand up, you dog. Who told you to sit down?" shouted the interrogator.

Yalo stood up, trembling, his eyes closed, before the interrogator allowed him to sit. Then the barrage of questions came at him.

Yalo wrote that when he gathered himself on the chair, opened his eyes, and saw the young man, he ached for his flashlight. This guy would never be able to resist a single point of light; he would collapse and crawl on the ground and say, "Take her, sir, and just let me go."

But the fiancé sat under the sun falling from the window behind the interrogator's head, lifted up his little nose as if he were apart from this story and from this whole country.

Yalo would write that when he saw Shirin sitting beside her fiancé, he suffered the third shock of his life.

The first shock was his mother with the mirror that swallowed her face and made her disappear, or at least made her feel that she'd died before her death.

His second shock was Tony Atiq, who vanished in Paris, taking the money with him, along with the French he knew, leaving Yalo alone with no money and no language.

Shirin was the third shock.

When they arrested him in his little house, the thought of Shirin never occurred to him. He assumed that the Madame had betrayed him. He had begun to notice for some time the hatred in Madame Randa's eyes. Even when he slept with her, he felt that she was no longer sleeping with him, but sleeping through him.

He said to himself, as he raised his hands in the face of the rifles pointed at him, that this was Madame's doing, and he laughed to himself. He would expose her and tell everything about his relationship with her. He would enjoy the way Monsieur Michel Salloum's face would wince as he heard the truth.

"My husband never suspects me, ever. I don't know what would happen if he ever found out about you. My husband's crazy about me. He could never imagine you bewitched me."

Yalo decided not to answer the questions in his house. He put his hands in the air and let them search the house. They confiscated the machine gun, the pistol, a box of ammunition, his overcoat, and the flashlight, while he waited quietly. There at the police station he would expose everything; instead of telling them about his exploits in the lovers' forest, he would tell them about the Madame.

Then he saw her in front of him, just as he had seen her for the first time.

He came with M. Michel to the villa in Ballouna. Yalo went to his house, showered, put on clean clothes, and went up to the villa. There he saw the most beautiful woman he had ever seen in his life. Randa was tall and dark with short black hair. Her lips were thick and full and her eyes green. He walked in and saw her embracing her husband with her bare arms. When she noticed Yalo, she took a step back. Yalo sensed that this woman's gaze fell on him from above. He detected a fugitive smile meant for him alone; embarrassed, he felt that his feet could no longer support him, so he closed his eyes and fell into the chair. Then he got up, wishing to leave.

"Just a moment, just a moment," said Madame.

Yalo stood in front of the door, confused, when Monsieur Michel motioned for him to sit. He sat on the soft red sofa and noticed that Madame had disappeared; then Monsieur also disappeared. Yalo was left alone in a spacious salon hung with various Byzantine icons.

When they returned, Madame Randa was wearing a blue dressing gown over her blue dress and bearing a tray on which she had placed a long-handled coffeepot and glasses of cognac. She poured the coffee and the cognac and offered them to the two men before sitting down. She crossed her legs so he could see the sole of her tawny foot and her calf rising and falling with the smoke of her American cigarette, which she exhaled into the air of the salon.

Yalo drank his coffee and cognac quickly and left with Monsieur Michel for his house, where he understood that his job would be to guard the villa as well as Madame and her daughter, that he must not openly carry a weapon by night or by day, that he would receive a monthly salary of three hundred American dollars in addition to the meals that would be sent to him from the villa.

But Yalo had erred, he would write that he had erred, and would feel moments of regret for the Madame during his long stay in detention. No, the truth was that his feelings of regret for the Madame began when he saw Shirin with her slender, trembling thighs in the interrogator's room. Suddenly everything ran together in his head and he tasted thorns, and saw before him the Madame's flirtatious calf, before he fell captive to Shirin's small eyes.

Yalo had erred that night two months before he was arrested and he was incapable of justifying or explaining his foolish behavior. Madame was wearing a white nightdress, stretched out on the sofa in the salon, her full breasts nearly exposed by the opening of her dress, emanating the fragrance of her perfume, Madame Roche. Yalo took his usual place on the floor beside the sofa. He told her he was tired and his eyes hurt, but she didn't believe him. She poured out two tumblers of whiskey and told him to drink. She picked up the remote control and started the movie, and began ruffling the hair of the young man sitting by her. That night Yalo did not wait for the end of the movie, just as he did not wait for her teasing – that slow sexual ritual that she imposed on him. Fed up, he took her on the sofa. He heard her voice pleading, "No, not like this," but he didn't stop. He had never before slept with her here. She would take his hand and lead him to the bedroom and there slowly undress, drawing him to her slowly, and when he took her she asked him not to come quickly. She languished and delayed as she gazed at her naked body in the huge mirror placed at the foot of her bed and Yalo was immersed in the fragrance of her perfume and writhed between her thighs and at the cleft of her large, firm breasts. He came near at a signal from her eyes and moved away at a signal from her hands, and when he heard her final sighs and sank beneath the water that flowed freely from inside her, seeming to disappear, he felt that he was shooting his whole soul into her and that he wanted to fall asleep in her arms. But Madame transformed quickly at the final moment into a stranger, covered herself with the bedclothes, and her dilated pupils began to shift feverishly, and she said that she was afraid that her husband would be showing up. Yalo would laugh and go back to her but she firmly resisted him and he understood that he had to go. He put on his underwear and his rumpled pants tossed beside the bed, and he felt that his feet were as rumpled and limp as his trousers. He would walk on trembling feet to his house, where he'd drink a bottle of red wine and fry three eggs, then take a shower and sleep like the dead.

That night Yalo felt nauseated and did not know how he had been able to get erect and feel desire. He felt sure that he would not be able to sleep with Madame Randa, but suddenly he got hard and was proud of himself. Yalo had wanted to ask her to postpone it but she did not understand his hint. He sat down on the floor like a dog, watching a movie that was like all those movies. All pornos were alike but possessed an undeniable excitement. He drained his glass in a single swallow, then jumped on top of Madame, took her in seconds, and got up. He did not take off his clothes. He unzipped his pants, flung himself on her, and finished. He refastened his pants, sat on the opposite sofa, poured himself another drink, and lit a cigarette.

Madame Randa got up and covered her naked thighs in a nightdress, left the television bright with the movie, and went into her room, dragging her feet. At that moment Yalo saw how Madame's gaze came from above and broke on the floor. He did not finish his drink. He put out his cigarette and went home.

In the days that followed, they spoke to each other. She scolded him and he scolded her, but she never uttered the words "I love you." She never once told him that she loved him, even when her water would spill in his arms. She'd rise like a ghost then sit cross-legged on the bed, her eyes dancing and shifting above her long neck before settling down and gazing afar.

In the course of that long week she still never uttered those words. Her pleading, broken eyes spoke but did not speak. Yalo felt a mixture of fear and pride. He saw her at the entrance to the villa and felt the bliss of that night. He followed her as usual to help her carry her purchases, but she did not look at him.

One night she summoned him to the villa. He went up, grumbling, sure that this would be another bickering session. He went in and saw her sitting alone in the salon, drinking whiskey. She motioned for him to approach and sit down. He sat on the floor beside her sofa and reached out to pour himself a drink, but she said no. She did not reach out to fondle his head. She drank and drank while he sat in his place. Then she turned to him and pointed to the door. Yalo left, stumbling, and realizing as he slammed the door that it was all over. He sensed that his days in the villa were numbered, and began to prepare for a new turn in his life, but he still could not let go of Shirin. He called her every morning, went to her house and stood in front of it, followed her to the company where she worked, and stood in front of the building entrance. Now he went home to the villa only at night. His hunting activities ended; he no longer had any desire to stand under the oak tree waiting for lovers who would fall prey to his flashlight. Ghada returned the books he had stolen for her from the Ras Beirut Bookstore on Bliss Street. Yalo would live sad and alone and would never stop buying the music tapes of Abd al-Halim Hafiz. He would spend his nights listening to the song "Her Beloved." He thought about writing a letter to Shirin, but realized that he could only write in Arabic, and doubted that the girl knew how to read Arabic. From then on, his encounters with her would depend on pure chance.

That is what he told the interrogator.

He said it was by pure chance that he met Shirin.

"And the telephone calls every day, you dog?" asked the interrogator.

Why did he ask him about the phone calls as if he didn't know the answer? People made phone calls because they felt lonely. Yalo wanted to tell the interrogator that he felt lonely because he had no friends. There was no one Yalo could talk to about his love story with Shirin because he lived with no one. From the day Tony abandoned him in Paris, he had lived alone, he and his shadow, he and his rifle, he and himself.

Yalo discovered his loneliness with Shirin when she left him there in the Albert Restaurant after lunch, and after having agreed to pocket the hundred-dollar bill, refusing the larger amount she had offered him. There, he felt lonely, and missed his friend Tony Atiq.

Why had Tony done that?

Why had he left him in an unfamiliar city where he didn't speak the language, why had he left him alone with no language and no money?

"There, sir, there, if you'd allow me to say so, it was cold. Real cold, sir, that makes everything in you shiver, every muscle in your body, every shudder of your eyes, everything. There, sir, the cold made you blue with fear and loneliness."

Yalo told Shirin about the cold. He tried to tell her, but she laughed at him: "You're the world's greatest liar!" she said, and refused to go up to Ballouna with him.

That was one week after the famous night in Ballouna. He called her house in the morning. Her mother answered the phone sleepy and yawning, and he heard her call to her daughter that someone named Yalo wanted to talk to her. Then came the tone of her delicate voice. Suddenly her delicate voice became broad and deep.

"Hello," she said in her delicate voice. Then her voice amplified, slowed down, and became scratchy, as if coming from an old recorded tape.

"It's me," he said, after hearing her ask, "Who is this?"

"Who is this?" she asked.

"Me, Yalo."

"Hi . . . hi."

"How are you?"

"I'm . . . fine . . . thanks."

"I miss you."

" . . . "

He said that he wanted to see her that day and she replied that she was busy. He said that he would wait for her in front of the Araissi office at nine in the morning and she said no. He said he would be there anyway.

"Fine, fine," she said.

"I'll be waiting for you," he said.

"No, not in front of the office. You'll find me in the News Café."

He said he did not know where to find that place and she told him it was near the Clemenceau Cinema.

"Okay, in an hour, so, at nine I'll be waiting for you there."

"No, no – I can't before five in the afternoon."

"Okay, I'll be waiting for you at five."

"Sure, sure," she said, and hung up.

When he met her at the café and they drank tea, he told her about the cold. She laughed and said, "You're the world's greatest liar!"

Yalo went to the café at four o'clock. He sat in a quiet corner, drank a beer, and waited. When the hands of the clock approached five o'clock, he felt nervous and fearful that he would not recognize her. He recalled all her features in his eyes, and waited as he sipped his beer slowly. But as soon as he heard her footsteps on the floor he recognized her, then scented the fragrance of the incense that preceded her. She paused a moment before sitting across from him and did not offer her hand in greeting. She pulled out the chair and sat down in silence. When the waiter appeared she ordered a cup of tea and Yalo also ordered tea.

She drank, and he drank.

She spoke, and he spoke.

Yalo did not remember what he said, or how the time passed in an instant, and then it was six thirty. Shirin looked at her watch and said she had to go.

"Should I give you a ride there?" he asked.

"No thanks, I have my car."

"Why don't we go to the mountain?"

"Where?" she asked.

"Ballouna," he said.

"Please, Monsieur Yalo."

"You still remember my name?"

"Please, please do me a favor, I'm very grateful to you. You were a gentleman with me. Please keep being a gentleman."

"Why am I, what did you say?" he said. "I wanted for us to go for a drive and get some fresh air."

"Please, let's just forget it," she said.

Then she asked him how he knew her name and telephone number, and he said he knew everything about her. He knew where she lived, describing for her the tall building in Hazemiya, and he knew where she worked, and he loved her.

Yalo did not remember when he had spoken of love, whether in their first encounter or the second. He remembered that he showed up at their first appointment stammering, and that when he saw her shivering in front of him in the café, he again felt like the hawk he was. He waited for an hour before she arrived, and he felt as if there were water trembling inside the muscles of his chest and inside his arms and legs, making him quiver in his chair. When she came and sat facing him and he saw the trembling of her narrow lower lip, colored red but almost pink, giving off a strong smell of perfume mixed with the scent of incense from her upper arms, his hawk feelings returned, and instead of being gentle, he felt that he had regained the power of words to say whatever he wanted without stuttering.

But he said nothing.

He noticed the trembling of the left corner of her lower lip. He lit a cigarette, sucked in the smoke, and exhaled it in a series of smoke rings. He shaped his lips into a circle and blew rings that landed against Shirin's eyes and dissolved on her lips.

Did she say then that she was afraid of him, or was that the second time they met?

Yalo did not remember the order of events exactly, but it was probable that she had said that at their second encounter.

She said she had begun to be scared to answer the telephone, or open her bedroom window, or walk home alone, or . . . because she saw his specter everywhere, and she was afraid.

He said that he saw her all the time in his imagination, and that her image had never left his eyes since they met in Ballouna, and that he could smell the scent of her body from his own body; that he had been unable to forget her, and that he loved her.

She said she was begging him.

He said he was begging her.

When she showed signs of standing up after paying the check, he caught her by the hand and felt everything inside him tremble. The softness of her hand cheered and intoxicated him. Yalo would write that there in the café he discovered a softness he had never known and would feel regret that he'd not discovered it at his home in Ballouna. There he felt a woman so light that she could have flown to the rhythm of the desire exploding inside him. It had not been sated. He said he had never felt her softness because he had been submerged in the scent of the incense from her forearms. In the café, an unspeakable softness spread through his limbs, as if her cold fingers were made of silk and stitched to her palm.

Why were her fingers always cold?

Once he told her, when he gently took her hand, that her fingers were as cold as ice and that when he took her hand he felt the urge for a glass of whiskey that he would put her icy fingers into and get intoxicated. She laughed; when she laughed at him or with him she was like someone trying not to laugh. The laughter erupted from her lips and fell back to them, then her lips contracted again, and her eyes emitted a ray of sadness.

She taught him how to read sorrow in people's eyes.

Once she told him that she could read sadness in people's eyes. They used to stand in front of the entrance of the building where she worked at five o'clock in the evening as sunset stretched streaks of darkness into the brightness. One day he waited for her for two hours in front of her office building, went down to Beirut but found nothing to do there, called her but was told that she couldn't speak to him because she was in a meeting, and then headed for the sidewalk in front of the company, and stood there without budging. He stood there unmoving for two hours or more without feeling the passage of time. When she looked out of the doorway she saw him and motioned for him to follow her. He followed her to her car without saying a word. When they reached her white Golf and she bent over to put the key in the lock, she looked up and saw him staring blankly, and greeted him, then he got in beside her and they went to the Café Chatila on the beach and sipped beers. Yalo could think of nothing to say. He felt the sorrow radiating from his eyes, felt alone, and decided to go and visit his mother. They drank beer and she said she had to go, and she went. She did not offer him a lift in her car, nor did he offer her anything. He let her go and he strolled along the seaside corniche road, seeing himself, in the mirror of his own eyes, enveloped in sorrow.

He learned from Shirin how to read sorrow in people's eyes – that is what he wanted to tell his mother, but he didn't tell her anything. He walked until he reached his car in Achrafieh, where he then drove to his mother's house in Ain Rummaneh. He did not know why he stood there without going in. He saw his mother through the window, sitting in the kitchen eating *burghul*. He did not approach to speak to her. He saw the sorrow in her eyes as well. He forgot what happened next; all he remembered was the bowl of *burghul* cooked with tomato and the taste of hot pepper piercing his tongue, and the sorrow that gathered around his mother's mucus-caked eyes, as if they had not been washed for days.

When he went back to his house, below the villa in Ballouna, he looked in the mirror for a long time and saw how sorrow had formed circles around his eyes. He imagined Shirin's small, honey-colored eyes and found that the

< 95 >

sorrow in her eyes was different from his. His sorrow formed circles around his eyes, whereas hers traced fine lines that spread out from her pupils. He decided to marry her.

Before seeing her again in the Café Chatila, he had not known. He went to meet Shirin as if he were continuing with a game he'd started, not knowing where it would take him, feeling toward her a love that emanated from his very ribs and seeped into his lungs, closing in, smothering him, and making him crave air. After he left her, his pocket filled with dollars, he drove home feeling smothered. He opened the window, breathing noisily, and when he reached the bend at Ballouna covered with pine trees, he parked the car and got out and began to devour the air. It was as if this love – he did not how or from where it had come to him – had cut off his air supply. He gulped down the piney air, drinking and drinking it in, until he felt sated and his blood began moving again. He went back to his car, drove home, and tried to forget. But after the meeting at the seafront café, that was when he decided that Shirin would be his wife.

When Yalo discovered that when he was with her he craved fish, he invited her to the Restaurant Sultan in Maameltein. He told her about the restaurant on the phone, how he had gone there once with Monsieur and Madame, and how they had the finest fish dishes, especially the small red mullet, better than any fish in the world, and cuttlefish cooked in its own ink. He told her that the cuttlefish wrote in ink in the sea and that this sea creature was the world's first writer.

She agreed to go. They met in front of her place and she rode with him in his car to Maameltein. This was the day Yalo was convinced that she loved him. It was the first time she agreed to leave her car behind to go with him. Usually it was the opposite, leaving him feeling that she would never in her life agree to ride beside him and let him drive. But that beautiful day in May she agreed to it.

She rode beside him and they went to the Restaurant Sultan, ate fish, and drank arak.

After they finished eating, they went down to the pebbly beach and he made her see the bay of Maameltein through new eyes. That's what she told him. She said that he gave her new eyes to see the world through. She laughed a lot, and let him steal a kiss on her lips, but when he wrapped his arm around her waist to pull her inside his kiss, she slipped away and said no.

But she ate the red mullet, not hesitating the way she had with the birds. Yalo told her to eat the whole little fish: "Cover it with lemon and garlic sauce and eat the whole thing." When she asked him about the head and the fish bones he smiled, took a fish, covered it with sauce, and gobbled it down. She did as he did and that was the first time in her life she had eaten a fish this way.

She ate with unusual appetite, drank arak, licked garlic sauce from her long, cold fingers, and laughed. Then the platter of cuttlefish arrived and Yalo announced that the real meal had finally begun.

She said that she would not even touch the black broth filled with pieces of the sea creature.

"Don't touch it," said Yalo. "I'm going to feed you."

He took a piece of bread, dipped it in the ink, and ate it. "Before the cuttlefish, you have to taste the ink."

"You're eating ink?" she exclaimed.

"The ink is the tastiest thing. Try it."

He took a knife and fork and cut a small piece of the sea creature, then put the morsel of cuttlefish into a piece of bread, dipped it in the ink, and offered it to Shirin, who obediently opened her mouth. When she began to chew the morsel, she closed her eyes and started humming a melody.

After the first morsel, Shirin got into the mood of the cuttlefish, licked the lemon and garlic-spiced ink from her lips, and thanked him for making her taste the most delicious food in the world. She was affectionate with Yalo in his car, allowing him to hold her hand on the Dbayyeh highway after the Dog River tunnel, and when they were in front of her house in Hazemiya, she let him place a long kiss on her lips, then got out of the car and bent over the window to tell him good-bye.

That was the day Yalo was sure he would marry her.

Yalo told himself in the mirror when he was shaving the next morning that he would marry Shirin; he would buy all the cuttlefish in the world and eat them with her, and live in her house. He had not said the words "her house," but when he thought about marriage and the house and children, he saw the entrance to her building and the sycamore tree on the sidewalk opposite and imagined himself under that tree, playing ball with a blond child speaking French. He remembered his grandfather and wondered how he would speak with his grandson's son, and in what language?

In his last days, his grandfather had stopped speaking Arabic and gone back to his mother tongue. He began to spend his time alone in his room, with a stack of papers by his bed. He copied the Syriac poems of Mar Ephraim and said that Mar Ephraim was a great poet and that he regretted that his only grandson was half illiterate, knowing only Arabic and deciphering Syriac letters only with difficulty.

"Come here and learn something, boy, I want you to become a writer like me."

Yalo laughed inwardly and said, "Only you're not writing, Grandfather, you're copying Mar Ephraim's poems. You're not the author."

"But I am Mar Ephraim," replied his grandfather, smiling at the foolishness of his grandson, who did not realize that all the writers in the world were copyists, that there was in the whole world only one book. This unseen book was not written from human inspiration but of infinite parts that revealed themselves to novelists and poets who would copy them down and rearrange them anew.

Yalo came closer to his grandfather and tried to read.

"Do you understand?" asked his grandfather.

"*Eluho hab yulfuno*," said Yalo as he stared at the words. "Kind of," he replied, "but why go to the trouble, Grandfather?"

Here the *cohno* went into his philosophy of books. He believed that books were like icons. Books were the windows that we open onto the infinite, and through them we can look into the other world. "That is, we don't see everything, we see fragments, as if we are peeking."

"Grandfather, people don't peek at books, people peek at women."

"Books are nicer than women, my boy, what do you know about books and women?!"

His grandfather, covered from head to toe in his black robe, and with his jar of ink placed on the table beside him, resembled a sea creature giving off the smell of ink.

Yalo wanted to tell Shirin about his grandfather, who resembled a cuttlefish, and peeking at books, and women who were like open books through which one might peek into the infinite, but he didn't tell her. Ideas vanished from his head when he was with her. He would begin to speak but then forget, and then knew nothing.

That was the story of his life.

The story was he did not say anything, he stammered in front of this girl; he became a little boy again, stuttering, forgetting, hesitating. Shirin was afraid of his stammering, and in listening to him, she sensed that his words could not be put together into a coherent sentence; she heard random words that did not belong beside each other on the branch of speech.

"Why are you talking that way?" she asked him.

"Don't you like my talking?" he answered her.

"Of course, of course, that's not what I meant. I don't know."

"You don't know what?"

"I don't know anything."

She said she didn't know anything.

I don't know anything either, Yalo would say. Only he didn't.

She had beaten him at announcing her ignorance of everything, so he did not know how to announce his own identical ignorance. Thus Yalo was, talking to her without knowing what to say, garbling his words, tripping over his tongue, and falling into a void.

There in the cell, where he sat alone writing the story of his whole life, he felt a void all around him. He saw the sheets of white paper and ink pens and longed for the smell of the ink in his grandfather's room, grasping the secret of the squid, which Arabs called the *habbar*, or inkmaker. He understood that this sea creature was the first to discover writing, because it wrote with its ink in self-defense and to resist death. Its enemies were completely misled by the ink in their faces, and the cuttlefish vanished from their sight in the dense black thicket that the ink painted within the seawater.

Yalo was alone in his cell. He had to release the ink onto his sheets of paper. He was like the cuttlefish, possessing no weapon but ink to release in order to deceive the hunters and save himself from death. But woe to the sea creature who fell into the fishermen's trap, because they would cook him in his ink. Yalo thought he would be cooked in the ink he was writing with now, that the black ink flowing onto the paper would kill him, and that he was powerless to deceive the hunter who awaited his sheets of paper in order to wrap him up in them, kill him, and devour him. He wrote and wrote, like a squid advancing toward his death.

"Hey you – animal!" shouted the interrogator.

". . ."

". . ."

< 100 >

How had the interrogator learned that Yalo called himself a hawk?
Had Shirin told him?

Had Yalo told her that he was a hawk?

Yalo had never spoken of it, so how did she know? What had she said? He had not told her, it was his secret, so how could he have revealed it?

He was a hawk. He lurked in the forest waiting for the moment to swoop down on his prey, and when he spotted it he would bide his time, determine the attack, stop. His black overcoat would fill with air and inflate, and the sleeves would stretch out. Yalo would lift his arms, which had become like wings, and hover with his bloated stomach, his rifle over his right shoulder, its dangling muzzle aimed at the earth, illuminate his black flashlight, and descend.

He felt as if he were swooping from an immense height, and once he trained the light on his prey he'd commence his descent to earth.

He was a hawk. A long black overcoat, and a narrow beam of light trained on the car swallowed by the night, two feet stepping lightly in rubber boots, a great nose picking up the scent of the perfumed victim, and two wide eyes that could see in the dark.

"Hey, you piece of shit – you're a hawk?"

Two men seized him by his armpits and made him stand. He felt as if he were flying and closed his eyes.

"You used to tell women that you were a woman hawk?"

They carried him by his armpits, spreading his arms out like wings, and the words began to rain down on his face and nose.

"Hey, you piece of shit, you think you're smart, you think you'll fool the justice system?"

The hawk under stomping feet.

"You told Shirin you love her and you want to marry her. Do you know who you are, and who she is?"

They stomped on his face, breaking his beak, and the blood flowed.

< IOI >

"You really think you're God's gift to women?"

He saw the boots through his blurry eyes, and the refracted sunlight, and the pain.

"We want you to confess to the gang and the explosives. Can you hear us?"

Blood, hawk, and pain. Suddenly his body left its owner and went to incalculable pains. He saw it fade away and sink into the pool of pain. He saw it go but he could not call to it. His beak was broken, his voice was hoarse, and his blood covered the ground. The body went to its pain, and Yalo felt that he had shed the hawk and taken on the tentacles of the cuttle-fish, and the pain stopped. He saw how he grew eight arms and seventy million optic cells stretched across his limbs, and saw his female, Shirin, swimming to his side in the depths, and he extended his fourth right arm to her, this arm was his sexual member, he pressed it into her feminine cavity, felt the eggs and fertilized them, and slept inside her.

The hawk was under their feet, and the cuttlefish mated with his female, who swayed around him and engaged in beautiful sport with him. His fourth arm was inside her and its thousands of eyes opened an infinite universe of colors to him. He saw what lay within the color blue and he saw colors that didn't even have names because humankind could not perceive them. Ink emerged from every part of Yalo, who had moved from his hawkish state to his maritime state and sunk to the depths, extending his eight arms and flying through the water. When he saw them and their boots, he fired his ink to mislead them and blood-colored ink flooded out.

They made him stand and shackled him. He saw the interrogator's face squinting into the sun and the red hue forming halos around his head, went out the window and flew away. The interrogator came close to him and spat in his face, and slapped him; then his palm filled with blood. He wiped his palm on the hawk's overcoat and ordered them to take him away.

< 102 >

The hands on the wounded hawk withdrew and they let him drop to the floor. Red lights plaguing his eyes, Yalo closed them, felt his tears, and sensed a salinity spreading through his body. Yalo became salty – he wanted to tell them that he needed some fresh water. He wanted to weep and leave his body to tremble and moan so that the heat of death would leave him before he died. He had the impression of falling into an abyss, felt that the valley swallowed him, and that he had become a pine tree. He smelled the pine sap and began to chew. The blood gushing in his mouth tasted like grilled pine. He curled his body up just before feeling himself being dragged out of the interrogation room, toward a jeep, where they sat him down among a group of policemen whose fat bellies hung over their leather belts.

Yalo did not know what or where or how.

Had he drunk anything?

Had he eaten anything?

Had he said anything?

Had he?

Later on, he wrote that he found himself in a pool of water, leaning against the wall, the water rising to his chest as he struggled to breathe, colors mingling with smells. His body intermingled with the smell of his blood, feces, and urine. He stretched out in water before curling up in it, and began to drown. Yalo vaguely remembered that a voice emerged from his limbs, remembered that he had become a voice, that he felt a mouth howling inside his mouth, and then he remembered nothing.

Yalo wrote that he did not remember.

When they took him back to the interrogation room, when he saw the interrogator's head by the window, when he saw the sun that had disappeared from the window, Yalo wanted to ask the interrogator where the sun had gone. He wanted to see the reflected light that veiled his vision but brought light. He wanted light, but the interrogator asked him for his opinion.

Why did he ask for his opinion?

"My opinion of what, sir?"

"Your opinion of what's happened to you," said the interrogator.

"Why? What has happened to me?" asked Yalo.

"The bathtub. Tell me, did you like the bathtub?"

Yalo understood that the bathtub was the name the interrogator gave to those vague memories filled with blood, water, and fear.

Yalo lowered his head and saw the interrogator's hand coming toward him. He recoiled instinctively, but the hand approached with the white sheets of paper.

"Take these," said the interrogator, giving him the sheaf of paper.

"Write the story of your life from beginning to end."

Yalo wanted to say that he didn't know how to write.

"I want everything. Don't forget even the smallest detail."

" . . ."

"I want whoever reads it to know and understand everything. Don't write me any riddles. Write things as they happened."

" . . ."

"I don't want you to make anything up. Sit down and remember and write down what you remember. I want the story from start to finish."

Yalo wanted to say that he did not know the start from the finish, and that he could not write, but the blood prevented him. Blood was dribbling from his nose and the air around him grew thinner. He tried to open his mouth to breathe. He closed his eyes.

Yalo was unable to write a single word. He found himself in the solitary cell and saw the sheets of white paper stained with the black light shining around him. He closed his eyes and decided to sleep.

"Write, you dog!" the man shouted at him.

He took up the pen and saw the circles of shadow pierced by the silver light emanating from the depths of his eyes, but he could not write. He threw the pen onto the small table they had put in his cell and heard the voice shouting at him again. The voice began to ring in his head as if it were stuck in the whorls of his ears, echoes rebounding toward infinity.

Yalo said.

Yalo would say, when he finished writing, that the echoes were his everlasting companions during that long year of ink.

They brought him a fountain pen and a plastic bottle of ink and ordered him to write.

He wrote because he loved life and awaited the end of the long tunnel of torture when he would leave prison and get his revenge.

Yalo felt, in spite of the excruciating pain from the torture sessions, a strange pleasure. His pleasure was his imagination. When he was being beaten or whipped, or suspended by his arms, he imagined himself in the torturer's place, and imagined his victims: Shirin, Emile, Dr. Said and Madame Randa, the lawyer Michel Salloum, Tony Atiq, and everyone else.

No, he imagined these things after the end of the "party," as they called his torture sessions. During the party he imagined the cell, and in the cell he held his own party. He was thrown into the cell, utterly exhausted, finding that imagination and role-play were the only means of restoring his body and vitality. He shifted his mind and imagined things as he wanted them to be. This restored some of his strength, and a few glimmers of his old hawk eye kept fear at bay. He tore the pain out of his parts and cast it into other bodies and saw how the pains left his fingers and toes to possess his victims.

At that point he fell asleep.

After the torture parties, Yalo's sleep was his revenge. He fashioned his slumbers as he pleased. He prepared the instruments of torture in his imagination, and made sure that he had not forgotten anything, then let his eyes close to the rhythm of chains or to the screeches of electrical cords, and saw how his victims fell under his torment, which had become their torment.

Even the final torture, which, when he experienced it, made him feel that his spirit was calling out to death and his body ached for the grave, even that torture was portioned out to others, and he dozed off to the sounds of their guttural groans and cries for mercy.

That was the grand party.

In that party, which he called the grand one, and still later gave several other names to, Yalo was seized with a terror that prevented him from opening his mouth, so he raised his arms in the air in a show of surrender, with tears streaming from his eyes, and began to wail savagely before the officer ordered that the canvas sack be removed from the suspect's lower body.

Even this torture took Yalo into his imaginary world. He decided to reserve this one for Dr. Said, who had abandoned Shirin in the forest and fled in his car, whose tires screeched loudly as they scattered gravel all around.

At first, Yalo decided to forget the sack, and excised it from his imagination's memory, but he found himself facing the scene with the sack whenever he closed his tear-moistened eyes. He heard the meowing and saw the bamboo rod and felt the claws tearing at him.

That was the moment of torture that drove Yalo to offer all his confessions.

Why were they now asking him to write his life story? Why did the officer not believe his confessions?

On that day, which entered Yalo's memory as the Day of the Sack, they dragged him from his cell at dawn and put him in what seemed to be a small room. He was blindfolded and his hands bound, palpating with his bare feet the long passageway he traversed, trying not to fall. When he reached the small room a hand pushed him forward and knocked him to the floor. He heard a voice ordering him to take his pants off. He tried to stand but his feet failed and he rolled on the floor. He heard loud laughter and felt a hand lifting him up. He stood and felt the hand unbuttoning his pants. He reached for the buttons on his pants and a hard slap landed on his neck and reverberated before the hand untied his blindfold. At first all he saw was darkness. A few seconds later a tall, broad-shouldered man in a khaki uniform appeared and ordered him to remove his underwear.

Yalo's tired eyes looked around and saw, beside the officer, three powerfully muscular men whose sleeveless jerseys showed off the glossy black hair on their chests and arms. He felt certain that he was going to be raped. The world blurred over and he froze in his place.

"Take off your underwear, dog!"

< 107 >

He sought the wall and tried to enter it. He remembered his grandfather's story about the archbishop who kept retreating and retreating until the wall opened up and swallowed him.

That was a legend of Constantinople. "When Constantinople fell to Muhammad the Conqueror, the archbishop entered the wall, and they are still waiting for him to this day," said his smiling grandfather. "Those Byzantines weren't very bright, it was as if they didn't know that they were the cause of the disaster."

"Is it true that the wall opened up?" asked Yalo.

"That's what they say," said his grandfather.

"And what was the disaster?"

"That they went into the wall, and are still there."

Yalo felt the hand that had unbuttoned his pants now reaching for his underwear and removing it. He bent over and his underwear slid off, and he stood before them naked from the waist down, humiliated, waiting for the order to bend over so that the rape could begin.

The tall officer was smiling behind his cigarette smoke, which had filled the small room, filling Yalo with dread and nausea.

"Let's go, guys," said the officer. Yalo backed up, terrified, his back square against the wall, trembling with fear and the cold. Two men with a canvas sack approached him. The first held the mouth of the sack while the other held the lower part of it.

"Come here, come on. Don't be afraid," said the officer.

Yalo froze where he stood, his behind pressed ever harder against the wall.

"I told you to come here!" said the officer. "Take the sack from these guys and put it on!"

"How am I supposed to put it on?" Yalo asked softly.

"Put it on like a pair of pants," said the officer.

"Pants!" said Yalo under his breath, without grasping what was being asked of him, standing rigid, not knowing what to do.

He rested his head against the wall and closed his eyes. The three men pounced on him, grabbed his shoulders, and pulled him to the middle of the room, then one stepped up behind him and seized him by the chest, pressing himself against him from behind. Then the two other men advanced with the sack and bent over while the third man raised him up erect and made him put his feet into the sack. After that the first man got up and tied the canvas sack shut around Yalo's waist with a cord threaded through the mouth of the sack.

The three men withdrew, leaving Yalo alone in the middle of the room. He felt something strange moving between his bare feet, but he did not understand the game until the officer came forward with a bamboo rod in his hand.

"Are you going to confess or do we begin?" asked the officer.

"I swear, I swear to God, I confessed everything, and I will do anything you want. I told you everything, but I'll say anything you want, whatever you want."

"Now you are still lying to us," said the officer.

"I told the truth, I swear, I swear to God, I swear to God I'm not lying."

The officer's bamboo rod descended and landed on the canvas sack between Yalo's feet, and the journey into torture began. The rod goaded on the thing inside the sack and the meowing and clawing started, along with his feeling of falling into the abyss. He goaded it one more time, so that the cat began to leap up and attack Yalo's lower parts from the bottom of the sack. The cat trembled with savagery, springing and butting, climbing up Yalo's member to bite and scratch it. And it had whiskers. Yalo could not see the whiskers, but he could see them nonetheless, gleaming in the dark.

The cat's eyes flashed in the darkness and its whiskers gleamed, and Yalo fell to the floor. At first his mind did not grasp what was happening, he heard the scratching and the yowling, but he didn't understand until he heard the officer ordering the cat with his rod to leap up; then he understood that he was at the mercy of a wild cat.

"Kitty, kitty, kitty – jump up! Up!" said the officer.

Yalo fell to the floor. He bent over with the cat's attacks and squatted, but then the animal grew fiercer. It leaped up to seize his testicles, at which point Yalo saw it and saw its whiskers and he felt that his testicles were exploding and that his member was trickling blood. He stood up wanting relief but the officer's rod never stopped goading the sack as he said "Kitty, kitty, kitty!" The cat squirmed and jumped frantically and Yalo collapsed.

With the sack Yalo discovered how fear erased pain and how a valley opened in his belly that stretched to the belly of the earth.

The officer with the swinging rod in his hand, and Yalo with the sack jumping between his legs, the sack with the cat that bit, scratched, howled, and squalled. The meows of the cat were like the crying of a thousand infants, and Yalo was like a lone child who had lost the power to scream.

When Yalo raised his hands in the air and his tears streamed down, he confessed to everything.

"I'll confess now," he wanted to say, but he did not say it. His voice came out like a throaty meow and he collapsed, and saw himself in a jungle of savage cats tearing at his body. He was like someone swimming, he would say that he was swimming in cats, and called the sack a pool of cats. He saw himself swimming in blood, howling, and meows.

And he saw his tears.

For three days and three nights his tears flowed, bathing his eyes and face. He did not wipe them away, he let them flow and take their course and channels, then drop to his neck and cover his whole body.

Finally, the pool of cats baptized him with tears.

"The true baptism, my boy, is the baptism of tears," his grandfather told him. "I am being baptized now. Leave me. No, I'm not upset with you, the tears come by themselves."

Gaby ordered her son to go to his grandfather's room to cheer him up. "Your grandfather the *cohno*, I don't know what's happening to him. Go to the Oilioto and talk to him so that he'll cheer up. Go on, Bro, God bless you."

"What am I supposed to talk to him about, Mother? He'll start speaking Syriac and shame me."

"Your grandfather is not well. Go in to him."

Young Yalo went into the room where the black clothing was heaped in the corner which had come to be called the weeping corner. His grandfather was sitting on the floor as if he were a pile of clothes; now that his body had shrunk and his bones weakened, he sat crumpled in his corner with tears streaming from his eyes.

"*Shlomo*," said Yalo.

"*Shlomo*," replied the *cohno*.

"How are you?" asked Yalo.

"*Shsfir, tade le-morio*," said his grandfather.

"What is it? What's wrong, Grandfather?" asked Yalo, but his grandfather did not reply.

The boy approached his grandfather, sat beside him, and the *cohno* covered his face with his sweaty, black-spotted hands, and resumed his soft wailing as the tears crept through his fingers. The boy stood paralyzed, listening to the drone of the silence broken only by the sobs coming from the depths of the man sitting in his "weeping corner." After a long while the grandfather brought his hands down from his face and told the boy not to be afraid of him, and told him about the tears of baptism.

"Do you want to know why I'm crying?" asked his grandfather.

The boy bowed his head.

"My boy, a man is baptized twice in life. The first time when he's young he is baptized in water, and the second time when he's old he is baptized in tears. I know that I'm being baptized before I go to join my mother."

"May you live long, Grandfather."

"I don't want to go, but I will go, and that is the sign, the sign of Ishmael, my boy. Ishmael is the ancestor of the Arabs and of the Syriacs too. Only the Arabs don't know a thing. Ishmael was the first human to be baptized. He was abandoned in the desert, with his mother, Hagar; he was baptized in tears, God sent water and did not let them die of thirst. You know why? Because he wept. The water came from tears, and water is life. 'And we made from water every living thing,' as it is written. I didn't know these things, but a Maronite priest named Joachim told me. He used to like to visit me to talk to me in Suryoyo. He said that there was no one left in this country anymore who spoke the language of Christ, so he practiced with me. I listened to stories, my goodness, how many stories he knew. You know, I am originally a layer of tile, but I studied and completed theology, but he was different, he studied in Rome, and knew more stories about Christ than are written in the Gospels. He told me about the baptism of tears. He said the Muslims are baptized in the tears of Ishmael too, and that's how he took me to the mullah, God bless him, and he said he wanted for me to return so that I could pass it on. Can blood be passed on? He wanted to bequeath me blood, only I refused. Later, Father Joachim reassured me, he told me that my father the mullah had also been baptized, that baptism is the way to forgiveness and that is how God forgave him."

"Your father was a Muslim?"

"*Lo. Lo.*"

< 112 >

"What was his name?"

"I was telling you about tears. Father Joachim said that baptism is not complete without tears. He was old, like your grandfather now, and when he spoke Syriac with me his tears would fall, and I had to hold my laughter back. Then one day I understood, and when you grow up you will discover the importance of the baptism of tears."

The *cohno*, whose face had been invaded by an immense white beard, sank into his final baptism. Yalo did not understand, nor did he dare to approach that sacrament of which it is said that the greatest event in the life of a man is his death, and that the *cohno* had woven his shroud with his tears, and raved about the mullah that wanted to bequeath him blood. Father Joachim revealed to him that the common legacy of humankind was its tears.

He asked his mother about tears, but she hushed him. "Do not speak anymore of this. We shouldn't be asking questions now. We should just be helping your grandfather." Yalo told his mother that he did not understand. She told him, "Later. Someday when you're grown up you'll understand." But he grew up and still did not understand.

On January 6, 1975, the eve of the war, when Yalo was thirteen, his mother asked him to help her take the *cohno* to the beach at Ramlet al-Baida. At first Yalo refused, saying that the man would be unable to bear the cold weather, that he might die, but eventually gave in to his mother's insistence.

"You still believe in fairy tales," he told her.

"Shut up. He can hear you," she answered. "Come on, take his hand and follow me."

They went in the night and the rain. On the beach, under a hard rain, as hard as bullets, the woman let down her hair and took her father's hand, and walked with him into the sea. The old man stumbled, fell into a wave,

< 113 >

swallowed the water and the salt and cried intensely, then he was quenched. Gaby cupped her hands and took some seawater to make the *cohno* and her son drink, and she said that the water had become sweeter than honey.

"I have seen the miracle," she said.

"Look at my hair, how it's become golden," she said.

"The water has become pure and sweet as honey," she said.

"Christ the Lord, peace be upon him, has said that you will be healed, Father Ephraim," she said.

But the *cohno* was collapsing. His feet were no longer able to support him, so Yalo and his mother worked together to carry him to the street, where they brought him home in a taxi.

"Don't die, I beg of you!" shouted his daughter.

Ephraim lived after the Ramlet al-Baida incident, after which fever struck him for a whole week. He died a year later, but Gaby lived the rest of her life with a bad conscience.

"I killed him," she said, "I killed the *cohno*. After that outing he couldn't walk anymore. He was consumed by weeping, his eyes shrank, as if he didn't even have eyes anymore, as if they had been rubbed away with only two black dots left, two little wells from which tears flowed, as if he had just bathed himself in his tears and died."

And Yalo now, or rather there, when he was extricated from the sack, sank into his tears. Yalo now, there, found that he was like his grandfather and like Ishmael, he traversed the baptism of tears and sank into his eyes.

He placed the white sheet of paper in front of him and decided to write, but he could not; yet there was no escape. The interrogator awaited him, as did his own fear. It was true that Yalo suffered greatly during the days of writing, but no suffering in the world could be compared to the pool of cats that had stormed over his lower half and cast him into a deep abyss.

The sack remained in his memory. As he wrote he saw two sacks, one above and one below.

The first sack was no problem, it was the war sack, the fighters controlled this sack and Yalo was one of them, so he did not fear this first sack they put over his head when he was arrested. He closed his eyes inside it and went with them. Of course he fell to the ground and felt that his legs had become blind, but he was not afraid. He knew that the game of shadows was part of the game of war, and that he was now entering the other side of a scheme in a world he knew all too well. He would say that he fled Beirut for Paris because the war nauseated him and he was utterly weary of the screams of the victims. But he did not say that. He was the son of a war that never lied because it never spoke. In the barracks he entered at the age of fourteen, Yalo learned not to talk, because the war camouflaged its words behind other words which fell to the ground like banana peels that people would slip on. The sacks were masks that covered everything. He wore the first mask after two weeks of training in the forested land around a mountain village whose name he had forgotten. He had gotten used to the mask. Then he discovered that speech wore a mask too, and that was a long story he would experience when he wrote the story of his life, as the interrogator had demanded of him.

The second sack, however, was different. The sack below was not a mask; it was an instrument of revelation, of scandal, of sorrow. Yalo awoke from what seemed like a coma and could not find the sack covering his lower half. He saw himself amidst his urine and feces; reached his hand between his thighs and felt a familiar warmth, he remembered Shirin and his tears began to flow. He understood at that moment the meaning of love and felt her tears in his own eyes, and the trembling of her lower lip in his lip, and her warm knee within his knee. He placed his hand on his own knee and the ghost of a smile appeared and as he saw how he had reached out to her small knee and rubbed his palm along it.

"What are you doing?" she asked.

"I'm lathering my hands. I like to be clean when I see you, and the best soap is your knee. Your knee is a bit like a little round soap, no?"

Her small eyes looked at him and a half smile escaped her lips before answering, "Yes, it's true."

Yalo laughed and Shirin asked him to remove his hand from her "soap" because they would be seen.

"I don't care about being seen. All I care about is you."

"Fine. Then for my sake, remove your hand."

He did so and rubbed his face with both hands as if he were scrubbing it with soap. Shirin screamed for him not to take his hands off the steering wheel, so he put his hands in the air, leaving the car to glide on its own on the Jounieh highway, before regaining control by seizing the wheel with his left hand, leaving his right hand on the seat, seeking her hand.

Yalo swam in his excrement, as he would say later, alleging nausea, but there in the middle of the pool where he found himself, he felt capable of doubling over against himself; he rolled up and became an infant, shrinking as if returning to his mother's womb. He reached out his hand, hungry and thirsty. He reached out and sucked. He closed his eyes and swallowed the sticky liquid, and craved sleep. He saw his mother's face and Alexei's face, and vanished amidst the tears.

Gaby tied up her loose hair in the kitchen and cried over her son who had sucked the life out of her and gone on to war and destruction. Yalo stood in the kitchen doorway and told her that he did not want to study and become a *cohno* like his grandfather. His mother had put him in the Atchaneh School near Bikfaya, but he escaped and went home to Ain Rummaneh. And from Ain Rummaneh he joined Tony and went off to war.

Yalo stood in the kitchen door listening to the woman tell her story. Why was she talking this way, saying she had eaten shit?

"For your sake, you little shit, I ate shit. My life is shot, what an idiot I was. When you were a kid I ate your shit, and now you want to feed me your shit again. Forget it!"

"Mother, please calm down. I'm like this because all the guys are like this."

Yalo's childhood had been full of the story of his mother, who had made a vow so that she would be blessed with a son. She went to the Church of St. Severus and made a vow. She was pregnant and sensed that her husband would not stand by her. He was like a phantom: "I knew he'd bolt, and I wanted nothing from this world except to have a son. I knew from the beginning, from the moment I married him. He was strange, he said he wanted to go to Sweden, and later on he'd send for me. I understood him all right. I understood that he'd leave and never come back. I made a vow standing before the icon of the Virgin. My father overheard my oath; he reprimanded me and said that was blasphemy. The peak of blasphemy. It was not blasphemy, it was despair, the peak of despair. I swore that if God gave me a son I'd eat his shit, and God answered my prayer, and I ate it."

Gabrielle spoke of the taste of milk, that "the taste of shit was milk, with something of my smell, because I was nursing you at my breast. And as I uttered my vow, there was the taste of milk in my mouth."

Yalo did not remember the story in words, but as a sepia photograph. A woman standing before a baby cradle, she was bending over, putting a finger in the diaper, and then sucking it. After bathing her baby and before putting him to her breast, she bends over her breasts, smells the odor, and is intoxicated by the two odors: the smell of her son and the smell of her milk. The woman kept up this rite of hers until the doctor told her that the child required real food: fruits, vegetables, and eggs, so she fed him and lost him,

< 117 >

– once he ate, the smell of his feces mingled with new odors. She began to sense the distance between her and her son; she could not smell the odor of shit, and she could no longer keep her vow. So she decided to disobey the doctor's orders and began giving her son nothing but milk, though the new odor had taken over the baby's body and feces so that she could no longer bring Yalo back to her. She felt that her son was separated from her.

Yalo saw himself now, that is, there, and saw the weeping. He was swimming in his own liquids and saw the tears streaming from his eyes, when he saw Alexei. What brought Alexei to this wakefulness that was so like sleep?

Blond Alexei, they called him. Tall, hulky, and blond-haired, he left the barracks to train on bodybuilding at the Sennacherib Club in Achrafieh. He enjoyed sodomy and formed suspect relationships with the young men he brought to the barracks on the pretext of training them to carry weapons. He denied the accusation and spoke only of his relationships with married women. He said that married women were practiced. "A woman has to be well-rounded, she has to be picked like an orange," he said, and he cupped his palms as if picking two small breasts and began to gobble them up and lick his lips as if orange juice were dripping from them. Yalo did not believe the tales of his married women, but he made sure not to tell him about Thérèse.

It was true why, when he listened to the stories of Alexei's conquests, he saw Sister Thérèse as if she were his tale, and he forgot the shop which smelled of wood, and over which revolved the blind man's eyes. He went with Thérèse to a faraway hotel, where the engineer Wajih had taken her, and discovered love and sex with her. Sister Thérèse's face was like a white light shining from the folds of her black clothing, pulling Yalo into it. Her soft white hand slipped into his black shorts and reduced the whole world to a fist holding the shaft of life that burned with desire. Thérèse had become

< 118 >

his own story. He told no one, and the secret that he never experienced became his personal secret, which he was proud of without ever putting it into words.

Blond Alexei was crazy and could not keep a secret. Yalo did not know how Thérèse's name had slipped off his tongue in front of Alexei, but the blond Russian began to refer to Yalo as "Thérèse's thing," and when the guys asked him about it, he did not talk as if he were hiding a deep secret. Then the name slipped out again in front of Shirin, but Yalo would not write about Thérèse when he wrote the story of his life. Once he told Shirin that she looked like Sister Thérèse and she asked who that was and he told her that she had been a nun who had taught him in school and that he was enthralled by her beauty and had a crush on her. He did not dare tell Shirin the true story.

Alexei was like a madman that awful night. No question, he had taken a serious hit of cocaine; otherwise why would he act like that? Yalo told Tony their first night in Paris that God would not forgive them because they forced that old man to eat his own feces. Tony laughed and shook his head, then he disappeared. He disappeared because he did not believe in anything. He stole the money and the language, leaving Yalo alone in that city.

Alexei appeared with cocaine powder traced in the red of his protuberant eyes, and told Yalo to come with him. They went to the underground floor of a building near the Hotel Dieu. They went down a flight of stairs and Alexei opened the door of the cellar with a key he had on him. There Yalo saw a lone blindfolded man, kneeling in the dark. Alexei trained the beam of his flashlight on the man's head, and the man looked uneasily toward the light but said nothing.

Then Alexei began his game. He fired his pistol in the cellar. The sound was like a cannon shot. The kneeling man started trembling. Alexei approached him and put the hot muzzle of the pistol against the man's temple and began to threaten him. When Alexei told the man that the hour of execution was approaching so he needed to prepare to meet his Maker, the man trembled and then sat back and stretched his legs out in front of him, and emptied his bowels. The stench spread quickly. Alexei approached the man, holding his nose, and ordered him to stand up. The man began to cry and plead, but when the muzzle of the pistol approached again he put his hands on the floor to push himself up, and Alexei saw the shit.

"You shit yourself, you coward?" shouted Alexei, guffawing. Then he told the man not to stand up: "It's not worth it. We'll execute you in your shit!" said Alexei. "And now before you die you must eat it!"

Yalo did not know why the man did it, since he was going to die anyway. Yalo saw the darkness and the smell, and the tears ran black down the sixty-year-old man's cheeks. The man's fingers reached out to his excrement, and he raised his fingers to his mouth and ate.

"You must eat it all!" shouted the blond Russian.

The man ate slowly, as if buying time before his death, and Yalo stood up. Suddenly Yalo felt a need to urinate and he was struck with a near inability to move, he thought he was going to collapse, he was suffocating, he couldn't get enough air. All of a sudden, he saw himself running outside, he reached the house dizzy and began vomiting. He went into the bathroom and thrust his head into the sink. Yellow vomit spattered out of his mouth and nose and the noise filled his ears. He heard Alexei's voice asking for him and laughing loudly. He wiped his mouth with a towel and opened the faucet to wash the yellowness out of the sink, then hurried out and went with the Russian back to the barracks, where he heard from everyone the story as the Russian told it, about the old guy they kidnapped and forced to eat his own shit.

They called him the Russian, but he was not Russian. He claimed he was

< 120 >

a White Russian, and said that all of Russia was red, with only a single white spot called Alexei. But he was a Syriac who had forgotten the language of his ancestors, like Yalo and the rest of the young guys. He was also a close friend of Said al-Mansurati, who composed odes and sang them, proclaiming himself to be the great new entertainer of Lebanon who would emerge after the war. Alexei brought a bottle of white wine and Said played his lute and sang, and the guys got drunk on the rhythms of Andalusian ballads. Said recited poetry about Achrafieh and sang it in his hoarse voice that was like Farid al-Atrash's, and the guys got drunk.

Said al-Mansurati disappeared, Alexei died, and Yalo found himself alone in his pool, listening to Alexei's voice in his ears.

He said he had found him upstairs in the office: "I didn't ask for his identity card or anything. I noticed that he had a foreign accent and I ordered him down to the basement and left him for about five hours on his knees and blindfolded. I swear to God I forgot about him, but after the line of cocaine I remembered him. When I bent over him, I saw that he had shit himself. What a coward! I forced him to eat it before he died. So he ate it. He knew he was going to die, and he ate it anyway. And you, you ran away, you coward. I swear to God, if your mother hadn't answered the door, I would have given it to you, I would have made you shit yourself. You never would have forgotten me your whole life."

"And him, what happened to him?" asked Yalo.

"Rest in peace," said Alexei.

"You killed him?"

"What do you think I should have done?"

"No, seriously, I'm asking you for real."

"No, I didn't kill him, I left him in the basement and came over to your place. Come back with me and we can take care of it."

< 121 >

"I don't want to go with you."

Alexei said that that the man died without his having to kill him. He let him finish his meal, then fired a bullet over his head and the man died.

"He died from fright, not from the shot," said Alexei. "When a man dies, he dies of death, he dies from fright. You too, you'll die one day from your cowardice."

Yalo did not believe that the man had died of fear of the gunshot. He was sure that Alexei had killed him for a laugh. Yalo thought that Alexei was right, he decided to get rid of his cowardice and laugh too. He was sorry that he had run home afraid and vomited on himself. He felt a desire to kill everyone and laugh. He couldn't imagine why everyone wasn't laughing, and laughed. He spent the rest of the war on the verge of laughter. Even death was funny and entertaining. Laughter was the highest state of life. Laughter was everyone being strange and deserving a good laugh. A stranger is laughable just by being a stranger. Even Alexei was strange, someone we could laugh at whenever we liked.

Faced with Alexei's corpse, something like a tremor of weeping swept through the young men, but Yalo felt like laughing. Alexei had not died the way most people die, but he was dead, and when they found him it was not him. He was a heap of clothes and pebbles and bones. Three months were enough for it not to be the man.

No one knew how Alexei had disappeared. Suddenly the blond Russian was just no longer there. They looked for him everywhere but found no trace of him. Their leader, Mario, decided that Alexei was a traitor and a coward. He gathered them all in the barracks and announced that he would turn him over to a military court as soon as he reappeared, but the blond did not reappear. The mill of the civil war kept turning. Mario called the war a mill and he bent over, naked from the waist up, like a mule, braying like a donkey, saying that he was carrying the millstone on his back.

"We grind people down, and they grind us down."

He drank arak and spun around, his eyes would spin too, and when he got drunk, he would grind himself down and grind down others. The guys in the barracks watched their hero Mario become a mule, and they laughed. His name became Mario the Millstone.

Mario issued a death sentence against Alexei without a trial. He gathered the guys together and said that Alexei was a traitor: "We don't know all the details. He said he was Russian but he wasn't Russian. He said he was Syriac but he wasn't Syriac. He said he was Lebanese but he wasn't Lebanese. If you see him you must open fire without asking questions."

"A word is a bullet," Mario said. "Aim, fire, and get rid of him for me, once he's dead we'll interrogate him. Just as for all the others, the investigation begins after death. First we execute him, then we question him. That's the way it goes."

But how? How did Alexei melt away in that faraway building?

Alexei's image would be burned into Yalo's memory. But the face was not a face, it was a laughing skull.

Mario knew it when he saw it.

A bunch of guys showed up and told Mario that in the Jeraydini Building, opposite the French Medical Faculty in the rue Damas, they had seen a decomposed corpse, and Mario ordered them to dump it before taking their positions on the premises. Then he noticed the fear and horror on their faces.

"Dump it and I don't want any bullshit. I told you to set up headquarters in the Jeraydini Building but you're a bunch of cowards looking for excuses."

Mario carried his rifle and marched ahead of them, and when they reached the heap of clothes and pebbles and bones, their leader bent over the remains and froze in place. In the middle of this dilapidated room, he looked like a taut bow.

Mario could hear their muttering about the remains and the bones. "Follow me," he said, and ordered Yalo to come with him. He ran ahead of them and mounted the steps to the building two at a time. When they reached the third floor, he froze in place. Yalo followed the noise, not hurrying along with those running, walking heavily and mounting the steps slowly, and in a corner of the dark room, where broken furniture was stacked, he saw everything.

"That's him," said Tony.

Mario looked at Tony irritably and stepped back. He rested his short stocky body against the wall before advancing again to lean over the remains. Yalo did not know how long the short man stayed there bent over, but he felt that time had stopped over Mario's back. Then his back began to quiver as though a wave passed through it from head to waist. He saw Tony step forward and embrace him, and he heard Mario's voice saying something unintelligible because his voice was stifled in his throat as if it were the captive of his Adam's apple that moved without liberating it. The back fell to the ground, Tony fell beside him, and Yalo saw himself fading away with the others.

"Where are you all going?" shouted Mario. "It's Alexei."

Mario's shouts combined with the shouting of the other guys, and Yalo wanted to escape. He felt his legs getting ready to run, but the voice froze him to the spot, and he saw them all staggering. The light was black, wrapped in the darkness of the buildings destroyed by the war. The shadow of the destruction spread over them and they bent over to discover what seemed to be a skeleton in clothes ragged from rot.

"That's Alexei," said Mario. "We have to take him away."

Yalo saw torn pants and a ragged shirt on a skeleton. The knees were bent and the bones bathed in black light.

"I recognized his belt," said Mario. "Let's take him away."

The leather belt was the only sign. The Russian kid was carrion.

"Who ate him?" asked Yalo, who felt a laughing fit coming on. He wanted to laugh, but he cried like everyone else. That day Yalo understood that laughter was the neighbor of tears, and that distinguishing between them was terribly difficult, since they had been so closely related since the beginning of creation. Both were surprising and alienating, and both surged in to fill the emptiness the soul felt.

There, facing this scene he would never forget, the tears were like a hemorrhage from a deep wound. Yalo saw himself bent over a pile of bones, which a brown, singed leather belt allowed them to identify, and he saw his comrades stripped of their clothes and their flesh. He saw bones bent over bones, and was overcome by laughter arising from tears, and understood what he had been unable to explain to Shirin, when he had been pursuing her with his love. He understood this mixture of laughter and tears was the hallmark of humanity, and that every human bore two souls with him, the first for laughter and the second for weeping. His problem was that the two souls worked together and that was why it was always impossible to define his feelings.

He told Shirin when she wept that weeping was a sign of happiness and love. She looked at him with her small reddened eyes as if she did not understand why he did not understand.

"Please, Yalo, understand me."

Getting up, she asked him to understand her. Shirin had the habit of getting up in the middle of their rendezvous as if she were preparing to leave, but when he looked at her with his hawk eyes she'd sit down again without a word.

< 125 >

She would tell the interrogator that she was afraid of his eyes and his long narrow eyebrows. She would say that she didn't know why she went out with him, that she was afraid of him, and that she agreed to meet him in order to persuade him to end the relationship.

The interrogator asked her why she went to meet him the first time, when the story had not started yet, and she said that she wanted to put an end to it with him.

"Okay, so you met him once, but after that why did you go back to see him so many more times?" the interrogator asked.

The girl stammered and said she didn't know, but she was afraid of him and felt sorry for him at the same time.

When she came to meet him, she would stand up to leave within minutes, but he sharpened his gaze and she'd find herself back in her chair. Shirin firmly believed that Yalo had two faces and that each face had a different set of eyes. When they'd met, first she'd see the first face with its drowsy, half-closed eyes, and she'd resolve to leave. She'd get up to say it was all over, then out came the second face with its eyes wide open, nailing her in place before forcing her to sit down again. She would weep listening to him speak words of love.

Shirin did not understand because she had not seen Alexei as a heap of bones covered with ragged clothes, and the young guys turning into skeletons and sobbing around him.

Yalo retreated, seeing how a human being devoured himself. This was the second truth of man. The first truth was the mixture of laughter and weeping, and the second was that he consumed himself. On the third floor of the Jeraydini Building, Yalo understood that what a human being offered himself at the final banquet was his death.

The voice was Yalo's but the question was everyone's:

"Who devoured him?"

Yalo looked around, expecting to find a dog or fierce beast. For in those days dogs ruled the war-devastated city. Yalo believed that it had been one of the wild or stray dogs that the fighters would shoot at for fun at the crossing points that divided Beirut from Beirut that had preyed on Alexei, but this had not been the case.

Mario said that Alexei had died from an overdose: "The bastard started wanting coke all the time. He started shooting himself up, too. Of course he was up there with one of his boys, he shot up and died. No one killed him, that's for sure, who would have done it? It was the needle. I just want to know who was with him? And how on earth they could have left him like this? Hell. We've become worse than animals."

Mario ended the discussion with his decree that Alexei had died of an overdose. But Yalo saw something else. He saw Alexei eat himself. He had bent over his death, and began his final banquet. He ate himself by himself. That was death, the last supper, when the dead man became the banquet and the guests at once. He ate without food, because he had become the food, and when the meal was gone he was gone with it, leaving behind only what was inedible. A skull, white bones, a laugh. That was what Alexei had become, a collection of bones, the remains of a meal. After Alexei had finished eating himself, he gobbled down his teeth. Nothing remained but a laughing skull. The mouth was a void, full of laughter and death.

The skull laughed and Mario wept and drank his tears. They all drank their tears and started coughing as if the tears were stuck in their throats and they could no longer swallow them or spit them out. So they sobbed and coughed and stood helpless before a corpse that looked nothing like a corpse.

"How are we supposed to carry him?" Tony asked, and pulled at Yalo's arm to make him help, but Yalo didn't budge from his place. He stood still, imagining the banquet Alexei had made for himself in this room with its

< 127 >

doors and windows ripped away. Alexei had refused to hold his banquet in secret. He had not entered the grave to eat himself in the dark, he returned as a child to eat his insides, as would happen with Yalo after the night of the sack, when, seeking warmth, he would lick his remains and drink his tears.

But Gaby did not understand the meaning of the final banquet. She clasped her son's hand and dragged him to the bathroom so he could see how her face had disappeared. "So, your image is consuming you, Mother," he told her.

"What does that mean?" she asked, frightened.

"How do I know? Go to sleep, Mother, and be sensible. Forget the mirrors."

But Gaby stood there as firmly as Mario stood before the bones spread out in the remains of the blue trousers and khaki shirt.

"Don't be afraid, Mother, come on. Go to bed."

"No, no," she replied. "Look closely. Do you see my face in the mirror or not?"

"I see you, Mother. The image is clear. Get these black thoughts out of your head and look."

"I don't see anything, I don't know what's happening to me. Please, Yalo, tell me what to do."

"God, what am I doing? Please just leave me alone and go to bed."

Yalo told the interrogator that he had run away out of fear of her and her speech: "I ran away from her and her mirror. I was afraid she'd kill me with her stories. I was afraid I'd go crazy because of her, because of this war, because of this life, so I decided to escape. When Tony said, 'Let's go,' I went with him to France."

"So what brought you back to Lebanon?"

"I told you, sir, Tony stole the money and left me stranded."

"And then?"

"Then Ballouna, from France to Ballouna. You know the whole story, sir."

"No, I don't. I want the true story."

"I told you the whole story with Shirin. I am guilty, I swear."

"You think you can make fools of us? I want the story of the explosives, I want the details of the activities of the gang and who its members are, and the sources of its funding, and who was giving the orders."

"It has nothing to do with me and I don't know anything about it," said Yalo.

"Your memory isn't so good, maybe we need to activate it. It looks like you won't talk until we work you over. Let's go."

He said, "Let's go," and Yalo was taken to the sack, and there amidst the pool of his innards that had gushed out, he opened his eyes to see Alexei's mother in front of him. Who had brought her to the prison?

The heavy, pale woman was sitting on the floor beside Yalo, smiling the feebleminded smile that had been on her face since she had seen her son in his coffin.

Mario and his two comrades, including Yalo, arrived at her house behind the Azarite Convent in the long, winding street that overlooked the St. Demetrius Cemetery in Achrafieh. The woman had seen death and the traces of weeping were etched on her face. Mario told her that Alexei had been found dead and that the burial rites would take place on the following day. The woman said nothing. She did not ask where he had been found, how he had been killed, or who killed him. She let herself collapse into the couch and apologized for not preparing coffee for her visitors because she was unable to get up.

Mario said that they would not bring the body to the house. She raised her eyebrows in disagreement and said that her son would go from his house to the cemetery.

< 129 >

Mario tried to explain but it was as if she were deaf. She consented only when Mario said that these were the orders of the command, which no one in the world could disobey.

"If that's how it is, do as you wish," the woman said. She said that she would meet them at the church. It would not be necessary for anyone to come to the house to accompany her there.

Mario said that they would have death notices printed, but Umm Alexei said that would not be necessary, since she was alone and there were no other family members here.

"He's a martyr," said Mario. It wouldn't be right not to print up some notices and post them.

Mario gave her some money in a small envelope and she smiled. She tried in vain to get up to see her visitors out, and Yalo noticed her thick, varicose-veined legs and fat body, which strained her large, tight dress.

"Never mind, ma'am, stay where you are," said Mario.

"Never mind what," said the woman testily. "Please help me up, I don't want to be paralyzed."

Mario approached her and extended his hand, she clasped it and pulled it toward her, nearly making him fall. But the woman could not get up, as if she were fastened to the couch, and her face flushed red. Yalo stepped forward and took her by the elbow and hand, using both his hands, and they tried again. Mario held her from one side and Yalo from the other, and the woman struggled with her arms but did not budge from her place. It was as if she had surrendered to gravity and was stuck to the sofa. Mario asked her to make an effort, "Push with me, mother, push," and the woman pushed and moaned more loudly. It was as if she were giving birth, thought Yalo. She pushed and gasped with three men standing around her trying in vain to help her. Suddenly the woman slipped off the sofa; her head struck the floor and her legs flew into the air.

"That's it, that's it," said Nina the Russian. "Leave me alone – that's it."

Yalo did not know why he thought that a child had come out between her thighs. He burst into laughter. He dropped the woman's hand and left the living room to stifle his laughter and wait for his comrades. And there too, as the guys had stood bent over the heap of bones, weeping, Yalo stifled his laughter and stood waiting for them.

"Pick him up!" shouted Mario.

"How can we pick him up?" Tony's hollow voice sounded as if it came from behind a mask covering his mouth.

Mario slipped his arms under the trousers and shirt to lift him up as one would lift a child, but Alexei fell apart. His bones began to drop out.

"Put him down, Mario," said Tony, his voice white and frightened.

Tony bent down and picked up the bones that had fallen from Mario's arms. Said al-Mansurati appeared with a wooden box resembling a coffin and put the parts of Alexei in it, then the box was carried to the headquarters in the Georges Aramouni Barracks at the Good Shepherd High School. There was no smell.

Alexei spent the night in the barracks, in a room no one entered. Tony suggested bringing in two big candles to put on either side of the box, as was the custom observed with corpses before burial, but everyone ignored his suggestion. So Alexei spent his final night in a dark room that no one had bothered to light up.

The next morning, Mario brought a real casket of brown wood, decorated with flowers in relief and with a metal plate attached bearing an engraved inscription: "Alexei, 1963-1988. Martyr." The guys carried the bier to the St. Demetrius Church, where Alexei's mother waited cloaked in black. The bier was placed before the altar between two large bright candles. The priest concluded his prayers, and the bier was carried to the Foreigners' Cemetery, as the public cemetery was called, though it was the

< 131 >

property of the church reserved for poor families, and at that moment the incident occurred that was etched in Yalo's memory. The bier was opened so that the priest might sprinkle a handful of earth on the corpse and say, "Dust to dust," and call for the burial. All the priest saw was a white sheet covering something, so he removed the sheet to sprinkle the earth on the face of the deceased, and what he saw was Alexei's grinning skull. The priest drew back in horror. The handful of earth dropped from his hand, and Yalo got up to close the casket and asked the gravedigger to lower it into the ground. At that moment Nina found her way between the priest and Mario, saw the skull, and screamed, "That is not my son!" And she began to curse. A stream of curses flowed one after another from her mouth, and her face turned pale and sallow: "That is not Alexei! Why are you doing this to me? Where is my son?" Mario tried to calm her down, but she threw herself onto the bier, determined to throw it down and scatter its contents. However, Mario and Tony were able to keep her at a distance from it, and the casket was lowered into the grave.

As to what happened next, Yalo could not recall. Something like a black veil fell over his eyes and everything was wiped from the screen of his memory, but he heard the story from his comrades. He heard how the woman had to be carried to her house because she refused to leave the cemetery, and how after that she sought help from the disabled shelter at Atchaneh, though she refused to live there because all of the disabled women there spoke Syriac or Turkish, and she did not understand either one, so she went on to die in the Orthodox shelter, near the Saint George Hospital in Achrafieh. The staff was sure that the old woman was deranged. For she was not Russian as she claimed, she didn't know a single word of Russian, and her son was not a saint and had not become a skeleton at the moment of his death, it was impossible, one of the signs of sainthood was the saint's body remaining uncorrupted even after death. So how could Nina say that

< 132 >

her son had shed his corporeal body, as a man sheds his clothes, to become a heap of bones?

Nina died, alone and sorrowful; she had come to believe that she was truly deranged, just as the old women at the shelter had whispered after hearing the story of the son who had shed his body. Nina would act out the scene; she'd begin by removing her clothes, then the screaming would escalate and the nurses would rush toward her to calm her down before restraining her. Nina tried to persuade the nurses to let her shed her body to become a saint like her son, St. Alexei.

Nina believed in her madness. She went to the shelter's church to ask the young priest who served at the Sunday mass for Beirut's small Russian community to cast the devils out of her. The priest pushed her away with the back of his hand to clear his way to the altar so that he could begin the early morning prayer that preceded the mass. Nina fell to the ground and suddenly all was confusion. She was carried back to the shelter after nurses and porters were summoned. She died two days later and was buried in the Foreigners' Cemetery beside her son.

The priest did not kill her, as Sister Blajiah, the supervisor of the shelter, had insinuated. For Sister Blajiah hated White Russians and didn't like the way they chanted their prayers. She said that the only acceptable manner of prayer was in Greek and in a Byzantine melody, because that was how they prayed in heaven.

The priest had nothing to do with it, the woman had come to the church to die there, and there were no devils to cast out. The Russian priest found nothing to liberate from her except her own soul. She left there, where everyone must leave one day or another, and that's all there was to it. As for the story of her son the saint, no one believed her. Struck by a bullet in his chest, the saint leaned on his comrade Yalo and told him he would shed his body the moment he died because he couldn't stand the thought of rotting

< 133 >

and swelling up like the rest of the dead that were eaten up by vermin and worms, then he bowed his head and gave up the ghost. His friend bent over to pick him up but did not find him; he found only a skeleton.

Nina said that Yalo was terror-struck when he saw the skeleton and ran to his comrades to tell them of the marvel. And when they came, that sector had come under fire from the enemy camp and no one was able to get to where Alexei had shed his body and left a skeleton so they abandoned him. "And when I found out I went out by myself and brought him back to the house. His bones were as white as snow, as if they had been scrubbed with soap and water. I went myself, under fire, and brought him back. All his comrades refused to come with me, afraid for their lives – what cowards! And to think that I'd taken them for soldiers of the White Army! I went by myself and brought back his bones so that his name would be remembered. His grandfather was an officer in the czar's army and I wanted him to become like him. The bastards, they let his flesh fall off his bones. They abandoned him there and no one saw the miracle, not even that tall Syriac, Yalo, Gaby's son, who'd seen the miracle with his own eyes, he stood there like a mute. Tall and stupid, what could he say? Alexei's grandfather told me, this is the kind of miracle that happened in Russia in the civil war times. He said that when an officer died he became a skeleton, the bones were as white as snow. That's what happened with my son. In Russia, they blessed the officer who shed his body at the moment of his death, and they declared him a saint. But they abandoned Alexei because they're cowards and they don't believe in the Holy Trinity. I offered him up to the Trinity. His father died when he was young, and I have no one left but the Trinity and that boy."

Sister Blajiah listened and wanted to believe her, but Nina began to make scenes in front of the other old ladies, she shed her clothes and her body.

The nun became certain that this woman was crazy and repeatedly told her that these thoughts were the work of the Devil.

Why did Nina come back from the old people's shelter in Atchaneh cursing the Syriacs? Sister Blajiah knew that her son was a Syriac, like all these youths, and that her family came from the Mardin region. Where had Nina come up with the story of the grandfather who had been an officer in the White Army?

The nun decided that the woman was crazy, and gave orders that she should be given strong sedatives that put her into a hallucinatory lethargy, which may have been the cause of her vision of the Devil that led to her death.

Yalo remembered nothing that happened in the cemetery, he had erased the scene from his eyes, and the woman was wrapped in what seemed like fog. He went back to his house and decided to leave his buddies, the war, and everything.

At first, Yalo saw himself as a hero, the war had come to teach him the secrets of life. That was what he felt in the training camp where he had become a Goat. He and his comrades, poor kids from the Syriac Quarter, became the masters of the streets. Yalo understood little of the complications and convolutions of the war that made talk of it seem so useless. He believed that he was fighting for the existence of a people who had disappeared into the darkness of history, as the *cohno* had described the continued migrations that had brought him from Ain Ward to Beirut. "We came from the darkness of history, and we will stay in the darkness, until the sun of justice rises." When Yalo asked him about the "sun of justice," the *cohno* replied that it was the Messiah. "My boy, we are awaiting the Kingdom of the Messiah, and He said that His kingdom was not of this world."

Yalo did not understand Lebanese politics or the language of war. He played along as if he were acting in a movie, and when he took part in a battle he felt as though he were a hero. But his feelings of heroism disappeared with time. He felt sad when he heard his mother, quoting the *cohno*, saying that war was useless. "We have to be yeast. We do not fight, my boy. The yeast does not fight the dough, but becomes part of it and leavens it so that it becomes bread. Leave the war and go to school. You should become a *cohno* like your grandfather."

Yalo was frightened by the image of himself he saw in his mother's eyes, for it had become a miniature version of his grandfather with his immense white beard. But what he feared above all else was the emptiness, not the sight of the bones covered with shredded clothes, but the profound emptiness of this war, which had become monotonous. The idea of war was seductive and gave you a feeling of heroism, but the war itself was tedious and repugnant.

Said al-Mansurati dreamed of becoming a singer. What a shame how he had vanished, no one ever discovered even his bones. And so Yalo agreed to go away to Paris. He saw his own apparition walking around in Paris before he became an apparition in the night of Ballouna, under the pine trees, among the sighs of lovers. When he found himself in prison, with the sheets of white paper before him, it seemed ridiculous. He had always hated writing, and hated being forced to write in school. But now he had to write a long story of his own life!

At the St. Severus School Yalo had not been a special student. He had been average at everything. He studied, managed to move from one grade to the next, but he did not possess the spark of faith that his grandfather the *cohno* had. He did excel at Arabic because of the books his mother had but did not read, and that was all. But Yalo did not hate school. His head rose above those of the other students in his class, because he was the tallest.

He sat in a chair at the back, and Malfono Halim told him that he was as beautiful as a pretty girl.

"I'm like a girl, Malfono? What?" Yalo asked in the office of the principal, who was always summoning him to give him books to read. The *malfono* stroked his pupil's wide eyes and told him that his lips were like cherries.

At that time, Yalo did not understand the meaning of sex, yet he saw something burning in the eyes of the *malfono* who taught them Arabic and mathematics. No, it was not true, what Said al-Mansurati told him: "We all dropped by Halim's – he couldn't get enough." Yalo remembered only the *malfono*'s hands on his eyes and lips. But his friends spoke of something else, they spoke of the *malfono*'s deftness, and drew with their fingers circles around their buttocks.

"Halim, oh man, Halim!" Tony said, after pouring himself a glass of arak. "I swear, there is no one in the world with fingers as light as his." He put his hand on his member and made as if to encompass it. "I swear – no one." The strange thing was that unanimity regarding the *malfono*, that he had been with all of them.

Yalo's memory said otherwise. It had not gone that far, in his view. The circumstances were innocent. The *malfono* would sit behind his desk and ask his pupil to come close in order to see his errors, and when he neared the desk the *malfono* had him squeeze in on his own side of the desk. The *malfono* would reach out and put his hand on the pupil's bottom.

"I swear, there's no one like him" exclaimed Tony. "Where are you, Halim, where have you gone!"

"Don't say Halim," said Said al-Mansurati. "We used to call him Malfono Halib because he was as delicious as milk. Good lord, what ever felt so good? His hand was wonderful, how he played. In all my life, I've never felt anything like it."

"What did you feel?" asked Yalo.

"Ha! Look, he's pretending he doesn't know. Of course he played with you the same way he played with all of us," Said laughed.

Yalo remembered nothing.

"You were the girl," said Said. "He used to say you were prettier than any girl. And once, I swear, once when he was fondling me, he started talking about you and how beautiful you were, and that might have been the most aroused I ever got."

"Over me?" asked Yalo.

"Yes, you. Halim did it with all of us. He said that was the philosophical way to discover life. It's what Plato did with Aristotle and Ahmad Shawqi with Abd al-Wahab, all the geniuses did it."

The *malfono* Halim used to place his fingers on the haunches of the boy to allow him to experience the bliss inside him. "*Malfono* the magician" is what they called him "because he made pleasure appear with a touch of the hand," Tony said.

But Yalo remembered nothing, though he remembered that he was more beautiful than a girl, and he attributed that to his mother.

Yalo experienced minor adventures with girls, adventures more like moments where he stole some bliss. It was true that he was able to find a link between stealing bliss during the war and the robberies in Ballouna, because in both cases he felt that he was picking a flower that had bloomed between his thighs. He felt around his flower preparing for that taste drawn by Malfono Halim's fingers on his lips, neck, and haunches.

Why now?

Why did the apparition of the *malfono* come as if to awaken him from his death and restore him to the life that Shirin had stolen from him and crushed under her feet?

It was the same feeling, the feeling of blossoming and bending like a bow.

A feeling that began with Elvira and continued with all the women. Even his randifying was part of that bow that bent him toward what seemed like death. When he felt the flower blooming between his thighs, he remembered Maron and saw the pain shining from his eyes, bending over Elvira and discovering the pain written on her white thighs.

"War erases names," he would tell the interrogator. No, he had not said that, he said that in war, you didn't ask anyone's name.

"And in the forest?" asked the interrogator.

"No, sir, never there, never once did I ask for names."

"What about Shirin?"

"Shirin was different."

"Didn't you make her kneel and threaten her with the rifle, and ask her for her name before you raped her?"

"Me?"

"You, you, who else?"

"Me!"

Yalo did not know where the interrogator got that story. He wanted to tell him that when he was with Shirin he forgot the pain, but he didn't dare. How could he talk about the pain that permeated his insides? Or about his flower that wilted under torture? How could he talk about his grandfather, the *cohno* Ephraim, who had sat facing him opening the Gospels and reading from the Apostle Paul: "A thorn in my flesh." He closed the book and said, "Watch out, my son, the thorn is sin, and sin hurts. Watch out for your thorn."

Yalo did not know how a man could watch out for his thorn, when it moved between his thighs every day.

"Maron got it moving," Yalo told Tony when they both had night guard duty at the Georges Aramouni Barracks and were talking about women. Tony was boasting about his adventures, and lying and believing himself.

< 139 >

He told Tony about Maron. He said, after chewing on his cigarette and taking a long draw on it that reached the depths of his lungs, that Maron, the son of Salma the cook, had guided him to his thorn. Yalo was ten years old when he accompanied Maron to the chicken coop in the backyard of the cook's house. Maron sat on a stone, pulled out his member, seized it, and began to repeat the name Marie. "For Marie, come on, pull it out and follow me." Yalo was taken aback by the size of Maron's penis, which was long, thin, and uncircumcised. Maron, who was fourteen, held his long thorn while a look of bliss spread over his face. He took it in the palm of his hand and shook it, shouting the name of their neighbor, the widow Marie. Maron stopped and looked contemptuously at Yalo: "What's wrong with you, afraid? Show me your dick." Yalo unzipped his pants and brought out his thing, which was small, thick, and erect. Maron looked at it and said, "It's still small. Don't worry, soon it will grow. Come on, follow me, for Marie." Yalo followed along with him, sitting on a rock facing him, holding his member and shaking it, and the pain came. Perhaps the pain came from the chickens, for Yalo felt nauseated at the sight of the black chickens standing frightened in a corner of the coop. But Maron didn't stop. He called out Marie's name and moaned and his shoulders shook, then the name came faster and with it his hand motions, and then Maron let up. His hand was full of the sticky white, and he shouted encouragement to his friend. To Maron's shouts, repeating the name of the black widow, the pain burst in Yalo's hand. "Get her," shouted Maron, and "Get her!" said Yalo, his hand motions accelerating, then unexpectedly something came from within him and his hand began to tremble at the convulsions of his member, but the trembling was met with a thick wall that prevented it, it hurled forward and then died out. The white liquid did not come out.

Maron laughed and began to chant: "*Qadishat Aloho, qadishat hayltono, qadishat lo yo moto.*" He told Yalo not to worry, he was still young, and when he grew up we would sow the bellies of women with the liquid that carries life in it. "Man starts to tremble because his soul is here, deep in the white," Maron said.

Yalo waited for his soul, which finally arrived. The wait was the reason for the pain that would accompany Yalo in his relationship with his inner soul. For that thorn became a flower, though its thorniness returned when the white liquid began to spurt, and he was bedeviled with pain.

"My thorn hurts," Yalo said, as he stood alone before the mirror in the bathroom. He saw Marie, swathed in black and carrying her son to the house of Edward the taxi driver; he grasped his thorn and shouted in pain. The woman did not shed her black dress after the death of her young husband, who had worked in the electrical extension project and died suddenly of heart failure, which deeply affected the Syriac community in Mseitbeh. He was in his forties and his wife, Marie, was nineteen. They had their first child, Najib, six months before he died.

"Heart failure," the *cohno* told his grandson.

"How does a heart fail?" Yalo asked.

"It stops talking," said his grandfather.

"It stops talking!"

"A heart talks by beating, it keeps beating and doesn't sleep, and when the heart falls asleep it means the person has died," the *cohno* said.

Yalo felt his heart pounding in his neck and asked his grandfather if he was afraid of dying.

"There is no death," his grandfather said. "We call death slumber. The dead sleep, they shed their bodies and sleep, and later on they awaken with Abu Isa."

"Who is Abu Isa?" Yalo asked.

"Abu Isa is God, my boy. He's the father of Jesus, of Isa, that's why we call God Abu Isa."

Edmond's heart fell asleep, leaving his young wife behind, dressed in black and carrying their baby, Najib, in her arms.

Finding herself alone without a provider, she turned to working at the Régie factory rolling cigarettes, they said. She became the lover of Edward the taxi driver, who told extraordinary stories.

She knocked at the door and Edward opened it. He had prepared a table full of every delightful and delicious thing, especially a bottle of country arak and small fried whitebait. She drank, ate, and danced. She wore an oriental dancer's costume and danced to the beat of Umm Kalthoum's singing, and Edward kneeled at her feet and sang.

Marie's image was seared into the memories of the young men of the neighborhood as an oriental dancer swaying like a cobra to a musician's melodies without ever tiring. This went back to what Edward used to talk about in front of Abboudi's shop when he was drinking beer with the guys and talking about horse races.

She came carrying her son in her arms, and before she ate or drank, she put a little arak on her finger and let the baby suck on it. When he fell asleep, she put him in the bedroom. She started to drink and her body shone. Edward recounted everything. He said that in the beginning she refused to take off her mourning dress and he would sleep with her in her clothes. Then, little by little, she became less modest, "and finally when she took it all off, heavens, what a beauty, how white she was! She was wearing a red bodice and red panties, and she said that she was allergic to the color black. Some red and some white and bring on the dance! My God, how beautiful she was, as white as milk, white filtered through white, white on white that made me melt. Then it was over and believe me, I was sorry. I told her from the start that I couldn't. The fact is I was afraid. I had decided to remain a bachelor, but then I don't know what came over me, I said to myself, Why not? I'll marry her. But then later, no, I couldn't, it was surely she who killed her husband. Who could handle a filly like that? I never saw anything like it. You just got near her and you felt the water coming out of her – a well, I swear to God, she had a bottomless well in her. Oh God, what could be better? But I was afraid. She told me that people were starting to talk, that is, I had to marry her. I told her I can't. I was afraid she'd kill me like she'd killed her husband. I asked her a hundred times how he died and a hundred times she didn't tell me. But no one saw the guy in the living room, my friends! They say he died in the living room after he asked for a drink of water and a cup of coffee. We ran over when we heard the noise and went in, and found ourselves in the bedroom, the deceased was in bed and covered with a white sheet. He was wearing a white shirt up top but no one noticed whether he was wearing anything below. Marie was standing beside the bed with her hair down. When the doctor got there he ordered us out of the room, and allowed only Marie to stay inside. After a minute the doctor appeared and said, 'May he rest in peace, it was heart failure.' He was almost smiling. What did that mean? It meant, this was not about a cup of coffee. I asked her a hundred times, and she smiled like the doctor, and didn't answer. She sipped from the glass of arak and something like fire came out of her chest. What did it mean? It meant, right, he died because he couldn't stand so much beauty, so do you want me to marry her and die too?"

The talk attributed to the driver came after Marie and her son left for parts unknown. It was said that she went to live in the village of Choueifat, where she dwelled in a cottage near the Régie factory. But Edward's account led to many fantasies among Yalo and his friends.

Marie's appeal was her white complexion embellished with a beauty mark high on her neck. A woman of thirty, her white face sprinkled with freckles leading down toward her sternum, of medium height, her hair long and black, pulled back like a cap on her head, walking with her infant in her arms, and lust accompanying her all the way.

Yalo, Maron, and all the neighborhood guys continued to milk their desire for her even though she had disappeared from the neighborhood. Maron gushed white, and Yalo with the thorn that had grown between his thighs cried out her name and cried in pain.

With Marie, Yalo began to look at women differently. He was possessed by sex. When he saw a woman walking down the street, he imagined that she had just gotten out of bed; he saw her naked walking beside a man with blurry features and closed eyes. Closed eyes had sex with all the women in Beirut. His imagination took him away to distant places; he no longer distinguished between young and old women. In his imagination all the women were naked in bed with their eyes closed. Even his mother entered the picture. He saw Gaby, her hair bound up in a round *kokina*, sitting behind a sewing machine in her pale yellow blouse, with the tailor Elias al-Shami hovering around and having sex with her. Yalo saw nothing but a world crowded with desires. It was as if all women had become one woman with many heads. He would be walking down the street or playing with his friends, but everything was obliterated when he saw a woman, and nothing remained in front of his eyes but the color white.

When the white came into his hand, Yalo was alone, and it was not Marie, it was Elvira. On that spring morning, Yalo awoke to water washing his lower parts, with a foolish smile on his face. Years later, when Shirin asked him why he was smiling, he would answer that love made lovers foolish, and he asked her when she would be stricken with idiocy as he had been.

When had he told her that? And when had she told him that he made her laugh? When did he feel a violent love for her that tore apart his insides and made him have a milking session before he was to meet her so that he would come to her transparent, with his pure love?

Tossed here, isolated from the world, Yalo was confused as to how he should organize his memory. He was confused because things came to him all at once and the images intermingled in his head, times overlapped in his consciousness, as if he were an old man. The *cohno* had once told him when he was trembling over his papers that the final stage of life was like a long sleep, and that the Syriac St. Ephraim had awoken from the sleep of death when he succeeded in transforming his body into solid, dry clay – like our ancestor Adam before God breathed a soul into him.

"How did they bury St. Ephraim?" Yalo asked.

"They broke him up. They could not bury him before breaking him up into small pieces, and that's how they lowered him into the grave."

"…"

"That's how I am," said his grandfather. "When life is over, a man becomes like clay, and can no longer distinguish between truth and illusion, or the past from the present. He becomes like a young child."

His grandfather smiled as he told his grandson how the body of St. Ephraim had become like clay, and Yalo saw simplemindedness written on the face covered with white hair, and saw the clay taking over his grandfather's hands, which emerged from the folds of the black robe. Old age was written on his grandfather's hands like sunbaked clay. Dark spots, thin fingers, bones like an interior layer of clay, and the smell of earth. When his grandfather's rheumatism worsened and his hands and feet got stiff, Yalo was frightened, seeing his grandfather as if he were a clay statue, and he began to imagine himself breaking up the clay body in order to put it into the casket.

Yalo's nights began to be filled with visions of clay. He saw his grandfather in many different forms. He saw him as a huge corpse bloated with earth that the sun had leavened, then he saw him in small pieces arrayed on the bed. He saw himself with a huge hammer he used on the clay body to shatter it, with blood streaming down his hands and clothes.

Faced with Alexei, of whom nothing remained but his white bones and

< 145 >

ragged clothes, Yalo saw his grandfather's face as he grumbled at his daughter's insistence on feeding his grandson morsels of raw sheep's liver to cure him of the anemia he suffered from. His grandfather held his nose because of the smell of the blood overflowing from Yalo's lips. Yalo was unable to push back his mother's hands, which besieged his mouth with a piece of raw liver with green mint and white onion.

His grandfather left the table repeating his graveyard theory: "Why are you treating the boy that way, daughter? A man's stomach should not be a graveyard for dead animals. Man is the image of God. What is this savagery, killing animals and burying them in our bellies so that we become like walking tombs. A man becomes a big graveyard. His stomach is a grave and his head and eyes are the gravestones. Then when a man dies he is devoured by the graveyard inside of him. His belly becomes his graveyard. Saints' bodies do not decompose and worms don't invade them because they do not eat the flesh of the dead. What is man, a graveyard?"

His grandfather spoke of tombs, and Yalo imagined his belly as a tomb for animals, and wept at his mother's firm hand, which did not pity the little lamb whose raw liver had become a morsel she thrust into the mouth of her son, who was a weakling. She would trick her son by preparing bulgur with meat, telling him it was potato balls. Yalo lived for some time on this disguised food. That is what his mother assured him when he started to go to the Sennacherib Club to practice martial arts and bodybuilding and ate only meat and sought nothing in food but protein so that he might overcome his weakness and develop his muscles.

The war made Yalo forget bodybuilding, but it did not make him forget his grandfather's stories about bellies and graveyards, or his life with the Kurds and the sight of slaughtered animals hanging at the entrance to the house and the smell of blood. The mullah lifted his cloak off the ground and stood with his feet apart to select chunks of meat he ate raw, with his womenfolk and children around him.

"I ate like them, pouncing on the slaughtered animal and dipping my hand in the blood. I was always hungry. The only thing that scared me was going hungry, I felt alone, a stranger among them. My brothers – his sons, that is – called me the son of the Christians and stole the food in front of me, so I was always afraid of dying of starvation. When I escaped, no, I didn't escape, my mother's brother came and offered to buy me, only my father, that is, the mullah, refused to sell me. He spat on the ground and said: "He is free to do as he likes." And I don't remember anything else until I was with my uncle in Al-Qamishli. There I felt I had made a mistake, so I escaped to Beirut and worked as a layer of tile. Then I received the divine calling and became a *cohno*. One day, kneeling at the hands of the lord archbishop as he was blessing me, I saw my whole life pass before my eyes. Don't they say that at the moment of death a man sees his whole life rush by like a reel of film? I saw my life at the hands of the lord archbishop and I saw blood. I saw sheep and calves hanging in front of me and I began to weep. I felt blood dripping out of my eyes rather than tears. Everything tasted salty, and I even saw the calves crying. Before a calf is slaughtered it cries like a little child. I felt as if I were about to be slaughtered. I finished praying and remained kneeling where I was. I should have gone to the altar to take part in the mass, but I couldn't stand up. I felt as if my legs were frozen, so I stayed there kneeling and weeping. Then the archbishop took hold of me, God rest his soul, by my shoulder and called me, 'Ephraim' – I had completely forgotten that they'd given me the name Ephraim, my name was actually Abel Abyad. And I said, 'Who is Ephraim?' 'Tell me what's wrong, my boy. Come, get up, your name has become Ephraim by the power of the Spirit. You must forget your old name. Spit on Satan and rise.' I got up, and I decided that day to stop eating meat. My wife fooled me, the way your mother fooled you. I did not become the master of my fate until after your grandmother died, may she rest in peace. She'd mix the meat in with everything else, and tell me it was vegetarian, and I knew no better. But later I discovered, because after she died my body smell changed – the rancid smell was gone. I decided then to become like clay, to eat nothing but the plants of the earth, my basic food must be greens, of which the most important is what they call Arabs' bread, or mallow. Eat greens and that's all. How did you get like this, my boy? When you were young you were like the saint. Now you've become a beast and your belly is a graveyard."

Alexei became a graveyard of his own, with nothing remaining of him but a set of bones and the ragged clothes around which gathered the sobs and exclamations of his horrified comrades.

Yalo saw himself as a tomb after the Alexei night, he saw his death in the form of shouts mingled with the claws that tore at his lower parts, and felt that death was a true mercy. The laughter of the officer who held the bamboo cane in his hand was like the echo of distant voices coming from beyond death. He tried to scream, but his voice came out as a feeble meow, then dizziness silenced him. There in silence he licked his excrement, unconsciously, as if consuming himself before sinking into the tomb.

That was the day Yalo confessed to everything.

What did he say? He no longer remembered, but he listened to his tremulous voice, knelt on the ground, and told the officer that he was ready to kiss his boots. He bent over the boots and kissed one. He did not see how the muscles in the officer's face tensed with pride and exaltedness. The officer was enjoying his triumph over this man prostrate before him, who had become a heap of shit and piss.

"You are shit," said the officer. "Listen to me. I'm asking you. What are you?"

"..."

"Answer the question."

"I'm shit," said Yalo.

The officer's guffaws spread through the room filled with a nauseating smell, they were like the lashes of the whip that had rained on Yalo's back.

Yalo discovered that a man was capable of anything. That was what Madame Randa taught him. With her he discovered his body as separate parts for pleasure. She taught him how to kiss. No, the kiss was the first lesson Elvira had inculcated in him – Elvira who married Isa, the director of the Banca di Roma branch in Hamra, even though she loved Yalo. But the women of the war made him forget the taste of that kiss until Madame Randa came along and randified his lips.

Elvira told him that she loved him but was going to marry Isa because he was rich. Yalo was not sad. It is true that he loved this girl who was five years older than he was, but when she told him that she was going to get married, he felt as if he had already heard the words before, and that he had been expecting them for a while. He looked at her with sad eyes and then lifted her dress to give her tan thighs a farewell caress.

Yalo forgot Elvira the moment he was plunged into the war and its women. Where did they come from? Why was love like combat? And why did everything taste like sawdust?

The first kiss happened at the girls' school. There Yalo and his friends spied on the girls as they played volleyball in short shorts that exposed their thighs. The boys' gazes infiltrated the chain-link gate, generating the shiver that made their pants strain and erected the thorn that needed picking. Elvira jumped, her smooth tan legs glowing behind the iron network. There, Elvira taught him everything. She went back to the neighborhood with him, hanging back as if she were afraid. He waited for her in the afternoon every Saturday behind the school gate, and when the game was over she put on her short dark blue skirt and found him waiting for her. They walked together from Raml al-Zarif, where the school was located, to her house in the Syriac Quarter. She held Yalo's arm and said, "You're five years younger than me. My goodness, if Auntie Gaby knew that I had snagged you!" When he told her that he loved her, she stroked his back and said, "Go play with girls your own age." She tightened her grip on his elbow and his thorn was inflamed with desire and he tried to kiss her on the neck. "Not here in the street," she said. In front of her house she invited him up but he hesitated. "Come up, I want to show you something." He went upstairs to find the house empty. He sat in the living room and she asked him to wait a little because she wanted to take a shower. She reappeared just after in a loose white dress, sat beside him, and kissed him on the lips. He bent toward her and put his lips on hers, and tensely imagined that this would be like a movie. Elvira pulled her head away and said, "Not like that. Close your eyes and don't move." He closed them and felt something probing around his lips. Again he pulled her close.

"I told you not like that. Sit and don't move."

She asked him to close his eyes and her lips began to ascend his face, then he felt a lip come between his lips and the flavor entered his mouth. He felt her tongue and began to feel dizzy. The lips withdrew and he heard Elvira's voice asking him to open his eyes and kiss her as she had just kissed him. She closed her eyes and leaned back on the edge of the sofa, Yalo's lips approached her face and began to scale it slowly, reaching her lips. He tried to put his upper lip between hers but didn't succeed. Opening his lips and taking hers inside his, he wanted to devour her two red lips. He felt her hand pushing him back, but he did not retreat. He took her mouth in his, and his lips entered the kissing game. He kissed her and was not sated until pain spread throughout his lips. Elvira waited for his kisses,

< 150 >

resting her head on his arm, her eyes closed, inviting him to the banquet of her lips.

"Ouch," said Yalo. "My lips are sore."

She got up and said she would make some tea. Yalo stood up and hugged her. At that moment, when his body clung to hers, he ejaculated, and Yalo shivered with the desire that had unfurled before he began. He felt the ache in his thorn and kept clasping the waist of the girl who whispered a request for him to move back a little.

"Please, please, you're staining my dress."

He moved back and saw the stains on his pants and the wet halos on her dress. She kissed him hurriedly and asked him to leave before her mother came home and saw him this way.

"What am I supposed to do?" he asked her.

"Don't do anything," she said. "Go for a walk before you go home, and your pants will dry out."

Walking had become his mandatory workout with Elvira. He'd walk her home and hug her behind the gate at the entrance to the building, then he'd walk around for a whole hour so that his pants would be dry before he went home.

Everything changed when Elvira took him to a discothèque called Le Quartier Latin in Ramlet al-Baida near the Egyptian Embassy. And there, in the dark, while they were dancing the tango in the dark, he felt his thorn grow and she told him, "No, not like this, today." She went back with him to the darkened corner where they had been sitting. She asked him to unzip his pants, she took the thorn in her hands and put it between her thighs, and there, in the dark, he saw her, he saw the short shorts and the girl who jumped with the flying ball, and his heart opened up and he wanted to shout, but she put her hand over his mouth and asked him to come. "Go ahead, love, come." When he heard the word "Come," everything exploded, and his white blood spread over her thighs. She snatched a paper tissue and wiped up the spill: "You're a true stud!" she said, wiping off the thorn and restoring it to its place inside his pants.

Yalo picked up the glass of wine in front of him to take a drink. "No," she said. "Not now. Now give me your hand." She took his hand and pulled it under her skirt, and began to move and moan, and asked him to kiss her ear.

"No, not here. Put it between your lips."

She put the curve of her ear between his lips, and he licked it with his tongue, and heard Elvira's suppressed cry, but kept following the movements of his fingers.

"That's enough," she said. "Hands off. It hurts."

He withdrew his hand, drained the glass of wine in one swallow, and told her that he loved her: "I love you more than anything in the world."

"You're still new at love," she said. "Enjoy it now and later on we'll see."

They started to go to the discothèque once a week, after her game. He would wait for her at the La Gondole Café, while she'd go home to shower, and then they'd head for the darkness of the dance floor.

Once he made love with her this way with the lights on. That was the day she informed him of her decision to marry Isa.

"But he's much older than you," he said.

"I'm older than you," she said.

She asked him to get dressed and go home. He left without having to walk through the streets; he left feeling his tongue. That day he had kissed and licked her breasts all over and discovered the map of her body. But she left him to get married. He went home to his mirror and tried to remember the black widow, burning with the fire of jealousy of a man he didn't know.

Yalo woke up looking at boots. He reached down below to make sure that his member was there, that the cat had not devastated it. He bent over, kissed the boot, and declared that he was prepared to confess everything.

"Do you confess to the rape?" the officer asked.

"I confess."

"And that you are agents of Israel?"

"I confess."

"And that you received orders from Abu Ahmad al-Naddaf."

"I confess."

"That you planted the explosives in Antilias and Achrafieh?"

"I confess."

"That you directed the network in Beirut and Mount Lebanon."

"I confess."

"Great. Now that you've confessed to everything, we're going to move you to detention. I'm sure the court will take into consideration the fact that you cooperated with questioning and will find cause for mitigating factors."

"Thank you, sir."

"Now you'll sign your statement, and later on the real sessions will begin."

"There are still more sessions, sir? I confessed just as you wanted."

Yalo had said that he wanted to confess to everything to get it over with. He said it was over, and the inside of his mouth tasted like rubber. He said that he was hungry, that he was thirsty.

"I'm thirsty, sir, and hungry, too. May I have something to drink?"

"You ate everything and you're still hungry?"

"I'm hungry, but whatever you say."

"You may eat and drink," the interrogator said, "but first you need to sign these papers. We'll read your confessions to you, and if you consent, you sign, and then everything's okay."

< 153 >

"I'll sign whatever you want. There's no need to read them. I'll sign everything."

The voice began to read. Yalo heard his name and his father's and mother's names. He heard about Ballouna and Shirin, about Emile Shahin and the explosives gang. He heard the names of the victims, and nodded in agreement.

The officer leaned over, handing him some sheets of paper and saying that the real sessions would pass in solitude, since he would be required to write the entire story of his life, from start to finish, omitting nothing.

In the cell, Yalo had been unable to write. He felt that he had fallen into a well and could not breathe. For after the exhausting interrogation sessions that had concluded with his admitting everything, Yalo could no longer remember anything. On top of that he didn't know what to write, what could he write? In the Paris Métro he had written on a placard and sat beside it like the beggars, under the merciless eyes of the passersby. There he felt the savagery of language. The French words whose meaning he did not understand landed on his head like the blows of a whip. He missed his mother, and he longed for anyone who might speak to him in Arabic, the only language he knew. In that Metro tunnel, Yalo wept when M. Michel Salloum spoke to him in Arabic, he wept because he heard the sounds of Arabic and smelled the scent of Lebanon. But here, in his solitary cell, he felt that he didn't know how to write.

They read him his confession in Classical Arabic, and the tall young man signed them in dialect. The first time he signed his name in Syriac. The interrogator took the sheet of paper and raised his eyebrows, eyebrows were raised in the Jounieh police station and again in prison when the interrogator visited him several times to rewrite what he had written. This meant that things were not going well, and that the investigation would lead Yalo back to torture.

"What is this?" the officer shouted.

"That's my signature."

"What, are you trying to trick us? You think you're pretty smart."

When Yalo explained his signature, the officer exploded in anger. "So now you're going to teach us Syriac? And you said you didn't know Syriac."

"I don't know it, but that's how I sign my name."

"No, that's no good," the officer said, looking around him and raising his eyebrows, and Yalo was certain that torture was now inevitable, so he said he was sorry for the unintentional mistake and that he was ready to sign as they wanted. The officer looked at the clerk and ordered him to recopy the final page so that Yalo could sign it in Arabic.

Yalo held the fresh sheet of paper in shaking fingers and signed it: Yalo. Once again the officer cursed him.

"What is this shit? Why don't you write your real name?"

"That is my name," said Yalo.

"Take him away," said the officer.

They put him into a truck and took him to a solitary cell, a small room four meters square with an aperture high in the wall covered by an iron grate, and to the right an iron cot with three woolen blankets on it. In the left corner was a green Formica table and white plastic chair. On the table were sheets of white paper, a fountain pen, and a bottle of ink. Yalo was to write his life story at this table.

Had he been a poet, he would have written that he'd fallen into a well of words, that he embraced the night, that his ink was blacker than the night.

Had he been a novelist, he would have written his memoirs in one single swoop and called them Ain Ward. The story would begin with the young boy who would become his grandfather, how he experienced the massacre of his village in Tur Abdin, how his feet led him to Al-Qamishli and from there to Beirut, how a layer of tile became a *cohno*, and how someone ignorant of the Syriac language became a fervent advocate of this language dying in his mouth.

Had Yalo been a storyteller, he would have sat in prison and told of the fearless Yalo, who'd fought like no one else, who was chivalrous and brave, then had experienced banishment much as his grandfather had, emigrating to France, from which he returned to become a lord among lovers, and, like all lovers, was betrayed.

If he had been.

But he was not.

He was Yalo, a young man trying to read in the whiteness of the paper his story, which he did not know how to tell, his language, which he did not know how to write, and his memory, which he did not know how to provide with a voice. He saw himself as a wild ass lost in the wilderness.

Had his grandfather the *cohno* not told him that Ishmael was the ancestor of the Arabs and Assyrians, the Christians and the Muslims?

"Yisma' Allah, Ismail, means 'God hears.' God hears nothing but the language of tears. We are the descendants of Ishmael. He baptized us in tears before Christ came and baptized us with water."

"He shall be the father of a great nation of people and shall dwell in the wilderness like a wild ass," the *cohno* said.

"Remember, my boy, this verse is from the Old Testament, from the Book of Genesis. Memorize it, because you too are a grandson of Ishmael, and you will become a wild ass."

Yalo wrote about this wild ass, tore up the pages, and started again. He immersed himself in the whiteness of the page that stretched before him like a vast desert.

My name is Yalo, Daniel Jal'u, the son of George Jal'u, nicknamed Yalo, from the Syriac Quarter in the Mseitbeh district of Beirut. My mother is Gaby, Gabrielle Abel Abyad. I am an only child, I have no brothers or sisters. I lived with my mother and grandfather. I never knew my father, and my grandmother died before I was born, so I don't remember her at all, and my father I never knew because he left when my mother was in her seventh month of pregnancy with me. That's what they tell me. They said he emigrated to Sweden, and that my grandfather kicked him out of the house when he found out that he wasn't a Syriac. I don't know anything more about him. I know that my grandfather, the *cohno* Ephraim Abyad, consented to my mother's marriage to him in order to solve a major problem. My mother was in love with a married man, twenty years her senior. She worked for him in a sewing shop. His name was Elias al-Shami and he was a famous tailor. I don't know him well. He used to visit us sometimes at home, and take me on errands with my mother. I remember his eyeglasses and his eyebrows, which were thick and gray. I was afraid of him and his black eyeglasses. Then suddenly he stopped visiting us, after my grandfather found out that my mother went back to her relationship with the tailor. My mother swore to my grandfather that I was not the tailor's son, but the son of George Jal'u. My grandfather didn't believe her, but what's the difference? Whether one or the other had been my father, it wouldn't change anything in my life because my real father was my grandfather the *cohno*.

My mother married my father when she was twenty, so my mother is only twenty-one years older than I am. I love her very much. My grandfather discovered that George Jal'u was a liar, and when my father decided to emigrate, my grandfather refused to let my mother go with him. He told him, Go and do your best and later on you can send for your wife. Now your wife is pregnant and has to look after her health. So he went and didn't come back. They say he had not gone to Sweden but had returned to Aleppo, because he was from a rich Aleppan family that went broke. They worked in dovetailing and inlaying wood, but the business failed. My father came to Beirut and worked in the shop of Salim Rizq, who was blind. Salim was a friend of my grandfather's, but my father robbed him. That's how my grandfather knew that my father was an Aleppan from the Greek Catholic sect, like Mr. Rizq, and a liar and a thief. When my grandfather got mad at me, he'd tell me I was turning out like my father and I'd be a thief like him and I should go to Aleppo to look up my family tree, because I had no origins. Then he came back sorry and said I was his only son, since God had not blessed him with a son, but had given him two daughters, my mother and my aunt Sara, who married Jacques Kassab and went to Sweden with him. There they speak Suryoyo in the street, and they have Suryoyo radio and television, but that's no good because a language separated from its land dies. God had compensated him with me; he sent him Jal'u's son so that he could have a boy, and that he was like the prophet Zachary. He was struck dumb before my mother gave birth to me. He remained unable to speak for three days. Later on, when my mother was in labor, he spoke, and said I was a boy, and that he had seen the prophet Daniel in a dream, and that's why they named me Daniel, and I was called Yalo.

My full name is Daniel George Jal'u, born in Beirut in 1961. I went to the St. Severus School in the Syriac Quarter in the Mseitbeh district. During the summer I worked in Mr. Rizq's shop. Then the war started. We had to move to Mrayyeh Street in the Ain Rummaneh neighborhood, and I went to school at Atchaneh and then transferred to the Taqaddum School near the Myrna Chalouhi Center in Sinn al-Fil.

In 1979 I joined the Lebanese Forces and became a fighter, and remained a fighter until 1989. I submitted to several military courses in Dhuhr al-Wahsh, but I didn't go to Israel for training; I wasn't qualified for paratrooper training because of my height. I am very tall – 191 centimeters. Some of the guys in my company, which was called the "Billy Goat Company," went there and trained, that is true, but me, no. My friend Tony Atiq took me to a training course and told me that Mr. Nabil Ephraim was recruiting Syriac guys and that we now controlled the biggest barracks in Achrafieh, the Georges Aramouni Barracks.

During the war I got to know a lot of guys, especially the Syriac guys who had come from Syria. They joined the war so they could get Lebanese citizenship. We fought, and a lot of us died, and we stole some, as everyone did who had fought, but we were afraid, especially the Syrian guys, because their dialect wasn't Lebanese, and there was the danger that they'd get stuck at our checkpoints, and it was a lot of work for Mario, our company commander.

In late 1989 I was depressed about everything. It was Tony Atiq's idea to move to France. Tony and I stole the money from the barracks and escaped to France. We went by sea from Jounieh to Cyprus, and from Cyprus we flew to Paris. That was the first time in my life I was on a plane. I enjoyed the plane a lot, but Tony drank a lot of whiskey and threw up, and embarrassed us. But flying in the plane was wonderful. In Paris, Tony left me in the hotel and took the money. He ran away and left me stranded. Didn't have a single franc. He was the money man for the trip, and the money disappeared. I don't speak French. I left the hotel and became a *clochard*. That's what they call homeless people there. I became a *clochard*, and didn't have the price of a bite of bread. That is, I became a beggar sleeping in the Métro tunnel at Montparnasse Station.

I met Monsieur Michel Salloum, may God honor him, in the Métro station. He took me to his house at 45, rue Victor Hugo, bathed me, dressed me in new clothes, and fed me. When he'd heard my story he offered me a job in Lebanon. He said he did not like young militia guys, but he saw in me someone different, from a good family, and that my grandfather the *cohno* had interceded with him for me. I went back to Cyprus by plane, and enjoyed it. I drank only one glass of whiskey, afraid that what happened with Tony on the plane would happen to me. In Larnaca I met M. Michel and we took the ferry together to Jounieh and from Jounieh to Ballouna, and I worked as a guard at his Villa Gardenia. I lived in a little house below the villa, and that's where I began a life of crime.

Yes, crime, I say it and I feel bad, and I hope God will forgive me, and I pray for my grandfather the *cohno* to intercede with God on my behalf, because I fornicated with the women of other men. I sat and watched the cars of lovers who came to the pine forest to make love in their cars. My grandfather would tell me that I was turning out like my father and I'd become a thief like him. That is what happened. The truth is that my main goal was pleasure, and I didn't want to rob anyone. I had a lot of fun watching those sexual exploits in cars. I'm ashamed now to write about those scenes that might offend a gentle reader's eyes, and lead him into sin.

The Devil tempted me, and I got involved in crime. At first it was stealing. I would come up to the cars with my flashlight and M. Michel's Kalashnikov, and when they saw me they'd be afraid of scandal or of dying, and they'd offer me anything they had just so I'd let them leave. I began to steal, then as things developed – and here I have to say it was not my fault alone, it was their fault too, because if they had resisted I would not have done the things I did, I would have retreated. Anyway, sir, the first time I raped a woman it happened by chance, without any premeditation or thought, but the man who was with her ran away, and she was standing there waiting. She was shaking with fear, and I approached her and made her sleep with me.

I am not lying. I promised the esteemed officer that I would write the truth, and the truth is that I misunderstood her shaking. I thought she was waiting for me to do it, so I slept with her, but I was mistaken. My feeling was wrong, because my situation was wrong. When I began to have sex with her she began to weep. She put the palms of her hands over her eyes and wept, but instead of stopping, I felt a strange pleasure. It was as if I were a beast. I swear to God, I don't know what happened to me, and now, after I fell in love with Shirin, I understood that that feeling is disgraceful and it is called rape.

After the first time, it was easier. I began to combine robbery and rape. Sometimes, however, I would be content with just robbery and I felt gallant, especially when I saw how the woman would thank me with her shamed eyes because I had done nothing more than rob her. I felt gallant and noble, and that restored some of my dignity.

I'll be content with the sentence the court will give me. Almighty God has already punished me for my atrocious deeds and I have been subjected to the torture I deserve, I now proclaim my penitence.

In Beirut I saw Haykal, who had been with us in the Georges Aramouni Barracks, and had tempted me with money. He gave me five hundred American dollars and said that it was from Abu Ahmad al-Naddaf, and he asked me to hide the stuff in my house or the cottage below the villa. I hid it. I didn't know Abu Ahmad al-Naddaf and had never met him. But Haykal had taken a paratroopers course in Israel, and that's where he came to know Naddaf. The stuff I hid in my house was ten kilos of gelignite, twenty detonators, and five hand grenades. Later on we got started.

Haykal came and said that the job was starting, and they began to take the explosives and went I don't know where. I paid no attention to the business since my main concern was Shirin. I made appointments with her and followed her from place to place, and I loved her. Don't ask me, sir, why I loved her, because love is from God. I loved her, and she became the light of my eyes and the warmth in my heart, and she loved me too, in her own way. I felt her love when she laughed with.me, but she was also afraid of me, and now I know she was right, because my behavior, what can I say . . . was not worthy of her. But for her to go and press charges, and ruin me, as she did, that I do not understand. It would have been enough for her, sir, to ask me, seriously, to break off our relationship, and I would have broken it off. Can one person force another person to love them? But she did not ask for that outright; I

< 161 >

felt she was hesitant. That's what made me continue with her. My goal was honorable. I wanted to marry her and put an end to the dog's life I was living. When my grandfather would get mad at me, he'd call me a son of a dog to remind me of who had abandoned me in my mother's belly and went I don't know where. Monsieur Michel told me that he didn't get a dog to help me guard the villa because Madame Randa was afraid of them. So he made me guard it alone. And I felt like a dog. I told myself, I work with al-Naddaf; I'll save a little money, marry Shirin, and live with her in a small, beautiful house in Hazemiya. But in the meantime I have to save some money to open a shop to dovetail wood. When I was a boy, my grandfather sent me to learn woodworking at Mr. Rizq's, that's how I learned the basics of the trade.

Then I got arrested.

I confess now, before God and the court, and I ask mercy for my soul. I have decided to repent and follow the path of my grandfather – God rest his soul – to take care of my poor mother, and not marry. I decided not to marry, and to give up Shirin, and love, and everything. I have also decided to stop eating meat.

This is the whole story of my life, from the moment of my birth until now. I wrote it myself in prison in February 1992, and God is my witness that I have been truthful in everything I have written. I am prepared to repeat in court everything I have said.

Yalo reread what he had written and felt frustrated. He had spent more than ten days writing these pages. He wept and suffered and felt unable to write. The respite would end in twenty days. The officer had given him the sheets of paper and had said he had only a month. "I'll give you one month, and you must write your whole life story. Write everything, and I wouldn't forget anything if I were you."

In his small cell, Yalo racked his brains, and tried. He longed to listen to a Fairuz or Marcel Khalifé song to get outside himself and feel like a human being again, but they refused to give him a radio. According to the guard, the decision was to keep him in complete isolation so that he could concentrate and write.

"But I just can't write!" said Yalo.

"Have it your way, but I'm warning you, there was a guy here before you who didn't write, and if you knew what happened to him."

"What happened?" asked Yalo.

"They beat him until he began to shit like a bull, and they didn't stop beating him until he was dead."

"Dead!"

"Of course not, I mean, it was like he was dead."

"And then?"

"And then he wrote. He sat behind the table and wrote about fifty pages."

"Fifty pages!"

"Of course," said the guard. "A guy has to write the whole story of his life. And a person's life needs at least fifty pages."

"How long did it take him to write it?"

"A month. Here all they give you is a month. Sometimes, if it's something important and the prisoner is into it, they extend the time. But usually it's just a month. And whoever doesn't write . . . misses out. So you're missing out, Yalo."

"I can't write like that. I need a radio and cigarettes. I can't write without cigarettes."

"I can get cigarettes for you," said the guard. "Give me some money."

"I don't have money. They took all my money away from me."

"Give me the receipt and I'll take as much as you need."

"They didn't give me a receipt."

"No way. Here they give every prisoner a receipt for the money they've taken from him, and his watch, and rings, and everything," said the guard.

"I tell you they didn't give me a receipt," said Yalo.

"Maybe your lawyer has it. Ask for a meeting with your lawyer, he must have it. And then I'll get you anything you want."

"But I don't have a lawyer," Yalo said.

"That's impossible. Here they appoint a lawyer if the accused doesn't have money. They appoint one."

Yalo felt regretful.

Now he remembered that the interrogator had brought him a lawyer after the night of the sack, but Yalo refused to talk to him, saying that God was his lawyer, and that he needed no mortal to defend him.

The lawyer signed the record without reading it or speaking to the accused. He whispered with the interrogator, signed the record, and left.

Yalo thought about asking for the lawyer to come back to help him write, and asked the guard to contact the lawyer, whose name he did not know, but the next day the guard gave him a single Marlboro cigarette and said that he could do nothing for him. He had brought him the cigarette out of pity. "The cigarette might help your mind open up. I swear that's all I'm able to do. Trust in God, take a deep breath, and try to write."

Yalo trusted in God, smoked the cigarette after breakfast, and felt extremely dizzy. It had been months since he had tasted a cigarette, so now the cigarette revealed its real taste. Tobacco was better than hashish; it took you to the tremors of lassitude and of dizziness. But people made a joke of smoking by turning it into a meaningless habit. Yalo decided that when he got out of prison he would smoke one cigarette a day and get drunk on it.

He went back to his pages and reread them and realized that they would not do. It was certain that when the interrogator read them he would think Yalo was trying to trick him and would arrange for him the fate of the bull the guard had talked about.

Yalo never asked the guard his name. He had learned in his solitary cell to hear the sound of the silence that rang in his ears. The short, hunchbacked guard with the pale, scarred face had never directed a single word toward Yalo. He unlatched the opening in the cell door to slide in a meal twice a day, at eight o'clock in the morning and five o'clock in the afternoon, and opened the door at ten o'clock in the morning, motioning for his prisoner to follow him to the bathroom. It was as if he wore rubber-soled shoes, for Yalo could not even hear his footsteps. The silence around the cell was like a sealed black wall, so that Yalo dared not cough or talk to himself aloud. He whispered to himself, looking to the right and left, fearing that some-one might have heard him. The silence remained unbroken until the day he finished writing the story of his life, which was too short and would not do. He didn't know how to rewrite it. It was then that he craved music and cigarettes. He didn't know where he found the daring to speak to the guard and ask for his help, but the result was not impressive: one cigarette and the story of the bull.

Yalo read what he had written and decided to tear it up. He shouldn't have written about his father and the blind Mr. Salim Rizq, because it exposed him. The interrogator would tell him that he was not Lebanese because his father was a Syrian from Aleppo, and this charge would be added to the charges of stealing, rape, and the explosives. He would be accused of falsifying his nationality and impersonating a Lebanese because his father, George Jal'u, had not been a Lebanese citizen. "But I'm Lebanese," he'd tell the interrogator. "The proof is my identity card."

And that was the problem.

They had not believed him during the interrogation when he said that George Jal'u was his father and the *cohno* Ephraim his grandfather. What was recorded on his identity card was different, as his grandfather had recorded Yalo as his son for official Lebanese purposes. On Yalo's identity card he was the son of Abel Abyad and Marie Samaho, and his mother, Gaby, was his sister. Of course this was not the truth. Cohno Ephraim had been called Abel in lay life and did not change his name on his identity card after he joined the priesthood and the bishop gave him the name Ephraim. The *cohno* had registered his grandson under his own name in order to give him Lebanese nationality, and to avoid the Lebanese citizenship law, which did not allow a woman to transmit citizenship to her son, even if his father was dead, vanished, had divorced her, or had left the country never to return.

When during the interrogation Yalo was asked whose son he was, and answered with the truth, he was considered a plagiarist and liar, and was brutally beaten before the interrogator was convinced.

"Fine, according to the identity card you are the son of Abel Abyad!"

"Yes," said Yalo, "but the truth is that Abel is my grandfather. My father's name is George Jal'u."

"That is a lie," said the interrogator. "We must summon Mr. Abel for questioning."

"Mr. Abel has become a *cohno* and changed his name. Now he is Abuna Ephraim," said Yalo.

"We'll summon Father Ephraim Abyad."

"But he died about ten years ago, sir, and I didn't do anything wrong here. It's not any of my doing. I had scarcely been born when he made up my identity papers. Let's assume that he adopted me, and consider that solved."

"That's what we'll assume," said the interrogator.

"So that when they ask my name, I have to say Daniel Abyad, right?" asked Yalo.

"Exactly. But – "

"But what?"

"I told you that's what I'll assume temporarily; that is, I won't consider you a Syrian citizen who falsified his papers to be Lebanese, I'll consider you temporarily Lebanese, and later on we'll see."

"Just as you say," said Yalo.

"No, just as *you* say," said the interrogator. "I mean, if you cooperate and confess, we'll forget about this."

"I will obey," said Yalo.

"But if you don't cooperate with us, you'll not only be humiliated and tortured, but you'll lose your Lebanese citizenship."

What should I write? wondered Yalo.

Should he write about his true father, about whom he didn't know much, or write his name as it appeared on his identity card? If he left out his true father, and later on he was accused of lying or concealing the facts, then what would he say?

The best solution was to stay out of it completely. He wouldn't write out his full name at any time. He would eliminate his father and after that he would eliminate the tales of Mr. Salim Rizq, who was responsible for exposing his father's origins. He would write that his name was Yalo and would eliminate his family name. He would cut Mr. Rizq out of the picture. But how would he explain his infatuation with Arabic script, oriental art, and the woodworking that had led him into Madame Randa's arms?

The blind carpenter, who saw with his eyebrows and read with his fingertips, occupied a great deal of the storytelling of the *cohno*, who wanted his grandson to learn a trade, and who during summer vacations sent Yalo to work in the blind man's shop near the St. Georges Hotel, where he sold the most beautiful authentic wooden Damascene doors with which wealthy Beirutis were then adorning their homes as part of the oriental ambience that was all the rage in Beirut in the early 1970s.

The grandfather wanted his grandson to learn to labor and toil, and to instill in him that by the sweat of his brow he would earn his bread.

Yalo worked three summers in Rizq's shop and began to like the trade. He now looked forward to the end of each school day so that he could go to his woodworking. Yalo decided that his future career would be in woodworking, and that he did not need more education. All he needed was to know how to read and write, and he had accomplished that. Plus, Mr. Rizq's son Wajih, who was called "the engineer," discerned in Yalo a gift for Arabic calligraphy and began to train him in writing Koranic verses in the Kufic script, which was very much in demand at that moment.

"I'm an artist," Yalo told his grandfather in the voice of the engineer that rang in his ears as the engineer trained him how to hold the quill and copy the Verse of the Throne.

But in the summer of 1974, when Yalo was thirteen years old, he did not go to work in the shop. His grandfather told him that he didn't need to get a summer job anymore. "Summer is for relaxation. You should read, study, and prepare, because the coming year will be middle school, which is difficult and requires preparation."

It was only years later that Yalo understood why he was not sent to the shop, when he put together the accounts his mother revealed of the circumstances of Mr. Salim's death, and of the engineer and Thérèse.

Gaby said that the engineer's wife did not attend the burial of her uncle, her husband's father. She closed up her house and took her sons to the mountain without performing her duties. "How shameful!"

"So where's the engineer?" asked Yalo innocently.

"Acting like you don't know, huh?" said Gaby, resuming her disjointed lamentation of the blind man who endured his son's offense with such magnanimity and courage.

She told Thérèse, "You are like a daughter to me. Come and live with me if you like. What more can I do?"

The son disappeared and it was said that he wanted to repent his sins so he went to Aleppo, where he decided to build himself a column near the column of St. Simeon Stylites, and sat atop it, like a Sufi, withdrawn from the world, until they arrested him and sent him to the insane asylum.

Mr. Salim told the story to his friend the *cohno*. Cohno Ephraim, who enjoyed a close friendship with Mr. Salim, begun after he arrived in Beirut, where he worked as a layer of tile in a workshop before adopting his priestly vocation. He told his friend to lay low if he felt tempted by disobedience, that was the secret. He volunteered to mediate with the abbess of Khanshara Abbey, but she refused to receive him when she learned that he was an envoy from the Rizq family.

The *cohno* did not like nuns, and spoke of the need for a total separation between monastic and public life. "What is all this silliness? They say they're nuns, but living like normal women. A nun's place is in the convent, not amidst the public. They must live apart from the community," said Ephraim to Salim Rizq as he told his friend about how the abbess of Khanshara refused to receive him.

The story that destroyed Yalo's vocational future began when Thérèse, a nun in her novitiate working as a teacher at the Tabaris School, came to the Rizq workshop to order frames for icons, and expressed her surprise at the beauty of the woodwork there, all without a single nail being driven. She asked the abbess's permission to take woodworking lessons from the engineer. And so, along with a nun called Sister Rita, she became a student of the engineer.

What happened after that? Why did Sister Thérèse claim that she went to stay with her family in the village of Ain Dara, and had she disappeared for three days with Wajih in the Grand Kamel Hotel in the town of Souq al-Gharb before returning to the school?

It seemed that the engineer Wajih promised to marry Thérèse when, in the hotel room, he saw her long hair draped over her shoulders. But why did the postulant confess her error and come with the abbess to the shop four months after the hotel incident? When Wajih caught sight of them entering, he slipped out the back door. Mr. Salim found himself looking at a scene his eyes, closed for twenty years, had never contemplated.

After listening to Sister Thérèse's confessions and her decision to abandon convent life to marry Wajih, who had taken away her virginity, Salim said that he did not know what to say.

The tall, fat abbess, who was more than sixty years old, said that Thérèse had incurred the convent's harshest punishments. She was sent to Khanshara and imprisoned for three months in the cellar below the convent, which was reserved in the past for nuns who had taken up with the Devil.

"We left her for three months bound in iron chains, and all she ate was bread and water, and we saw that that was enough. We asked her what she wanted, and she said she wanted to come here. And I came with her to reach an understanding with the engineer Wajih."

"But Wajih is married," the father said, and burst out in a peal of hysterical laughter. "Wajih, my bastard, you've turned out worse than your father. Is this story true, *ma soeur*? I find it very difficult to believe."

The blind middle-aged man approached Thérèse, whose tawny face twitched with fear and disgrace, reached his hand out to her face, and then grasped her small, perspiring hand. He told her to come and live with him, for he was prepared to do whatever she wanted.

"Come closer, Thérèse, my girl, what I want to say to you is, we are Catholics, so we don't divorce. My son Wajih is married with two boys, God bless you and bless them, only, what do you want me to do? Come and live with me. My wife died so I live alone, and I'm blind. I'm ready to make good for my son's mistake, if that's what you want and if it's God's will."

"You!" shouted the abbess. "You want to marry this virgin girl, a bride of Christ? You're old and blind. Aren't you ashamed of yourself!"

He tried to explain to her that he had not meant marriage, even though marriage was a shield for beautiful girls and a shield against scandal.

"How can you see in the first place, to say she's pretty?!" said the abbess, her voice quavering and irritated.

"Yes, *ma soeur*, I can see beauty, because beauty sees me." He pointed to the treasures of woodworking that filled his small workshop. "Do you see those? Those are me. Even now I'm still the one who designs the difficult jobs. I read with my hands, *ma soeur*. What did I say to upset you? I promise I have a good heart. I shouldn't have said a word. What business is it of mine? It's Wajih. And Wajih isn't here. Please tell me what you'd like me to do and I'll do it."

< 171 >

The abbess said that they would come back at ten o'clock the next morning. "Tell the gentleman to expect us," and the two of them left.

When Wajih came back to the shop and his father confronted him with the truth, at first he denied everything and said that Thérèse was crazy and that she had made up the story, and that it had nothing to do with him.

"We'll take care of everything," his father said. "Just tell me how you slept with her. She's a nun, how did she agree to it? Tell me what you did with her in the hotel."

At first his son insisted that Thérèse was not a nun but a postulant, and there was a big difference, and that she must suffer from a touch of dementia because she had made up this story from A to Z. But when his father told him that the abbess would show up the next day, he broke down and admitted everything. He said that he didn't know how he would get out of this mess.

"Don't worry, my boy, if you can't, I'll take her."

"You pathetic old man, you want to marry a nineteen-year-old girl?!"

Salim told the *cohno* how his son had hit and kicked him, and how Wajih had all of a sudden been possessed by a diabolical rage. "My son is lost, lost forever, my father. I can assure you I did not want to marry her. I'm not up to that, and anyway she was a child. I thought that way I'd be able to protect her and my son at the same time. And anyway, why did the abbess speak to me that way? Wajih told me he did not deflower her, she was already deflowered. Anyway, I don't know anything anymore."

Wajih disappeared and it was said that his wife had thrown him out of the house so he went to live in a cheap hotel in Bourj Square until his fate took him to the insane asylum in Aleppo.

Yalo did not sleep that night, after his mother recounted some details of the story, how the postulant came to the shop every day at ten o'clock, how she finally disappeared leaving no trace. Wajih's wife had a nervous breakdown and then asked Salim Rizq for her husband's share of the business and completely broke off relations with the Rizq family.

The scandal made its way to the family's birthplace in Aleppo. Wajih went to build his pillar beside the pillar of St. Simeon Stylites of Aleppo, and was arrested, then sent to a hospital for the feebleminded. Now, the father could find no trace of his son, neither from his relatives there nor at the hospital, so he became certain that Wajih had started the rumor of the pillar to get rid of his wife and live in peace with his virginal nun.

Yalo did not sleep that night. He saw the beautiful tawny-skinned nun and reincarnated himself as Wajih the engineer as he took her to the Grand Kamel Hotel in Souq al-Gharb, breathing in her long hair that fell to her shoulders, immersing himself in the incense-fragrance emanating from her neck. He stayed with her for three days without ever leaving the room. Their meals were brought to the room. They bathed, ate, and slept together. She told him she loved him and that she loved the Lord Jesus Christ. She asked him to kneel beside her because the Lord blessed their love. And Yalo, or rather Wajih, drank in her youth, which dripped forth drop by drop from her pores into his own, and recited her prayers with her; he took all of her and she engulfed him.

Nor had Yalo seen the blood of her virginity.

"Where's the blood?" he asked her.

She pointed to what resembled butterflies drawn in a floral color on the white sheet. He pulled her to him and told her she would remain a virgin forever.

Yalo must not refer to Mr. Salim and his son the engineer in the story of his life, so how could he explain his infatuation with wood inlay and Arabic calligraphy?

"I am an artist," he told his grandfather when the *cohno* proposed that he join a religious seminary. "No. I don't want to be a *cohno*. I am an artist, and someday when I'm older I want to be a calligrapher."

But he did not become a calligrapher. His grandfather died a year after they left West Beirut during the war. Yalo joined the barracks and became a fighter, like thousands of young men who left their studies and met the fate that the war had fashioned for them.

How would he explain to the interrogator his beautiful script, his infatuation with wood, and its connection to Madame Randa?

It was true that the name Randa had not been spoken during the two months of questioning he had spent in torment. But who could guarantee for him that the fortyish woman would not appear at any moment and claim that he raped her? And how would he explain his knowledge of woodworking if she were to acknowledge her relationship with him?

Yalo lived alone in the Kesrouan village of Ballouna, which experienced a major revival during the Lebanese civil war, as was the case with many villages in Kesrouan, the heart of the Maronite area in Mount Lebanon, which was peripheral in the war. So it became a refuge for people fleeing other regions of Lebanon. There was a neighborhood of Greek Orthodox who had left Mseitbeh in West Beirut, which resembled their old quarter in Beirut. They built a church to which they gave the name St. Nicholas, which came to be called Mar Nicholas, in which served Father Seraphim Azar. There, Beirut accents, which overburdened the letters and were pronounced with both cheeks, mingled with the Kesrouan accent, which twisted Arabic and melded its letters together in a strange manner.

Yalo lived alone in his cottage and got acquainted with boredom. One day Madame summoned him – M. Michel had traveled to France to take care of some business of his there – to ask him to help her repair one of the valuable mother-of-pearl inlaid chairs; it had tipped over, breaking one of the legs. She asked him to carry the chair to the car so that she could take it to the carpenter.

"Why the carpenter?" asked Yalo. "I know how to fix it."

Yalo sat on the floor and began mending the chair. When the Madame saw him at work, she asked him why he was not using nails, and he explained to her that this kind of wood did not need nails.

"How do you reattach it? With glue?"

Yalo told her about dovetailing and how wood could be made male or female, and how once the pieces were joined, they clove together permanently.

"Male and female, huh?" she said.

"Come, look, Madame," Yalo said.

She leaned over the back of the slender young man who was bent over the wood, giving off the scent of jasmine.

"That's what you call the joining of tenons and mortises?" she asked.

"Yes, it's called *ta'shiq*, the coupling of wood," he said.

"So wood is like people, it cleaves together?"

"Wood is better than people, Madame. Because it stays together."

"Without getting bored?" she laughed, and left the living room. At that moment Yalo sensed the ghost of randification, and he would call that year the year of *ta'shiq*.

She told him that she fell in love with him as he was joining the wood, and that she wished he had taken her just as the wood took the wood and stayed that way permanently.

He would have to eliminate Mr. Salim, his son, and the *ta'shiq* from his story. It was true that he had spoken to Madame Randa about the old blind man and his infatuation with Arabic calligraphy, and how Wajih the engineer had made him memorize whole verses from the Koran so that he could engrave them on the wooden doors. But what should he do? If he wrote the story, he might lose his Lebanese citizenship, and if he didn't write it, he might end up in an endless labyrinth. Yalo was aching for a second cigarette. He put the end of his pen between his lips, and began to suck at it and blow imaginary smoke in the cramped cell. He got up and paced, trying to organize his memory. "I have to tie the story together with a single thread," thought Yalo, and before his eyes appeared a line of blood extending from Ain Ward to Beirut – "My line," Yalo said to himself. "I began there with my grandfather the *cohno*, all of whose family members were killed in the massacre. Who could account for a massacre victim? I'll write that I was slaughtered. I, Daniel, am the descendant of the victims of the massacre. My grandfather was born in blood, and began to drink blood Sundays with every mass he celebrated. And I've gotten drunk on blood. What does it have to do with me? Did I start the war myself? Everything you say is true, but me too, I am true. Anyway, there were no explosives. I swear to God this business of explosives, of Haykal or Abu Ahmad al-Naddaf, is a frame-up. They made me confess so that the sack torture would stop. It was either I confess to being in with the explosives gang, or I get more of that wild animal in the sack that attacked me from below. I either agree, or eat shit. And the way it turned out, I agreed and ate shit anyway."

Yalo sat down behind the green table, took the pen posed between his lips like a cigarette, looked at the blank sheets of paper, and wrote his story again.

< 176 >

My name is Daniel, but everyone calls me Yalo, I'm from the Syriac Quarter in Beirut. I was born in 1961, I'm an only child, I have no brothers or sisters. We left the Syriac Quarter in Mseitbeh in 1976 because the war had intensified and we were afraid of the religious feelings that were mounting. We had a big house surrounded by a garden with every kind of tree – loquat trees, almond trees, acacias, China trees, and date palms. We left our house without taking any of our belongings and went to the neighborhood of al-Mrayyeh in Ain Rummaneh. There my mother rented a furnished apartment from one of her clients. My mother is a seamstress, and her customer arranged the place for us at two hundred fifty lira per month and said it was temporary. I moved from the St. Severus School to the Taqaddum School. My grandfather the *cohno* was unemployed because in our new neighborhood there were no other Syriac families. My grandfather died of grief. My mother was without work in Ain Rummaneh, so she started to go from house to house to do day work. That is, she would go to a house and spend the whole day there, sewing whatever they needed, lengthening or letting out their clothes, raising hems or cutting cloth. She was paid by the day, not by the kind of work. Our situation became very difficult. I did not fit in well at my new school. The grades were all mixed together, and most of the students were from families that had fled from Damour. I left the school and joined the war. Tony took me to Achrafieh and there I got to know a guy named

< 177 >

Alexei, who was a White Russian, and one of the leaders of the Billy Goats Battalion. Alexei asked me if I wanted to become a goat and I told him no. I told him I wanted to fight to defend my country. Tony laughed at me and said that I did not understand the language of war. He told me, say that you want to be a Goat. I said I was willing to be a goat, and I became a fighter, and I fought.

I fought because my grandfather urged me not to emigrate. He told me that emigration kills a man's soul and makes him a wanderer. He told me about his emigration from Ain Ward to Al-Qamishli when he was fifteen years old.

My grandfather told me not to emigrate. But I left for France, and that was the cause of all my troubles. The truth is that I was tired, tired of the war, and poverty, and my mother. My mother had become like a maniac with her mirror and the ghost of my grandfather, whom she saw every night in her dreams. It was Tony's idea to emigrate, and I was enthusiastic about it. The name on my identity card is Daniel Abel Abyad. But people call me Ibn Jal'u. I was born in Beirut in 1961. I worked as a guard at the Villa Gardenia, which is owned by Monsieur Michel Salloum, in the village of Ballouna in Kesrouan.

I started my new job at the end of the war. My friend Tony Atiq and I traveled to France. We fled after we stole the money from the Georges Aramouni Barracks in Achrafieh. In Paris we stayed in a small hotel in Montparnasse. It was a great place, and it was the first time in my life I had my own room. In our house I slept in my grandfather's room. My grandfather decided it would be that way when I was five years old, when he ordered me to move from my mother's room to his. He said that the regimen in the house had to be strict: men in one room, women in another. So I moved in with him, but nearly every night I would sneak into my mother's room to sleep in her bed.

We stayed in the hotel for about two weeks. We did nothing. We strolled around Paris, ate in restaurants, and drank French wine. Once we went to the Pigalle district, and a French woman, I mean a whore, made me wear a condom when I slept with her. I hated it, and something almost happened then that never happened in all my

< 178 >

life, which was going soft at the last moment. I hate wearing a condom. But here in France they force people to do that out of fear of AIDS.

I began to worry because we weren't working. Tony reassured me saying that he would get in touch with some of our friends here to find us work, but we were in no hurry because Tony had plenty of money.

Then Tony deserted me.

I don't know how or why. I didn't even realize he was playing a trick on me. I was walking along with him, following blindly, and suddenly I noticed that he had disappeared. So I was alone in Paris, without a single franc.

The proprietress of the hotel, a respectable Frenchwoman, took pity on me. She communicated with me through gestures and with a few English words, and managed to explain that Tony had paid her for two nights for me before he left the hotel. She added that she was prepared to let me stay one additional night for free, and would give me breakfast for three days; after that I was on my own.

Tony spoke French but I didn't. When that woman started talking to me I felt like she was throwing stones at me. I had that feeling until I was back in Lebanon. In France, I understood that words were like stones. When you don't understand the language, it is as if people are stoning you or torturing you. With the Syriac language it was different. True, I did not understand it, but I felt it and I knew that I could get between the words and sentences to grasp some meaning. My grandfather used to talk to my mother in Syriac and she would answer him in Arabic and told him to stop speaking Kurdish. It really provoked him. My grandfather was Kurdish, no, what should I say, he was not Kurdish, but he spent his childhood among the Kurds after the Ain Ward massacre, and he spoke their language. Then he emigrated to Beirut and worked in tiling, like so many of the Syriac youths who ended up in the Syriac Quarter in Mseitbeh in Beirut. It was in Beirut that he began to learn the Syriac language. He had not studied the colloquial Suryoyo that people used every day; he learned the formal liturgical language. When he became a *cohno*, he began to use the formal language, but with me he spoke colloquial Arabic with some Syriac

< 179 >

words sprinkled in. When my mother called him "the Kurd," it got under his skin, especially in his last days when he would have long crying fit, and my mother didn't know how to soothe him. After my grandfather became a *cohno* he stopped eating meat. Then his wife died of cancer and he became very inflexible, almost unbearable, especially in matters of diet, cleanliness, and morals.

My grandfather's inflexibility caused a major problem in the family. I had not paid much attention to it, but my grandfather told me how Elias al-Shami had been castrated, and my mother went crazy. She went crazy not because my grandfather had castrated her lover, since that didn't concern her, but because he had told me about it and exposed her.

I don't know how, but when I heard the story, I had a feeling that I'd heard it before. Mr. Elias had been a presence in my life, even though he rarely visited us. My mother would take me to the amusement park, and he would be there. I would always ride the Ferris wheel, and they'd stay down below. I would spend an hour or two looking out at the sea and the city from above. As the world twirled around, they sat down there drinking coffee and talking.

Once, I got lost. I remember it now as if it had happened to another person. I had thought that the idea of this other person who resembled me was just a childhood thing, I mean, when I remember my childhood, I feel that the child who was me, was some other person. But now, after my experiences being imprisoned and tortured, I began to see Yalo's whole life as if it were someone else's. I do not know how to describe these feelings, sir, but they are true feelings. I look at myself in the mirror of my self and I see a different man and fear him, his thoughts, and his acts. No, I do not say this to dodge my responsibilities, because I know that I am now paying the price of my sins, and I seek the pardon of Almighty God.

I do not seek the pardon of people, nor do I write these lines in order to gain the favor of his honor the judge, because life no longer concerns me. I know that I will be sentenced to death on the charge of planting explosives and killing innocent people, but I am innocent, I swear to God, innocent. Even so, I will accept most willingly the sentence handed down against me. I tell myself that this is my destiny, that it was written well before I was born. I can't do a thing. I see my grandfather crying before me and I ask him to intercede with me with St. Ephraim the Syriac. All I ask for myself is mercy and relief in the next world.

I got off of the wheel, or the whirl – I don't know what that ride is called – and could not find my mother or Mr. Elias below. I began crying and people gathered around me and asked me whose child I was and where I lived. I didn't know how to tell them where I lived, but I told them I was from the Abyad family and that we lived in the Syriac Quarter, that's all I knew. I kept on crying among people who didn't know what to do with me. I was crying. Then someone I didn't know recognized me and said, "That's the priest's son," and took me home in his car. And there was my grandfather, and the scandal that bound me to him. It was then that my grandfather realized my mother was still involved with the tailor.

In Paris I was very afraid. Suddenly I found myself on the street in a city where I knew no one and didn't know the language. So I resorted to the art that I did know. I took a piece of cardboard from Madame Violette, who ran the hotel, and wrote in beautiful Naskh script this phrase: "I am a Lebanese youth, homeless and alone. I seek mercy because I cannot afford the price of a crust of bread."

I sprawled out with my cardboard in the Montparnasse Métro station and stayed there several days, and all I had to eat was a dry piece of bread given to me by a French tramp, homeless like me, drinking wine straight from the bottle, his body giving off a putrid smell. It was there M. Michel met me and saved me. He brought me back to Lebanon, gave me work, treated me well, God bless him, and I betrayed his trust. A man who trusted me with his home and his wife and yet I did not deserve his trust. Instead of being his watchdog, as he asked of me, I became a stray dog and started a life of my own. I began by spying from the pine forest located below the St. Nicholas Church.

I want to tell the truth for the sake of my conscience. In the beginning I had no desire to rob people or rape women. Everything started when I discovered by

< 181 >

chance the cars that parked in the forest. I monitored them to guard the villa, thinking that there might be suspicious things going on here, and my duty as a guard was to be aware of everything. But the activities turned out to be sex and necking. I could not see things clearly from far off, but the glimpses I saw and the shadows of men over the shadows of women set my imagination aflame, sir.

My story began with a love of voyeurism, no more and no less, then I made my decision to go down to them, to get closer to the scene for a better look. Why did I do the things I did after that? I don't know.

I know that the first time I went down I was carrying a Kalashnikov rifle and a flashlight, and I saw how fear overwhelmed the lips of the man sitting in the car, and I learned that fear started at the lips. I rapped at the car window with the muzzle of the rifle and the man opened the window and tried to talk, but he couldn't speak. His lower lip trembled. Then he reached into his pants pocket and gave me a handful of dollars and Lebanese lira. It was not part of my plan to rob him or force him to pay. I had no set plan, all I wanted was to watch. He reached out his hand with the money and I took it, and stood there by the window. He took off his watch and ordered the woman beside him to remove her watch and gold necklace with the cross hanging around her neck, and he gave them to me. I took them and remained at the window, and heard the voice of the woman saying, "Please God, don't hurt us, sir." I don't know why I responded, "Shut up, whore," and instead of her getting upset, or the man getting angry or getting out of the car to defend her, the man bowed his head as if in consent, and the woman smiled, a kind of grimace. At the moment I lusted for her but I didn't do anything. I was strangely aroused, but I walked back to my house below the villa and heard the sound of the car skidding in the dirt and speeding off.

After that things developed naturally, and I began to hunt once or twice a week, no more, because I wasn't that ambitious. I was afraid that if I overdid the hunting, people would stop coming to the forest. My prey was always the last car, I mean, the car that lingered the latest at night.

I saw things I cannot describe, which taught me so much about human nature and made me understand my mother's madness. My mother was an unfortunate woman whose misfortune was loving a man who wasn't worthy of her, and she went all the way with her love. I take after her in that. It is true that it is disgraceful to compare my stupid behavior and my despicable desires to those of a respectable woman who was a victim of love, but God fated me also to taste love, and to be a victim of love, and for my life to end the opposite way it began. For I began in sin in the forest, and ended in love. I am my mother's opposite and an extension of her. She drowned in the mirror, and I don't need a mirror. She no longer saw her image in the mirror, and I can see my image without one.

I saw a few things, sir – how can I say it – some of them came in broad daylight, but those were the minority, of course. One of them came at ten in the morning. He must have been the most shameless man in the world. He came in broad daylight, parked his car by the huge sycamore tree, and had sex with the woman. I could see her big breasts through the branches. He didn't get her totally naked. He opened her blouse and her breasts came out and he slept with her on the seat of the car. He sat on the seat to the right of the steering wheel and she got on top, and her breasts jiggled. They arrived, with her beside him, in a red Peugeot. He got out of the car and undid his pants. She opened her door and stood waiting for him. He sat down on the seat, then she got back into the car and straddled him.

One of my first experiences was with this woman. I saw her open the car door and stand there waiting for him, and I could not control myself. The sun was every-where, I saw myself holding the rifle, pulling my cap down low so that my face was hidden, and charging toward them. I didn't rob them. I got to her before he did, he saw the gun and froze, I gestured for him to get lost, and he went away without putting up any resistance. I sat down and ordered her to get on top of me as she had got on top of him. I undid my pants and pulled her breasts out, and took her exactly as he had done. I left the car then to go back home and I saw the man return to the car and leave.

Things began taking on a new direction, for in addition to my first pleasure – observing people and robbing them – I had a second pleasure until God made me a passion addict.

I read many of the books I used to find in my mother's room. But the book that especially influenced me was the book *The Victims of Lovers*. This was the only book I reread several times. On the first leaf of the book was an inscription in red ink: "To my little darling, so that she will know," with a scribble that looked like an illegible signature. I don't think my mother read the book, she did not like reading. She didn't even read the newspaper. I believe the scribble was the signature of the tailor who loved my mother, but didn't marry her. I used to tell Shirin when we met that I was a passion addict, and she would laugh because she did not understand what the words meant. I explained it to her and told her stories of lovers who had died for love, but she laughed at me and at them. That is how I imagined the tailor, too, telling my mother the stories in the book, with her laughing too because she didn't understand.

I became the victim of this girl who filed charges against me and put me in prison. When I saw her in the Jounieh police station, I thought that revenge was her way of proclaiming her love for me – and this often does happen in love stories – because she was incapable of ending it with me except through revenge. So my love and passion for her increased. But when I saw her fiancé, Emile, that idiot jackass who knew nothing of the truth, I understood that her love was gone. I am sure that Emile was not with her. When I took her to my house, a different man was with her, a doctor in his fifties, I don't remember his name anymore, but he's a famous physician. Why didn't they bring him to the interrogation? He would have told the truth, and then everyone would see I was innocent. I am not a rapist. Not really, I swear to God I don't know. But now I confess before God and before you that I used to rape women, because you call this rape, and because after I fell in love with Shirin I discovered that it was rape compared to the beautiful sex that a man can have with a woman he loves. I slept with Shirin very little, but I made love to her whenever we met and it was a beautiful and wonderful thing and could not be compared to the sexual relations I had with women in the forest. Love is a humane thing, like praying, while sex in the forest was like war, and that's what made her think it was rape. I confess that I did commit rape, and I seek pardon for that and mercy on my soul, for the sake of my poor mother who lives alone with no one to look after her. She really needs her son. And I'll rededicate myself to her service.

I confess that I stole, plundered, and raped, and I am certain that God is punishing me through you.

As to the final chapter in the story of my life, it is the strangest one, sir, because I don't know how I got involved in the affair. Haykal contacted me – I don't know his family name – and was with us in the Georges Aramouni Barracks. He tempted me with money. He gave me five hundred American dollars and told me that it was from Ahmad al-Naddaf. He asked me to hide the stuff in my house, and I agreed. I never knew this Naddaf, but I had heard of him because he was famous in the border strip Israel occupied. He was in charge of explosives training, and he'd trained many of our guys. Haykal gave me ten kilograms of gelignite, twenty detonators, and five hand grenades to hide, and after that we started. Haykal came and told me that the job had started, so they took the explosives and went away. But I didn't pay much attention to it. My only concern was Shirin, making dates with her and following her from place to place, and loving her. My plan was to marry her to put to an end to the dog's life I was living. When my grandfather the *cohno* used to get angry at me, he would call me the son of a dog, and Monsieur Michel told me that he had not gotten a dog to help me guard the villa because his wife, the lady Randa, was afraid of dogs. I said to myself, I'd work with Haykal, make a little money, and marry Shirin, and we would live in Hazemiya, but before that I would have had to save a small amount of capital with which to open a woodworking shop, since I had learned the trade of dovetailing wood at Mr. Salim Rizq's shop when I was young.

I now confess, and proclaim that I have decided to repent, and follow the path of my grandfather – God rest his soul – and take care of my poor mother. I have decided not to marry and to relinquish everything else. And I have decided to stop eating meat.

This is the whole story of my life, from the moment of my birth until now, written in prison in February 1992, and let God be my witness that I have been truthful in everything I have written. I am ready to repeat all I have stated in court.

< 186 >

Yalo read the pages he had written and put them aside with a feeling of deep relief. He had succeeded at writing the whole story of his life. Now, when he was summoned for interrogation, he would say that he had admitted to everything and written everything down, forgetting nothing.

He wrote about his boyhood, his youth, about the war and Michel Salloum. He wrote about his mother and her lover the tailor, and about the *cohno*. He wrote about Shirin, whom he had loved, and hunting in Ballouna. It was true that he had been compelled to write a fake story – the story about Haykal, Naddaf, and the explosives – but there, there was no avoiding fakery. Yalo felt that he had outsmarted the interrogator because he remembered the names of two men no one would ever find. Haykal had committed suicide in November 1991; it was said that he had hanged himself because he could no longer obtain cocaine. Naddaf had moved to Brazil and never been heard from again. Yalo had confessed, as they'd wanted, but he hadn't opened up a crack allowing them to ravage his soul and his body again. The interrogator would read these names, research them, and decide to close the dossier due to the impossibility of following up the case with two men who no longer existed.

Yalo sat on the floor of his cell and rested his head against the wall, feeling hungry. It was as if the words he had written had opened up a gulf inside him that could only be filled with food. He saw a fish before him and his mouth began to water. He would have told Shirin, had she been there, that he no longer feared anything once he had discovered blood in fish.

He told her, or would have told her, about Munir Shammo, who had brought a big sea perch home, wriggling in the throes of death.

What happened that day?

As Yalo recollected the story for Shirin's sake, he felt that speech was not possible without love. When he gave in to love, he felt the taste of speech. Speech was full of flavor when it was spoken with love. It was true that now he no longer loved her, and that he felt capable of killing her because she had shattered him by betraying him; written on her bare thighs in the interrogation room was a flagrant sign of her treachery. Yet now when he sat down to write, he felt her presence, and remembered how he had become an open book to her. He had tried to seduce her with words, with stories, true or fictitious, but she remained indifferent. He had written his life in front of her but she refused to read it. She was always in a hurry with her mind elsewhere, as if she did not understand or didn't want to understand.

Now she was here, as if she were sitting beside him in the cell, listening to the story of the fish. But his mind strayed a little because of her lipstick. She began to eat, curling her lips so she wouldn't smear the red; then, when she realized the impossibility of that, she wiped off the red with a tissue. Yalo cried, No! and wanted her lips. He imagined himself rubbing his lips against hers and licking the red from them. He knew she did not like Arabic songs or Arabic poetry, but he could not control himself, so he told her to listen, and Shirin put the tissue on the table and looked at him, waiting for him to go on.

"Listen to this poem," he said. "Mansurati used to sit in the barracks and sing, and we'd sing with him. He immediately entranced with his voice and his lute. Never in my life was I able to hit the right note, my voice was terminally off-key. But Mansurati – my God. When he picked up his lute and started singing, I felt the soul of the world, I can't even describe it. Don't you feel that way when you hear music?"

She replied in a murmur that the kind of music that moved the soul of the world was classical music. She said she loved Bach, and thought that songs were a violation of music.

"You don't like Nizar Qabbani?" he asked her.

"I'm not talking about Arabic poetry," she said. "Even Jacques Brel – you know Jacques Brel?"

He nodded to say that yes, he did, but his incomprehension was clear from the way his eyebrows knitted together in his effort to show he knew.

"What are you talking about?" he said.

"I was saying that even with Jacques Brel, whose songs are complex, I feel like he's lowering the standard of music when he puts in words and meanings."

"But listen to what I'm going to recite for you," he said. "It's the most beautiful song in the world, even more beautiful than Abd al-Halim Hafiz. Listen."

And he drew his head back to rest his temple on his right hand before reciting the poem in a heightened voice:

> *In Achrafieh, the day I was there and came to her,*
> *I surrendered my life to your lips*
> *And I tasted the fruit, what a taste!*
> *If not succulent grapes*
> *Something very similar.*
> *Were it not for her sweetness in love and*
> *My tenderness in love,*
> *I would have eaten those lips and feasted on them.*

He began to tremble: "– feasted . . . fea . . . sted . . . on . . . them. Isn't that lovely? That was our song in the barracks. We sang "feasted" and everyone interpreted it his own way. Alexei took out the *f* and put in a *b*, and Mansurati got mad. I swear to God he was a great artist. I don't know what happened. He said that he was fed up with the war, that he wanted to be a performer. Of course all of us were fed up with the war, but not everyone who got fed up became a performer, it's not like that."

Yalo laughed, thinking he had said something funny, but when he saw no trace of a smile on her lips, he became serious again and told her about the fish and the war.

When he recalled how he remembered this incident, he was dumb-struck. For the fish full of blood had sunk into his memory as if it had never happened, and when she tried to wipe the red from her lips so she wouldn't mess up her lips, the fish woke up and the story came back.

He remembered the fish's head, its two quicksilver eyes, and its mouth opening and shutting as if it wanted to say something but couldn't. The *cohno*'s friend Munir Shammo, who was retired from his tiling work and now spent his days fishing, showed up early that Saturday morning with a fish in his basket. He put it in the kitchen and left. When Gaby came into the kitchen, she cursed her luck for being the one who had to clean the hideous black fish, full of bones, the fish called in Lebanon "the Bolshevik." But she froze in her tracks and screamed when she saw the fish wriggling and flap-ping on the kitchen floor. The fish had flipped itself off the counter to the floor. Hearing his daughter's cry, the grandfather hurried in and saw it too.

"The fish is talking to God," he said, and knelt to pick it up, but the fish slid out of his hands. The fish was almost a meter long, its gray scales were spattered with white spots, and its eyes were shining with life. Ephraim bent to the floor and took it in his arms as if he were picking up a child, and said that he was going to return it to the sea, but the fish fell from his embrace.

The *cohno* backed away and said he was going to fetch the fisherman. Yalo could not remember where his mother had disappeared to, but he found himself alone with the fish in the kitchen. He approached it, but slipped and fell, landing on the head of the fish, and blood began to flow. Of the black coffee grinds his mother used to stanch the blood and of the carnage that had spilled across the sink, Yalo couldn't remember a thing. All he remembered was his grandfather weeping over the fish whose blood had splashed and stained the sink and the kitchen wall.

"You butchered it!" exclaimed the *cohno*. "Why, daughter? Who butchers a fish?"

Gaby had sliced open the fish's belly, scooped out the insides, and begun to pare off the scales with a large knife when the *cohno* came back accompanied by Munir Shammo.

Blood streamed from the butchered fish, which continued to tremble in Gaby's hands, which were busy scaling it as she commented that this was the best fish she had ever seen in her life. She said that she'd get three meals out of it. She'd fry the bottom half for lunch, grill the upper half for Sunday, and the huge head would be cooked in a rice pilaf — a fisherman's dish.

"Bless your hands, Uncle Munir. Please join us for three meals of fish."

The grandfather kept lamenting the butchered fish, and left the house with his friend. He came back late in the evening and announced that he had given up eating fish.

"That's how my grandfather stopped eating fish, even cuttlefish he wouldn't eat, although cuttlefish are full of ink – there isn't a drop of blood in their veins.

"You know that in France they eat blood?"

"What?!" Shirin exclaimed.

"I'm telling you, they eat blood. M. Michel let me taste something called boudin; he said they stuff a pig's intestines with blood and eat it."

"You ate it?"

"Of course. Why not? And then I lived in a house where they drank blood almost every day."

"You all ate blood?" she asked, a look of nausea on her face; she turned away and scowled, and then grabbed a tissue to wipe the red from her lips.

"No, don't wipe off the red. I love the red."

She looked at her watch. When Shirin looked at her watch it meant she had made up her mind to leave. He surprised her then with his question about whether she believed in God.

"Of course. Of course," she said.

"And you go to the *'atdo?*"

"The what?"

"You go to church?"

"Not all the time. But of course at Christmas and Good Friday. So, like everybody."

"And you take the sacrament?"

"Kind of. Sometimes."

"And when you take it, what do you feel?"

"What's with these stupid questions? C'mon, let's go."

"No, let's not go. I'm asking you a question. Answer."

"Fine. I open my mouth and I eat the host."

"And blood!"

She said that it was just a symbol. The wine did not become blood in the mass except symbolically.

"That's not true," said Yalo. "The mass is a sacrifice, which means a slaughter, a real slaughter. I know that."

"You don't know anything," she said.

She said that she didn't like discussing religion because she didn't understand anything about it, but she believed in God and that was enough.

"Of course that's enough," said Yalo. "But I was telling you about the *cohno*, my grandfather, being vegetarian, but he drinks blood every day."

"He drinks blood?"

"Of course he drinks blood, he's a *cohno*. At mass he drinks the blood of Christ, he puts sweet wine and water into the chalice and drinks it."

"That's wine. You scared me. I don't know why I still believe you."

"No, it is not wine, it becomes blood," said Yalo, but he didn't tell her that he was afraid at mass. He would close his eyes and open his mouth to take the host, he would feel the taste of blood, and become dizzy. He wanted to tell her about his grandfather's wonders, about the miracle of the Kurdish mullah, about Alexei and his mother the Muscovite. But he felt that every conversation with Shirin opened up innumerable empty spaces within him, and he was incapable of filling them. The words would pour out of him, yet he realized that he was saying nothing because he was unable to speak of a clear and simple concept – his love for her.

"But you don't know me," she said.

"I know everything," he answered her. "Love is the greatest knowledge." He wanted to tell her that her smell never left him and that he was ready to change his life for her, and that he was not just a thief or villa guard; circumstances had made him what he was. He would open a fine woodworking shop. But he didn't say any of that. Speech needed something, something beyond what Yalo was going to learn in his solitary cell. Speech required a ruse, and ruses only came to him here, when he was trapped between two walls: the gray prison wall with its peeling paint, with numerous fissures and gaps that took on human shapes at night, and the wall of the white pages placed before him so that he could write the story of his life. Yalo had not known that this method of extracting confessions from a suspect was the most prevalent method in the Arab world for political prisoners, after the traditional torture parties. A prisoner found himself facing an empty cola bottle, and was forced to sit naked upon the bottle. If he succeeded in avoiding death by septicemia or blood loss, he was given a sheaf of white pages and was asked to write the story of his life. This was when the real torture began, for the act of writing became an instrument of death and a path to suicide. The words became like knives stabbing the one who bore them. So the prisoner tumbled into the pit he had dug himself, slipping on his words, falling into his blood, which had taken on the color of ink, and sniffing his own blood.

Yalo had not known the smell of his own blood, before he went to prison. Even when he stood in front of Alexei's bones, bereft of their flesh, and listened to the stories of Nina the Russian, he did not smell the odor he now smelled in his cell as he tried to cheat death by writing the story of his death.

The image of Nina came back to him in the cell, as if she had sprung from the wall.

"Are you Russians, auntie?" Yalo asked her as he drank the rosewater mixed with sugar specially prepared by the Muscovite.

"It's for the feast day of the living prophet Elias," the woman said, pointing to the rosewater. "We drink rosewater with crushed ice – not because the feast day comes in July, when it's hot, no, because Elias is the prophet of fire. He ascended to heaven in his chariot drawn by steeds of fire. Ice with sugar for the fire. Before the feast of the prophet Elias I can't make rosewater. Rosewater, my son, is the essence of our local red rose whose hue is like fire. We pour fire over ice and drink it on the feast of fire. Drink up, my son."

"Thank you, thank you," said Yalo, and took a sip of the magical drink that refreshed the soul, hesitating a little before returning to his question.

"Are you Russians, auntie?"

"And you, my son, where are you from."

"From here."

"And before here?"

"We're from Ain Ward, that's what my grandfather says. That's a village in Tur Abdin."

"Abu Alexei, may God have mercy on him, was from Mardin," said the Russian woman. "That's why he didn't speak Syriac. The people of Mardin speak only Arabic. When he proposed to me, I told him I would not have a Syriac. He told me he was Syriac but at the same time he wasn't Syriac, and we were married."

"So you are Syriacs?" asked Yalo.

"They are, sort of, my husband's family. Me, no."

"Are you Russian?"

"That's what they say. They call us the children of the Muscovite, but we're Arabs. Someday I'll tell you the story of my grandmother's grandmother. She was the Muscovite, and it's from her time that the label stuck to us, and that's why I named my son Alexei. His father wanted to name him Iskandar, but I said, No, Iskandar means Alexei, this way the boy will have a Russian name, like the czars. What's better than the czars?"

Yalo entered the cloak of sleep. He wrapped himself up on the iron cot in the corner of the cell, closed his eyes, and saw the specter of the pregnant woman running in her long dress stained with blood. The woman had emerged from the wall, he saw her. The image of her began with her belly, stained with blood, a belly distended with a fetus in its sixth month, it emerged from the cracks in the wall in its black dress spotted with black blood.

The image began with the color black, soon replaced by white. The dress became white and blood spread into its folds, as if the blood were tracing the fetus's head and its stupified expression in the face of death, while the woman's face was indistinct, as if covered by a pale yellow stain.

The woman emerged from the wall and started rushing through narrow streets. Suddenly the streets vanished and the woman was alone in the wilderness before she reached the outskirts of the city of Tyre. She stood before a walled structure. She knocked at the gate and a nun opened it, then slammed the iron gate in her face. But the white, bloodstained dress sounded again, emitting a noise like the cry of a baby. The nun reopened the gate, grasped the woman by the arm, and brought her into the convent.

The morsels of the story Yalo had heard from Nina the Russian became a picture on the wall of his cell. At night, the picture came off the wall and rushed off in search of the convent of Russian Orthodox nuns in Tyre that would take her in with her fetus crying in her belly, and that would save its life and hers.

Yalo couldn't remember the story in a coherent manner. Nina gave the name of the village, and told how the man had been slaughtered, his head upon his wife's belly, but now Yalo couldn't remember the name, nor did he know how to explain what happened in 1860, in the massacre that inaugurated a chain of massacres throughout Lebanon. They said that when the Russian Orthodox nun heard the crying of the fetus in the pregnant woman's belly as blood flooded around it, she went into a stupor. She had no choice but to reopen the gate and allow the woman to stay at the convent, where she gave birth to her only daughter.

"That girl was my great-grandmother, and they used to call her the Muscovite because she was born in the Russian nuns' convent in Tyre. Her children and grandchildren were called the children of the Muscovite. That became our name."

What happened on that hot July day in 1860?

Yalo drew a picture of the village in his mind and called it "Nina's town." There in the village that slumbered on the slope of Mount Hermon began the massacre in the house of the woman in her sixth month of pregnancy.

A man with a rifle came in and told the pregnant woman's husband that

he was his friend, so he would be the one to kill him, rather than letting anyone else torture him before killing him. He placed the man's neck against
his young, pregnant wife's belly, and slaughtered him with a knife, like a
sheep. The blood spurted and penetrated the woman's insides, and she lost
the power of speech. She ran out of her house, to find herself in the convent
of Russian nuns in Tyre, where she gave birth to her daughter.

Before the story got to the part about the rich man who asked the abbess
for the orphan girl, who died leaving a huge fortune to her and her daughter, there were many things that needed clarification. But Yalo did not dare
tell Nina that it was hard to swallow the story of the man placing his head
on his pregnant wife's stomach before being slaughtered, or that some of
the things said to have been said sounded more like something from a novel
or a movie than like something that had really happened.

Yalo was certain that over the course of this war the Lebanese had dug up
the history of all their past wars to justify their madness, which made talking to them impossible. It was true that he himself behaved like a Lebanese
during the war, and he was Lebanese and wouldn't allow the interrogator
to trick or threaten him with his father who was not his father and whom he
had never known. Yalo had fought under the banners that had been raised,
and swallowed everything he was told, but when Nina the Russian told him
about her grandmother, he felt that he had taken in too many stories and
couldn't bear it any longer. Nina told the story as if she had been an eyewit-
ness, and even repeated the same words the killer spoke at the moment he
committed his crime.

"You're my friend, I'm the one who's going to kill you. Don't be afraid.
You won't feel anything, just a little hornet's sting."

She said that the killer said "hornet's sting" and that the night before
the crime he'd come to the house of the victim and reassured him, saying
that nothing would happen in their village, that their coexistence there was

sacred. The man slept reassured despite the smell of fear that pervaded the village. The next morning he heard a knock at the door, opened it, and beheld the face of death. Suddenly the man was struck with horror and never uttered a word. He bowed his head, laid it against his wife's belly, and died.

"A hornet's sting," he said before taking the knife and slashing the neck upon the belly of the pregnant wife who had not yet turned seventeen. Then he left, leaving the young woman to wander like a madwoman for days and days on country roads before arriving at the Russian nuns' convent.

"It couldn't have happened that way," thought Yalo, as he watched the woman emerge from the wall with her distended belly, as she began running toward the convent in Tyre.

She knocked, and the nun opened the iron gate a crack. When she saw the round belly stained with blood, she slammed the gate shut.

She knocked again, and the fetus cried in her belly.

Nina said that had the Russian nun not heard the sound of the fetus's crying coming from the woman's belly, she would not have opened the door a second time.

"The fetus cried in its mother's belly," said Nina.

"Is that possible?" asked Yalo.

"Of course it's possible, my son. It was a miracle, and the proof was that the nun was a saint. The other nuns began to kiss the nun's hand that opened the door, because she'd heard the voice that no one but Elisabeth had heard. No one but a saint can hear the voice of a fetus."

"But maybe it's your grandmother who was the saint, because it's the fetus in her belly that spoke," said Yalo.

"No, my son, that wasn't my grandmother, that was my great-grand-mother. She didn't hear the fetus crying in her belly, because God didn't open her ears to it. Only divine intervention can open ears."

Yalo said that he understood, but in fact he didn't understand a thing. The young woman had fled her village and taken shelter at the convent, where she gave birth to her baby girl, and they lived there together, the mother serving and the young daughter studying. When the girl turned fourteen, the gentleman Nakhleh Sadeq met her; he was a Tyrian merchant of fifty who had emigrated to Argentina and come to Lebanon to marry and then return to his new country. He saw the girl once in front of the convent and fell in love with her. He asked her mother for her daughter's hand, but she refused to discuss the matter with him. She said that she and her daughter belonged to the convent and that he had to speak with the abbess. The abbess summoned the girl, feeling certain that she would refuse the marriage – being the child of the miracle – that she would choose a vow of chastity and become a bride of Christ. So the abbess was surprised to see the girl agree to the marriage. Her conditions were that her mother should live in the house with them, and that Mr. Nakhleh not return to Argentina. The even greater surprise was when Mr. Nakhleh agreed to both conditions. The rich merchant married the girl, and she gave him her only son, Musa.

"That is how we became the Musa family, only everyone called us the children of the Muscovite," said Nina.

"So you are not White Russians," said Yalo.

"Our hearts are white and we love Russia," said Nina.

Yalo saw the young woman emerge from the wall with her distended belly, whose bloodstains had taken on the shape of a fetus attached to its mother's belly. The mother rushed into the forest and hid behind the first pine tree she found, then got up to run toward the convent of Russian nuns.

Yalo did not ask what happened to the corpse of the husband whose wife was forced to remove his severed head from her belly before gathering up her blood-drenched dress to go. Did the woman discard the head? Or did the murderer-friend not sever the head from the body but merely slaughter the man by slitting his veins? Who then buried the body? Was it buried at all, or left to rot by itself in the abandoned house?

To Yalo the story seemed impossible, but when he saw the pregnant woman emerging from the wall of his cell, coming toward him, and anointing his forehead with the sticky blood dripping from her long dress, he felt that writing this story was easier than writing the story of his life.

How could he write? What could he write? He didn't know how to put the necessary distance between a word and its image. He wrote the name Nina and saw Christians and Druze drowning in their own blood. He wrote his name and saw his image affixed to the name, so he was forced to erase the image in order to keep writing, but the name vanished along with the image. Yalo found himself in the silence of black ink.

Tomorrow when the interrogator came, Yalo would give him the pages he'd written and say that this was everything; all the confessions were written down, and that was enough.

"I don't know how to write, sir," he would say.

Yalo closed his eyes and fell asleep, and that featureless woman appeared. She came and sat down beside him, and wept. Yalo became both men, the murdered husband and the murdering neighbor. He placed his head on her distended belly and heard the beating of two hearts as they mingled in a strange rhythm, and he understood what his mother had said about the sensations that men were incapable of feeling.

His mother was drinking coffee in the living room with her friend Catherine, telling the story of Elias al-Shami and her father, and weeping. After disparaging Elias al-Shami and throwing him out of the house, the *cohno* raised his finger in his daughter's face and told her, "That is enough fooling around. Now I think you need to take control of your feelings, and cast Satan out of your body."

< 200 >

She said her father was a man, and men understood nothing. The *cohno* thought that she was like him and that the incentive for her establishing that long-standing relationship with the tailor was to satisfy her sexual urges. Even Elias thought that. "He'd sleep with me and finish, and then he'd look at me and ask, Did you come? At first I'd tell the truth and would wonder why he'd ask when he knew that when a woman comes she's like a fountainhead. When I said that I hadn't come, he'd get upset and pout. Later I began lying to him and saying that I had come, so he'd relax and light a cigarette and puff himself up like a rooster."

"So you never came?" asked Catherine.

"Of course, lots of times, what do you think?" Gaby's peal of laughter came from deep in her throat. "But not at the push of a button."

Gaby said that men did not understand desire, that they thought of it as a circle fixed around the head of their member. "That's why men finish before they start. They don't know the feeling of the wave that rises inside, taking your body to unknown places with infinite zigzags."

"I didn't want anything from Elias. My father misunderstood everything. It wasn't about sex, it was about tenderness. I knew he couldn't marry me. It's true that I suffered a lot and I hated him when he told me about his wife and children. I told him, "Please don't speak of this because I can't stand it, these are things that I already know, but I can't stand to hear you speaking about them. When you talk about your wife and her illnesses, I hate you and I hate myself."

Gaby said that she forbid him from talking about his family because when he started talking about Evelyn, his wife, he became another person. He lost his manhood and his attractiveness and became a middle-aged man giving off the rotten stench of his false teeth.

Gaby told no one this.

How could she say what could not be said? How could she say that she no

< 201 >

longer remembered anything of that day except for the scent of the man's words that had spread over her body? How could she say that when she was naked in his arms, she emerged from the darkness? She rose like a hidden sun from the darkness of her shroud-like clothes.

Gaby was eighteen when she went to learn her trade in Elias al-Shami's tailor shop, and it was there where love blossomed to the point of dominating her whole life.

She remembered that he had said something about the need to sew a new dress. It was a November evening with dusk falling, but Elias al-Shami did not turn on the electricity. The two assistant seamstresses had gone home, and Gaby was busy with the day's last chores in the shop before going home. She sensed Mr. Elias at her side saying that he wanted to make a new dress for her and that he had found a beautiful piece of fabric just for her.

"For me?" asked the young woman.

"Of course for you. I want you to wear a dress that shows off your beauty. It is a crime that you wear these old clothes that hide you. Clothes aren't supposed to cover the body, they are made to be an extension of the body. That is the secret of dressmaking. That's what makes it an art. Come closer so I can see," said Elias.

The young woman came closer hesitantly. He took the measuring tape and started to take her measurements. He measured her height and then her hips, he then brought the tape measure to her breasts and she saw her dress fall to the floor without her even feeling the hands that had undone the buttons in front. The dress fell and Gaby stood in her underwear under the gaze of the tailor, a gaze that crept across her body and never left her. She crossed her arms as if to cover herself, but actually she was trying to calm her body hair, which stood on end as if a magnetic field surrounded her.

He left her standing there before him and drew her body with green chalk on tracing paper, then looked at her breasts and said, "What kind of camisole is that? Tomorrow I'll buy you a new one." Then he sat down on the chair and asked her to come to him.

The camisole fell to the floor, and Gaby saw herself standing before the seated man. She felt his breath on her breasts. He put his head between her breasts and took a deep breath. He said that he smelled flowers. She felt his lips taking in the nipple of her left breast before starting to suck the nectar. That's what he would later say whenever he brought his lips to her breast. "I want to suck the soul of the rose." The young woman felt her breasts between the man's lips crawl, climb, retreat, and advance. Something deep within her rose up and then sank down again, and made her tremble.

His head pulled back, and he rose from the chair and went into the next room. Gaby didn't move, not knowing what to do. Her insides throbbed with contractions that came and went. Time stood still as she stood motionless. Then she bent over, picked up the camisole and her dress and put them back on. When she saw him coming, she said, "Do you need anything, sir? I'm going." She felt that she was hearing her own voice for the first time; her voice emerged like the voice of another woman. It felt deep and rose straight from her chest. She asked him if he wanted anything. He shook his head but said nothing.

Suddenly night fell. She bent over to retrieve her camisole, and while she was putting it on, night fell. When she'd bent down, a pale white glow was enveloping everything, but when she picked it up and stood in front of the mirror to put it on, she saw only darkness and no longer could see herself in the mirror. She was not in a hurry and decided to go back home. She saw him standing at the door of the room like a phantom and asked him if he needed anything, and hearing her own voice, she went out. Once at home, she went into the bathroom and washed, and when she covered her breasts with soapsuds, the sensation of the magnetic field that had taken her to faraway places now came back to her and made her discover that the

< 203 >

kokina anchored with safety pins no longer suited the beauty of her nakedness and that from now on she needed her long hair in order to possess her own shadow.

In the days that followed, Gaby felt frustrated. Every evening after she finished sweeping and straightening up the shop, she waited for the green chalk and the dress project. But Mr. Elias ignored her as if she didn't exist, as if he hadn't taken her breasts in his hands and said that her beauty tormented him. "Your beauty is tormenting me, and you, is all this hurting you?" he asked her after waiting several days. He saw her as a little girl and was afraid for her. "I swear to God, I feel like a sinner. You're my daughter's age. I don't know what I'm doing with you."

She waited for him for more than a month before he came back to her with the new dress. She had finished up her work and was getting ready to leave when she saw him coming toward her carrying the yellow dress that glistened like the sun.

"What do you think?" he asked her.

"Oh, how beautiful," she said.

She took the dress and turned her back to him so that she could undress and try it on. She heard him say, "No, not like that," and he asked her to bathe before putting on the new dress. He pointed to the bathroom.

Gaby looked worriedly to where he was pointing.

"I'm supposed to bathe here?"

". . ."

"But I don't have my things with me."

He left her standing there, hesitant, and returned with a towel and underwear, walking ahead of her to the bathroom. She followed him as if entranced. He turned on the shower in the tub, the hot water shot out, and the steam rose. The man leaned over, put liquid soap in the water, agitated it with his hand, and the soapsuds frothed up, and with it the fragrance of apple. Gaby felt intoxicated. The steam got in her eyes and enveloped her in a white cloud. Two damp hands removed her dress and underwear and she stepped into the water. The man knelt at the edge of the water, picked up a bath sponge, and began to rub her body with it. If Gaby had been able to recount it, she would have said that she saw a man bent over as the branches of a tree bend, over and around her. Her body slid into the suds and fragrance and swayed to the rhythms of the water. He then took her by the hand to help her stand up and began to kiss her, lower and lower, as if discovering her with his lips and eyelashes. He pulled her out of the water and embraced her, and the water dripping from her body stained his shirt and pants. Gaby had not seen him naked. Her eyes were closed, but she felt his nakedness, and how he was united to the water. She became, with her medium height, her white body and fragrance, an extension of the man who stood embracing the woman's body freshly emerged from the soapy water. He dried her off bit by bit, then dressed her in her new clothes and asked her to look in the mirror. Gaby saw how her image was born in the mirror and a new woman emerged, one with a new body, new eyes, and a new voice. She stood in front of the mirror and undid her chignon, letting her hair hang loose down to her ankles.

"What's this?" asked Elias al-Shami. "Come, come, you need another shower."

She started to tie up her chignon again and asked him not to touch her hair.

"What are you doing?"

"I'm tying up my hair."

"You're crazy!"

He said she was crazy. He said that this hair needed to be draped over her shoulders, and when she tried to explain to him that she could not because her hair had to stay tied up in a bun to crown her head, and that it was let

< 205 >

down only for the miracle of the Epiphany or her wedding day, the tailor laughed and said, "What nonsense! Hair is the soul of a woman."

She tied up her hair again, fastened it with several pins, and wrapped it around her head. "Incredible," the tailor said. "Incredible, you should leave it loose." "It's not done, Master Elias, it's not done!" she replied.

She wrapped her *kokina* and left without looking back, but she discovered that her heart had fallen on the ground and she felt the urge to bend over and pick it up, but she got hold of herself and walked home.

And so Gaby began. She renounced the old Gaby, and put on a new image along with her yellow dress. She would discover in the street that led to Talaat Shahhada Street, where the tailor's shop was located, in the Syriac Quarter where she lived, that the sound of her footsteps on the street had changed. She felt her hips and the curve of her pelvis, and her neck that drove her forward.

Elias al-Shami initiated her into the secrets of the world where her navel became the secret of life. There he had begun, explaining to his young love that the art of tailoring began at the navel. For when man first tied a baby's umbilical cord at the moment of birth, he discovered that he could knot hides, devise fabrics and fibers. He told her the story of the navel and the dog. He said that he had read it in the Epistle of Barnabas. When the girl asked her father about this Gospel, the *cohno* cursed Satan and spat, and told his daughter to spit on Satan.

Spitting on Satan was a custom of the Abyad family in Beirut, and Yalo carried on the custom everywhere. Even here in prison, when he wrote a sentence wrong or he had an inappropriate thought, he'd feel a strange taste rising in his throat, up to his tongue, and would say, "I spit on Satan!" and spit. Shirin hated spitting, and her features contracted in disgust whenever Yalo cleared this throat to prepare his spit. When he tried to explain to her that he had to spit on Satan, because he was the one who had first spit on humankind, the look of disgust around her eyes grew even more intense. But Yalo felt that he had to spit in order not to vomit. Then he understood that he had earlier suffered from stomach ulcers. The ulcers were accompanied by his scalp turning dry and scabrous, and both conditions derived from terror. Yalo did not deny that during the civil war, he had begun to distinguish between terror and fear. Yalo could never forget his first night at the Sodeco checkpoint on the Green Line in Beirut when the shooting started and he felt unable to control his bowels and that his knees were going to give out. He crept over to the corner of the checkpoint, squatted, and defecated. No one saw him. All the guys were busy fighting while he was busy shitting, as Alexei told him the next day when the odor was obvious. The word *shit* would have become part of his name had the Goat Battalion not withdrawn from Sodeco and taken up a new position near the museum. There, at the museum line, Yalo learned how to be afraid without losing control of his bowels, though at the beginning of every exchange of gunfire he felt the need to urinate. He controlled himself in the beginning, then when he was nearly losing control, he joked to the guys that he was going to piss on the enemy. When he saw their looks of bewilderment, he came out from behind the barricade, squatted, and pissed under the volleys of bullets.

"Why do you piss that way, like the Bedouin?" asked Tony.

Yalo replied that this was the humanitarian way to urinate: "We have to squat rather than flaunt what God has given us," said Yalo, repeating his grandfather's saying.

It was during the war that Yalo learned the difference between fear and terror. A fighter might be afraid, but an ordinary person would be terror-struck. That was why Yalo chose to be a fighter. He fought to inflict rather than feel terror. It's true that he was afraid, but fear was nothing compared to the terror that paralyzed a man and made his mind a blank.

< 207 >

When Yalo was eleven, and a shell landed in the street where he was playing, he was not afraid, but he was terror-struck and froze on the spot. A few days after that, white scabs formed on his scalp and everyone said that he was in danger of going bald, and a burning taste was coming up from his stomach. His mother took him to the doctor, who said it was caused by terror. He asked Yalo what had happened, but the boy could no longer remember. The image of the girl Najwa, with whom he had been playing ball in front of his house, had been erased from his memory when the shell landed and the girl had been torn to pieces. Yalo didn't remember the incident. He listened to his mother tell him about it. She told the doctor that her son had been deaf and dumb for two days, then began to vomit a green fluid and the white patch started to grow on his scalp.

The doctor said it was terror and prescribed a yellow ointment for Yalo's head and a black liquid for him to drink every morning before breakfast for the ulcers. This was the cause of the small white puncture prominent on Yalo's right temple, which he called his third eye.

"I have three eyes," he told Shirin.

"How did you see me?" she asked.

"I have three eyes," he said, and pointed to the white puncture on his temple.

"I have a white eye in my black hair, but someday when I go gray, I don't know what will happen to this eye," he said smiling. Shirin grimaced before letting out a smile and accepted his offer of a cup of coffee in a nearby café.

She asked him about the eye that resembled a white puncture and he told her that he didn't remember the incident, that he had even forgotten the features of the girl who was killed. He told her he had not heard a thing – he hadn't even heard the impact of the shell. "That is terror," he said. "Terror is when you forget." The young woman lit a cigarette, took a deep draw, coughed, and then the cigarette trembled in her fingers.

"So you mean to tell me that you were terrified, and that's why you don't remember a thing about the incident?"

"I told you I forgot because of the terror. Why don't you believe me?"

"And why don't you, too, believe me when I tell you I forgot everything that happened in Ballouna? You have to understand – I was terrified, too."

"Terrified!" He repeated the word several times, softly. "But you reached out, and your arms smelled like incense."

Had Shirin said that, or had Yalo heard, in his solitude, silence, and grief, voices coming from the depth of his imagination, meaning that he could no longer distinguish between reality and illusion?

Yalo did not tell her about the shell and the girl's death. He said it was his third eye; a third eye only grew for those who possessed the ability to see things from their various angles, then felt the green rising from his insides up to his esophagus, so he spat on Satan, and asked her to spit. Shirin irritably put out her cigarette in her coffee cup, swallowed her own saliva, and then left.

When Gaby told the story of the navel, and cited the Epistle of Barnabas, her father told her, "Spit on Satan, daughter." The *cohno* spat, and his daughter spat, and his grandson spat. But Gaby was convinced that the Epistle of Barnabas might all be false, except for the story of the navel.

Elias al-Shami said that God was the first tailor because when he ordered the angel to remove spittle from Adam's body of clay, he also ordered him to sew a puncture in the belly of the first man. So the puncture became a navel, and the navel became the mark of man.

"Do you know, Gaby, what the navel is?" Elias said.

She was standing naked the way he liked her to be. He asked her to undress and walk naked around the workshop, then he knelt on the floor and started to kiss her navel before devouring her body with his hands.

"Do you know what navel means?" he asked her.

"Of course I know. It's the intestine retied to the placenta."

"No, no, Gaby, listen, my love, I'll tell you, but this has to remain a secret between us, because the navel is the secret of man."

Elias al-Shami rose and went into another room and then came back carrying a green book. He sat on the chair, put on his glasses, and began to turn the pages, then when he found the passage he was looking for, he said, "Listen," and began to read:

"'Then God said, one day when all the angels were assembled: "Let each one that takes me for his Lord straightaway bow down to this earth." They that loved God bowed down, but Satan, with those that were of his ilk, said: "O Lord, we are spirit, it is not just that we should bow down to this clay." Whereupon God said, "Depart from me, O ye accursed ones, for I have no mercy for you." And Satan spat upon that mass of earth as he departed; the angel Gabriel raised up that spittle with some of the earth. So that therefore now man has a navel in his belly.'"

"Did you understand the story?" asked Elias.

She said that she understood, but he wasn't convinced. The tailor always treated her as if she didn't comprehend. He would tell her something, and ask her whether she understood, and when she answered yes, he would begin to repeat it. He would repeat himself several times to the point where the young woman was ready to explode, and she would gaze at him with narrowing eyes. Only then would he realize that he had gone too far, and he'd gather his sentences, shorten them, and drop his commentaries.

In this repetitive manner, Gaby learned the art of tailoring and the art of love, and all the Damascene arts that the master ascribed to his family, who left Damascus for Beirut after the massacres of 1860.

Master Elias always surprised his young love with one question: "What is the most important thing in life?"

When she gave the answer she had learned from the last time he'd asked the same question, she discovered that this time he had another answer in mind. In the beginning the most important thing in life was the art of tailoring, then it became the navel, then dogs, but in the end she wasn't sure.

Master Elias al-Shami was infatuated with his young lover's navel. He read to her about the navel of our lord Adam, peace be upon him, from a forged book written by an Italian monk who embraced Islam in the sixteenth century, wanting thereby to solve the complex problem that humankind invented when they had wanted to divide up God among themselves. He'd lean down then to caress and kiss her navel.

"God is indivisible," said Elias. "That is the most important thing."

He bent over the young woman's navel. A small navel resembling a rose tucked into a smooth belly. He knelt and said that the navel was the first icon God made, an icon fashioned from the elimination of the stain of Satan's spittle.

She said that she understood. She suddenly felt the need to sit down; she had been standing before him naked, listening to him explain that love was the first lesson a man received when suckling at his mother's breast. He moved closer to her breasts, but, all of a sudden, a glacial fear came over Gaby and she said that what they were doing was a sin, the sin that her father the *cohno* had repeatedly discussed when talking about women: "God blessed me with only two daughters, one gone off to a faraway country and the other divorced yet not divorced, a widow yet not a widow. May God save us from sin."

Gaby said that she went back to him after her husband had disappeared and she had given birth to her son, not for the sake of the navel or for sex, but because she felt alone and the night weighed down on her body. She went back and wanted him at night. She told him: Just one night. I want to sleep the whole night beside you in bed so that I won't feel that the night will swallow me like an abyss." Gaby was unable to describe to the man the

< 211 >

signs of her fear of the night, not because she did not know how to speak, but because speech came only when the other was ready to listen. Speech. Without this readiness, it fell into the gulf that separated one human from another. That is what Yalo learned from Madame Randa. In the beginning, when his magic randified her, she never stopped talking, and he drank in her words and her love. He did not talk much because he didn't know how to talk as she did, though her speech began to seem as if it were his. When their talking ended, their love ended. Yalo understood that a man spoke only when the other became a part of his speech. That was why Shirin left him sad. He tested her silence with his speech. He told her about his adventures, his wars, stories he had experienced and some he had not, in order to throw her a line to draw her in toward him; she approached the line, grasped the end of it, then let go.

Elias al-Shami was different. When Gaby went back to him, he felt that he was awakening. He said that he didn't want to lie to her, that he did not want to be like all the other men who lied. He said that when she got married, she fell off the edge of his life. He said that he'd forgotten her and was relieved. "Why are you coming back? I was calm. It was over."

What could she say? At six o'clock in the evening, she felt a gale stirring inside her, and this gale commanded her to go to the tailor shop. She knew that the master would be by himself now. He opened the door and rubbed his eyes as if he didn't believe them.

"Come in, come in," he said hesitantly.

She entered and stood in the portico where she had always stood at six o'clock nude beneath his gaze, and he would take her in his arms. She stood there, hesitant, stammering.

"You're still beautiful, Gaby," he said. He lit a cigarette and sat in the rocking chair without inviting her to have a seat. So she remained standing, arms folded. He told her how he'd forgotten her to return to his normal life

< 212 >

and reconnect with his clients. He went back to his innocent sexual banter with the women workers in the shop, which never left him troubled, and he never had to undress. He burst out laughing: "Do you know, Gaby, you're the one who taught me how to strip? Maybe I taught you everything, but you taught me how to take off my clothes. I don't like taking off my clothes, I feel self-conscious. Even with my wife, I never – "

"I don't want to hear about your wife," she said.

Gaby didn't know where this old talk came from. When they had been in love, she had never allowed him to speak of his wife or his three children. And now, even though she had come here for work, and she didn't want to rekindle their relationship or be maddened by jealousy again, she reverted involuntarily to her old way of speaking.

When Gaby agreed to marry, it was as if she were throwing herself into an abyss. She saw the man coming to the house and heard her father giving his consent. She closed her eyes, said yes, and fell from a great height. She said yes and went to the shop the next morning. She went to Master Elias's room, where he was drawing with green chalk on a piece of fabric, and she said, with no preliminaries, that she was engaged and was going to get married. The man raised his head from the piece of fabric and looked at her from beneath his glasses. "Congratulations," he said. "I can't say anything but congratulations, my darling. It's your right, I have no right over you. I pray that you'll be happy."

She left his room and went back to her sewing machine, immersing herself in her work. That evening, she did not linger, as had been her habit; instead, she was one of the first to leave the shop. When she was at the door, she heard his voice calling to her to stay a little longer because one of the dresses needed altering. She said, "Sorry, but I'm in a hurry. Tomorrow."

She did not return to work. She told her father that she had lost the desire to work, and the *cohno* said that it was for the better. It never occurred to him that his daughter, who had closed her eyes as she agreed to marry George Jal'u, was throwing herself into an abyss of despair after having given up on her true love.

She said that she had not come here for the sake of the past; now she was a married woman and had come for work; she asked him whether she might get her old job back.

"Everything will be like before," he said. "You can start tomorrow morning." Then he came near her and reached his hand out as he had done before, but she didn't offer him hers or come near him.

"Thanks, boss," she said, and left.

But this *thanks, boss* evaporated quickly, and Gaby slipped back into their old story. And there he was again insisting: "What is the most important thing in life?"

Gaby couldn't understand how this man never bored himself with his own talk. She was with him now because she needed a job and because she dreaded the heaviness of the night. She wanted him just one night, for which they would go to a hotel or anyplace he wanted. He promised her that they would go to the Grand Hotel in Sofar, and he set a rendezvous with her there, but at the last minute – after she had invented a plausible lie for her father – he said that he couldn't make it and had to postpone. Whenever she got upset, he would shrink with sorrow and anger, and in the end she would console him, as if she had committed some sin that needed his forgiveness.

"You still haven't told me what the most important thing in life is."

She knew that he was waiting for the same answer about the navel and the art of tailoring. But the last time, he surprised her with the dog. He said that dogs were the most important thing. And he went back to the Gospel of Barnabas to recite how God had created the dog.

"Listen," he said.

She stood half naked, yawning, certain that she would hear the story of Adam, the spittle, and all the rest. ·

He opened the book and recited:

"'One day Satan approached the gates of Paradise, and when he saw the horses eating grass, he told them that if this mass of earth received a soul, they would suffer from it; therefore it was in their interest to trample on that mass of earth so that it would be ruined. So the horses, stirred up, violently commenced to assail that bit of earth among the lilies and roses.

"'And so God thenceforth gave a soul to that unclean part of the earth upon which fell the spittle of Satan, which Gabriel took from the mass. And dogs were created, barking, and the horses were frightened and fled. Then God gave a soul to humankind and all the angels sang: Our Lord, may His holy name be blessed.'

"Did you understand?" he asked.

"God bless you, please, that's enough. I want to go home, I'm tired."

"You understood that God created dogs to defend humankind? That is true, but it's not the most important thing – ask me what the most important thing is."

"Whatever. What is the most important thing?"

"The most important thing, my love, is that man and dog come from the same clay, and when sin takes hold of man, he becomes a dog."

"So we're dogs?" she said.

"Not at all. Love is not a sin," he said.

When he spoke to her of dogs, she realized that everything had become bland and monotonous, and that she no longer loved him. Gaby told Catherine that she no longer loved him: "But I stayed with him, and that's the worst thing. When you don't love someone but you stay with him, even if he's not your husband. I mean, I understand, a married woman or a married

< 215 >

man, she's the one who's judged, and the judgments always favor the man. But me, what do I care? I don't know what came over me."

"So how did you leave him?" asked Catherine.

"I didn't leave him. I stayed with him to the end, even after my father went after him. I don't know, things eventually just died a natural death."

Gaby told of what happened between her father and Elias al-Shami, and how she felt, as she listened through a partly closed door to the conversation between the two men, that her father had devoured the man.

"Devoured, yes. That was the first time in my life I saw how a human being can become a predator. It was as if my father was chewing him up, and the other shrunk more and more. He devoured him with words. I don't know how to describe it to you. Finally, it stopped. I was happy. I pretended to be upset, because I should have been upset, but deep down, my anger was sweeter than joy."

Gaby said that she had been happy to see her father devouring Elias with words. He did it as if he were spreading out a tablecloth before gobbling up a feast. The *cohno* ground up the words as if he were grinding up the man himself, and the man shrank and nearly disappeared.

He asked her the question but she did not know what to say.

She thought of saying that it was velvet. The tailor used to love velvet so much, he used to ask her to put on blue velvet slacks so that he could unbutton the buttons, and let his hand wander between the velvet of her slacks and the silk of her white breasts.

"Look in the mirror," he said when they had finished making love. "Look how beautiful you are, look how beautiful love makes you."

She said he was a dog. "Dogs are the most important thing. It's dogs who come out of mankind's navel."

No, he said, and the little hollow that sliced through his right cheek expanded. Gaby used to love this scar that was the mark of her teacher's manliness, when he was struck with a razor on his cheek by a swindler playing a shell game in Bourj Square. Elias told his story of the shell-game player many times, and each time the story ended with the blood that streamed down his face, and how he successfully arrested the swindler and drove him to the police station. Then he'd touch his cheek and say, "Ouch."

But now she no longer responded with "May God be with you," because she no longer cared. Love was waning and expectations were gone, and all that remained was a deathly feeling of solitude with a man she couldn't leave because she didn't know how.

Gaby told no one that she felt an indescribable yearning for the man and that the yearning began in her arms; a shudder would invade her arms, which would become nearly suffocating waves pressing against her rib cage. She didn't understand this sensation, since she hated him and hated his odor. "At first smelling his odor disgusted me," Gaby said. She did not realize that through all those years it was her own odor she was smelling. When she was near the man, she gave off a feminine smell that overwhelmed everything else. When Gaby's desire died, she began to smell his odor, the odor of cracked skin mingled with decay.

Yalo, no.

Yalo smelled his own odor only here, when it mingled with his excrement. Yalo realized suddenly that he might be unable to prove his innocence, and he grew terrified of the words he was writing.

Yalo said that he had to get out of prison in order to accomplish one goal. He would go to Shirin so that he could smell the fragrance of the incense that her arms gave off. That fragrance was love, and Yalo wanted to remember love to restore the scent of life. He tried to write everything, but he wrote only very little. He read the pages and felt the lashes of the whip and the electricity that tore out his fingernails and toenails. The interrogator would grab the pages and throw them in his face because he had not written his whole life story. Yalo did not know how any person could remember his whole life story, and even if one could remember it, the time needed to write it down would be no less than the time it took to live it. Yalo smiled at that thought. He would say "Yes, sir" before explaining his theory about how no one in the world was capable of writing the whole story of his life. Even Jurji Zaidan, whose books Gaby brought home but never read, even Jurji Zaidan, all of whose books about the history of the Arabs Yalo had read, wrote a million pages about others, and then when he wrote his memoirs, he had nothing to say.

Yalo did not understand why they tortured him this much, or why there had to be the period of waiting before more unimaginable torture set in. Was this because of Shirin and the cars, the night in Ballouna? Why didn't they prosecute the whole Lebanese people? Yalo was sure that everyone in Lebanon made love in cars. So why just him? Why were the other lovers not prosecuted? Was it because he stole? And who didn't steal? His grandfather told him that everyone stole, and that one of the saints wrote that all the rich were thieves, so people could get rich only by stealing from others. "Look, my boy," said the *cohno*. "Look well. Everyone is putting his hand in someone else's pocket. Look well, my boy. You have to see behind things, and a man cannot see what is behind things unless he has the grace of the Gospel. Look, and learn how to accept grace, and then you will see. And when you see, you will discover that the greatest curse on mankind is the hand. Sin lies in the hand, and when a man puts his hand in his neighbor's pocket, and the neighbor into yet another's pocket, and so on, then that is society. That is why the saintly fathers withdrew from the world."

"And you, Grandfather, why didn't you withdraw?"

"Because I'm not a saint. I am just a poor soul. I don't know why my life has unfolded as it has, or if it has any meaning."

Yalo laughed when he saw how the fear of God make his grandfather's hand tremble. For Yalo knew that things were different; the discovery that Yalo made in Ballouna was greater than all his experiences in the war. The war taught him death, but Ballouna taught him that everything was death, or resembled death, and that the hand was in fact an extension of the penis. He learned this with Randa, before discovering the darkness in the forest where the differences between the parts of the human body were erased. The lovers in the cars taught him that man could be like a sardine covered in the oil of sex. The cars were like sardine cans, and the people were curvy fish swimming in oil. He liked this idea and decided to add it to his first idea about writing. He took out a blank sheet of paper and wrote. This was the first time he had written anything beyond what the interrogation required.

He wrote, first, that a person could not write his life; he had to choose between living and writing. Yalo had chosen to live; therefore he wrote what the interrogation required. But he did not want to end as Jurji Zaidan had ended, excavating the lives of others; he preferred that writers excavate his life, that is if they wanted to write a love story unlike any other.

He wrote, second, that everyone desires everyone, and that his experience had taught him, as he observed the lovers in Ballouna, that most lovers committed betrayal or accepted it. And that even he himself, when he loved Shirin, would betray her when he got the chance, because "the scent of treachery is the sweetest scent." He had stolen this idea from Madame Randa, who told him during one of her randifications with him that betrayal was the sweetest thing, and that she had begun to worry that she would get used to it and would no longer feel treacherous when she was with him.

Third, he wrote that all ideas were stolen, and that people spent their time stealing ideas from one another.

Yalo was cheered as he wrote down these three thoughts in the form of three consecutive sentences:

1. No one is capable of writing his life.
2. Desires are in desires.
3. All ideas are stolen.

He felt a strange relief, and decided to revise the story of his life. He would write it in a condensed and clear form and would offer two versions to the interrogator the next day: a detailed version, and a condensed version eloquently relating his life.

He sat behind the green table puffing at his pen as if he were smoking a cigarette, and began.

Sir, respected judge.

I want to add these pages to the story of my life that you requested me to write, and which you will find in the personal file of the accused, Daniel Abel Abyad, called Yalo.

Sir, I want to seek a pardon. For in the two months I spent in solitary confinement, with nothing but white pages and the Holy Bible to keep me company, I discovered that I am not Yalo the criminal.

No, no, I am not pleading insanity as criminals do to escape the noose. No sir, I am no longer that Yalo. I discovered, as I was writing the story of my life, that I am no longer him. The days I spent in interrogation, and my reading of the Bible, made me discover that I was reborn. For this, sir, I go back to the Gospel and all the holy books. When they say, In the beginning was the Word, that means the word was the first thing. And when I wrote the story of my life, I discovered the word that created me anew. I do not know how to explain that in plain Arabic, but as I saw my entire life pass before me from beginning to end, I was convinced that I had become a new man, just as I was convinced that the old Yalo was not conscious of the things he did. I mean, he did not fashion his life as he would have liked, he was like a hypnotized person and it would not be fair for a man to pay the price of deeds that he did not chose to perform. Yalo the tall phantom in a black overcoat,

< 221 >

who descended upon lovers' cars, Yalo who fought and killed, laughing all the time – he is gone for good.

I can assure you, sir, judge, that I have become a new man. I know my story because I wrote it, and I will write it again if you wish, but here, in prison, I feel that I no longer have any connection to the past. All I learned from the past was love. Yes, sir, Yalo's life began when he discovered love, but this love was also the cause of his death. That is, Yalo fell when he stood up, and became despicable when he became human. Yes, sir, he mistreated Shirin and pursued her, but he discovered love. A human being, sir, is a man who loves. That is what my grandfather the *cohno* taught me, God rest his soul, yet he was the cause of our ruin. He forbade my poor mother from staying with the man she loved because he was married and cowardly and did not dare divorce his wife. Should my mother have been deprived of love because her beloved was a coward? My mother was deprived of love, and a woman deprived cannot give. I believe that this was the root of the disorder I experienced.

Sir, I fled because of the war, not because of the money stolen at the Georges Aramouni Barracks. In any case, I was tricked in Paris, because my friend Tony stole the money and left me stranded.

I fled the war because I no longer understood it. No, I was not a coward; I never once ran away, even when I was afraid. I would control myself and tell myself that I wasn't afraid. Isn't that courage? So I was courageous, and I abandoned the war because I was fed up with it. In the beginning I was like all the young guys. I wanted to defend Lebanon, and then I found out that I was fighting the impoverished, like me, and that I would remain an outsider no matter what I did. A human being is an outsider in this world and my grandfather would say it's precisely because he was a human being. When I discovered that I was a human being, I fled to Paris, and I was tricked, and Monsieur Michel Salloum saved me. He gave me work as the guard at the Villa Gardenia in Ballouna.

Everything I wrote about my life is true, but there is one thing I want to clarify, without meaning to hurt anyone, God forbid. I am now as pure and white as this

< 222 >

white page upon which I am writing the story of my life. I just want my conscience to be clear, and to close out my past life by confessing everything. This is not to degrade M. Michel, as I hold the greatest respect for him, but the truth must be told.

I want to confess to something I tried at every phase of my torture and confinement not to confess, to preserve the reputations of these people. But I discovered that confession was my only way of becoming a human being again and beginning a new life, and I was confident that you would take my circumstances into consideration and pardon me. It would be unthinkable for the amnesty to include all the war criminals while I should spend my life in prison because I slept with a woman, or with several women.

I was desperate, sir, when I returned from France and started working at the villa. Everything seemed black before me, I could no longer distinguish colors. Now I feel remorse for those days. I was living in a villa amidst a green pine forest but wasn't seeing the colors of nature. Is there anyone who cannot see nature?

Yalo did not see colors, he was living with his eyes closed. Yes, sir, I kept my eyes closed, I wanted to stay in the heart of black. Black was my life, I lost all sensation, I was living as if in a long dream. Then a woman entered my life, a respectable woman for whom I had nothing but esteem. This woman, whose home I lived in as a guard, viewed me as a poor and solitary kid, she had compassion for me. She then taught me to love my body. Had it not been for her, my black and blocked pores would never have opened. The first time she spoke with me, she asked, "Why are you a shade of blue? I am olive-skinned and tan easily, and I didn't know that my skin had turned such a deep blue-black. When I went back to my house below the villa, I looked in the mirror and discovered that my skin had turned as black as the things I had seen. This mirror had restored to me my color and my sense of life. The sex and love I tasted with Madame Randa Salloum were greater than the love tasted by all the men in the world. Her love brought me back to life, but opened in my heart a bottomless well. I became, when I stood in the garden and breathed in the scent of pine, I felt excited. Yes, sir, I became a part of nature, and nature knows

< 223 >

no boundaries between things. That is what led me to the cars and all the trouble. Right away I felt as if I were living in a dream – up at the villa, with the lady teaching me the subtle art of love, and down in the woods I felt as if the cars were animals constantly mating with one another. And the odor of sex was everywhere.

I lived in the Villa Gardenia, which belonged to Michel Salloum, near the Church of St. Nicholas. I only went to mass once, because I missed the icons and the fragrance of the incense. Ballouna became like a triangle: the villa, the forest, and the church.

Yalo went astray by stealing, but stealing was not his objective. He stole by chance; he stole because they made him steal. That is, when he went down to watch from up close. He fell into the trap of money, and the lure of jewels, and that is not right, sir, not only because stealing is a sin, but also because money distorts things and dilutes pleasures.

As for rape, it is true that I raped, but I did not know that it was called rape. I thought that was what sex was – you came upon a woman and didn't need to explain anything. That was stupid.

Yes, Yalo was stupid, because later on he discovered, when he was stricken by the affliction of love, that this sort of sex was meaningless. Even so, not even love could prevent him from having this sort of sex, because human beings are sinful by nature.

I was confused, sir. Yalo was Shirin's lover and thought only of her, but even so continued to take lovers and have sex with women whenever the circumstances permitted him to. Perhaps it was the place – the place, sir, the forest was full of devils that swarmed around the fragrances of pine sap and wild grasses. I don't know, I never lived on the mountain. My grandfather lived in a village that was said to resemble Paradise, but me, I have only lived in the city, in the Syriac Quarter in Mseitbeh and al-Mrayyeh in Ain Rummaneh. Our first house had a yard full of trees, mostly acacia trees with white and yellow flowers that have a beautiful scent. But the smells of our yard have nothing to do with the smells of the Ballouna forest.

When the fragrance of pine mingled with that of cypress, the place became strange and lust-inspiring.

I am sure that Shirin loved me. My problem is that I didn't understand her love and I didn't know how to deal with it. The girl had a nervous breakdown after her fiancé left her, and she fell in love with the doctor who gave her an abortion. Yalo's relationship with her would have worked if Yalo had shown his true personality, but he played games with her and scared her away. He had a true passion for her and dreamed of marrying her. When in love, a person takes risks, sometimes everything is lost, and this is what happened. Shirin was afraid, and she was right to be. When a person wants something too much, it escapes from him. This is what happened to Mme Randa with me, I began to feel like an object in her hands and that she could no longer do without me, that's why I took off. The same thing happened with Shirin, only she loved Yalo. I can assure you, sir, she loved me. She would tremble with love whenever we met, I realize that now. Before I thought she was trembling because she was afraid, and that I would make her even more afraid, but now I know that she loved me and was jealous of Ballouna. Instead of telling her that I was an artist, a calligrapher, and educated – that is, an intellectual – I told her about the crimes I had committed, and some that I had not committed, which made me fall from grace with her, and that's why she wanted to be through with me by any means possible.

Sir, I am sure she is tormented now. Shirin and I committed a grave offense against love, and I want her to know that I am ready to correct it. I am ready to turn over a new, clean leaf with her, and if she wants marriage, I have no objection. I want Shirin to know that I am ready to marry her whenever she wants, and she'll know I am saying this because I love her.

I did not sleep with her only in Ballouna, when I surprised her in the car with that worthless doctor; her fiancé was not with her, as she claimed, but I don't want you to interrogate her because I know how fragile she is. Her delicate body could not bear torture. But I slept with her several times after that in a hotel in Jounieh. I beg

< 225 >

you to forgive her for lying and saying she was in the forest with her fiancé, Emile, – a despicable coward, that guy – he shook with fear during my interrogation, even though I was the one who was being tortured, not him.

And concerning the explosives, I am prepared to go along with my confession about Haykal and al-Naddaf, if you judge it necessary. That would be my sacrifice for the sake of civil peace in Lebanon.

I hope, sir, that this new information will be useful, and helpful toward closing my case and proving my innocence. I rely on you, sir, for I am an orphaned young man. I do not know my father, my grandfather is not my father, and my mother is not my sister.

Finally, sir, I would like to thank you, to thank the interrogator and all of his assistants who permitted me during this period in captivity to make peace with myself and discover things that had never come into my mind.

Yalo closed his eyes and spat on Satan. He was sitting in the interrogation room, his insides churning. The interrogator's face reached him
through the glow of the dim fluorescent bulbs fixed in the ceiling. Yalo
stood under the light and looked around. The interrogator's gray hair had
a yellow tinge to it, his small face seemed planted on the table, he turned the
pages and looked at the tall specter under the fluorescent light.

Yalo closed his eyes and saw with his third eye. He felt a tremor move
through the muscles of his arms and legs, and spat on Satan. In prison Yalo
had learned how to spit in his heart, he no longer puckered his lips to eject
a clot of phlegm onto the ground. Now it was enough to say "I spit on
Satan" and promise himself that the day he was free of this nightmare, he
would spit on all the devils he had been forced to deal with. He said "I spit
on Satan" to stop the tremor in his heart and muscles, but the trembling
spread in gentle waves through the body of the tall specter from his head
to his toes. And before the interrogator had spoken a single word, Yalo
understood that he had fallen into a trap.

"What's this – you're the king of sex?" said the interrogator, spacing out
his words to suggest that his words implied a variety of threats.

Yalo was not afraid, or so he convinced himself; after all this what could
he fear? What could be more terrifying than the sack, than the feeling of

< 227 >

being castrated, than being rolled like a ball under boots? So why should he be afraid? He put his hands firmly on his thighs in an attempt to stop the tremor in his body, but in leaning over he heard a cracking in his neck. How had the interrogator gotten behind him so fast to slap him? Yalo straightened up again and saw the short interrogator standing behind him, waving the pages.

"You're screwing with us, huh, king of sex?" the interrogator said, circling the tall, bewildered man, who didn't know where to look to acknowledge the words of the interrogator. Yalo spat on Satan and closed his eyes. He thought of suggesting that the fat-thighed, round-faced interrogator stand on a chair to face him so that they could communicate. But before Yalo could open his mouth, the interrogator punched him in the stomach so that the air was cut off from his lungs and he doubled over, his mouth wide open as if begging for some air to breathe before closing his eyes to die.

Yalo would say that he felt death coming on. When he was in the sack, under the whip, in the leg braces for a beating, or in the pool of water, he had not felt final death. Perhaps he died without knowing it, but he was certain that he would make it, but now, faced with the circling interrogator holding the pages, punching him in the stomach and kicking his buttocks, Yalo entered the labyrinth of death, despising himself for being unable to draw a breath.

The interrogator went back to his chair behind the table and his head reentered the fluorescent white. Yalo found himself trying to reconnect the words coming from the interrogator's mouth so that he could grasp their meaning.

Yalo heard the names Michel Salloum and Randa several times and gathered that the interrogator was asking him about the few pages he had added to his confessions. However, he did not understand the question sufficiently to answer it. He heard the names splintering between the interrogator's thin lips.

"Why aren't you answering me, you dog?"

"I don't know, sir."

"You don't know? So who does know?"

"Sir, I wrote that I would start my life over, give me a chance. I swear to God, it's over."

The interrogator said that he understood the game, and that Daniel was going to taste whatever torture would force him to tell the truth.

"You think you're pretty smart, huh? You think that you can screw with us, you dog? We gave you paper so that you could write the truth, not so you could make up stories, make accusations against honest people and destoy their families. Do you dare tell me, bastard, that you slept with Madame Randa? Go ahead, say it! What are you afraid of?"

Yalo said nothing, but he felt the urge to dance, for the interrogator sputtered his sentences as if he were singing along to discontinuous music from his throat. A smile formed on the lips of the thin specter.

"Are you laughing, you son of a bitch?" he asked, signaling with his hand.

Three giants appeared. Yalo had not been unaware of their presence in the room. The fluorescent light gave a yellowing glow to the inspector's mass of gray hair falling into his round face. Yalo gazed for a long time at this face and suddenly a shudder of fear ran through him. It was as if this face, the crack in whose lower half emitted words, was not a real face at all. Yalo had never before seen a face like this one: a soft nose that blocked the lips, as round as a ball. His activities in the forest had made him an expert when it came to faces. He could tell a good face from a wicked face with no trouble: a big nose meant fear, thin lips meant wickedness, a fat face meant surrender, and so on . . . He would judge them by their faces, which he'd

< 229 >

read in the light before deciding how to proceed. Should he use violence? In that case, he'd frown with his eyebrows and rap against the window with the muzzle of his rifle. Or should he be polite, lowering the rifle and signaling with his head? Or perhaps be apathetic, lowering both his rifle and his head? Yalo knew all the faces, but this face . . . Before, he hadn't looked at the interrogator's face; he had been the prey and the prey does not see the hunter's face. But that day, after Yalo had written his story so many times, he shivered with fear when he saw the interrogator's face: a soft nose that disappeared in the fleshy, round face, lips like two lines drawn in green, oval eyes that didn't appear to have pupils, and a voice coming from some mysterious slit in this ball resting on the table.

When Yalo finished writing the story of his life, he felt sure that his journey through torture had ended. He wanted the story to end so that he could go back to the life he had left behind. Yalo discovered, when he sat behind the table, broken by physical and spiritual pain, that his life had been unreal. The life he had written down came to him like dismembered, incomplete stories. He saw himself in these stories as someone else, and so Yalo hated writing and hated himself. "Shit!" He closed his eyes and said, "Shit! This Yalo whose story I am writing will go from these pages to the hangman's rope, will stand under the noose, will dangle from the end of the rope like an unreal specter." This is how he saw himself, as if in a nightmare, and now he was coming out of his sleep and standing before the interrogator. He would say that he had written down everything and that he had nothing new to add, so there was no need for torture.

Yalo stood before the interrogator to tell him that he wanted to become a real person again and leave the stupor where his memories and the story of his life had taken him. He had become a shadow like his grandfather Abel Ephraim Abyad. The grandfather, who had become a shadow of himself in his last days, used to talk about his life as if it were not his own, and Yalo would listen to him with only half an ear. Here in the cell, Yalo discovered that he had not been able to listen to him because the *cohno* was dying, and the living could not listen to the dead unless they died with them. But fragments of his grandfather's voice came back to him in his solitude, and he heard in his cell the words that his ears had refused to hear, and lived with death, and his story became a shadow of his life. Yalo lived in the shadows and hated the color black that spread ink on the page, but then, all at once, he decided to come back to life.

He stood before the interrogator to speak, but the interrogator didn't look like a real man. His head was on the table and he spoke in a soft, almost inaudible voice. Yalo felt that he was still ink on paper, and that his soul had not yet come back to him, so he closed his eyes.

The interrogator did not shout at him, telling him to open his eyes as he had done previous times, he left him in the dark. But the young man sensed the three large men standing directly behind him. He saw them with his third eye, which suddenly came back to him. Since his arrest, this eye had gone dark and no longer saw. In prison he tried to make it see the way it had seen in the forest when he'd felt like he was an elevated tower looking down on the world and seeing in every direction. Was it true that he really saw himself that way, or did the idea come to him there in the café in Achrafieh when he was trying to convince Shirin to believe in him and in his love for her. There he told her how this third eye of his had grown, and how he had tried to see through it after he'd heard the *cohno* tell his daughter that the boy had a third eye, and how he would close his eyes so he could see with this new eye. Shirin laughed, and her small eyes would widen. There Yalo had become a tower; with Shirin he had three eyes, and could see what he liked. He carried himself as if he were an elevated tower pouncing on its victims, and was full of visions that mingled with his desire to possess all the women in the world.

< 231 >

But here, before the interrogator, in this room whose fluorescent white was tinged in yellow, he saw with his third eye three men standing behind him, and could smell a beating coming and felt sure that he was still in the mousetrap. He saw his shadow break on the wall as he bent over to avoid the blows coming at him from behind.

"You dare say you slept with Mme Salloum?" said the interrogator.

"I . . . said . . . no . . ."

The blows rained on the shadow that Yalo saw with his three eyes. The shadow squirmed with pain, and the pain spread from the wall to his third eye, which suddenly went dark.

"You?" said the interrogator. Then he got up, came out from behind the table, and approached Yalo. The interrogator stood up, and the blows stopped. Yalo listened to the interrogator read a letter that the accused had written asking that the judge pass it on to M. Michel Salloum.

I want to direct this message to the lawyer M. Michel. I feel gratitude toward this honorable man who saved my life and brought me back to my homeland, Lebanon, after the torment I endured in France. I want to apologize to him for everything. I abused his trust and bit the hand that was extended to me in kindness, I devoured the flesh of the man who fed me, gave me shelter in his home, and restored my dignity. Not only did I put the machine gun he gave me to dishonorable uses, I used the small Colt 7.5mm pistol he hid in his car in the assaults I committed. I hid the pistol in my room below the villa; it was under the fourth flagstone to the right of the entrance, wrapped in cloth and a sheet of plastic.

I would like to ask M. Michel, the attorney, to forgive me for my sins. I know that he has a good heart and that he will forgive me, but, here, I hesitated so much before deciding to confess. But this good, decent man must know the truth, that is my moral duty, I must tell him the truth, however difficult or cruel, so that he will know, and so that I will feel that I have repaid a small part of his favor. I slept with his wife, Mme Randa. She seduced me. I am not saying that it's her fault and that I'm innocent, because I'm a sinner too, and I believe the Devil tempted us both. And I ask M. Michel to forgive both her and me.

I thought at first that it was Mme Randa who betrayed me, because I decided not to continue this shameful and immoral thing we were doing. She threatened me, humiliated me, and forbade me from speaking with her daughter, Ghada. My relationship with Ghada was limited, I would buy books for her. Ghada was an excellent and refined girl. I bought her Agatha Christie novels. And our relationship never went further than discussing detective novels. I don't like detective novels because they scare me. To me they are exercises in scaring the reader, but Ghada found intellectual pleasure in them.

I ask M. Michel the attorney to forgive me, I ask him also to tend to his life and to the morals of his wife. This will ease my conscience for good, I am ready to receive the punishment I deserve, and I ask God to help M. Michel since his problem is greater than mine.

Yalo saw the face that was reading and felt a pang of sorrow. The truth he had not wanted to be revealed had been revealed. He did not know how his pen slipped and he wrote those things. He would tell the interrogator that he also repented what he had written and that he withdrew his confessions, but he was not prepared to write everything over again. He couldn't. The beautiful two-story villa must by now have become a hell, and the staircase connecting the salons on the ground floor to the bedrooms upstairs must have been wrecked by the footsteps of M. Michel, who just found out that his whole life had been a delusion.

"Who do you think you are, you piece of shit? First we confirmed the presence of the pistol and M. Michel showed us the gun permit and that's how he slipped out of the trap you had set for him. And then, you know what M. Michel did when he read these inept tales about Mme Randa?

He burst out laughing and said, 'What a shame, I knew something was wrong with that boy, but it's my fault because I took pity on him. What ingratitude!' And he laughed, and we all started laughing, and then he shouted, 'Ah.' He fell to the ground and turned red, muttering something incomprehensible. We took him to the hospital, and there they discovered that he had angina. But God saved him from your infamy, he had open-heart surgery and his condition is improving, thank God. He refuses to sue you because he never wants to hear your name again, and he begged us to close the file relating to him in this investigation. Are you happy now, you dog?"

"..."

"Answer!"

Yalo heard a moan coming from his shadow on the wall. The interrogator began to read passages taken from an investigation with men who had reported crimes Yalo had committed in the forest, after the newspapers reported that the suspect had been arrested. Yalo heard the interrogator tell him to rewrite everything, putting in the details given by those people, and to give explicit details about about the explosives network.

"Listen, you dog, to how you must write!" The interrogator picked up some pages and began to read.

"'My name is George bin As'ad Ghattas, my mother's name is Angèle, born in 1961 in Ballouna and living on my father's property, file number 20 Ballouna, Kesrouan. I hereby inform you that on May 16, 1991, at about ten thirty at night, I was driving in my car, a black Mercedes 220, license plate number 1713620, from the neighborhood of Christ the King in the direction of Ballouna. When I arrived at J'eita, I saw a young woman I did not know standing by the side of the road waiting for a car. I pulled up beside her and she got into the car with me, and she told me that her name was Georgette. I do not know her full name or where she lived. After a

< 234 >

conversation I parked the car in a neighborhood in Ballouna near the Greek Orthodox Church, and we began to interact inside the car. Approximately five minutes after I had parked in the area I mentioned, a person I do not know approached me and tapped at the car window on my side, pointing a military rifle, a Kalashnikov, in my face. He ordered me to give him all my money and jewelry. Afraid that he would harm me in some way, I immediately gave him one hundred eighty American dollars and thirty thousand Lebanese pounds, which I had in my possession. He also took from the girl accompanying me a pair of diamond-studded gold earrings. He began to threaten us and curse. He also stole the girl's watch, and when he saw that it wasn't valuable, he threw it from the car and began to threaten to kill me. He ordered me to get into the trunk of the car. I refused and a discussion ensued with this armed man. He also had pulled the girl out of the car and asked her to strip. When she refused, he put the muzzle of the gun in my stomach and said that he would kill me if the girl did not strip. So she began to scream that she didn't know me and didn't know anyone. He then dragged me from the car and kicked me in the testicles. I fell to the ground in pain, and saw the girl undressing, then everything went black because I lost consciousness. When I came to, my head hurt terribly. I saw the empty car. The girl wasn't in it and the armed man was no longer there, so I drove home, took two aspirin, and fell asleep. In the event I should see this person again, I would be able to recognize him. I may also inform you that he is tall, lean, about thirty years of age, and wearing a long black overcoat. When you showed me photographs of one Daniel Abel Abyad, I recognized the man who held me up.'

"Now do you understand how you should write?"

" . . . "

"Listen, you dog, I have here the accounts of all the people you attacked, raped, and robbed. Only they have gaps and I want you to fill in those

< 235 >

gaps. So – write down what happened when this guy was unconscious, you understand?"

Yalo said, he tried to say, that he was no longer able to write. He said that he didn't know how to fill in the gaps. He said that he'd confessed to everything. He said that he didn't know.

"And afterwards!" shouted the interrogator. "Afterwards, don't leave out the details about the explosives network, and don't go slandering all the women in the world, you understand?"

"I understand," said Yalo.

"So now fill in the gaps," said the interrogator.

"What gaps, sir?"

"About Georgette, and you kicked that guy, and what happened then."

"I did not kick anyone, sir."

"Here we go, he's starting to lie again! Watch it – we know everything."

"If you know everything, why do you need me to write? Just give it to me, sir, and I'll sign it, but please, please let this be over."

Yalo saw three men approaching the tall specter trying to protect his head with his hands. Then he saw how the specter rose up. It rose and did not feel pain, Yalo transcended pain. He rose higher and higher. He saw the world like a circle, and saw his soul circling inside him, and felt something stabbing him in the heart with one blow, and stayed there, where everything was a smothered moan, and smothered sobs, and smothered screams, and agony that penetrated the bone marrow and muscle membranes.

The interrogator ordered them to seat him on the bottle. The tall phantom heard the order but didn't understand what it meant. He saw the interrogator take a cola bottle, open it, then put his thumb in the opening and pull it out, making the sound of a bottle being opened. The interrogator drank from the neck of the bottle, then put it back on the table in disgust saying he didn't like cola except with ice.

"And you, how do you like it?"

". . ."

The interrogator approached him and ordered him to stand up. Yalo guided himself along the wall, but his hand slid down the wall and he fell again.

"Help him up," said the interrogator.

They stood him up, and two men supported him under his armpits to keep him up.

"Come over here," said the interrogator.

The two men advanced with Yalo, dragging him by his armpits

"I asked you how you like your cola. Tell me."

"Me?" said Yalo.

"Yes, you! Who do you think I'm talking to?!"

"I like it a lot," said Yalo.

"I know you like it, but how? Cold or warm?"

"Normal," said Yalo.

"Fine. Let him stand on his own."

The men left him, and Yalo felt the pain in his back and shoulders spreading down to his calves, and he said, "Ouch!" before finding his balance. The interrogator gave him the bottle and asked him to drink.

"Me?" said Yalo.

"I want you to drink the whole bottle so you won't be thirsty."

Yalo drank, and the reddish brown liquid ran down his gullet to his digestive tract, causing successive spasms. Yalo stopped swallowing because he felt the need to throw up. The interrogator shouted at him to raise the bottle again and drink it in one swallow. He felt the two men near him. The first seized his shoulders while the other grabbed the bottle and poured it down his throat all at once. Yalo was suffocating. He wanted to vomit. He realized suddenly that he was naked from the waist down, and the two men

< 237 >

were forcing him to sit down. He didn't see the empty bottle placed on the raised wooden bench they called "the throne." The first held the bottle while both of them sat him down on it. He was invaded with spasms that quickly eased as he let out screams from his throat and mouth, involuntarily. One scream and Yalo was on the throne. Shards of glass came out of the neck of the bottle and mingled with his blood, and he began to ascend, hearing only voices coming from distant places.

When Yalo awoke in his cell, he was a mass of agonies. He remembered that a doctor visited him and gave him a black ointment, he remembered the doctor telling him how that part of the body was very sensitive, as a major mass of nerves met there. He advised him to wash the wound.

Yalo lived with his long torment. His visits to the toilet were the most painful, because the constipation he had during the first days following his descent from the throne soon turned into diarrhea. His days became pure pain; he could neither sit nor sleep, not even on his stomach. Yalo mounted a column of light that penetrated him from below, and climbed it, and found himself far from the prison, writing as he pleased, not as the interrogator had ordered him to, but as he saw with his three eyes he had the feeling that he was perched on the highest place in the world.

I want to write the story of my life from start to finish.

My life is over. Now I understand, sir, that I was unable to write because I was clinging to a cord of hope. I was convinced it was possible, that something could change, maybe Shirin, M. Michel, or Mme Randa. Maybe one of them would take pity on me and help me rid myself of this torment.

Now it's over. Hope is gone, and it is up to Daniel George Jal'u, and Yalo Abel Abyad, to write his story from start to finish.

Yalo is on the throne, as if it were a minaret, and his three eyes are beams of light reaching the end of the story. He sits on the column like St. Simeon Stylites, who sat on his column a thousand years ago in Aleppo, the city of my father, George Jal'u, a city I have never seen except through the closed eyes of Master Salim Rizq.

Yes, sir, I see Yalo there and I envy him, I mean I envy myself, because my soul knows how to contact the souls of the dead and to talk to them, and discover that *vanitas vanitatum et omnia vanitas*. Man lives in a lie and believes in lies, and makes of his life a lie to add to all the others.

I write now about Yalo, whom you elevated atop a bottle called "the throne." Yalo is on the throne, like the King of the Dead. Yes, sir, I see him dead, and the dead do not write because they are dying.

You were wrong to ask him to write the story of his life. Yalo cannot write because he has gone to another place, where they do not write, where they have no need to write. I, Daniel, am writing, and will write everything you want about him and about me and about everyone. But Yalo, no. I want to be frank with you and say that Yalo left me and went far away. I am body and he is spirit. I suffer and he soars. I got down off the bottle while he still sits on the throne.

I see him before me. I approach him, question him, but he doesn't respond. He says that his words no longer understand his words. He mixes Arabic with Syriac with languages I do not know. So how can I understand him?

I write in Arabic, not only because you asked me to, but because I am an Arab. For even if George Jal'u of Aleppo is not my father, Elias al-Shami of Damascus is. There is no third possibility. I lean toward the second option, even though this is an issue of no importance to me. My mother kept the secret from me. She said many times that she would tell me something, but she was afraid it would shock me. Every time she began the story she would stop with the disappearance of her husband or with his departure, and when I asked about the secret she would yawn. I never knew a woman who yawned like that; she hid the secret in her open mouth, which she would cover with the palm of her hand, then she'd walk through the house bent over as if she were looking for something she had lost.

I know that my poor mother was no longer able to see her image in the mirror because she wanted to erase her secret. She thought that her life had been in vain because Mr. Elias had not proposed marriage to her. But when I asked her, she said that she had not wanted him. She said that she wished he had asked her to marry him so that she could have refused him, but he never asked. How strange, Gaby – is it possible that the sorrow of your life was that you were not given an opportunity for refusal?

Yalo did not pay much attention to his mother and her problems because

< 240 >

he was seized with the idea of leaving Lebanon. We must understand him, he is a victim, sir, and a victim will become even fiercer than the torturer when he finally gets the chance. The war was Yalo's chance. I agree with you, the civil war and the chaos are detestable, but imagine with me the situation of this kid whose father was his grandfather, and his mother his sister; imagine with me what the war could do to him. The war was his chance, but he lost it, and instead of straightening himself out as many others did, he dropped everything as it was and left for France.

I do not think that my mother's tragedy was because of Elias al-Shami; Elias was the result. For the cause, we have to look to Cohno Ephraim, a maniac obsessed with delusions and the idea of death. Gaby lived with him after the death of his wife, and became his daughter, his wife, and his mother. Gaby knew Syriac but preferred to speak Arabic. She told me that Syriac was like a rosebud that blossomed and became the Arabic language. She would close her five fingers into a fist and then open them as she told her only son not to cry when his grandfather beat him for not remembering Syriac words.

Yalo fell in love with Shirin the day he met her on the mountain. I prefer to say that he met her because I do not like to use the word rape, which you have imposed on the poor guy. Yalo did not rape Shirin, because a man is not capable of loving a woman he has raped. Rape, sir, is an abominable thing. Ask me, because I know. Yalo knows the meaning of rape because he engaged in it. I did it and regretted it, but not with Shirin. I loved Shirin because she reordered my soul and my body.

Gaby did not believe her son when he informed her that he decided to quit his studies for good. She thought it was just a whim. But the lad stamped his feet nine months after the death of his grandfather, and said "That's it!"

My mother lived like a lost soul in her new house, after the war forced

< 241 >

her to move from West Beirut to East Beirut. And there, the outskirts of East Beirut, Yalo decided to join the war. He never returned home without smelling of blood. Gaby lived alone. She wended her way around the houses in her new neighborhood to revive her career as a seamstress. Elias al-Shami had vanished from existence; she didn't look for him, but she asked around and was told that he had bought a house in Ballouna along with others from their old neighborhood who had all left Beirut.

Yalo's story, sir, has a name – war.

How can I describe to you what happened to Yalo after M. Michel Salloum in Paris offered him a way back to Lebanon and a job as a guard at his villa in Ballouna? At the time, Yalo saw this village as a word written on the forehead of the middle-aged tailor. He saw the specter of Elias al-Shami that had occupied his youth with the smell of his false teeth, a smell like that of rotted mint, and he was afraid. Yalo wanted to refuse M. Michel's offer, but he had no other option.

But the truth, sir, the truth that only God knows, is that my memory is distorted and I don't know. Did Yalo hear from his mother that Elias al-Shami went to live in Ballouna, or did he hear the name of this Kesrouan village for the first time from M. Michel? But for some obscure reason, he associated that Kesrouan village with the tailor, that was the association in his head. His mother gave up the tailor when she fled West Beirut for the al-Mrayyeh neighborhood in Ain Rummaneh; she said that she thought that he had gone to Kesrouan, but it wasn't certain she had actually named the village. So why had Yalo seen the name of the village written on the man's forehead? Why had his feet led him to commit his first offense one month after starting his new job?

I should clarify things so that we understand what happened. When Yalo returned to Lebanon with Michel Salloum, and lived in his little cottage,

< 242 >

he lived his life at night, because night was his cover. In daylight he felt naked, and his long black overcoat was not enough to hide him. He went out during the day only once, in order to get the equipment necessary to fix Mme Randa's wooden chair. The mistake which was the beginning of all mistakes was the one he made in church. No, sir, the mistakes did not start with Shirin. All he did with Shirin was to be totally naked under the light of day, as if he were unaware of the dangers surrounding him. For love blinds and leaves on our faces tracks of foolishness. The mistake started in church. What made him go that Sunday morning, wearing his long black overcoat, to the Orthodox Church in Ballouna, to look for Elias al-Shami? Had he really wanted to kill him as he claimed when he told Shirin about his love of killing? Of course not. Yalo lied to Shirin all the time. He lied and believed his own lies. I swear to you that he lied, which is why there was no need for the torture party he endured when he was tied to a chair for three days without having the natural right all of God's creatures have, from animals to humans, to discharge his need. That torture was useless. I lied to Shirin. I told her that I went into the church carrying a gun and a hand grenade because I wanted to shoot Elias al-Shami then throw the grenade at his corpse to blow it into pieces. Yalo was not carrying a pistol or a hand grenade when he went into the church and drew a few looks. Entering the church was his first mistake, then this mistake was linked to the confessions of Mr. George Ghattas, a resident of Ballouna, about a man wearing a long black overcoat whom he had previously seen in the church. He suspected him of being the same man who attacked him when he was in his car with a woman named Georgette. It never occurred to Yalo that a resident of Ballouna would fool around in the forest of the town where he lived. But what would bring someone like that to church? He fooled around, and then came with his wife to mass? What shamelessness! said Yalo, before receiving

< 243 >

a barrage of slaps and kicks. Truly shameless, sir. What do you want with M. Ghattas? I am ready to confess to everything, because things no longer have any meaning.

The interrogation about the church was trivial, and forcing Yalo to confess that he intended to kill Elias al-Shami and blow up the church was meaningless. Yalo went to the church to see the man who might be his father, but he saw nothing. He went into the church when the priest was moving around with his censer among the worshippers, so all he saw was smoke. He began to cough and his eyes teared up before he made the sign of the cross and left.

Yalo lied to Shirin, because – how can I say it – because love makes a man talk. Love is a fountainhead of talk. Without talk love does not exist. In order to keep talking, Yalo had to make up stories. Shirin spoke only rarely, which forced Yalo to perform alone on the high wire of talk. He made up stories for her so that love would continue. For talk is the bed in which lovers sleep. That is the truth, and that's the reason for the ambiguous situation in which the interrogation took place.

Yalo, up above, did not respond. His three eyes saw in all directions: north, south, east, and west, the past and the future. The future was clear to him: it was death, and Yalo needed no more than a small leap to get there, the Kingdom of Death. The past was a problem. The past frightened him and frightens me because events intermingled so strangely. He says yesterday and means twenty years ago, and he says a long time ago and means a week ago. It's this state of loss that I am experiencing and he is experiencing. Yalo's loss did not begin on the throne where he sits now, his loss began when he was not covered by the night.

Yalo lived in the night of Ballouna, not because he was afraid, but because he was looking for safety. Even if he was afraid, what was the crime? It was his right to be afraid. Who among you, sir, does not get frightened? It was

Yalo's right to be frightened or upset because he stole money from the Georges Aramouni Barracks and left for France. That was the truth he did not tell M. Michel Salloum. He bathed in the residence in Paris and shaved his beard, put on clean, pressed clothes, drank a glass of French red wine, and told M. Michel Salloum that his friend had stolen the money and fled. The gentleman laughed and said, "A thief who steals from a thief is like someone inheriting from his father. Good for him!" Yalo tried to explain that he was not a thief, but M. Michel did not want to listen and gave the impression that he knew everything but decided to close his eyes.

The truth was that Yalo was covered by the night because he did not feel safe. The war, when it ended, left an immense void in his life. The war locked its doors, and the vague fear of the fighters started. The war was like a great barricade they hid behind, and when the barricade fell, every one of us felt naked. It is very difficult for a human being to find himself naked. Madame Randa taught me that. She got naked when her lust began to gleam in her eyes; she stood before the mirror, contemplating her tan skin that shimmered with lust. And when everything was over, she covered herself with the blanket and refused to get out of bed until Yalo had left the room because she was ashamed of her nakedness. We were like Mme Randa, sir – when the war was over, we felt ashamed of our nakedness, and we went looking for cover.

No, sir, I was not afraid, because the war was over and there was no one to hold me accountable for the stolen money. I had stolen it and then it was stolen from me, no one could accuse me of a thing. I covered myself with the night because I felt naked, not out of fear. Even with Mme Randa, Yalo ended his relationship with her fully clothed. The relationship ended as it began, with clothes. The first time she took everything off, but he only took off his pants and found himself shooting inside her very quickly. That day Mme Randa stood before the mirror contemplating the beauty of her nakedness, and Yalo discovered the difference between a cooked woman and a raw woman. He told her she was a woman cooked and she burst out laughing because she thought he was joking. Yalo smelled the fragrance of sun and spices and he saw how a woman ripened in her desire. That's how he started the process of classifying women, which he never told anyone about.

Now, sir, even as he is suspended between the earth and the sky, the rapture runs through Yalo's veins when he remembers the difference between a cooked woman and a raw woman. This theory was devised by my grandfather, God rest his soul. No, sir, my grandfather had no women, for he was a man riddled with complexes, but he divided food into two categories: meat and vegetables. After giving up the eating of all variations of meat, he assigned vegetables to three categories: defective, uncertain, and perfect. The defective do not ripen to be fit for consumption until they are cooked over the fire, like zucchini or beans or okra, and so on. The uncertain also ripen by fire even though they can be eaten raw, like eggplant, spinach, fava beans, and chickpeas, etc. As to the perfect, they ripen in the sun and need no flame, because they have interior fire. These were all varieties of the finest fruit, grapes, figs, and tomatoes. My grandfather chose the perfect vegetables, and he ended his life eating nothing but raw vegetables. He even gave up eating bread. He began to shrink, he got very thin, his bones grew as pourous as clay, and his flesh grew as rough as bone. He died with the intention of becoming a clay figure, that is, earth baked by the sun.

These are digressions, and there would be no need to bring them into the story of Yalo's life had his grandfather's culinary theory not played a decisive role in defining the young man's view of women. I can affirm that one of the causes of his voyeurism was his desire to see cooked women. Yalo's theory did not have the same symmetry that his grandfather's theory had. The *cohno* hated the cooked and preferred the raw ripened by the sun. Yalo preferred the cooked. Cooked women ripened over the fire of their desire. The raw ones had no fire in them. What he hated most were the efforts raw women made to ripen themselves artificially using makeup or silicone, which had become so prevalent in Beirut after the war.

Yalo had mulled over his grandfather's words at length, and in the end adopted that view himself without realizing it. Cooked women did not require external fire; the sun of their desire sufficed to ripen them, and in this they resembled perfect vegetables, which were ripened by their inner fire.

When Yalo found a cooked woman, he was struck with an irresistible desire, and in those cases he did not rob or in any way insult the man escorting her, but showed a resolute desire. The other man understood that he must retreat, otherwise his life would be in danger.

So I can say for sure that when Yalo found himself with Shirin – and Shirin was a raw woman in every sense of the word – he felt no desire. The gray-haired man fled, abandoning the young, light-skinned girl, thus forcing Yalo to take her to his cottage. In the cottage all his and his grandfather's theories about fruit and women dropped away. He smelled the fragrance of the incense coming off the girl's outstretched arms, grew intoxicated, and entered the passionate unknown that led him to his miserable end.

I question him, but his face turns away as if he is living in another world. Once he wanted to ask Mme Randa her opinion about men and whether they could be divided into two kinds, the raw and the cooked, but he was embarrassed so didn't ask.

Yalo did not give up his theory. He considered Shirin to be an exception, and believed that women, too, categorized men the same way. Of course, I believed that I belonged in the cooked category, and I wanted to hear that

< 247 >

from a woman. Yalo didn't bring up the subject with Shirin because she forbade him to talk during sex. Even when they went to the seashore and ate fish and he put his arm around her waist so that she could lean back to await his kiss, even at that moment when he felt on top of the whole world, he didn't ask, afraid that Shirin would get upset. For the young girl was vulnerable and easily hurt.

How had this angelic creature become his adversary?

In the interrogation room, Shirin wore a mask of cruelty and indifference. The tenderness was gone from her eyes, and her small nose, which ran as much as her eyes teared, was like a thorn planted in her face.

Why did her nose suddenly get bigger?

His grandfather, God rest his soul, complained in his final days of his nose and ears. Every part of him had shrunk, he was shorter, and his skin hung on his bones because he was so emaciated, but his nose grew bigger, and his ears grew wider and longer. He gazed with disgust at his face in the mirror. Once he said that he wished he could trim his nose and ears the way people trimmed their fingernails. That frightened me. I, who had never been afraid in my whole life, was afraid of the *cohno's* nose and ears because he said that they were the marks of death. A person's body parts stopped growing, except for the nose and ears. Death was a mercy, for if a man kept living, he would turn into just a long nose and two giant ears, that is, a cross between an elephant and a donkey. God forbid.

I believe, sir, that I have explained the circumstances that drove Yalo to make his mistakes and commit his crimes. Now I will try to write the whole story from start to finish. Consider me to be his voice, which he lost when he sat on his throne. He is there, not complaining or moaning. I am positive that he is experiencing a tremendous moment no one has experienced before, except those who have undergone the gravest tortures.

Do not say that he gets no credit because he climbed his column by compulsion. It is true that you forced me to drain the cola bottle and sit on it. But Yalo's achievement was his decision not to get off it. I got off; he didn't. I am in pain; he is not. My pains are great, sir, because fire burned the gate of my body. But I am convinced of the need for us to write the whole story so that we can remove ourselves from this predicament.

< 249 >

I want to write, but I am lost.

When I write about my life, must I write about my grandfather, my mother, and my father, or about my life that concerns me alone? I do not know. You want everything, especially the stories of Ballouna, the women, and the explosives. I think the story should begin with those events. But I cannot. Because ever since I . . . since when? Since the cat sack, no, since the bastinado, no, since the throne, no . . . since the torture I experienced, I can't distinguish between the beginning and the end. By the way, I can only congratulate you on your original methods of torture and your ability to extract a suspect's confessions, as if you were extracting his soul. That is, he feels as if his soul is leaving his body and he is back in his mother's belly, which makes him confess everything. Though the torture is violent, the bodily signs of it vanish quickly, leaving only the spiritual traces that make you feel that your soul is about to leave you. I congratulate you, sir, especially for the bottle. The bottle is the conclusion after which there is no conclusion, because it's long, I mean it makes time long, even endless. I sat on the bottle for about a thousand hours, or a thousand times longer than that. You say that it was just half an hour, and you are right, because you know more than I do, because you wear accurate Swiss watches on your wrists. Me, alas, no. But the bottle changed the meaning of time. I mean, I

< 250 >

felt as if I were in eternity, that time was frozen, and that I was living the last moments of my life; yet that my life was long – never-ending. I wanted it to end so that the pain would be over, but it stopped ending. That is eternity. I will not mention the pains that are still with me even now, especially when I go to the toilet. It is not polite to talk about these things. But the truth, and you want the truth, the truth is that what frightens me most is my feeling that I need a toilet. There I go back to experiencing eternity again, and I smell my own smell, and I feel that pain has a smell. Yes, pain has a smell, and its smell is shit. That is what I feel and what I smell.

But I am very lucky, I feel that my grandfather's prayers for me were not in vain. One of the prison guards here told me that many suspects died from the bottle because it broke in their backsides and they got gangrene in their large intestines, and all their insides grew inflamed. Thank God that did not happen to me. On the contrary, the bottle helped me a great deal. How can I explain to you – I don't know. But your experience with prisoners must have made you capable of understanding what I am writing. For I was not the first to have ascended the throne of spiral glass, and of course will not be the last.

When I ascended the throne and the pain pierced me from bottom to top and from top to bottom, I was sure that I would die. I mounted it and death began, that is, I felt death. Death is violent and has a sound; something explodes inside you, and you hear a sound no one else does, and after the sound your body tingles and you sense that you are being dragged beyond white sleep. You are not sleeping, but you float beyond sleep. And then it's over – Stop. Everything is dark, and it's over. That is exactly how it happened with me. I am not lying. I am telling the truth, sir. Something snapped and I was beyond sleep, I mean, sleeping yet not sleeping, and then I woke up.

You took me into eternity and made me understand the meaning of life,

< 251 >

because I tasted death, and drank it, from the top and from the bottom. I want to say, sir, that through all of these experiences, when I reached the essence of things, I saw him before me. Would you believe, sir, that my grandfather, who was also my father, was waiting for me everywhere? What did I want with him and his absurd story? But death, sir, when death approaches, it imposes its conditions. Death means that we experience things we never experienced, and the stories we have heard become facts. When I approached death, I became my grandfather and my grandfather's grandfather, and all the descendants of men. I speak now from experience, so my mission is very difficult. I cannot write you the stories of all mankind that I know, but I wouldn't know how to write them. Therefore I ask the respected interrogator to be a little patient with me. I will be brief and get to the heart of the subject you are looking for, but I saw another heart, just as essential, that I cannot ignore, so I will write it with the fewest words possible in order to be truthful to myself and to my soul suspended there on the throne of death.

When I thought that the story had to begin with my grandfather, I hated it, for I did not love my grandfather – he embodied cowardice and selfishness. My grandfather was afraid of everything, perhaps because his conscience reproached him so much after the death of my grandmother Marie Samaho, God rest her soul, of whom it was said, died because of him. My grandmother died before I was born, which was why my grandfather was imposed on my father – or my mother's husband – to come and live with him in his house. I believe that the husband couldn't bear it from the very first day, so he packed his things and fled the unbearable atmosphere of that house. He left because he never once felt that he was in a home of his own. The bed was not his bed and the life was not his life, and the woman was not his woman. My grandfather claimed that he had discovered by chance that my father, or my mother's husband, was not Syriac but an Arab from Aleppo belonging to the Melkite Greek Catholic sect. Fine, what does that change? Where is the crime? And why did the *cohno* not discover the truth before his daughter married the man? My grandfather killed my father and trampled his shadow. Do you know, sir, that I do not possess a photo of my father? He was even torn out of the wedding pictures. Nothing remains of him – even his name is gone, because I bear my grandfather's name. My identity card says that I am from the Abyad clan. So what am I supposed to say when even now I don't know the difference between a person being Syriac or Arab. A person is a person, and we all come from Adam, and Adam came from dust. So why all these tricks? I do not understand my grandfather's pains that made his mouth a graveyard of Christ's language. What kind of foolishness is that? What, Christ does not understand Arabic, Greek, or Latin?

My grandfather's fear cannot be described. My mother said that it came from his childhood, as a result of the massacre that was committed in the village of Ain Ward at the beginning of the twentieth century. But I am not sure of anything. Perhaps my grandmother's death was the cause. I heard the news of my grandmother from other people, not from my mother. My mother spoke only rarely of her mother, but I sensed the presence of a dark shadow hanging over the silent relations between my mother and grandfather. Suddenly silence would fall between them and they would converse without words. I understood that true dialogue between people goes on without talking. Words do not express things – they cover them over. Now, sir, I understand why writing is difficult for me, because what is being asked of me is that I cover up the story, and here I feel deficient, for whoever wants to write must possess a double text, he must dub speech over the silence. As to when speech is your life, you speak in silence.

I understand, sir, that you are asking a man to write the story of his life for the purpose of ethics and retribution. But what is the use of my story? And why am I telling my grandfather's story instead of my own? Is it because the *cohno* killed his wife? Is it true that Abel Abyad, known as Ephraim, killed his wife, and that was the cause of his fear of everything?

The *cohno* used to say that a man's body was a temple of fear. God created for the soul a body of clay to calm its fear of fear or of God. But the corporeal temple became a new cause of fear, because of the original sin. Man died because he sinned, and death is his greatest fear. We fear the body, therefore we must dissolve it before it dissolves our souls. We must restore it to its clay state and not be overly solicitous of it, see to it as a potter cares for his clay, by watering it and setting it in the sun. The body needs only water and a few vegetables cooked by the sun. All else is vanity.

In the beginning, the *cohno* tried to defend himself. He said that he didn't want the woman to suffer. But when suffering came after the disease spread to her bones, he didn't know what to do, and had to get help from doctors. The woman was taken to the Greek hospital in Achrafieh, where she died amidst doses of morphine, which failed to ease her suffering.

Yalo did not understand the silence between the *cohno* and his daughter – which constituted a dialogue between them – until he heard their neighbor, Mme Mary Rose, threaten her husband by saying that she would let him die the way the *cohno* let his woman die, without getting treatment for her. Yalo imagined the scene and saw it through his mother's eyes, and understood how a person could be capable of reading that which had been erased.

When his grandfather described the massacre that took place in Tur Abdin, he said that he could read what had been erased. We have to learn how to read words that have been erased, that is our story, we, a people whose story is erased and its language erased, so if we do not learn how to read what has been erased, all will be lost.

In the past, I did not believe the *cohno* could read books erased by time and torn by history. But now I am beginning to believe him, because I have seen how Yalo read silence and erased words.

< 254 >

My mother began to speak erased words before her image in the mirror was erased. She used silence so that the *cohno* would understand that she knew.

Yes, sir, it seems that my grandfather left his wife to die. He took her to the doctor who diagnosed cancer in her left breast, but instead of checking her into the hospital to remove the affected breast, he took her home, bought a box of aspirin, and let her die. He told his daughter that there was no medicine for cancer and that it was better that the doctors not be allowed to cut up her body; his only concern was that she not suffer.

But she suffered so much!

Gaby did not use that expression, but she looked at her father and he read it in her eyes, and his tongue lost the power of speech. That day, Gaby invented the language of silence, and tried to use it to address Elias al-Shami, but the tailor did not possess the gift of silence. Only Yalo learned it, and his relationship with his mother proceeded in silence. He came home and read her sorrow, solitude, and love for him in her eyes, and replied, without speaking, that he wanted to live his life and could do nothing for her.

Gaby lost the taste for food. She told her son that the taste had stayed behind in the old house in Mseitbeh and that she had been unable to cook because she no longer could distinguish flavors. All foods now tasted the same to her, all having the flavor of bulgur. "That's how my father was at the end, and now maybe I'm at my end, and can no longer feel the taste of my mouth."

Gaby did not tell her son how she answered her father when he said he had lost all taste, because she was afraid she might anger the *cohno* in his grave. For the *cohno* was greatly insulted when his daughter answered that he yearned for Kurdish flavors because he was a Kurd. Yalo did not know why his grandfather was so sensitive about the subject of his Kurdish origin. For his grandfather, when he came to Beirut fleeing his uncle in Al-Qamishli, spoke Arabic and Kurdish, and became fluent in classical Syriac only here. He said that he had forgotten Kurdish, as if it had been erased from his memory, even though he had spoken it when the Kurdish mullah came to their house in Mseitbeh, to witness his son's rejection of his heritage.

Was this story true? Or did my mother make it up? I don't know.

What has been asked of me is simple, I must write out the details of the crimes I committed, with a short introduction about my growing up and my experiences in the war.

I am trying, sir, to exclude the details that do not concern the respected interrogator or do not serve justice. Therefore I will concentrate on just two points: the crimes in Ballouna and the crimes related to the explosives, as you asked me to. But when I ask Yalo I find him silent. So what should I do? I ask him a question and his silence answers me with another question. Is that possible, sir? If everyone spoke they way he does, there would be no more speaking!

I asked him, and he asked me, whether the crimes in the forest were more serious than his grandfather's crimes.

Yalo did not kill anyone. He was capable, if he wished, to kill whomever he liked and bury his victims in the forest, and no one would have asked any questions. If he'd killed Shirin, would she ever have filed a complaint with the police? Or would Dr. Said al-Halabi have had the nerve to go to the police station to file a complaint against a young man who had caught him in suspicious circumstances with a girl younger than his children?

Now Yalo was a criminal, which was natural, and his grandfather was a saint in the eyes of people, which was also natural, but where was justice?

I was found out, sir, because I had not killed anyone, while my grand-father became a saint because he killed. Do you call that justice? I don't think that we can justify the *cohno*'s crime as being well-intentioned, just as Elias al-Shami's crime against my mother cannot be justified by his claim that his wife was ill and he didn't want to offend her.

Does my mother have to die for his wife's sake? Did my grandmother die because the *cohno* was ambitious and wanted to be an archbishop?

And then what was my father's story? My grandfather claimed that Mr. Salim Rizq said my father was not Syriac, but an Aleppan. So what? I worked three summers with Master Salim and his son, the engineer Wajih, and no one told me anything like that. I think my grandfather seized on this story about my father because he knew, deep in his heart, that I was the son of Elias al-Shami. The tailor was from Damascus, and Damascus is not so far from Aleppo. That is how I became a son of the Aleppan, or in other words, the son of al-Shami, the Damascene. But this is not the question. The question is how George Jal'u agreed to marry a girl who was not a virgin. What did he do when the virginal blood did not flow? Or did Gaby wound herself and cry out in false pain so that the man would have the impression that he had opened her? Did she shout like a whore to give the impression that she was a virgin? I do not say this because I have any-thing against non-virgins, I am convinced that there is just one virgin in all human history, the Virgin Mary, Mother of God, glory be to her. There is no need for virginity because Mary suffered for all women. But Gaby's false virginity led George Jal'u into a trap. The man lived in the *cohno*'s house like a stranger. Even sleeping with his wife was done secretly and quietly, as if Gaby were not his wife, as if she were her father's wife. He told her that she was her father's wife before turning his back on her and vanishing, which proved to be correct in the sense that I too became the son of her father. But how could the *cohno* register me as his son, bearing in mind that his wife, that is, my actual grandmother, who is my mother according to my identity card, died before my mother's marriage? The only explanation is that my grandfather went and dated my birth before the death of his wife. That is, he committed forgery, which is punishable under the law. It is most likely that I was not born in 1961, as officially recorded, but in 1962. That would explain my backwardness in school and my stammering as a boy, and much more . . . but, how did he succeed at that? Didn't the identity registration official notice that he was sixty years older then I was? So, how? Was he the prophet Zechariah as he claimed, when he told everyone that he was struck dumb three days before my birth? Where did he come up with this criminal fantasy?

I said that I hated my grandfather but that is not true. How could I hate him with his body like a clay figure and his failing memory? He is the spirit returned to the source, the spirit indifferent to stories. I will tell the story from start to finish. The beginning is over there, with my grandfather, who, returning to his beginnings, had stopped eating and had begun living out his deficient memories. At this point in his life he told me everything, but I did not believe a thing. How could we believe a crazy man who tied a rooster by its feet to a fig tree and then killed it, because the way it mounted hens disgusted him? The story was unbelievable, sir, and I am not asking you to believe it.

We lived in Mseitbeh, in a small house with a big garden. My mother raised chickens for their eggs. We owned one rooster and a dozen or so chickens, I don't remember exactly how many, but I do remember how they died, and that's the story.

One day, my mother came home to the surprising sight of our rooster tied up to the tree, humiliated. It was a huge rooster with yellow feathers and colored wings, and its crowing deafened the world. She didn't ask who tied up the rooster because she knew. She went to the fig tree and untied him. The rooster surged up and laid into the hens, and what happened happened. I heard the crowing of the rooster and ran to the yard and saw an unforgettable sight. The rooster was screwing all the hens at once. I don't remember how old I was, perhaps I was eight, and of course I counted my age by my identity card, being unaware of my grandfather's forgery, which I discovered only here in prison, thanks to your plan to make me write the story of my life, which has allowed me to remember things I never remembered existed. Therefore, sir, I offer you this thought, for writing is the only way to remember, otherwise men's lives would be limited to the present and they would live without a memory, like animals. I discovered that when I write, the gates of memory open before me. I know that you want me to write a short story, so I will be brief, but I am amazed at my memory, which opens up and takes on the memories of my mother, grandfather, father, Tony Atiq, Alexei, Mario, Shirin, and all the people I've known in my miserable life. My greatest surprise was ink. For ink flows involuntarily. Ink does not come from somewhere else. Ink flows from between my fingers, without stuttering, as if I were the cuttlefish that Shirin consumed. Now Shirin consumes me, and I see her gobbling the cuttlefish that feels terrible pains from my bottom to the bottom of the world. Ink spills from between my fingers and teaches me Arabic. I am writing now because Jurji Zaidan taught me language and writing. Had it not been for him, I would have been like so many who do not know the beauty and magic of language. My mother brought the al-Hilal novels from Elias al-Shami and I read them. Master Elias was infatuated with history books and with my mother, so he gave her the books as gifts, but she didn't read them. In reading I found a distraction from my solitude. At first it was difficult, then the lines that resembled anthills transformed into words and penetrated my head. This was what was behind my success in Arabic in school. I have asked the guard here to bring me books, but all he brings me is the Gospel. I've nothing against the Gospel, but I wanted the books of Jurji Zaidan for inspiration. I mean, it is true that the story I am writing now is not historical, because Yalo is not one of the heroes of history, yet he is a hero; I mean, there is some heroism in his life. One hundred years from now this story will be part of history. But fine, I will try to write what I know, without forgetting my debt to Jurji Zaidan. He revealed to me that the Ghassanid kings had been Syriac, that is, they were Jacobites and Monophysites. When I learned this fact, I teased my grandfather, telling him that the Arabs were Syriac and so there was no need to blame me for my origins, and that I would not study Syriac because the Ghassanids prayed in Arabic and their faith was righteous. When he did not answer and tried the silent treatment on me, I said that he had lost his power. At that, the *cohno* seized on the word *haylo*, he asked me what *haylo* meant. "*Haylo means haylo,*" I told him. "Listen," he said. "*Qadishat Eluho, qadishat Hayltuno, qadishat lo yo muto.* Translate that into the language of the Ghassanids, like a good boy." So I translated it, though the truth is that I didn't know how to translate, but I knew the meaning of the sentence because we prayed it every Sunday in church. I said, "Most Holy is God, Most Holy is the All-Powerful, Most Holy is the Eternal." He said that *hayltunofo* came from the Syriac word *haylo*, which meant power. "Now, you are using a Syriac word without even knowing it. Half the words people use are Syriac. Those Ghassanids did not know what they were saying." And he began to enumerate the words that were the names of the months, from Qilaya to Soka, Nahlo, and so on . . . he could find nothing to defend himself and his dead language save admonitions that supported my mother's theory about the flower that had bloomed.

The flower was now blooming in the ink covering my pages. The flower was blooming inside my body, which rose with Yalo and embraced the souls of the dead and sympathized with my mother. Sir, I must take her back to her house in Mseitbeh. If am not sentenced to death because of the affair of the explosives, which I will tell you about in detail, and I get out of prison, the first thing I do will be to take my mother home so that she may live, dignified and honored. Then I will go back to my first job, dovetailing wood. I thought that I had forgotten the craft, but *ta'shiq* is like swimming, it is not forgotten. You must know how to divide wood into two types, male and female, and join them as a man joins a woman. Nails kill the spirit of wood, whereas dovetailing returns its life by marrying it to itself and restores the fluid that flowed out when the trees were cut. Engineer Wajih told me that wood never dies because *ta'shiq* gives it a new eternal life.

Instead of getting upset with his son, Master Salim offered himself to solve the problem, a sign of blind Mr. Salim's fine moral qualities – he was Cohno Ephraim's opposite. Truly, how was it they were friends? Instead of Salim's tying his son to the trunk of the fig tree, he took it upon himself to defend him, then tried to save the situation, which won him only ridicule. As to my grandfather, when he saw that my mother had released the rooster, he shouted that he had tied up the rooster because it was insatiable. We endured three days of quarreling, him tying it up and her freeing it, saying that he was just jealous. On the third day, my mother came home to find the rooster tottering around, tied to the fig tree. Its yellow feathers were dropping, and the rooster was dying. She asked him what he had done, and he said he had beaten the rooster not in order to kill it but to teach it a lesson and temper its sexual voracity.

The rooster learned its lesson for good and gave you its life. The rooster died alone in a corner of the yard. Early the next morning, we awoke to strange sounds. The terrified hens were swarming around the rooster's corpse, screeching. Yes, the hens were screeching as if they were hoarse roosters, and they did not stop screeching until my mother went down to the yard, took away the rooster's corpse, and buried it in the garden.

After the death of the rooster began the misery of the hens who turned the garden of our house into a slaughterhouse. The slaughter started after the death of the rooster because the hens began getting dizzy, tottering around, and falling to the ground. Had anyone besides me seen a hen in love stumble in her walk, then spread her wings to regain her balance so that she would not fall? I began to fear my mother's return home in the evening because that meant that a hen would be slaughtered. My mother would go down to the garden, sleeves rolled up, grab a hen and break its neck, then finish it off with a knife and throw it down, shaking off the blood. My mother's pretext was that the hens were sick and would die of sorrow over the rooster, so they had to be slaughtered before they died and would be inedible as carrion.

For a whole month we ate nothing but hen, and my grandfather peered into the chicken broth and grumbled about the globules of fat spread over the surface. Now I have come to understand my grandfather's position, who abstained from eating meat, given the rancid smell of blood. The sole embodiment of my solidarity with my grandfather came directly after his death, when I stopped drinking wine for good, because wine reminded me of the smell of blood. Now I know that I was wrong, that abstaining from wine and drinking arak instead really damaged my stomach.

Shirin loved wine, but I forced her to drink arak, and that was a mistake. I made so many mistakes with Shirin, as if a beast had awakened inside me, and I interpreted things as I chose. I understood her fear of me as a lover's fear of commitment, and her refusal to eat as the contentment that comes along with passion. That's what happened with me when I was in love with Madame Randa. I do not deny that I loved her – that woman deprived me of my right mind, and all because of the calf of her leg which appeared and disappeared in the slit of her long cloak. I wanted her every day, night and day. I waited for her and I burned. I was literally burning when M. Michel came home from Paris. That was when she dealt me a card and began ignoring me altogether, her voice grew flat and she started treating me like a servant. She'd put her nose in the air as if she smelled something bad while I stood before her like a dog.

My intention was not to steal, sir. I was searching for my self, which this woman had taken possession of. By coincidence I discovered lovers' cars, and there I found my entertainment and consolation. I am not a dog willing to accept that kind of treatment. Yes, I accepted the unacceptable when I was in the shadow of the tawny calf of her leg which was damp with the sweat of lust. With the car game in the forest, things began to change. My life changed in the forest, and gradually I began to move away from Madame. But, may Almighty God be praised, my lust for her ended only when I fell in love with Shirin.

I know, sir, that you want three things from me: what I did in Paris, the women in the Ballouna forest, and the explosives gang I was connected to.

I will tell you Yalo's stories in detail. I want this story to be a warning for those who might need one. So when I sit in the chair before the table holding the fountain pen to write, I feel fright. For this ink which fills the pages is my soul. I want my soul to flow. I am not like the cuttlefish, which uses its ink to deceive fishermen and predatory fish. I don't want to deceive anyone. I know that in the end you will cook me in this ink, but I will go to my fate with perfect acceptance.

I do not fear death, sir, nor do I use my ink to deceive you. But I would be lying if I confessed to what you are demanding of me. Would you agree to my leaving some pages blank for you to write whatever you want there, with my acceptance of everything you write? Of course I will not do that because I do fear your anger.

After Yalo viewed the world from that steep height, it became unthinkable to take him down from his throne to torture him. I tried to mollify him. I told him not to be afraid, because I would write everything, and from now on would not allow him to taste physical torture.

I knelt before the window where he sat in exaltation and asked him to help me a little. I cannot write these things by myself. Excavating a skull hurts, and makes you incapable of putting words in useful sentences.

The *cohno* knew that, so he took words just as they were and copied them. He copied the odes that Ephraim the Syriac had written, or the Syriac poems that Hanno al-Ainwardi wrote to eulogize the people led to the slaughter, and his blood became a long line stretching to the border of the heavens.

The *cohno* wrote a line of red blood in black ink, and said that when he copied odes and Syriac poems he became the author without any harm to the words or phrases. I wish I had before me a book telling Yalo's story so that I could copy it and be done with all this. I said to myself that my soul must remember, but every time it remembered, it forgot, and I discovered that I had to remember all over again, and that I was still far from the essence of what I had to write, that is, a frank confession of my crimes, a statement of readiness to accept responsibility for them, and acceptance of the just verdict that will be rendered against me.

The fact is, sir, that I did nothing in Paris. I spent three weeks there, which felt longer than an entire year. I learned about misery and hunger there. Had God not sent me the lawyer M. Michel Salloum, I would have died like a dog on a Métro station platform. I confess that my greatest crime was that I spat on the hand that reached out to help and comfort me. Instead of being the slave of that decent and honorable man who saved my life, I betrayed him. Yes, I betrayed him, and that is my worst crime. I'm not talking about my relationship with his wife, who was destined for me – I had no hand in it – for the betrayal happened long before that. I betrayed him in Paris, and it was a deed I will have to regret for as long as I live. I do not care if M. Michel made his fortune dealing in arms in Lebanon, Europe, and the Gulf. He can do as he likes and his money is his own business. We in Lebanon should be the last people in the world with any right to condemn arms dealing. Had it not been for arms dealers, how would we have been able to fight? He is an arms dealer and we resorted to arms. What more can be said?

I stayed for a week at M. Michel's residence in Paris, 45, rue Victor Hugo, where I saw something unbelievable before being sent back to Lebanon to work as a guard at the Villa Gardenia in the village of Ballouna in Kesrouan.

M. Michel pulled me from the jaws of death. I was sitting in a tunnel in the Montparnasse Métro station holding a piece of cardboard upon which I had written my name. M. Michel stood in front of me for a long while before asking me to get up and follow him. I could not believe my ears. I had heard Arabic words, and I understood. O God, how sweet it was to understand. There in Paris, when they spoke to me in that language I did not understand, I felt as if they were beating me with words, and I'd involuntarily put my hands to my face to ward off the blows.

He asked me to get up and follow him. At first he asked me who I was, and the noise of the trains drowned out my voice. He ordered me to follow him and I remembered what Christ had told one of his disciples: "Take up your cross and follow me." I said that I would follow that man to the ends of the earth and would never leave him, and would be his slave.

M. Michel stood in the Métro tunnel and asked the tall, thin young man why he was sitting there, like a beggar. Yalo tried to tell his story, but he did not know what to say. He sobbed. No, he didn't sob, but his voice was choked. The gentleman asked him whose son he was. He answered that he was the son of the priest Ephraim Abyad, and the gentleman exclaimed, "Son of a priest and lying around here?" Yalo said that the priest was his grandfather. "Come on, come on," the man said. "What evil luck. Now your father or grandfather is weeping in his grave. Come on. Get up and follow me." So Yalo followed him and found himself in an elegant house.

< 267 >

He bathed, put on clean clothes, and met Ata. M. Michel gave his guest no chance to ask questions. He ordered Ata to come forth and bless Daniel, son of the priest Ephraim Abyad. The short, big-bellied man with small hands approached and greeted Yalo. Then M. Michel asked him for oil. Ata hesitated a little before turning his back. He stood facing an icon of the Holy Trinity, which showed three figures with halos of sainthood around their heads sitting in a semicircle around a table bearing three goblets. Ata turned his back to Yalo and approached the icon, looking like he could have still been seated, his legs were so short and his posterior so wide. Ata extended his arms, and a few moments later, oil began to leak from his palms and Mr. Michel exclaimed, "Holy! Holy! Holy! Did you see the oil, my boy? Rise and receive the blessing. Make the sign of the cross and rise." Yalo hesitated a little, but he followed M. Michel, who approached, his head bowed, and took a little of Ata's oil to touch it to his forehead and make the sign of the cross. Yalo imitated his new master and did as he had done, not believing his eyes. It was as if he were dreaming. When Ata turned around again, the oil stopped dripping from his hands. He looked at Yalo, and seeing the look of surprise on his face, winked. All Yalo could do was wink back.

This was how the betrayal started. Yalo didn't tell his master about the truth he knew, not because Ata had given him money, but because he was afraid. He was afraid he would say something that his master would not believe and he would find himself out on the street. This was the betrayal Yalo regretted having committed. Yalo had met Ata in the alleys of the war in Beirut. Ata Ata – that was his full name – had been active in a group of Jehovah's Witnesses, a religious group that had greatly expanded during the war before slowly disappearing. It was a group claiming to belong to the Protestant sect and whose members were forbidden from smoking or drinking alcohol. Their women were not allowed to adorn themselves or use perfumes or cosmetics. Their main teaching was to prepare for the imminent end of the world. Ata carried around religious books and distributed them door-to-door. Yalo encountered him for the first time in his house in al-Mrayyeh as Gaby threw the swarthy-faced missionary out of the house, because, "God forbid, we were the followers of James the Saddler and the Syriac Saint Ephraim, and here these types came to preach to us the religion that was born in our own country and speaking our language? How shameful!" Then I encountered him a second time in the Karantina Prison, where it was said that he was imprisoned for stealing jewelry from a house he had entered to preach in. He was released only after he publicly repented and severed his relationship with the Jehovah's Witnesses.

Yalo answered Ata's wink with an involuntary wink of his own after witnessing the miracle of the oil, which reoccurred with the visit of Archbishop Mikhail Sawaya to Michel Salloum's residence in the rue Victor Hugo.

M. Michel was agitated that evening. Archbishop Mikhail would come to visit him in order to confirm the miracle of the oil that dripped from the hands of his servant Ata. A French chef had come that morning and prepared dinner, and a Filipino servant turned the apartment upside-down to clean it. In the evening His Eminence arrived with his staff, and no one was in the house but the three men.

I was sitting by myself in my little room when M. Michel opened the door and asked me to come out and greet His Eminence. I felt extremely ashamed. M. Michel must surely have told the bishop about my story, and now the Q and A would start and I did not feel like talking. I thought of slipping out of the house because I'd had enough of the phantoms of the priests, and now came this fraud performing miracles, with an archbishop presiding. Only where could I go? I understood, sir, that my grandfather was the reason I was saved from degradation in Paris. Had M. Michel not fallen under the spell of miracles, he would not have looked after me. When

< 269 >

he found out that my grandfather was a priest, he said, "Get up and follow me." I got up and found myself sitting alone in a corner of the salon while Ata turned his back to his master and the archbishop sitting on the sofa facing the icon of the Holy Trinity. Suddenly the oil began leaking out of his small outstretched hands. M. Michel exclaimed, "Holy! Holy! Holy!" and the archbishop made the sign of the cross. Ata seemed to shrink while the shadows drawn by the candlelight on the walls created a strange ambience. The lights had been turned off on Ata's orders. The electric lights were turned off and candles were lit. The shadows fell onto the walls and the oil started. Ata's feet disappeared and Yalo trembled when Ata's feet disappeared, and he nearly believed the miracle. Then he noticed that the man was kneeling and the oil was gushing more freely. Ata stood there, not turning his back to the icon, and walked backwards, his face to the icon and his back to the archbishop. When he reached the archbishop he suddenly turned around and bowed before His Eminence and kissed his hand, but the archbishop took Ata's hands in his, then raised them to his beard and massaged it with the holy oil. At that point M. Michel fell off the sofa and knelt before Ata asking him to place his hands on his head. Ata placed his hands on his master's head and then raised them up, retreated two steps, and folded his arms.

The archbishop asked why the oil stopped, and M. Michel replied that the oil stopped when Ata turned his back to the miraculous icon.

The archbishop stood and approached the icon, bowed before it in such a way that the fingers of his right hand touched the floor, then he kissed the icon and exclaimed, "Holy, holy, holy," and fell on his knees. M. Michel fell on his knees beside him, and I heard the archbishop say that the icon was leaking oil, and then his voice was raised in this prayer: "Now release your slave, Lord, according to your saying Peace, because my eyes have witnessed your redemption." Then the archbishop stood and asked Michel to turn on the lights. The living room chandelier lit up, and Yalo saw the three men shining under the effect of the oil.

I saw tears in the archbishop's eyes as he was trying to sit down. Ata held him by his arm and helped him back to the sofa. The archbishop said that he felt dizzy, so M. Michel offered him some orange-blossom water, but His Eminence refused with a twitch of his narrow eyebrows, and asked Michel and Ata to sit by his side.

I was sitting alone in the corner, seeing them without their seeing me, and the idea came to me that His Eminence plucked his eyebrows like women do, and I nearly burst out laughing, but the archbishop's voice froze the blood in my veins. I heard a broad, deep voice, which seemed to rise from his chest, say: "The Father, the Father, I see the Father. Look, Michel, look, my sons, the Father seated in the middle of the icon is moving, he is carrying the goblet and bringing it to his lips. No one has seen the Father without dying. The Father calls us to his kingdom and brings news of the second coming of the Lord." He said that the Father raised his goblet a second time and the icon was erased. "The icon is erased," he announced in his resounding voice, before falling to the ground.

I thought the archbishop was going to die. He flopped off the sofa and fell in a sitting position on the Persian carpet covering the floor, then walked toward the icon and knelt down, placing his forehead against the floor. Michel and Ata knelt on the floor, and I found myself kneeling and gazing at the icon without seeing any change in it. I don't know how long I knelt but I felt that it would never end. We knelt in silence, hearing nothing but the breathing of the old archbishop, which sounded like snoring, then he began to breathe calmly. I thought that we would remain kneeling like that forever, and my knees were aching, and my eyes began to hurt, so I closed them, and after a long while, I heard Ata's voice saying that dinner was served. It seemed that he had left us kneeling and went to set the table.

I opened my eyes and saw that they had arisen, and I followed them to the dining room. The table was set, there were five place settings, five goblets, a bottle of wine, a bowl of salad, and a steaming platter giving off the fragrance of mutton. After the archbishop pronounced a blessing over the table, he turned to the empty chair and asked M. Michel whether we needed to wait for another dinner guest before starting. M. Michel glanced toward Ata, who explained that the extra place was left for the living St. Elias. The archbishop said that this was a Jewish custom, and asked that the place be removed. But Ata resisted, saying that the plate had appeared to him in a vision. He said that he had heard the voice of St. Elias asking him to leave him a place at the table. Then Ata's voice started rising until it sounded like a little girl's, begging the archbishop for permission for the prophet Elijah to sit with us. Annoyance showed plainly on the archbishop's face as he devoured the mutton but said nothing. Silence fell and His Eminence took only one swallow from his goblet, so no one else drank.

When Ata and I cleared the table I saw M. Michel bend over to kiss the archbishop's hand, and I also saw him slip something into his hand. The archbishop took the thing and said, "May God always bless this house." I wanted to say to M. Michel and to the archbishop that Ata was a fraud and had nothing to do with faith, but I wasn't sure that my voice would make it out of my throat. I was afraid my voice would come out sounding like Ata's did, thin and like a little girl's, so I said nothing.

In the kitchen, while we were washing the dishes, Ata gulped down all the glasses of wine, saying that it was the finest wine in the world, then he drained the bottle and smacked his thin lips. He then handed me some money without daring to look me in the face.

Yalo did not attend the following oil sessions, which were held three times a week in this Parisian residence. He guessed that Ata had decided to exclude him from them, and thanked God for that, because he was sure that had he been summoned to a second session he would have burst out laughing and exposed the whole trick. But the trick was eventually exposed at the villa. Ghada told me how the deacon Issam succeeded in exposing it.

Ata exploited M. Michel's faith and milked him. Yes, milked him. Ata was a fraud, and thank God it was not I who exposed him. I saw how he left the villa in the February cold. He was naked from the waist up as if he were walking on his knees. I thought he was kneeling, and guessed that he had moved his miracles from the living room to the garden, but I was mistaken. Ata stood under the illuminated balcony for shelter from the rain. I called out to him and he looked back, and when he saw me his teeth flashed from his rain-wet face before he ran into the darkness and was swallowed by it.

Ghada told me how the deacon Issam exposed him. As usual the ceremony took place in the dark, by candlelight. The oil began to leak out of Ata's extended palms. The deacon leaped up and grabbed him from behind and called for the lights to be turned on. Before Issam joined the clergy he had been a gym teacher in an evangelical college. Once he caught Ata, his poor victim could not move. The lights came on and the deacon asked Ata to take his shirt off, but Ata resisted. But the deacon rendered him unable to budge, and tore his shirt to pull out from under his armpits two tiny plastic bottles filled with oil. Then he turned to M. Michel and said: "This imposture must stop!"

Ghada laughed at her father's credulity and said that Ata was a crook, that he must have gotten a lot of money out of her father before he took off. I didn't tell her what I knew, afraid that she would tell her father and that he might think I was an accomplice. All I knew of Ata was that he was a Jehovah's Witness and that he had nothing to do with me. It is true that he winked at me and gave me some money to buy my silence, but I would never have said anything anyway. My relationship with him consisted of no more than my having seen him, as dozens of others had seen him at

< 273 >

M. Michel's residence in Paris, just as Archbishop Mikhail Sawaya had seen God the Father, which of course was impossible. I know from my grandfather that no one can see God the Father; even Moses did not see him in Sinai. Only Christ saw him. No one saw the Father but the Bro, for Christ is the true Son.

That is all that happened in Paris. I know that you asked me for the Paris story because you suspect that my relationship with the explosives gang began there. But I swear to God this is everything. And Monsieur Michel had nothing to do with it.

Yalo wrote in his previous confessions about his meeting with Haykal. The truth is that the explosives story started with that meeting, which probably took place in Achrafieh when Yalo was in front of the building where the offices of the Araissi Advertising Company were located, waiting for Shirin.

At first Yalo ignored Haykal, but the gang leader approached him. After a forced greeting and embrace, a conversation started. Haykal began to browbeat and threaten Yalo because of the money taken from the Georges Aramouni Barracks. Yalo didn't pay much attention to the man because he was waiting for Shirin. He wanted to protect her, so he agreed to everything. He made an appointment to meet Haykal at the Badaro Inn. He said they would meet there tomorrow afternoon, shook hands, and left. Yalo claimed that he left the area, but he settled in behind the Empire Cinema to wait for Haykal to disappear. Yalo went back to where he had been waiting and stood under the acacia tree that shaded the sidewalk. Suddenly he felt a hand on his shoulder and turned around to find Haykal, and knew he had been caught. Haykal asked him for his address, and Yalo found no way out of giving him the address of the villa. Haykal said that he preferred to meet with him in Ballouna and so cancelled their meeting in Badaro Street and went away. Yalo was sure, however, that he would hide himself somewhere to watch him. So he too decided to leave. He looked at his watch and mut-tered as if he were waiting for someone who didn't show up, then left.

Yalo went into the café next door to the Empire Cinema, drank a cold beer, and then went back to the building to wait. But Shirin didn't appear. She must have left while he was away. Again he looked at his watch, mut-tered, and shook his head before leaving.

This, sir, is how Yalo got entangled with the gang. I am not saying that Shirin was the cause, but I will say that this was fate. Yalo got entangled with fate and was forced to store explosives in his cottage, but he did not take part in the bombings because he was preoccupied. Yalo was a lover, sir, and that's all.

I made you a promise and I've kept it, but I cannot resolve the subject of the explosives better than this, or answer your question – the one that cost Yalo so many kinds of torture and beatings – "Where did you hide the explosives?"

After Yalo confessed to the explosives because of your insistence, you searched his cottage, turned the villa inside out, and dug up the garden, but you found nothing. I cannot guide you to their location, not only because I don't know, but also because my imagination does not permit me to play this game. What you require of me is truth, not imagination. I have said what I can on the subject of the gang, but I cannot imagine more. Now I am remembering and not imagining, and there is a great distance between the two. Remembering is imagination too, as memories come back to me like fantasies and bring me into a long night, but I cannot lead you to the location of the explosives because I am not writing a story but the truth. I know that if I point you to any specific place, you will go there and search, and if you do not find anything, and of course you will not find anything, my punishment will be disastrous.

I swear to God, I can imagine anything you want, but I cannot lead you to the location of the explosives because this spot does not exist. Even the story of Haykal's meeting with Yalo in front of the building where Shirin worked I would not have been able to concoct, had something similar not happened to me when I met Najib Mansurati.

I was standing under the acacia tree waiting for Shirin to leave work when I felt a hand on my shoulder. I spun around and saw a smiling face that I didn't recognize. He said he was Najib, but I did not remember who this Najib was. I thought he was one of the dozens of modern beggars proliferating in the streets of Beirut. One of them would approach and address you politely; you think he is going to ask you something, but instead he launches into a long tale about the illness of his mother, wife, or son, the point being that he wants a U.S. dollar from you. This phenomenon of the dollar bewildered me, why did they not beg in Lebanese currency? Even beggars, sir, had lost faith in the national currency! I thought he was one of those, so I felt annoyed again. But then he said my name – he called me Mr. Yalo. Now, my name has never been used with the title Mister. I am just plain Yalo or just plain Daniel. Where did this guy come up with this Mister to tack in front of my name? I turned to him and he said that he was Najib Mansurati, the brother of Said the singer. He brought his face close to mine to give me a kiss. Then he asked me whether I knew anything about his brother's fate. I understood from him that Said decided to become a professional, so when the war ended he went to Al-Qamishli to work as a musician in the Khabur Hotel, which was owned by a Kurd named Muhammad al-Haytah, and that Said then disappeared. Najib said that they'd looked for him everywhere, that his mother had gone to Syria and visited all the prisons but found no trace of him.

He asked me what I thought and I said I didn't know. I mean, a guy who'd been one of the Billy Goats, and then goes to Syria to be a singer? Wow – what a jackass!

"Maybe they sent him," I said.

"What?" asked Najib.

"Nothing, nothing, I was just remembering the song 'I would have eaten and feasted.' Do you remember how your brother used to sing it?"

"In Achrafieh, the day I was there, and came to her
I surrendered my life to your lips . . ."

The brother began to sing the song and I almost joined in with him, but I remembered we were standing in Tabaris Square in the middle of Achrafieh, and people would think we were crazy.

I wanted to tell him it was probably all over for Said, but I said I didn't know anything. He invited me to visit them at home. He stood beside me and pulled a pack of cigarettes out of his pants pocket and offered me a cigarette, I told him no thanks. He lit his cigarette and smoked it quietly. He was waiting for me to ask him how he was, so he could ask me, but I didn't say a word. I wanted him to go away so my relationship with Shirin would not get mixed up with my past life. Shirin had to be the beginning of a new life unconnected to memories of the war. But Najib remained standing there in his carefully pressed dark green pants. Through his pants I could see his white, hairless thighs. In my memory I saw him as he was when he visited his brother in the barracks, wearing shorts, and Alexei's winks and comments about boys and the incomparable pleasures of life. He finished his cigarette and I finished ogling his thighs, but he kept standing there. Then I decided to leave. I looked at my watch and muttered. He asked me if I was waiting for someone, and I told him I had to get out of there. He threw himself on me to kiss me, and a crazy rage ran through me; I could have bitten him instead of kissing him, and the voices raged in my head, but I kissed him with lips trembling with anger. I hurried away and went into the café near the Empire Cinema, where I soothed my nerves with a cold glass of beer, then went back to the sidewalk to wait, but she did not appear, which meant that she had left while I had been sitting in the café.

This is the true story, sir. I never did anything with young Mansurati in the barracks because I know that it's not just a sin but a crime as well. Even with the *malfono* Halim I never did. Others maybe. I don't know and I don't want to make accusations, but me, no.

Therefore I suggest that the subject of the explosives be closed at the point we reached before, that is, when Yalo met Haykal near the Araissi Building in Achrafieh, in Tabaris Square. I believe this confession should be seen as clear and sufficient evidence by the court. The judge can use it against me, or can find mitigating circumstances. Let's suppose that Yalo was blackmailed by his former comrades, that he wanted to protect his relationship with Shirin, and got mixed up with that, but he was not directly involved in either the planning or the execution of the operations. Plus, his relations, or the relations of M. Michel, with one Ata Ata do not go beyond the business of the miracle. Poor M. Michel – he's the last one to blame, that decent man who saved my life and made me human again after my misfortunes in Paris had turned me into the lowest kind of animal. It was enough that he was made a laughingstock, and his visits to Lebanon after the scandal of Ata in the villa became rare. I think the Ata incident ruined his influence in his home. Just think, sir, his daughter, Ghada, who had looked up to him like a god, started to ridicule him. If that was how his daughter acted, just imagine what his wife had to say – Madame Randa, who had always mocked his infatuation with Byzantine icons and the little flask he sprayed the icons with to keep them clean and bright. It is certain that the lady came to despise him and that she chose me as the right address for expressing her contempt for him. I was just a tool, sir, and this realization helped me to recover from that love. I am Randa's tool and she was a tool for her husband, who was Ata's tool, and Ata was a tool for I don't know whom. Or I am my grandfather's tool, and he was my mother's tool, and she was Elias al-Shami's tool, and he was his wife's, and she was her illness's, and I do not know. Or Shirin was Yalo's tool and he was M. Michel's, who was a tool of arms smuggling or of the war, and the war was the tool of I do not know . . .

We are all tools, sir. No one exists by himself or for himself. So why did God create us? To torture and be tortured?

Yalo does not agree with me that life is meaningless; it's as if he's just discovered some other meaning of life, which he doesn't want to tell anyone. Even I don't know it. I come up close to him and read to him, he'll turn his head toward me for a moment and then will return to his private world, which takes him someplace I do not know about.

Yalo, sir, discovered that a man does not exist until he sinks to the lowest of the low. And from there, no one returns as the tool of another. There he becomes a lamb to be slaughtered in place of all, and his soul flies above the world because it has been freed.

But I am afraid for him. I am writing because I am afraid for him. I feel a tremendous pain rising from my posterior to my neck, choking me. I sit on the place of pain and write about him, for him, and beg him to get off and come back to me. But he is there, above, not hearing or seeing, though of course he hears voices coming from within, and sees when he closes his eyes. I envy him and fear for him and am afraid of him, and I do not know. Do I have a right to ask him to come down so that he can return to me, so that we can leave this prison together and start our life anew? I want to begin my life. Now I know the meaning of life. When I leave here I will open a little workshop for dovetailing wood, take care of my poor mother and console her, and I'll forget Shirin, the story of Shirin, and my love for Shirin.

The story has become clear to me now, for you, for him, and for me. Poor Yalo. Do you know, sir, that no more than ten, or a few more, rapes were attributed to him, in the space of a year and a half? Of course, we must add to that about twenty counts of premeditated or unpremeditated theft.

The charge is unfounded, sir.

I know that one count is sufficient for you to incarcerate me and curse my forefathers, but things have to be understood within their context, and mitigating circumstances should be taken into consideration. And in my view, the only charge on which I should be tried is the charge of voyeurism.

Here I would like to examine closely the charge of rape. Who is the real accused here, sir, Yalo or the men and women who used their cars in the forest of Ballouna for fornication? Lebanese law is clear and candid, it outlaws fornication in public places. It might be said that it is an unjust law because it infringes on individual rights. That is true but it is not legally valid. The law says that a woman found in suspicious circumstances in a vehicle in a public place is to be dealt with as a prostitute until proven otherwise. So why do you apply the law only to Yalo?

I know that you do not want me to philosophize. The officer told me when I was on the throne that he wanted the story without philosophizing

< 281 >

or bullshit. I am relating the facts as I lived them and witnessed them. But do you not agree with me that I have been wronged in this case?

I do not want it to be understood from what I am saying that I want to pin the blame on Shirin. Shirin is pure and innocent, and came to the forest with that pimp Dr. Said al-Halabi only because she had despaired of life and her fiancé's stupidity. You saw him, sir, how he sat in the interrogation with his fat thighs rubbing together. He said that he was an engineer and a graduate of the American University. What would this jackass with his fat thighs know how to engineer? How could she choose him and abandon me? Can't her eyes see? Is it possible to dump a tall, slender young man, who walks on tiptoe so he won't disturb the dead that cover the face of the earth, for this bastard afraid of his own shadow? Plus, how could he say he had been with her in Ballouna? What a despicable liar. He was happy to show off his consort in order to see me in prison. I swear to God, sir, if I had seen this idiot with her I would have shot him and planted his corpse in the forest and left his soul to lament forever among the pine trees. But I did not kill anyone. Had Yalo been a criminal, he would have killed all of them and made a forest for the dead like the jungle in Ain Ward.

I will not digress from the topic now, in spite of the shadows of my grandfather that fill my head and the gravelly voice of his last days that still rings in my ears. I will not digress and tell you about the willows of the dead from which the weeping of the trees was heard, but I will tell you the truth of Yalo's passions and burglaries, and how he would descend upon the cars with their lights off amid the piney night and plunder the money, watches, and rings that God apportioned to him. Yes, the ring that he offered to Shirin was one of the spoils of Ballouna, and when he saw it inside the interrogator's handkerchief, he came undone; the tears gushed from his eyes, not because he felt guilty, nor because he was seeking sympathy as you'd believed, but because he was upset that Shirin had betrayed their covenant. He'd given the thick silver ring with engraved pharaonic symbols to Shirin as a symbol of his love. They sat in the Rawdah Café, by the sea. That day she took the ring, her heart was open, and he felt her love. She took the ring and thanked him and spoke as if she were an open book. She spoke of her family, of her brothers who had immigrated to Canada. She said she was weary of people who didn't know how to enjoy life. She said that she envied Yalo, yes, she told Yalo that she envied him, because he was living life to the fullest and enjoying it. She thanked him because he had taught her how to eat and savor. She spoke of her mother, who only cared about plastic surgery and face-lifts, and of her father, a contractor who went to the Casino du Liban every night to gamble. She said that she'd decided to go back to college to study French literature, and she recited to him the poems of Jacques Prévert that she loved. Yalo saw himself climbing her words, rolling in them, and embracing them. Then she reached out her hand and he clasped it. She said that she thanked him for everything before looking at her watch and saying that she had to go home.

The ring of love became the ring of accusation. Shirin no longer wanted it, preferring to wear her fiancé's gold wedding band. She is free, and I will not discuss her freedom, but why did she give the ring to the interrogator?

The interrogator knew that the ring was worthless. Had it been worth anything, she would have held on to it. Why had his excellency the interrogator not asked her why she accepted a ring from a man who had stalked her, hated her, and wanted to get rid of her? The interrogator saw the ring as criminal evidence, and he was right, but had he asked Shirin when she had received it from Yalo? Of course not. Even had he asked her, she would have lied rather than confess that she had taken it six months before she pressed charges against me. I will not request that you ask her what happened during those months, and how many times we ate fish and *kibbeh nayeh* and drank arak.

But please be patient.

I confess that I stole, and the penalty for stealing is prison, and I confess that I committed adultery with women in Ballouna, and my punishment will come from Almighty God. I will write about how things happened and I will try to remember, and I hope you will forgive me for the gaps in my memory. A man's memory is full of gaps and no one but God can fill them. God alone possesses a perfect memory, whereas a man remembers only to forget.

You want the beginning of the story, and the beginning was Ballouna.

The story began when one night I saw a car park in the forest for half an hour and then leave again. As a guard, I was worried. It was pitch-black; in my head I drew up all sorts of plans to defend the villa should it come under armed attack. I know, from having overheard M. Michel, that the villa might come under threat. As you know, he was involved in arms trafficking, owned a hotel in Ras al-Khaimah, did business with the biggest fashion designers in Lebanon, arranged for Lebanese fashion models to visit the Gulf, and the like . . . I was crouched in the dark, ready to face the worst, but nothing happened, thank God.

The next night I heard a similar noise and witnessed almost the same scene, although things took a more complicated turn. A first car had turned off its lights, then a second car came and parked not far from it, also turning off its engine and lights. The first car left after a while, while the second waited another half an hour before leaving. That made me fearful and suspicious. I said to myself they must be surveillance cars, and that two cars together meant that the operation had been carefully managed and coordinated.

I thought I might go over to the second car, but I was afraid of being the victim of an ambush. I decided to wait and watch with my hand on my weapon. But the second car suddenly turned on its lights and drove away. So

I resolved to tell Madame what I had seen, but then changed my mind. The man had trusted me with his home and his family and made me understand that he was relying on me alone. So I decided not to stoke her fears and to do my best under the circumstances.

That went on for about two weeks. I proclaimed a state of alert every night and built imaginary fortifications along the pine and willow trees in my head, until the truth took my by surprise.

The moon was full. A car came and parked under the willow tree as if it wanted to camouflage itself. As usual, the engine and the lights were turned off. From my hiding place behind the wall of the villa I couldn't see. I didn't know what to do. Should I move toward the car, leaving my machine gun behind the wall, and walk as if crossing a street, so as not to get into a premature battle with this gang that had planned out the assassination of M. Michel, or the kidnapping of his wife or daughter for ransom? Or carry my gun and advance stealthily so that they could not see me, despite the risk? Then I remembered what our trainer, Costa, told us about a fighter's relationship with his rifle. There were three things a man never left behind or lent, even to those closest to him: his woman, his rifle, or his horse.

I took the rifle and advanced slowly and cautiously. I moved away from the villa wall, adopting the duck waddle that I learned in my military training. I moved in like a duck and concealed myself under a pine tree from where I could see the car clearly, and who was inside it.

That was when the surprise happened.

I was expecting to see armed men, but I saw no drawn weapons. I found a man and a woman. I said, this is it, they are pretending to be lovers so that they can surveil and make plans, but no, you couldn't fool Yalo so easily! I decided to stay and watch until the end. Heck – it was like watching a movie!

But little by little I began to forget the gang, because I sensed that the man and the woman were not role-playing, but seemed to be having sex, I mean, like teenagers. I got into it with them. No, in the beginning I was not aroused because I was afraid, and a guy who's afraid, can't. But gradually my fear faded and I controlled my breathing and began enjoying myself. That was the first time in my life I saw people actually having sex. I got very aroused and I was afraid I'd fall to the ground because I was squatting and my knees hurt, but I decided not to get up at all. That time, I finished before the guy in the car finished. I let my rifle slip down in my hands and rub its wooden hollow against my erect member until I shot. I never saw anything like that. A man fondling every part of a woman's body, her breasts coming out of the top of her dress, and more . . . my friends told me how they had spied on their families at night and how lust came to them amidst the whispers of their fathers on top of their mothers; me, alas. My father had left long since, Elias al-Shami did not sleep with my mother in our house, and my grandfather was a dried-up tree stump.

There, under the pine tree, lust seized me. I saw that man, whose features I could not make out, sucking two big breasts, then playing with them, then . . . I don't know how I can describe it, but it was an extraordinary sight. After I heard the sound of the engine turning over, I rushed back to my cottage so I could clean myself up. And a strange thing would happen. I would get aroused again and touch myself under the shower, and since then, I'd get aroused as soon as I step into the shower.

After that moonlit night, and from my ongoing act of surveillance, I understood the whole game. It had nothing to do with gangs and assassination and kidnap attempts, as it appeared to me in the beginning, it was all about sex in cars. I decided to pursue my observation. I never abandoned my machine gun, though I also started bringing along the flashlight Madame Randa had given me, and would pull a white woolen cap that I'd found in the cottage over my head.

The story of the flashlight is tied up with the electrical current being cut off. Two months after I had started my job, the electricity died and I heard Madame Randa's screams. The villa's electricity did not fail, as a rule, since when it was cut off in the area, it would come back on automatically from a huge generator that circulated electricity to the houses in the village. But it seems the generator was down, so darkness spread, and Yalo heard Madame Randa's voice asking him to come up. She had a lit candle and a slim black flashlight in her hand. She gave him the flashlight and asked him to start up the villa's own generator, which was in the garden. Yalo went down to the garden, attended to the generator, and kept the flashlight. No, it was the Madame who'd asked him to hold on to the flashlight in case of emergencies. So he put it in his coat pocket and it became his constant companion since his life was filled with emergencies.

Yalo did not initiate the adventure, the adventure came to him. What could he do? His adventure had been spying on blind cars that parked among the trees, with the steam of lust rising from them above the green pine branches.

A man goes to his fate, as they say. And Yalo's fate was the forest. Yalo waited for the night, lived the night, and breathed the night. In his eyes, the cars started to resemble animals having sex in the dark. He liked this idea and he decided to tell no one. When he told Shirin the story for the first time, he omitted the part about him putting the rifle against his thighs and what happened after that. Shirin believed him. Yalo was convinced that Shirin believed every word he told her. That is why he was so surprised to see her in the interrogation room – and that's what led to his caving quickly and his confessing to everything. Yalo was not such a coward as to confess so easily, but he confessed because Shirin's presence threw him off balance; he found himself in a maelstrom he could not pull himself out of before grasping that they wanted him to confess to the explosives, so he did. But you found his confessions lacking, which was true, but not out of an effort to obstruct the investigation or to mislead the court, as they said, but because he didn't know. This is a story I have set out for you in detail, sir, and I ask that no more be demanded of me, for I have resigned myself to the will of God.

The first time it happened by chance.

Yalo was squatting in his usual place, behind the villa wall under the pine tree, when a car came and parked in the forest. The car's headlights went out, so he could no longer see a thing. He spent most of his nights that way, sitting in the dark, counting his breaths and imagining. He never really could see unless the moon had risen, and so he came to love Fairuz's song "We're Neighbors With the Moon," and he would sing with her, "His home is behind our hills, he comes up before us." But the moon did not follow Fairuz's orders; the moon shone only when it was full. And because the moon waxed and waned like the breasts of his beloved Shirin, or so he imagined them that strange night when she gave off the scent of incense, he called them "moons," and gave them the name *sahro*. Every time he uttered this Syriac word, he had to explain its meaning to Shirin.

That night, with the two heroes of the scene totally shrouded in blackness, Yalo heard a scream and saw what seemed to be the shadows of struggling arms. Then he heard sobs mixed with the moans of a woman. That was when Yalo the hawk was born. He saw himself racing, pulled the flashlight out of his overcoat pocket, and turned on the beam – catching the man between the eyes.

Yalo strode along as if flying, and descended on the car with the wind that filled the sleeves of his open coat so that he looked like a bird spreading its wings. A few seconds were not enough for the driver to regain his composure and run away. Yalo was there and saw how the man's jaw was slack from fear, and saw his arms. Yes, the man was halfway out of the car window, with his hands raised in surrender. But Yalo continued his approach with the beam aimed between the man's eyes. He reached the car and signaled with his rifle. The man pulled himself back into the car, bent over, opened the door, and got out with his hands in the air, saying, "I'll do whatever you want. Whatever you want. You want her, take her. She's a whore. Take her, but . . . please."

It hadn't occurred to Yalo to take her. He had rushed down because he heard the sound of a quarrel, and crying. But the man standing before him, half bowing, did not stop talking: *Please, anything you want, take her if you want, but let me go.* Yalo ignored the man, approached the window, and trained the light on the woman. It was a young girl, or so she appeared to his hawklike eyes open in the dark. She sensed the light and her moans increased. Yalo felt sure that she was not what her friend, who was around forty, had described her to be. Yalo retreated a step, kicked him between the legs, and spat on him. The man, doubled over with pain, started to empty his pockets of money. He held it out for Yalo. Yalo saw the money, but instead of pocketing it, again he kicked the man in the balls and spat on him. He gestured with the flashlight in his left hand for the man to go. The man got into the car, started the engine, and drove off, with the girl bent over beside him.

Yalo was surprised at how the girl had been content to stay with a man who had called her a whore. He should have rescued her from that bastard. But what would he have done with her?

He went back to his cottage and decided to wash up, and under the shower he imagined the girl to be with him, and what had to happen, happened.

That is how it began, sir.

The first time, Yalo did not steal or rape. The first time, he realized, after coming out of the shower and drinking a glass of arak and a tomato and onion salad with oil, that he was an idiot. He should have taken the woman and the money and maybe even the car, too. He got drunk and talked to himself, and laughed at his naiveté.

After the first time, things took a different course. Yalo did not plan out his operations, as his main preoccupations were observation and voyeurism But he still descended on lovers every once in a while, and took whatever plunder God granted him. Yalo was not greedy; had he wanted to, he could have stolen whatever he wanted and had sex with whomever he wanted, but he was rather reserved in his operations and he savored them serenely. It had nothing to do with being afraid of the police, as he felt certain that none of these people would file a complaint with them. What would they say? Would they say that they were having sex in cars? What would their fate be, and the fate of their companions, if Lebanese law were applied?

Those whose testimonies the interrogator read had not told the truth. I am not saying that their testimonies were totally false, but they were incomplete. The police, sir, did not question them in a serious way, I mean c'mon! They all came with girls they didn't know? That's a lie. I swear to God, in my whole time there I only found one prostitute and I shared the money with her that I took from the man. As to the rest of the women, they were not of "unknown identity," they were ordinary women. But the investigation was not serious because all that would have been needed was a single bastinado to beat the truth out of them, and they would have confessed the names of the women. I am not saying they should be tortured with water, the sack, the chair, or the bottle. That would be a sin, but if you had interrogated them, sir, you would have learned the truth of the lovers' forest. But you were not interested in the truth itself. You were only interested in condemning me and pinning the crimes of rape and the explosives on me. So you let them all go their separate ways, and only your humble servant was left to mount his heavenly throne.

My forest stories are not all the same, but I will not relate them all because I do not know how to describe the difference between one fragrance and another, between one taste and another, so I will settle for spelling out the headlines, which is enough, because I am writing my confessions here, not an imaginary tale.

First:

I do not know the women's names because I did not ask their names. I did not ask because I did not want to be asked; that is the rule of the game. So torturing me to compel me to name them will do you no good at all, because it will compel me to lie. And that is what I promised myself, and you, and God that I would not do.

Second:

I only stole what was offered to me. I confined myself to whispering, "Hand over everything," and taking what came from their pockets. I did not demand their watches or jewelry, but I didn't refuse them. Once I threw a watch away because it looked like a child's watch, not worth anything; I saw the man bend over and pick it up, so I ordered him to give it to me. Then I saw that I had guessed right, it was worthless.

Third:

I would speak very little, and in a whisper, because I was intent on no one remembering my voice or my features. I would cover my head and face with the white woolen cap, and I spoke in a low voice because I think a low voice terrifies people.

Fourth:

I did not commit rape in the true sense of the word, only once. The man threatened me and treated me like shit, so I was forced to make him get into the trunk of the car, which I locked him into, then I dragged the girl over to the pine tree and tried with her, but she stubbornly refused and tore my shirt, so I threatened her with my weapon. The experiment was no fun because the woman was pretty well locked-up. I felt like my member was leaking, so I decided to stop having sex with the woman, but I didn't succeed in sticking to my decision.

Fifth:

Only once was it actually fun, with a woman in her forties who was with a guy no more than twenty-five, or at least that was my guess.

Sixth:

There were more incidents of robbery than of sex.

Seventh:

I kept none of the stolen goods because I had decided from the beginning that it would have been a mistake to do so. That's why I sold everything at pathetic prices and on any terms. I sold them in the jewelers' market in the Aisha Bakkar neighborhood near the highway of the television studio. I determined not to deal with any one jeweler to avoid being found out, and I also spent all the money I had gotten very quickly.

That is, in brief, my story with the women in the forest. As you see, sir, what I did was not even one percent of what any other man in my position might have done. The wages were ample, and the automobiles thronged into the forest like mad.

As for the engineer's story, which alleged that he was with Shirin in the forest, it is baseless. He was not her fiancé and did not come with her. Had he been with her it would have been completely different. Of course, sir, you noticed his greed and his rottenness when he was in the interrogation room, sitting like a deaf person at a wedding. He would pull a cigarette out of his suit pocket as if he were stealing it, instead of putting the pack of cigarettes out on the table in front of him like everyone else does. You, sir, put your pack on the table in front of you, and offered cigarettes to your colleagues and visitors – you even offered me a cigarette, but I didn't notice it because my eyes were closed, a habit from my childhood. But him, sir – he reached into the inside pocket of his suit and pulled out a cigarette, because he is vile. I swear to God if I had seen this idiot in the forest, everything would have been different because I would have killed him. But God help us, had I killed a single person and buried him in the forest under the willow tree, the killing would not have stopped, and the forest would have become a graveyard like Ain Ward, where children were not allowed to play because of the cries that came from the tree branches.

My grandfather said that the reason he agreed to leave with his maternal uncle Abd al-Masih, when his uncle returned to the village to make an offer for his sister's son, had been the laments of the willow forest and the white poplars that grew on the banks of a little river whose name I do not remember. That is where the whole story began, where I, your humble servant Daniel Abel Abyad, known as Yalo, was linked to the thread of blood reaching from Tur Abdin to the end of the world.

My grandfather said that I was born under the sign of death because the umbilical cord was wound around my neck. The midwife, Linda Saliba, saved me from death by a miracle. She let my mother scream in pain, because she forgot the placenta in her belly, and began to undo the umbilical cord from around my neck. It had blocked my cries, making everyone think that I had been born dead.

I was born strangled, and the rope of blood is my one legacy. So it will not surprise anyone if I wrap the rope around my neck in the end, making my beginning my end, making my life no more than a dream.

The story was born in my memory only here in prison, once I sat on the bottle, which allowed me to savor that man lives outside of time. It is true that the pain was great, but living outside of time was an incomparable pleasure. This explains, in my view, Yalo's insistence on remaining there in the memory of the dead.

I do not know, sir, why I am writing this story now, in spite of my being aware that you don't care about it and it will add nothing new to the investigation. For all the crimes have been confessed to, and all you have to do is render a verdict. I am writing it for the sake of poor Yalo, for this would be the first time he'd hear the whole story of his grandfather.

The story begins with a child named Abel Gabriel Abyad, born in the village of Ain Ward, near Tur Abdin, in a country with no name, because it was the country of a people who did not yet exist. There, at the onset of the twentieth century, the Turks committed a dreadful massacre, killing about a million and a half Armenians. This was the massacre that our brothers the Armenians commemorate every year. My grandfather's massacre, however, no one remembers it because it was a minor massacre incidental to a major one. Woe unto a people butchered in a peripheral massacre, because the butcher will not even find it necessary to wipe the blood from his knives. And this is what happened early in the century, when the small Syriac population was massacred.

The armed hosts attacked a small village called Ain Ward, the Spring of Roses because of the red damask rose that grows on the banks of its stream, from which sprang water turned golden by the sun. (That is how my grandfather described his village to his daughter, before adding that he spoke like the poets, and that he had wasted his life by neglecting his poetic gifts.) There the massacre was committed that killed all the inhabitants of the village. Sensing the imminent danger, the villagers took refuge in the Monastery of St. John, about three kilometers from their village, but the attackers, who surrounded the monastery, settled for nothing less than the surrender of all of them. After negotiations led by Cohno Danho, the villagers were promised safety. They came out with their hands raised after throwing their rifles to the ground, and the massacre began. The attackers used swords on every neck, both women and men without distinction, and only a tiny band of villagers survived, who slipped through the valleys and fled in the direction of the city of Al-Qamishli.

My grandfather didn't remember the massacre, because he was less than three years old. He told the story of the massacre as he heard it from the uncle he hated. So I am not compelled to believe the story, not the story of fleeing to the abbey nor the story of the villagers being massacred and buried in a mass grave dug under the willow trees. What can be believed is that the children under the age of three were not harmed, and that the attackers pillaged the houses in the village before deciding to move into them. So the image of blood that became my great-grandmother's *kokina* might be merely a metaphor by which my grandfather wanted to prove his poetic gifts.

The children wandered the streets of their village, begging. Their terror and hunger left them no time to weep over their murdered families.

Then Mullah Mustafa issued a decision.

I know only his first name, because my grandfather refused to talk about him. The mullah decreed that children should not be left wandering in the streets and issued orders to distribute them among the Kurdish families who had taken over the houses in the village. It was my grandfather's great luck to be taken to the house of Mullah Mustafa. The boy's name was changed from Abel to Ahmad, and he became a Kurdish boy, speaking Kurdish, Arabic, and Turkish, and living in the bosom of the mullah's family, as if it had always been so. The willow forest was the only remaining witness that remembered what had been. The children were forbidden from playing in it because of the moans that seeped from among the branches of the trees that grew so remarkably after the massacre.

The story might have ended here, with Abel Abyad forgetting his origins, or even becoming an officer in the Turkish army like so many children who were snatched from the arms of their mothers and raised by the Ottoman Army, becoming pillars of the Janissary corps whose very name evoked terror.

But destiny had a different view.

Ten years after the massacre, and after the Ottoman defeat in World War I, with the dissolution of the state, some of the Syriacs in the regions of Tur Abdin, who had fled to Al-Qamishli in northern Syria, began to look for their children. Here my grandfather's uncle, named Abd al-Masih Abyad, appeared.

Abd al-Masih arrived in Ain Ward, went to Mullah Mustafa's house, and said that he would buy the boy for any amount they named. The mullah swore that he would return the boy to his family, community, and tribe. The mullah said that he was ready to give the boy Ahmad back to his uncle without compensation if that was what the boy wished.

The mullah called over Ahmad, who stood between his Kurdish father and his Syriac uncle. He heard his story from his father's mouth and understood that the mullah was making him choose between going with Abd al-Masih Abyad and staying here.

When my grandfather got to this part of the story, his tears used to stream down and his voice would choke up, and he began to stutter and stammer. He would fall silent for a long time and ask for a glass of tea before relating how he went away with his uncle without looking back.

Instead of the story ending here, it took a new turn in Al-Qamishli, because the lad felt redoubled banishment. He did not speak Syriac, and he hated the job his uncle found him as a bakery worker. He felt that people treated him as a Kurd.

In Al-Qamishli, my grandfather regained his original name but lost his identity, because in people's eyes he had become a Kurd. He felt banished.

The world had closed in his face, and he had lost the smell of the trees that had filled his life in Ain Ward. And in this house he had to contend with his uncle's spates of madness. When his uncle drank arak, he turned on his wife and three daughters and beat them, then he'd start in on his sister's son, whom he had wanted to be a son to him, as God had not granted him a son, and beat him savagely.

Abel did not know what to do. He could not go back to Ain Ward, nor could he stay in this small, dark house. Nor could he leave the exhausting job in the bakery because that would mean dying of hunger. So the only salvation he could see was in the Church of St. Ephraim. He attended Sunday mass assiduously, and took part in cleaning the church after mass, which brought him to the attention of the deacon Shimon, who assigned him to the Sunday school he held in the church's vault to teach his pupils the religious rituals.

Here, my grandfather said, God saved him. A love of learning blossomed in his heart, and he excelled among his peers, memorizing all of the Syriac prayers without understanding a word.

Once again fate intervened because the deacon Shimon advised Abel to go to Beirut, where the world would open before him. The boy made his decision right away, collected his weekly pay from the bakery, and instead of going home, took the bus from Al-Qamishli to Aleppo and onward to Tripoli and then Beirut. Abel arrived in Beirut carrying nothing with him but the address of the St. Severus Church in Mseitbeh. He searched for the church for a long time before finding himself before its locked door, where he spent the night.

In the morning, a new chapter of the story began. Cohno Hanna al-Dinohi arrived at the church and saw the boy sleeping on the sidewalk. He woke him gently and asked who he was, and Abel gave him Deacon Shimon's letter. The *cohno* read the letter carefully, took the lad into the church, and led him to a side room where he could stay until they decided how to handle him. The next day he gave him a letter of introduction for Mr. Mitri, who ran the Yazbek Tile Factory, suggesting that he not talk much because his dialect might seem too strange to the Lebanese ear.

Here, sir, was the beginning of the grandfather I knew. That is, he became Abel Abyad. He worked in the tile factory and helped in the church. He studied Syriac and religion, and the *malfono* marveled at his ability to memorize his lessons with record speed. My grandfather was the best student in Cohno Hanna's night school, in which a number of Syriac tile workers, who had come from Syria, studied. Then the *cohno* married him to his sister's daughter, according to the official family narrative. The truth is that the *cohno*'s niece fell in love with my grandfather and went on a hunger strike for his sake. This forced her family to consent to her marriage to the young Kurd who became, with this marriage, a legitimate son of the sect in Beirut. Eventually the *cohno* asked Abel to quit his tile work and help him manage the affairs of his parish, as he was growing old. My grandfather had grown in stature and knowledge, and had turned to glorifying the Creator, which had elevated him in the eyes of the three times regretted Bishop Daoud Karjo, to become an assistant *cohno* in the Church of St. Severus, and later was bequeathed the position after the death of Cohno Hanna.

My grandfather studied a great deal. My mother said that he studied Syriac at fifteen and was fascinated with theology and the debate over the One Nature versus Dual Nature of Christ. He went to study in Damascus, to return with the highest theological degree. His ambition then emerged because he felt that God had chosen him from the netherworld, and just as Christ had chosen his disciples from among fishermen, the Lord had chosen his disciple Ephraim from among the children of the massacres.

The story has to end here. My grandfather's story ends, like all stories, with the death of the hero. My grandfather died, ages ago. The story truly ends here, because all the events that would occur after the death of his wife were expected. The man aged all at once and discovered that his life was futile. He began to invent books that he had not written and to impose strange rituals on his daughter and grandson.

Gaby, however, believed that the story did not end entirely with the death of her mother. My grandfather had begun to change before his wife's death; her death had been just an additional factor in a transformation that had begun with that strange visit Mullah Mustafa had made to the *cohno*'s house in Mseitbeh. What a strange story! Why did the Kurdish mullah come to the house of the Syriac *cohno*? Was it true that he asked him to go back with him to Ain Ward, and that he promised him his inheritance, offering to marry him to his cousin after he repented to his Lord and returned to his true faith?

My mother said that had she been told that story, she would not have believed it; but she saw it with her own eyes and heard it with her own ears. She heard a rapping at the door, and saw the old man with his white beard and black cloak speak to her mother in strange Arabic, asking for Abel. The woman asked him to come in and sit down, and she called her husband, who was in his room putting on his priestly robe in preparation to go out. My mother and her sister, Sara, went into the living room to look at the strange man who had hugged and kissed them.

My grandfather came into the living room and saw the old man fidgeting in his armchair, about to get up. The *cohno* ran toward him like a little boy, took his hand and kissed it, and put it against his head. He kissed both the top and the palm, and the old man kissed him on the shoulder and sat down again. The *cohno* remained standing, head bowed, before the old man. The mullah ordered him to sit, so Abel sat down on the side of the couch, as if ready to get up again at any moment. The men had a strange conversation

< 300 >

in a strange tongue. They drank tea and smoked rolled cigarettes the mullah brought in the pocket of his cloak. The *cohno*, whose lips had not touched a cigarette since he joined the clergy, smoked like a practiced smoker. The *cohno* wept and the mullah wept. Then when the mullah stood up to depart, the *cohno* bowed over again and kissed his hand.

My mother said that the mullah proposed that his son return to Ain Ward because he wanted to bequeath him land and also proposed that he marry the mullah's niece. But my grandfather refused the offer and said he could not.

They did not speak much, for a man such as the mullah, whose authority extended over the whole region of Tur Abdin, was not used to talking much. It was enough that he took the trouble to come. His honoring you with his presence could hardly be repaid. That's what my grandfather said, yet even so he told him that he could not.

The *cohno* cried bitterly, my mother said. The mullah cried quietly. The two men's tears ran into their beards, then the mullah left and the *cohno* stayed, dazed, as if he were blind and deaf.

My mother said that her father remained practically mute for seven days, and that on the Sunday after his visit, he did not go to church on the pretext that he was ill. And that he refused to receive any member of his parish. He spent a week in bed eating nothing but bread and water.

My mother said she discovered that day that her father was a Kurd, and that when she saw him speaking Kurdish with the mullah, she saw his true face, which she never saw again until the moment of his death.

The *cohno* was very changed after that visit, as if a strange spirit had entered his body, as if the Syriac language had possessed him and he had become dazzled by all the names of the Lebanese, Syrian, and Palestinian villages that started with the word *kafr*. He would interrupt conversations

< 301 >

countless times in order to trace the Arabic words to their Syriac roots. He said that the very air spoke Syriac, and he stood before an icon of Christ and spoke to it in the language only the two of them understood.

Only once did my grandfather relate his conversation with his Kurdish father to his wife. He said it was a test. "Just as Satan tested Christ, the mullah was sent to me so that my faith might be tested." He said that he was afraid of himself, especially when his Kurdish father told him about the torments the Kurds experienced in Turkey and the oppression they felt and how their villages were violated every day. The mullah, whose mere footfall made everyone shudder, seemed hesitant and sad, as if he had come to be rescued by his son. Both men cried a great deal, laughing only when the mullah reminded his son how he had memorized the Holy Koran at the age of seven, which in Ain Ward was considered a virtual miracle.

But the greater miracle, the *cohno* told his wife, was that he was able to forget. The mullah had come to awaken in his heart all that he'd forgotten.

Up above, Yalo refused to descend from his throne and come to me. I tell him not to be afraid because he is right. Yalo committed only one mistake for which he was very sorry, but he was unable to make up for it, and did not understand that this mistake would drive him to his end.

The mistake was not Shirin herself, but Shirin's voice.

The girl he loved to death could not forget. She went out with him so many times; she laughed, cried, ate, and drank. She held his hand and kissed him, and slept with him in the little hotel in Jounieh. She loved him yet did not love him, but she could not forget that he had broken her voice.

"My voice broke in Ballouna, that's why I can't love you right," she told him. He didn't understand what she was talking about. He thought of a china plate falling to the floor and breaking. But he didn't understand that when a woman's voice broke, it meant that her heart had been irremediably derailed. And a derailed heart could not love.

She said that there, when Dr. Said fled in his car, and she remained alone in the forest with the tall man, she tried to scream, she did scream, but terror paralyzed her so that her voice never made it out of her throat. The sound was broken in her throat and it broke her.

She said that she was ready to do anything for him, but she was unable to restore her broken voice. That was why she couldn't continue with him. She had decided to go back to her former fiancé. She begged Yalo to understand.

Yalo did not understand and that was a mortal sin. He hung on to the cords of her broken voice, and pursued his game with a broken woman.

That is how he got to prison, ascended to his torments, and lost his soul.

I approached him and tried to read to him, but I stopped reading because I saw his tears. I read to him about his grandfather and the Kurdish mullah and the broken voice, and the tears streamed down his cheeks and wet his neck.

How can I bring him down off his throne and gather him to my chest?

Yalo is coming down, now, sir. I see him coming down from the throne and walking in my direction. I see him along the window, I see him approaching. I rise, open my arms to him, and let him enter my eyes.

Yalo gazed at the pages, read a little, and asked me to stop writing, because the story was over.

I t was noon.

The officer entered the solitary cell and ordered Yalo to follow him. The young man picked up his papers and walked through the dark corridors. He descended one steep step before finding himself inside a large room underground. The young man with knitted brows, long tan face, and tall, slender stature stood in the nearly dark room, holding his papers in his hands as he waited to offer his story to the interrogator. He had made it to the end of his long journey of torment, he had reached the end.

I stood, and did not see.

The darkness was dense; no, it was not the darkness, but the lights I bore in my eyes were blocking my vision and creating patches of darkness and light. I closed my eyes in order to see, as I always did, I closed my eyes in order to let the light retreat from them, then I opened them to see.

I stood in heavy silence that resembled darkness. I stood and waited with the pages in my hand. I was sure that everything I wrote was correct, and that I had written the story of my life from start to finish and would never after this day be subjected to torture.

I heard his voice: "Open your eyes!"

I opened them and waited to be asked for my papers. But the white man sitting behind the iron desk did not ask me for anything. I saw puddles of water on the floor and smelled the rotten odor that filled the place, and felt that I should go back up above. I should never have believed them and come down off my throne.

I felt that I was on the verge of collapsing. I heard his voice saying things I couldn't understand. His words were slurred, and I wasn't able to disentangle the letters from each other. I heard questions about a man named Richard Sawan and a woman named Marie. My answer was only that I had never heard these names before. I understood that I would be moved to the Roumieh Prison and that now I was in the lower level of the interrogation building of the intelligence service in Sinn al-Fil.

The interrogator said that my story was laughable, and his laughter rang in my ears. I approached him and offered him the pages. My hand remained suspended in the air. The story of my life from start to finish was in my hand, and my hand was in the air, while the interrogator laughed.

"Come here so I can see," said the interrogator. "What's that you have in your hand?"

Why did he ask me, when he knew the answer? Yalo thought, then said to himself that this was interrogation. They asked you about things you had already confessed to, and when you repeated your confessions you made mistakes, which was an unavoidable thing because you cannot tell the same story the same way twice. But this time, no. I will not answer a single question. All my answers are written down on paper. I will not tell my story all over again. I wrote the whole thing down from start to finish, so there is no margin for error. Black on white, and everything is here. I will not rewrite it or retell it. This is my story, so let them take it and do to me, and it, whatever they want, but I will not . . .

Before Yalo could finish his sentence in his head, he felt a pain in his tongue and felt the answer forming in his throat, and words solidifying on his lips. He wanted to answer, but he could not. He held out his hand with the pages and stepped forward.

"I'm asking you, what is this?" shouted the interrogator.

"This . . . this . . ." said Yalo.

"What?"

"This is the story."

"The story!"

"Yes, yes, the story."

"What story?"

"The story. My story. This is the story of my life."

He waved the pages, but the interrogator did not reach out to take them.

"The story of your life!" said the interrogator in amazement, and got up from behind the table.

"Yes, sir. You all asked me to write it, and I wrote it from start to finish."

Here the interrogator burst out laughing and asked Yalo to come closer.

Yalo stepped over the hollows filled with stagnant water and saw the interrogator's hand reach out to snatch the pages, so he drew his hand back instinctively, tightening his grip on them.

"Those are the pages?" asked the interrogator.

"Yes, yes, these are the pages."

"Why did you go to so much trouble?"

"Sir, you asked me for everything, and I wrote everything. At first, the officer sent me to be tortured because I left things out. There's nothing missing in these."

"Great. Great. You're really something, after all. A jackass – you are a jackass," said the interrogator.

"I am a jackass," said Yalo.

"What, are you making fun of me? Are you being clever?"

". . ."

"Who do you think you are?"

". . ."

"Maybe you thought we were waiting for your story so we can know the truth? We know everything. Anyway, who do you think you are? Do you think these papers will save you? You are nothing! You are less than nothing! Let me have a look at those pages."

Yalo held out the papers and heard a burst of laughter.

"You're a jackass and a fool! Do you know who you are?"

". . ."

"Answer when you're asked a question."

"Yes, I know."

And I saw. I closed my eyes so that I could see, and I saw. The pages flew into the air before falling into the hollows filled with stinking water. I heard the interrogator's voice.

"Excuse us, Monsieur Yalo, excuse us, we've gone to a lot of trouble with you. Your story is stupid and a waste of time. We discovered the explosives gang and they confessed to everything. You have nothing to do with it. You're just an asshole. Why did you get smart on us and write those endless stories? That's what made us doubt you. But you're just an asshole, a bastard, a nothing. You're going to be tried on the charges of theft and fornication in the Ballouna forest, that's why there was no need for all these confessions."

Yalo saw the pages fall to the ground and heard the interrogator's voice say, "Come on, get him out of here!"

The pages were on the ground. The story of my life from start to finish was on the ground. Water, ink, and a bleeding story. His voice said, "Come on, out of here!" and there I was, wanting to ask him not to step on them, but he crushed my voice. The words hung in my throat.

"Look at what a shit he is," said the interrogator. "He thinks he's a big shit. Come on, get him out of my sight!"

I saw myself drop. I saw myself down on all fours trying to gather the sheets of paper. I saw his feet stepping on my hands and fingers and the heel of his boot grinding the pages as I tried to gather them. I sank into the water and the odor and felt my buttocks being kicked, and heard loud laughter. I saw my forehead bumping against the floor. The smell of my tears resembled the putrid odor rising from the water-filled hollows.

" . . ."

And I saw him.

He exited from my clothes, mounted the iron desk, and jumped out of the window. I saw him up there, as he found his throne once again.

They dragged me along the floor.

Two muscular men appeared and dragged me. I clung to the floor because I could not leave Yalo here. I would not leave the story of my life torn under their boots.

I saw myself being carried off and I saw myself inside a military jeep that took me to the prison. My tears streamed out of my eyes, my hands, my ears, my nose, my face, and my chest.

I entered the cell where they had left me a blanket on the floor near the door. I looked at the small, high-set window with its metal bars, and when I saw him my tears stopped.

Yalo was there waiting for me.

Verdict

The Criminal Court of Mount Lebanon, consisting of Judge Ghassan Diab and counselors Nadim Juha and Nicola Abd al-Nur.

Having reviewed Accusation number 223 of the date 18 March 1994, and the arguments of the public prosecutor of Mount Lebanon number 9355, dated 2 August 1993, and all the documents relating to the action.

It is clear that the accused:

Daniel Abel Abyad, also known as Yalo, son of Marie, born in 1961 in Beirut, of Lebanese citizenship, has been transferred to this Court. He was apprehended in person on 8 June 1992, and remains in custody.

He will be tried in accordance with the jurisdiction of Articles 639 and 640 of the Criminal Code, for committing, in the quarter of Ballouna, on dates within the statute of limitations, multiple instances of robbery and rape, involving the use of a firearm, at night.

Hence in open and public court, the following is clear:

1: The Findings

It is clear that the accused, Daniel Abel Abyad, was employed during 1991 and 1992 as a guard at a villa located in the town of Ballouna, the property of M. Michel Salloum, attorney, on an exposed height overlooking the surrounding side roads, which for their part were a place frequented by lovers, indeed there usually would be found there young men and women exchanging caresses and kisses. Given that the villa overlooked the side roads, the accused regularly witnessed what occurred inside any car parked on any of these roads.

It is clear that the accused, Daniel Abel Abyad, repeatedly engaged in acts of robbery in the manner described approximately thirty times, and raped approximately three women, and that among the victims were N.S., A.F., and M.D.

It is clear that the accused, Daniel Abel Abyad, received from his employer, Michel Salloum, attorney, a military machine gun, a Kalashnikov, registered to the latter, to assist the accused in guarding the villa, within its confines. He also had access to a military pistol belonging to his employer, which the latter kept permanently in the glove compartment of his car. He gave the car keys to the accused, Daniel, so that he could maintain and clean the vehicle. Both the pistol and the machine gun were registered to Michel Salloum. Members of the Jounieh Police Department recovered the machine gun and pistol and restored them to their owner.

It is clear that the accused, Daniel Abel Abyad, confessed to the acts described above, in the presence of the Jounieh Criminal Court, before the investigating judge, and wrote a manuscript text of his confessions. However, he retracted his confessions before this Court, claiming that he had confessed under torture, although the report of the forensic physician proved the accused underwent no physical or mental torture. Daniel advised that the plaintiff Richard Sawan had tried to rape the young woman in his company, and that he had prevented him from doing so, and did not rob him.

Richard was questioned in his capacity as plaintiff and asserted that the accused, Daniel, was the one who undertook to rob him and rape a certain Marie who was with him in the car and whose full identity remains unknown.

Daniel advised that he did not rape the plaintiff Shirin Raad, but that she had requested that he allow her to stay with him after her fiancé, Emile Shahin, fled. It is clear that the plaintiffs Shirin Raad and Emile Shahin forfeited their personal rights to the accused, Daniel Abyad, were questioned in their capacity as witnesses, and asserted that the accused threatened to kill Emile Shahin before the latter left the forest, then raped Shirin Raad three times in his cottage located below the Salloum villa.

It is clear that the representative of the public prosecutor made a motion to charge the accused, while the accused's court-appointed counsel argued his innocence, pleading insufficient evidence. The last word was given to the accused, Daniel Abel Abyad, who left his fate to the Court.

Thus we are certain of these facts:

1. A charge and a request to drop the charges.
2. The first police investigation, and the recovery of the overcoat and flashlight from the residence of the accused.
3. The testimony of the hearing.
4. The accused's confession during the first investigation, and before the judge in the hearing, and his handwritten confessions.
5. His proven statements in court.
6. The statements of witnesses.
7. The recovery of the machine gun and military pistol and their return to their lawful owner.
8. The trial, and the sum total of documents of the case.

II: THE LAW

In that it has been proven to this Court, through the confession of the accused, Daniel Abel Abyad, before the Jounieh Criminal Court and before the judge in the proceeding; through his written confessions; through the recovery of the machine gun and pistol and their return to their owner; through the recovery of the overcoat, woolen cap, and flashlight; that the accused, Daniel Abel Abyad, undertook, alone, to commit multiple acts of armed robbery at night and multiple acts of rape involving the use of a firearm.

Given the testimonies heard before the court of: Michel Salloum, Randa Salloum, Shirin Raad, and Emile Shahin, and that of the plaintiff Richard Sawan;

Given that the accused, Daniel Abel Abyad, committed multiple acts of armed robbery and rape at night involving the use of a firearm, he has perpetrated a felony as specified in Articles 639 and 640 of the Criminal Code;

And given that the Court, after giving due consideration, views the granting of the accused the mitigating circumstances, based on Article 253 of the Criminal Code;

Therefore the court decides,

After hearing the arguments of the public prosecutor, the defense, and the accused;

1. The accused, Daniel Abel Abyad, is convicted of the felony in accordance with Articles 639 and 640 of the Criminal Code, and is condemned to twenty years of hard labor, based on the first provision, to increase this penalty to hard labor for life based on the second provision, and reducing the sentence to ten years of hard labor, based on Article 253 of the Criminal Code, and to consider the time he spent in detention.

2. The sentenced party will be responsible for the payment of all legal costs and fees.

Duly judged against the sentenced party, publicly issued and informed in the presence of the representative of the public prosecutor on 6 June 1994.

< 312 >

I live in this cell with a large group of prisoners. But I am alone and don't deal with anyone. I asked the guards for paper and pens but they refused. One of the guards, named Nabil Zeitoun, took pity on me. All the prisoners here ask for food and cigarettes, but not me. I have no desire for food; cigarettes, on the other hand, I do crave, but I don't ask for them. I asked for white paper. I want paper like my pages that were destroyed in the interrogation vault. When I look at my life, I feel that it is a story. I want to read the story so that I will be able to bear the pains that come back to me. I can't tell my story to anyone, because they'd think I'm crazy, and also no one would understand. I wrote my story by myself and for myself.

The prisoners here watch me with strange eyes. They think I'm the "king of sex" – that's what the head of the cell named me. He's a professional hashish smuggler who lives here as if he were in a palace. The prisoners serve him as if he were not a prisoner like them. When I entered cell 12, Mr. Abu Tariq al-Arnaut – that's the name of the head of our cell – gave me a cot on the side of the room near the door, and told the prisoners to watch out around me because I'm an insatiable sex fiend.

I do not want any of them. I look at the steel-barred window and I see him, and I feel like crying.

After the verdict sentencing me to ten years in prison, I was moved to this elongated cell stinking of male sweat. Odor, not fear. For I no longer fear anything. I was publicly proclaimed innocent of the explosives crimes. The incidents in the lovers' forest, and the circumstances, made the judge laugh several times, especially when I was asked to supply the details. I felt sure that day that my sentence would be light. But when they told me that the sentence was ten years, I fell into a depression that would not go away. My only request of the court was the pages that the interrogator trampled. That too made them laugh.

I could not explain to them that I wanted my papers for his sake. How could I tell them about Yalo, who has returned to his heavenly throne, near the window, and who doesn't answer me?

The prisoners give me strange looks here, because they yearn to hear my story, after all that was said about my sexual exploits, and that I had not only raped women, but men too! Horrible! I see the prisoners' eyes widen with lust for the stories without any of them daring to come near me out of fear of being suspected along with me.

I do not want them, nor do I have the slightest desire to talk with anyone. I want to talk to myself and cure myself of its pains. I look toward the window and address a person that only I can see, and I try to remember the stories I wrote, but my memory fails me.

No one can claim that he has done me a favor. I have paid the price for everything. Life and me, we're even now. If you put us on the scales of a balance, we would balance out. That is why I have no pangs of conscience or regret over what I have done, not because I am pleased with what I have done, but because it was bought with my own suffering and blood.

I long for the smell of pine sap and the fragrance of incense that surrounded the Villa Gardenia. I long only for those two smells. As for the people who passed through my life, I feel nothing toward them. Even my mother, I do not long for her in the real sense of the word. I knew true longing when I was in love and stupid. Longing bites and hurts. But now I long for my mother without pain, I miss her because I pity her. The poor thing visited me once in prison. Visits here are strange. The prisoners stand behind iron bars while family members face them from the other side, and the shouting starts. My mother came once and brought me nothing, unlike the other family members who brought food and cigarettes to their imprisoned sons. She came and stood with the rest of the group, and did not see me. It was truly strange – I am the tallest prisoner here, and I feel that I am growing taller, even though that is scientifically impossible, since a man stops growing when he is in adolescence. Yet I'm growing taller and thinner, I know it and I am surprised by it, yet my mother didn't see me. She stood

< 315 >

there with her mussed *kokina* and looked to the right and the left looking for me, while all the time I was standing right in front of her. I shouted out to her and then she saw me and wept. She covered her ears with her hands and bowed her head. She covered her ears because the clamor hurt them, it was like my grandfather whose ears grew larger in his last days and who would spread his palms over them so that the sound wouldn't enter his brain and crush it.

I shouted out to her and she blocked her ears and asked me to lower my voice. I asked her how she was doing and she answered me quietly, but I did hear her. I heard her voice through all the other voices and understood that they had evicted her from the house in the al-Mrayyeh quarter in Ain Rummaneh. When she went back to her house in Mseitbeh, she found it inhabited by a family she didn't know. She told them it was her house, but they threw her out and threatened to call the police. She said that now she lived in lower Mseitbeh. She had rented a small room in the neighborhood of huts inhabited by housemaids, Syrian construction workers, and Kurds. She also said that she was paying a hundred thousand lira a month for her room and that she was going to end up begging in order to eat because she didn't have a cent.

Nabil Zeitoun, one of the prison guards, took pity on me. He noticed that no one visited me, and that I put nothing in the trust, and seeing my insistence, he gave me twenty sheets of white paper and a ballpoint pen, saying that was all he could manage for me. I decided to write the story of my life all over again, in tiny script, with words like ants, so that no one else could read it. I saw with my own eyes how the interrogator had trampled my pages and how he drowned the pages in the foul stagnant water. I can still smell it, mingled with the smell of men's sweat and urine, which keeps me from remembering. I want to remember everything. I try, but I see everything black on white, I cannot read, it's as if I were reading in a dream. I see letters whose riddles I cannot unlock.

On these pages I'll write very small letters, squeezing an entire page into one line. The pain has not left me. The prison doctor diagnosed me as suffering from a rectal prolapse because of the bottle and said that it might require an operation. But he advised me to be patient and not to have the operation in the prison hospital because the outcome was not guaranteed.

I am not writing for my own sake but for his sake and his mother's. I want him to come back to me for his poor mother's sake. We must find a solution for her, because she will be the heroine of the story. I don't like stories where the heroes are men. Gaby will be the heroine of my story, with her *kokina* and her long hair that turns golden before the sea, and her lover the tailor, her father the *cohno*, and her son who wasted his life.

My mother visited me only once, I'm worried about her. I haven't heard from her for a year and I have no way of getting in touch with her. That is why I wrote only one page. A whole year in which I wrote just one page. This was not out of laziness but out of confusion. I want the story to have a happy ending. I don't want my story to end with the heroine, Gaby Abel Abyad, my mother and my sister, walking alone through the city streets, tripping over her shadow.

I want some other ending.

I try to imagine a different ending, but my imagination is no help. I don't have enough imagination to find for Gaby a dignified ending worthy of her love story. And if I don't find the end of the story, how will I be able to write it?